John Sadler is a British historian specialising in the Anglo-Scottish Border conflicts during the Middle Ages. Sadler is a regular contributor to military and historical journals and has published a number of books on the subject. He has taught and tutored history as well.

PRAISE FOR JOHN SADLER:

'...you close Sadler's (book) with a shake of your head and a sense of mourning for the dead.' – Toby Clements, *The Telegraph*

'A fascinating history ... in which the author transports readers back to the events of the day, giving a feel of what it was like to participate in combat then.' - *The Scots Magazine*

'Written for a popular audience, the narrative is always lively and entertaining.' - *The Journal of Military History*

BLITZING ROMMEL

JOHN SADLER

ENDEAVOURQUILL

AN ENDEAVOUR QUILL PAPERBACK

First published by Endeavour Quill in 2018

This paperback edition published in 2018
by Endeavour Quill
Endeavour Quill is an imprint of Endeavour Media Ltd
Endeavour Media, 85-87 Borough High Street,
London, SE1 1NH

ISBN 978-1-911445-63-0

Typeset using Atomik ePublisher from Easypress Technologies

Printed and bound in Great Britain by
Clays Ltd, Elcograf S.p.A.

www.endeavourmedia.co.uk

Dedicated to Henry Gabriel Meadows and all that life holds for him

An officer should be comely, sprightly and above all else, confident in his own dress and bearing. He should, where possible, eat a small piece of meat each morning with molasses and beans. He should bear himself gracefully when under fire and never place himself in a position of difficulty when being shot at. He should eat his meals comfortably and ahead of his soldiers, for it is he whom is more important tactically on the battlefield and therefore he who should be well nourished. His hair should be well groomed and if possible he should wear a moustache or similar facial adornment.

When speaking to his soldiers he should appear calm and aloof and give direction without in any way involving himself personally in the execution of arduous duties or those inappropriate for an officer. He should smoke thin panatelas except when in the company of ladies, where he should take only a small gin mixed with lemon tea. He should be an ardent and erudite gentleman and woo the ladies both in the formal environment and in the bedroom, where he should excel himself beyond the ordinary soldier with his lovemaking and virile prowess. These, I say to you, are the qualities of an officer that set him apart from the lay person and the common soldier.
Major S.T. Meadows, of the Royal Gurkha Rifles

Table of Contents

Prelude

The Blooding

During his first retreat, the long attrition towards the beaches when he was just a novice in the art of military catastrophes, Joe had kept a kind of journal. With the stench of burning materiel and abandoned vehicles, heralds of defeat, the Second Battalion of the Fusiliers commenced its withdrawal at 01.30 hours — he remembered the time but not the exact date; this would have been in May, the third week perhaps.

Darkness was lit by the fires of an army in retreat; flames from the ancient chateau at Ottenburg seared the night. Everywhere roads were clogged with a mass of men and vehicles. The Battalion could muster around 450 effectives, there was a shortage of both small arms ammunition and grenades, and all non-riflemen were integrated into four somewhat ad hoc fighting companies; mortars were left behind. A new line was chosen and as quickly abandoned.

Captain Pearson, the Quartermaster, performed prodigies to provide hot food for the desperately tired marching men. Two companies became detached in the enveloping fog of retreat and were not seen for several days. Fifth columnists appeared to be active in the Forest of Soignes as the Fusiliers passed through, the leafy canopy of spring leaves offering shade from a warming sun. Somebody shot a nun on a bicycle — apparently German spies were dressing up as nuns, but this one just looked like a dead nun

In forty-eight hours, the companies marched nearly as many miles. Transport scheduled to arrive never did, and those drivers they had were falling asleep at the wheel, adding to lengthening tailbacks. As they tramped across the Brussels–Charleroi Canal, engineers were already packing demolition charges. It was a total bloody shambles; naturally, we blamed the French.

Joe and his platoon of riflemen marched with the rest He'd written: *I was attached to Battalion HQ. The enemy was dropping three-inch mortars around us, terrific bangs but little else. Oddly, I wasn't afraid; I had a belief I'd be alright as long as I stayed standing, didn't dive for cover — daft, you might think, but it worked. Getting out was tricky; whilst we were fighting adrenalin kept us going but now we were all dead tired. We hadn't sustained that many casualties, none in my platoon, apart from one bloke who'd been injured. Nobody was giving us any orders and, frankly, we were afraid of German tanks. The only weapon we had was the useless A/T rifle — couldn't penetrate the armour, it was there for morale not effect; anybody who said it would work should have been made to use one against a Jerry tank.*

Early in the morning on the nineteenth of May — he remembered *that* date — Tournai was engulfed in flames. To add to the prevailing madness, inmates from the local asylum were wandering the shattered streets; they had to be rounded up and secured in the museum. A surreal experience, dazed and bewildered patients, in their ghastly institutional uniforms, strolling wonderingly yet unconcerned over debris and dead flesh. The sane ones had already left. Now, the battalion was expected to hold the line of the Escaut Canal. An uneventful four days, largely undisturbed by enemy activity, save for random long distance shelling and a barrage of rumours, a short lived re-run of the phoney war they'd all got so used to. Well, it wasn't phoney anymore.

These barrages were alarming and so accurate that bridges were blown in near panic, and more precious vehicles abandoned. Joe and his weekend warriors were attached to 'D' Company.

We were commanded by Lieutenant Gregson now. Captain Hutton had been injured; his kneecap blown off. We had a full company with everyone added in, now in three platoons. We still didn't know where we were going, but everyone, officers and men, were behaving well, no signs of any panic anywhere. We crossed some ground where 'C' Company had put in a bayonet charge, blood everywhere, lots of it, blood and bodies; one of my best friends was killed there. A lad called Rutherford, a fireman I think before the war, was collecting in abandoned rifles, most with bayonets attached, thick with blood.

More withdrawals followed and the Battalion was soon marching through a landscape they'd advanced over barely ten days earlier; no cheering crowds this time. On the twenty-fourth, Bethune fell and the fog of war shrouded more closely. Nerves were stretched taut as enemy fire could erupt at any time — Germans or fifth columnists.

We came under MG fire and dived into ditches. I could see a fellow apparently directing fire from an open hayloft. I was getting ready to pot him when the CSM stopped me, said the fellow was probably just a farmer. I wasn't so sure, but I didn't shoot.

Later we came across the French — what a shambles, you never saw anything like it: some were barefoot, their clogs around their necks, some pushing prams or carts, no sign of order. It was disheartening, I tell you, none of them was going to fight! None of what we did bore any resemblance to our training. We were told to prepare to ambush tanks. How do you ambush tanks? I improvised a barricade across the road, just took the French farmer's cart and bales; he was very unhappy about it! I put a couple of men in a hayloft ready to drop grenades into the tank hatches. We couldn't dig in, we had no tools, our ammo was down to what we had in our pouches and we'd few grenades.

When the Brits entered Calonnes-sur-Lys, locals warned that Axis forces had already preceded them. Confusion prevailed and the Battalion moved up to occupy St Venant the following evening. The enemy was very close; any daytime manoeuvre was accompanied by an unhealthy overture of mortars and MG fire. It soon became apparent the Fusiliers' left flank was rather in the air — the ominous and unmistakable resonance of German armour could clearly be heard.

That night it seemed to the men of Second Battalion, as it had to Homer's Greeks before Troy, that enemy campfires ringed them all around and more hard fighting loomed. Joe had recorded that *the place was just a scattering of farm buildings along a single road with one big house. We dug in around this — I say "around" as we didn't go into the houses. The British Army didn't like to disturb residents and people were still in their homes. Not like Jerry, he'd have turned each house into a fortress; we should have done the same. We weren't receiving many orders, so I went out for myself to do a recce.*

I came to a small humpback bridge; the whole area was waterlogged, with deep streams and generally uncultivated, mainly animal pasture. I went round making contact with the other platoons; we had no Brens, only rifles. Jerry started shelling and again I was lucky. I met our officer, Lieutenant Gregson; he had his briar walking stick, I remember. He asked me what I was doing there and I told him — suddenly there was a terrific bang as a shell landed nearby and he went down. I ran over to him, he was screaming and a bowl-shaped lump of shrapnel was wedged into the base of his spine. He was in terrible pain and I saw he was trying to pull out his revolver, I think to shoot himself. I took the pistol away and tried to pull out the shrapnel, but it was red-hot!

We had no field dressings left by then and I ran to get stretcher-bearers. Sergeant-Major Metcalfe sent out a party and gave me a cup of tea. The CSM said, "Look Milburn, there are no officers left; I'm in command and you're now Second-in-Command." I protested there were PSMs [Platoon Sergeant-Majors] *senior to me. "Doesn't matter", he said, "that's it." They brought Lieutenant Gregson in, carried on a five-barred gate; poor fellow, he died. Later, I remember his mother sent out five embossed silver cigarette cases for the stretcher party.*

Joe now had to tell the other PSMs that he was in charge; *and they didn't all take too kindly to that. I sent Corporal Donaldson and a patrol forward, sent out the "bad boys" — those who were habitually in trouble. Private Whitely, the battalion boxer, went with them. They were back in two hours, said they thought the whole German army was out there, and on this side of the canal as well. I let CSM Metcalfe know and he said we'd defensive fire behind us, guns and mortars, ha …*

In the filtering light of dawn 'A' Company was attacked when the Fusiliers brushed a fighting patrol. A savage firefight erupted and though Jerry was driven off, we lost men too. He had plenty more, we had none. Next came armour; the British two-pounder A/T gun was largely ineffective — those that existed were rapidly knocked out, leaving only anti-tank rifles, which were about as much use as a fart in a thunderstorm.'

The CSM ordered stand-to at dawn, there was a terrific enemy barrage and we could then hear tanks in the distance. Well, rifles were no good against these steel monsters; men weren't willing to fight. It wasn't cowardice; there was just nothing you could do. The German infantry came on in the usual way, small groups using cover. I had a German rifle then, as I'd given

5

mine to a fellow who had lost his. I got up into a corner of the barn; I was a canny shot and I put down seven Germans.

A lieutenant — never mind his name — came in and asked if he could fire a shot. Well, he did, and next thing he was squatting in the corner, trousers down, doing his business. Now I never saw that before — the books and films talk about that, but it never happens in reality. Never seen a fellow fill his trousers; I just got on with the shooting. Men were starting to run from the tanks, there really was nothing you could do; men were running everywhere.

Second Battalion HQ was concentrated in a stout barn just off the road passing through St Venant and south of the canal of that same name. Barricades were hastily flung across roads and track ways, the available gunners were firing over open sights as German tanks, like hungry sharks circling, closed in on the position. A brace of panzers began pounding from the left bank of the canal whilst more stormed 'A' Company's position. At least one Axis crew was dispatched by fire from an anti-tank rifle, but the end was never in doubt. They hosed our blokes with MG fire and ground remorselessly over slit trenches, some of whose occupants died, crushed into a mess of bloody pulp, yet others miraculously survived.

'D' Company was also being pulverized and soon down to single platoon strength with Joe the senior man still standing. Despite these mounting odds, the Geordies were still fighting. Joe ordered Sergeant-Major Pearson to counter-attack with his shrunken platoon and seal a looming gap on one flank. This attempt cost all their lives. When, via the Berkshires, orders came to fall back, Joe could barely muster twenty-five men and retreating meant somehow getting over the canal.

Saw my platoon running back now as well; one of our men had been shot through the head by a sniper and killed, this had unnerved the rest. I was disgusted. Some, a couple, were wounded, the blood running in channels

down their trousers. CSM Metcalfe called for a counter-attack. "But with
what?" I said. The Germans were coming on, they had automatic weapons,
Tommy guns. I was out of ammo for my German rifle and had only my
pistol. I gave the order it was every man for himself.

For the rest, the Axis net had already tightened too far. Some B
echelon transport had managed to cross the St Venant Bridge and escape
the trap; for the remainder it was now a question of selling their lives as
dearly as possible. They possessed not a single anti-tank weapon and a
handful of Axis tanks were rumbling through the shattered village. One
simply stormed the bridge, gunning down any defenders, pumping high
explosive into buildings. An eighteen-pounder, WWI vintage, somehow
knocked out this first panzer, but there were plenty more behind.

Joe was with those who were still able and prepared to mount a final
stand around the barn and Battalion HQ. Colonel Simpson fought with
his revolver, despite injuries. Smoke and fumes clogged the air; hay and
straw were everywhere on fire. It soon ended: German tanks and infantry
surged over the dwindling remnant; for Second Battalion, the battle
was over. Joe and his few survivors made a run for it across corn fields.

I think it was corn, standing crops, anyway.

The men ran anyways and I ordered them to zigzag, run and lie flat.
Whitely was one of those hit. I went back to him; "Leave me," he said, "I'm
finished." He was: I could see his injuries. He was a very brave man. As we
crossed the field we came across a lorried Vickers MG section, just sitting
around, calm as you please. They pretty soon mounted up and scarpered.
"Don't go that way," I yelled, "you'll drive into an ambush." They went
anyway. Of 120 men in 'D' Company, nine of us got out.

Their trials still weren't over:

We came to a canal, the Lys I think; half the men, including CSM
Metcalfe, couldn't swim so I removed my webbing, got into the water and

swum across. It was difficult; the far bank was concreted but I found a small boat and managed to paddle back over, so we got everyone across; never got my webbing back though. After exhausting marching, catching up with our own 'B' echelon and being under near-arrest in a barn, accosted by an officer who clearly had not seen action, our tiny group was saved.

Chapter One

A Call to Arms

When I go home people will ask me, 'Hey Hoot, why do you do it man, what, you some kinda war junkie?' You know what I'll say? I won't say a goddamn word. Why? They won't understand. They won't understand why we do it. They won't understand that it's about the men next to you, and that's it. That's all it is.

Black Hawk Down (2001)

*

Barely a year earlier, war had seemed far more congenial.

'And now ladies,' boomed Sgt. Storey, 'we will dig trenches, so hands off cocks, pull up yer socks and let's see how well you can sweat.'

'We're sodding infantry,' Private Hinckley muttered, 'not the bleedin' RE, why can't those idle bastards dig the damn trenches?' He was a thickset young man with a flabby, potato face topped by an unruly shock of dead black hair. His greatest passion was the consumption of beer and his battledress bulged, like a wet sack, in all the wrong places.

'Because, Private Hinckley,' the NCO had excellent hearing, 'the Engineers, fine fellows as they may be, are not here whilst you my heroes *are*, and moreover, Private Hinckley, you will dig because I bloody well tell you so.'

Joe had seen trenches before. He'd trained the previous year up on the artillery ranges by Otterburn in Northumberland — a bare, windswept moor, ablaze with the rich purple of summer heather. Then the platoon had been spared the chore of actually digging the beastly things, others had performed that service beforehand. Now the heavy, heathery soil of Coquetdale capitulated beneath the onslaught of shovel and pick.

The men were a mix of manual and office workers. Some came from the land and more from the mines, to them digging was second nature. Those from more sedentary backgrounds suffered accordingly, hands soon raw and blistering, sweat in damp torrents soaking their thick flannel shirts.

'God,' Neville Forster managed, his lean face blotched and glistening, 'this is no work for a gentleman. I may write to my MP, if I can still hold a pen, that is.' Neville was from minor gentry; one of those families who'd cashed in on the coal mining bonanza. Tall, sandy haired and with even, almost aquiline, features, he looked like a product of one of the better public schools even though, on cost grounds, he'd ended up at the Newcastle Royal Grammar, which was not quite the same.

'It's 'cos you're doing it all wrong lad,' Ernest (Ernie) Thompson, thickset bantam and pitman from Earsdon, explained good-naturedly. 'Give us that bloody spade. Now watch and learn.'

With practised ease and a degree of economy bordering on the graceful, he slid the sharp-pointed tool into the tricky ground, his cut as sure as a surgeon's incision. With a deft movement of his foot he rammed the blade deep into the earth, then applied back and shoulder muscles to drag the load free and swung easily to unload. 'If you're going to do this for eight hours a day lads, you might as well do it right.' To watch such a consummate professional was almost a joy and Joe felt the prick of conscience at the way his ambitions led him to look down on others.

They chewed down into the ground as the trench began to take shape, the sharp, rich scent of the peaty soil filling their nostrils, its dark elasticity and subtle texture hinting at ancient secrets. 'Learn to love your trench, me boys,' the sergeant enthused, all the more so as his exalted rank excused him from the labour. 'If we're ever doin' this for real, then it's mud or death.' He'd been in the previous war and never let them forget it.

Dug down to eight feet through the heavy peat, a fire-step was cut into the front wall of the bay. 'Now then my lads,' Sgt. Storey continued, 'here we have an excellent field of fire, whilst the enemy has no clear view of your position. As you will note, your rifles command the ground in front and should the air fill with the sound of enemy projectiles you can always hope they fall on the bay next door.' Separate pits were dug to accommodate one of the company's Vickers machine guns, fat-barrelled weapons that were lovingly fussed by their owners but ate up rounds at an alarming rate and spewed death over the ranges in a rapid stuttering roar, mangling and collapsing wooden targets with lethal abandon.

That night they slept in the trench. Men crammed in anyhow, ground-sheets and webbing festooning the newly dug walls. 'What the hell are we doing all this shite for,' Hinckley continued with habitual grousing, 'what's the bloody point in training infantry to cover ground when we're stuck in a bleedin' hole?'

'Nobody is suggesting you spend the whole war in trenches,' Neville wearily explained, exhaustion weighing heavy. 'We use trenches to attack from. Would you rather we just stood out in the open and let Jerry's gunners enjoy themselves?'

'As I'm not going east of Alnmouth, I can't see it matters and there's not much point digging trenches round Roker Gasworks.'

'Jerry will never get as far as Roker,' Joe commented, 'especially if he knows you're waiting for him.' This drew a ripple of laughter, but they were all too tired to care.

Next morning they awoke after fitful dozing, still tired, rank, aching and unshaven; mess tins of warm, sweet tea, dark as treacle swigged with relish. Odour of frying bacon lifting weary spirits, skies fine and clear, reveille of birdsong in the line of trees behind and placid sheep unmoved by all their earlier effort and this strange, fresh scar upon the otherwise timeless landscape.

Yesterday they dug. Today they would attack and defend. A and C Platoons in the trench, B and D seeking to dispossess them. Happily, the defending platoons were using blank rounds and the machine gun, due to the scarcity of blanks and its prodigious appetite, stayed silent which was a blessing. B Platoon came forward in good order, the ground rose gently toward their objective, lush and undisturbed by bombardment. After a day's hard labour the mock attack was practically a recreation though they sweated afresh beneath the weight of their stiff webbing and laden bandoliers.

They moved fast, ten to a dozen paces between each man, avoiding bunching. 'Remember,' Storey bellowed, 'machine gunners love a group, spread out you're a waste of lead.' And so they advanced, sweeping over the easy terrain with sheep, rather reluctantly, moving aside. They jogged, using ground as they'd been taught, one section covering the rush of another, pausing to loose snap shots at the parapet ahead. Then a final surge to the sandbags; leaping amongst their grinning comrades a deal of tussling and cries of 'Had enough, Jerry?' and 'Well done the Fusiliers!' It was all rather exhilarating. Nobody died.

Afterwards they had lunch, a hearty mutton stew, served hot and washed down with cans of tea, ardent warriors basking in the glow of their achievement. Hinckley was moaning about his feet, Jackie Dodds, aspiring journalist, furiously scribbling notes; no doubt this morning's exercise would feature, in suitably re-mastered dramatic tones, in a forthcoming edition of the *Newcastle Chronicle*. Second Lieutenant Ridley was consulting with Sgt. Storey, wondrously pink and scrubbed, his tailored battledress looking distinctly more box office than their own standard issue heavy wool serge.

'Odd mix,' observed Neville, 'the battalion, I mean.'

'Be alright if it wasn't for toffs,' Hinckley groused but without malice.

'You've got university men, aspiring professionals,' a nudge to Joe, 'office workers, miners, farm-lads, shop-boys, tradesmen ...'

'Don't forget us creative types,' Dodds reminded, 'likely I'll be the one who writes the official history.' He was thin; vaguely ascetic-looking, aside from the acne, constantly squinting though thick glasses like a myopic field mouse. God knows how he'd got through a medical.

'Best learn to write first,' Hinckley sneered. 'Journalism isn't writing, it's just sensation. Besides, I can't see the War Office rushing to the man who wrote up the 1938 Alwinton Village Show when they'll be needing a proper historian, one wi' letters after his name an' all ...'

'This war, if it ever does happen, will be the greatest journalistic event of the century,' Dodds portentously predicted, 'and I'll be front of the queue, best stay civil if you want a good word said ...'

'Bloody good of Adolf to lay on a war just for your effing career; what makes you think you'll last long enough to land a job as war reporter?'

'I'm lucky me, well as talented. That's a hell of a winning combination.'

Joe and Neville were left alone as their mates headed to the latrines.

*

'Do you want to marry her?' Neville enquired blandly. 'My sister, I mean?'

'Christ, I know who you mean and how the hell do I know? Your bloody father wouldn't be overly impressed …' Joe was caught off guard, his tentative advances to Evelyn Forster were, in the marital sense, embryonic and burdened by the disparity of caste.

'A formidable impediment to be sure, he knows you for an ambitious and amoral social climber, and he's something of a practitioner, even a specialist, in that area himself …'

'Thanks …'

'Still, if you were to get a commission, dress nicely like Ridley over there, polished Sam Browne, swagger stick and a decent pair of boots, you'd be a different class of suitor. You'd need to learn to talk some recognizable version of the King's English of course, wash and shave more often, go to church of a Sunday, that sort of thing …'

'Fat chance,' Joe snorted.

'Well, between Adolf and Benito you might just manage it. If this war does kick off, and it will, there'll be a proper shortage of officers. Even the better class of oik like you might stand a chance …'

'I can't see the army recruiting its young gentlemen from tenant farmers' sons, Neville. You, on the other hand, would get a commission just for the asking. You're almost gentry, been to Oxford — even if it was only for the weekend — and your dad's an impressive record in abusing his workers, bastard that he is, sorry… no offence.'

'None taken, and he's all of that, but I'm not officer material. You, my lad, very definitely *are*, and I've seen you looking at all that smart kit. Don't tell me you haven't thought about it.'

Neville, with his habitual insight, was spot on. Joe couldn't help contrasting his own shapeless khaki with the officers' precise and expensive outfitting. He'd seen the way girls looked at them in the streets of Newcastle. As a mere, if not so humble, private he could never compete. If there was peace rather than war, he would anticipate qualifying as a solicitor. In time, he might go on to a partnership in a respectable firm.

But Joe was impatient. Whiffs of glory and a couple of decent decorations could catapult a man through the ranks of society quicker than a lifetime's graft. And *did* he want to marry Evelyn? Well yes, he did, partly as he fancied himself in love and partly because he was, if he was honest, determined to leave his peasant farmer pedigree as far to the rear as possible.

'Imagine yourself strutting through Morpeth, even the metropolis of Newcastle, gleaming and brushed, perhaps a gong or two, the odd scar, nothing to detract from your astounding beauty of course. That'll make 'em sit up and take notice.'

'Don't know who'd hate me more, my dad or yours.'

'There'd be some competition there, I'll grant you. My old man would hate you because firstly, he always has, second he'd be jealous and third, he'd know your evil designs on his daughter would be getting closer to realisation.'

'My dad would consider me a class traitor, betraying the oppressed peasants' struggle and joining the ranks of the county bourgeois. He'd be bloody right, too. Besides I'm not sure how Evelyn would react. It won't be that easy.'

'Did I say it would be easy? First, you've got to persuade someone you're worth a commission, and even then some nasty German might ruin the whole scheme by uncivilly blowing your pretty head off.'

*

In the afternoon, with sun high in a perfect blue, they went for a run, swapping their uniform for gym kit, glad to be free of itching wool and stiff flannel. Strung out in a long, irregular column the battalion pelted along the valley floor, worn path shaded by birch and alder, river flowing lazy over a riot of slick stones. They angled up in a diagonal across the flank of the hill, following sheep tracks, ground harder, leaving the patchwork of fields behind. The afternoon sun was fierce on those first days of August, heather bright and purple, swathes of bracken, air like wine. And on they ran.

'Come on lads,' urged their officer, already reclining against the rough stone cairn that marked the summit, 'don't let those dozy sods in C Platoon show you the way.'

'More bloody trenches,' Hinckley puffed, 'hardly think you'd need 'em all the way up here.'

'They're not trenches.' Joe gestured at the ring of ancient ramparts around them. 'It's an Iron Age fort, probably been here since before the Romans came.' He had a fascination with history and the more ancient stuff especially, fuelled by reading Howard Carter and Mortimer Wheeler. Douglas Fairbanks and Errol Flynn had helped.

Here, where even in high summer a chill breeze rode over the slab of moor, there was no sound except the mournful cadence of the curlew, keening as though in search of lost souls. The village with its huddle of steadings clustered so very far below. They took a breather, the rippling of a mountain breeze plucking at their soaking shirts, lighting up sly woodbines. 'Bugger me,' said Hinckley, gasping puce and perspiring, dragging on his fag, 'thank Christ they don't have hills like this in Sunderland.'

'Typical Mackem,' Neville snorted, 'absolutely no idea. Just look around you man, this is God's country, even the sheep are impressed.'

'I went up Penshaw Monument once, that was quite high enough. If God had wanted us to climb bleedin' mountains he wouldn't have dumped 'em all in bloody Northumberland.'

'How'd you get up Penshaw?' queried Dodds, whose notebook was again in evidence. 'You shin up one of the columns? I thought Hartlepool was where the monkeys came from?'

'Hartlepool's where they *hang* monkeys, stupid, reporters too if they've got any sense. I got up Penshaw by the stairs, like any civilised being. There's a spiral in one of the columns an' if I read that in the paper, I'll sue.'

This was the pattern of their days in training, mock attacks, route marches, drill, trench digging and PE. It was pleasant enough, air warm and enlivening, the camp dry and comfortable. Food was plentiful and generally hot. Officers ate in the mess, a large pavilion-like tent out of bounds to ORs but silver and china much in evidence. Bottles of hock (still in fashion despite the prospect of hostilities) were chilled in the stream, crystal decanters of dark-red port which glowed richly in the evening light — the more Joe gawped, the more envious he grew. The more he felt he could cheerfully take his place at the polished boards, covered in fine white linen, gleaming glassware ranked in precedence. Bugger, that beat warm beer and stale baccy.

'You wouldn't think we'd already had one world war, would you?' Neville cut across his jealousy. 'Looks like Queen Vic's still on the throne and us with a bloody great empire on which the sun never sets, silly sods.'

'Well, we do still have a canny sized empire.'

'It's bust laddie, all just show, too many snouts in the trough and we're still paying for our fathers' war. This one will cost a bloody sight more.'

*

Barely a day later and Joe was on the train approaching Newcastle, chuffing into the elegant curve of Central Station with the grimy majesty of the medieval keep rising incongruously between the maze of lines. News that war was imminent had not come as a particular shock to the men of B Platoon, nor to the rest of the battalion for that matter. Debate had, however, raged over the potential deployment of territorial battalions in offensive operations. The brigadier, when he'd addressed them, had finished by suggesting that though they were not obliged to fight in France or anywhere else beyond 'our shores,' there was an expectation that, should they be called upon, they would volunteer.

'Any man who would not willingly fight for his country then, let him take a pace to the rear,' the brigadier had challenged. Hinckley and a few others, ignoring their NCO's hostile glares, shuffled embarrassedly backwards but the majority, very nearly all, stood firm. When the officer finished with 'God Save the King,' the echo resounded down the valley like a roll of thunder. Joe and Neville, with Dodds and the rest of the platoon, had remained in their ranks.

When Joe had set off for camp he was determined to become a solicitor, work hard, rack up some cash and status — but this bland ambition was dulled by the opportunities war had opened up. For young men like him, burdened with a poor background, the lure of martial glory was enhanced by the possibility of a significant hike up the social ladder.

'I bloody well joined up to defend my home, not fight for somebody else's.' Hinckley had vehemently justified his stance as they struck camp, the tented city disappearing as fast as it had arisen, canvas folded and stowed onto Bedford trucks. 'That was the contract I made and I'm sticking to it ...' His petulant self-justification failed to impress his fellow squaddies, still bathed in patriotic glow. Other members of the platoon looked darkly on the dissenter. 'You'll be bloody conscripted anyway, an' go where you're bloody sent...'

'What about you?' Joe discreetly asked Neville, 'I thought you didn't believe in war?'

'In truth, I don't. It's all very stupid really, a bunch of tyrants and gangsters pissing on each other's boots, but you can't really object to the absurdity of something unless you're a part of it. Besides, how'd you manage without me?'

Joe had first come up to Newcastle a year ago, very much the hick. Even now, the scale of the big city with its vast and sprawling industry stirred a chord. The Tyne shipyards produced the cream of the world's warships and men o' war were frequently seen amongst the flotillas of shipping crowding the quays. Upriver, at Elswick, Armstrong's gun foundry had swelled to become a metropolis, a town within a city. It had been Lord Armstrong who'd paid for the construction of the new swing bridge back in the 1870s, freeing up the river passage. His workshops and foundries built the great guns that gave the navy its teeth. Looking eastwards, the quayside appeared dwarfed by the mass of vessels, oil tankers, tramp steamers, colliers, pleasure craft and a couple of sleek-hulled destroyers.

Central Station was a heaving scrum. Beneath the wide sweep of the cast iron and glass vault, a tastefully grandiose statement of the city's Victorian prosperity, men and women jostled. A few were already in khaki and the treatment afforded them must have made those in civvies wish they wore uniform. Men slapped him heartily on the back or pumped his hand, earthy and encrusted navvies with a grip of calloused iron, city gents immaculate in morning suits. Girls glanced coyly and invitingly, hints of promise in shining eyes. It was all very gratifying. All the more so for one who'd campaigned no further away than Rothbury.

Messrs Wingrove, Templeton and Hicks had their offices on the corner of St Cuthbert's Chare, off the Quayside. Sixty years before, the river-frontage had been spectacularly re-modelled by the massive explosion of an old soap-works on the Gateshead side which had demolished a warren of sagging tenements and scattered the disassembled remains of their inhabitants over a large area. Now the Quayside was the heart of the mercantile city, with the classical thoroughfares of Dobson and Grainger sweeping upwards. Tall and elegant facades, fine ashlar clouded by the black stains of unchecked industry.

The law firm occupied an entire building, its occupants stacked in ascending order according to their station in the hierarchy. Joe, as an articled clerk, shared a crowded office on the first floor with half a dozen others. A couple, he knew, were in the Terriers like himself, Mason and Goodyear were privates in the Fifth Northumberland Fusiliers. A third, Johnston, had enlisted in the more fashionable yeomanry, Northumberland Hussars, now equipped with anti-tank guns rather than chargers. Johnston was also in the office, sleek in his old-style cavalry uniform that was just that bit better cut than the infantryman's, sporting a leather bandolier that afforded the wearer an altogether more dashing look. The booby was even wearing spurs.

Perched languidly on a desk and working his cigarette with panache, Johnston, Joe admitted grudgingly, looked the part, and a pair of twittering secretaries was hanging on every ounce of military wisdom. He was tall, rather gangling and owed his place in the elitist yeomanry to his brother-in-law, a successful accountant. Though he had cultivated that languid drawl befitting a cavalryman, the distinctive rolling lisp of the coalfield occasionally escaped. He acknowledged Joe's arrival with the merest nod.

'All of us accepted service overseas when we joined up,' he was openly bragging, 'wouldn't have it any other way, not much fun being stuck at home guarding the public loos when all the action's going to be in Belgium. What about your lot, Joe?' he enquired. 'You'll be deployed to watch St James' Park, no doubt?'

'Same as you,' Joe retorted. 'You won't catch the Fusiliers sitting on the sidelines. We volunteered to a man,' he exaggerated. Johnston snorted, but any further exchange was interrupted by the office manager, sober in black, who curtly informed Joe the senior partner wished to speak with him. That shut Johnston up.

Arthur Templeton, great-grandson of the founding member, had his office on the top floor, as befitted one in his exalted position. The room was large and formal, heavily panelled with glass-fronted bookcases; shelves groaning under the impressive weight of leather-bound law reports. Joe knocked discreetly — normally an interview with the senior partner was a rare, and not infrequently terrifying, experience. Templeton was a grave and austere character, impeccably formal and not renowned for his sense of humour.

When he answered the summons to enter, Joe found his employer looking out of the full length sash windows that commanded a superb view of the river and its constantly changing traffic.

'Well, Joseph,' he began, turning round, 'you've taken the King's shilling and very soon you may be called upon to earn it.' With this he almost smiled. The knot of his tie was perfect, Joe noted, cuffs shot forward precisely the required length, discreet gold cufflinks.

'We are all so very proud of you, our young men', the older man continued 'and I'm giving you the same assurance as I gave to Johnston and the others. Your place here with this firm is secure for the duration of hostilities, and your career may resume thereafter as though uninterrupted …' Joe mumbled his thanks. 'Assuming war does come,' his employer went on, 'and it will, God help us, the government is sure to introduce conscription straight off. I can't see any vast queue of volunteers forming up like *we* did, last time.'

It seemed, for a moment, as though the interview might be finished.

Templeton seemed hesitant, as though not quite sure how to tidily dismiss his junior. Joe was about to save any embarrassment by excusing himself, when the older man unexpectedly continued.

'You will take a glass of sherry?'

This was indeed an honour, normally reserved for partners and then only at Christmas. 'I should be very pleased,' Joe dutifully responded, though sherry reminded him rather too much of maiden aunts, daft little yapping dogs and acres of chintz.

A moment or two was lost in the ritual of pouring the amber liquor into thin acid-etched glasses. The sherry was certain to be good, the firm did not stint itself where such important refinements were concerned. Joe wryly considered that the decanter from which they were drinking had probably cost the equivalent of several weeks' wages for a lowly articled clerk. War had a way of opening doors.

'You will understand, Joseph,' — his Christian name, another rarity — 'that we are all very proud of you young fellows, very proud ...' Templeton was still not entirely at ease, seeming to stumble over the conventional platitudes. A gulp of sherry. 'It will be no easy matter though, this war, possibly even worse than the previous madness ...'

Now, and for the first time, he looked directly at Joe. 'I fear the business will not be done by Christmas as the gutter press predicted back in '14, I make no secret of the fact I find their incitements as odious as they are dangerous. Are you prepared, do you think, for the rigours that lie almost certainly ahead? All of us who went through Flanders prayed our sons would be spared the same, but it rather looks like we were wrong ...' Joe realised the older man was absolutely sincere, his voice betrayed that and an edge, more than a hint, of bitterness.

'I shall try and do my duty, sir,' he responded (earnestly, he hoped).

'There's no choice, really. If war comes each one of us must do his bit, however tough it gets.'

'But are you prepared for service overseas? I take it you volunteered when called upon? That will be no sinecure.'

'I'd deem it an honour to serve my country in any capacity,' Joe dutifully and stolidly replied. Hitler or not, he wasn't going to damage future prospects.

'Whilst I am no soldier … oh, I did my stint in the Yeomanry last time round, like your colleague young Johnston. We crossed over in September '14 and never rode our horses again after that. Since the Armistice I have made something of a study of war. I'm no armchair general either, mind you, but I'm bound to say that I wonder if our general staff appreciate the nature of this fresh conflict.'

Joe listened; he had considerable respect for his boss' intellect, which he suspected far surpassed that of most of the part-time officers in his battalion.

'This will be a very different kind of war. The Boche has learnt from his mistakes, but I wonder if we and the French have. They boast of their great Maginot Line — impregnable by Great War standards but putting your faith in fortresses has rarely worked. I'm having this conversation with you, Joseph, as I feel you will understand. I certainly believe a commission to be within your reach and you may count upon my endorsement …'

Joe murmured his gratitude.

'Without wishing to seem unduly censorious, I'm having this conversation with you rather than Johnston or any of the others, for although I don't doubt their eagerness or their spirit, I am less assured of their native wit. You, I suspect, are different.'

'You believe we, that is to say the army, is unprepared?'

'Unready, I'd say, in the sense that we've prepared for a conventional campaign of trenches and I suspect the actual nature of this war will be very different. Germany has created a huge new tank force, fleets of bombers, and they've had the chance to try all these out on our unfortunate Spanish friends. Dear me, I do hope I don't depress you too much but I would believe I was failing if I did *not* acquaint you with these ideas. I may be completely wrong, of course.'

Joe had not really thought about the actual course the war might take. When he'd thought of it at all he'd supposed it would revolve around trenches and great set piece battles, the sort his father had fought in.

'Well, we've trained pretty hard, I daresay we're as proficient as we can be. I'm sure though that the Fusiliers are ready for any test.'

Their sherry was consumed and Templeton poured another, though their conversation turned to more mundane matters of files and workload, lodgings and rent. When it was time for Joe to go they shook hands formally and he was surprised to see the older man's eyes were full.

'God bless you boy,' was all he said.

*

That summer he was lodging in Heaton, a couple of miles from the city centre, one of those prosperous middle-class suburbs that had sprung up during the preceding reigns in response to the city's rocketing riches. The houses were ponderous, semi-detached villas with deep gardens to the rear of tree-lined avenues, red brick and pebbledash, coloured glass and grey slate. He had a room in number fourteen, Whittingham Terrace, each road being named after a Northumbrian market town.

Mrs. Musgrave was his landlady, darkly handsome and rather operatic in appearance. She'd been widowed some years previously and, finding her late husband's pension uncomfortably frugal, was obliged to take in 'young men of good character and professional prospects' as lodgers. The same sign proclaimed 'No Irish need apply'.

His room was on the first floor, nice enough and well-proportioned, with a view over the neat and well tended garden, floral wallpaper, brass bedstead and mahogany washstand. This was grander than he was used to at home and so he counted himself fortunate. There was only one other lodger, a commercial traveller who, unsurprisingly, travelled a great deal and was seldom seen; a rather seedy little man in a well-worn tweed suit.

She greeted him at the door. He later thought she might have been waiting. Adele Musgrave was a woman of indeterminate age, probably some years older than her carefully tended appearance would suggest, of ample proportions and something of a leading light in local amateur dramatics. He imagined her to be much sought after by the rather sad older men or, worse, sadder and more hopeless young men, who were drawn to such vapid posturing.

'You'll be off then,' she enquired. Her dark hair was piled luxuriantly and the abundant orbs of her splendid bosom beckoned imperiously from a high necked silk blouse, her wide hips in a well cut grey woollen skirt.

'Well, we're not at war yet.'

She drew her breath in sharply, perhaps imagining him bound immediately for France, 'and probably no further than Wearside, I'm afraid, guarding the gasworks, not exactly *Under Two Flags.*'

He was aware that she read some romantic fiction and that her voice, clear and well-modulated, might disguise a social origin not entirely consistent with her present position. She was, he thought, a good-looking woman and her flowing curves had featured regularly in his nocturnal fantasies.

'I will keep your room if you want, the war can't last forever.'

'You're very kind, but really I don't know what to suggest. Obviously, we might be called on to go to Belgium or France, who knows?'

25

'I did have a German lodger once,' she confided over tea she had made, sitting in the airy conservatory. 'Nice enough chap, awfully polite, not like some,' she teased; all part of their informal ritual. Though they both behaved well, staying within the bounds of propriety, each was acutely aware of the other. 'I think he was buying guns or shells from Armstrong's, probably about to start shooting them back at us, seems so odd we're nearly at war with them again. He didn't seem at all beastly.'

'Most Germans are pretty much like us I guess, though not if you believe the press. Is that a new play?' He gestured toward a bound manuscript lying on the cane seat between them.

'Oh yes, seems a bit frivolous I suppose, what with war looming. A Jacobean tragedy,' she smiled. 'Not exactly cheerful, I'm a rather naughty married duchess who has an affair with a younger lover, not the sort of stuff the vicar normally goes for.'

'A happy ending?'

'Oh no, I end up fighting a duel with my estranged husband and he stabs me with his sword, I fall down dead at his feet, in doublet and hose, too,' she added coyly.

'Sounds intriguing, I hope the sight of you in costume isn't too much for the vicar.'

'Be careful, or I'll make you help me learn the lines ...'

'Only if you promise to wear your hose...'

*

He put his better suit on and shaved at the washstand with some care. What was looking back at him from the mirror wasn't really that bad. Not quite a gentleman perhaps, but not necessarily far off. His teacher had once described him as 'Anglo-Saxon.' A decent squarish face, hair a darker tint of fair, eyes blue and features regular, mouth not too wide, nose pretty straight, if not completely, been broken a few times boxing, inside the ring and less formally out. He'd a decent build, just over six feet which was tall for mid-Northumberland, more yeoman than pitman, agreeably wide of shoulder and narrow at the hips, a regular Douglas Fairbanks.

That evening, they dined in some style. The commercial traveller was away, travelling in commerce presumably, and the maid discharged for the evening. He did not particularly like the dining room, with its dark burgundy flock paper and mock-Tudor furnishings, but Adele had dressed for the occasion in a fitted satin gown which, though high necked for ostensible modesty, showed her assets to advantage.

If Mr Musgrave had chosen to die at an injudicious moment from the pension perspective, he'd at least had the decency to leave a reasonable cellar. Joe, bred to ale, was not particularly familiar with wine, though Neville had made some efforts to educate him.

'I did think of a Riesling,' Adele confided, the soft and artful glow of candles showing her dark eyes as shining pools of light, 'but it seemed somehow unpatriotic, I suppose I can't drink German wine till the war's over. It's a shame really, as I prefer it to French, even if they are our allies.'

They were eating blanquette of chicken with a potato border — somewhat superior to the grub he'd consumed in camp — followed by a pierrot pudding. 'I suppose I should, strictly, have served white wine,' she continued, 'I do hope that's alright?'

It was, in fact, really *very* alright. Adele had liberated rather a fine claret and Joe was savouring the richness of taste, a warm smoothness that seemed suited to the balmy summer's evening. 'It's really very nice,' he confirmed, somewhat lamely, he felt, cursing that he'd not paid more attention when Neville was extolling the virtues of various vintages.

Even though the French windows were open, there was no hint of breeze. Next, she plied him with cheese and good brandy, further booty from her deceased husband's stock. The fiery spirit, properly served in a heated balloon, trickled delightfully mellow into his full belly.

A certain innocuous flirtation had been a part of their relationship since he had taken lodgings with her the previous year. This had been enjoyable whilst remaining within the strict bounds of convention. She was, after all, a respectable widow and he had rather vaguely hinted that he was spoken for. Guiltily, he realised he had not thought of Evelyn all day and this beguiling matron was now entreating him for help with her lines.

'You're not in costume,' he gently chided.

She gave him a long look which held immeasurable depth, then briefly excused herself while he kept his attention fixed on the brandy.

When she reappeared in full stage rig, he was transfixed. Her hair now hung loose in a dark, seductive curtain that made her look younger and her full figure was encased in a dark satin doublet, laced and pleated but which clung to the curves and light coloured hose that left very little to the imagination. She blushed slightly, aware of the effect.

'I am supposed to be trying to look like a boy,' she suggested.

'I'm not sure that's entirely convincing. I imagine your vicar needs the odd cold shower.' At this point, Joe certainly did.

'Well he plays the madly possessive husband, the one I have the fight with. He keeps apologizing every time he stabs me.'

They went through her lines, which she delivered with gusto. He supposed she was probably a natural actress. When it came to her death scene, she provided wooden rapiers with thin 'blades' of a couple of feet or so. When she was disarmed he hesitated briefly — killing her seemed rather ungallant. 'Stab me,' she commanded and, when he still hesitated, she took the point of his foil and placed the tip against her left breast. 'Push slightly,' she commanded, leaning forward as though impaled.

He obliged with a rather feeble lunge and she arched dramatically forward with a loud gasp. She remained stricken for a long moment; one hand cupping the fictional wound, then took a halting pace forward as though about to drop, treating him to an unfathomable glare. She sank abruptly to her knees before him and then flopped forward, the adulterous slain, her percheron buttocks shuddered in a final, compelling quiver and then she went limp.

Adele didn't move, as though killed in earnest. Joe remembered suddenly that in the play the husband contemptuously rolls his faithless wife's corpse over. He was experiencing some minor difficulty, in that he was hugely erect. He nudged her gently on one hip. She obligingly threw herself over as though unceremoniously kicked so that she sprawled immodestly on her back, arms out-flung, heavy thighs spread in an apparently involuntary invitation. He bent, as he'd been instructed, to close her eyes, which were currently dramatically wide. As he did so she circled an arm around his neck, and drew his lips to hers.

'Dying woman's prerogative,' she suggested, her silk-encased legs still wide.

'Is this what they mean by active service?' She murmured huskily as they drew breath, 'The things a girl has to do for king and country.'

Chapter Two

Operation Mercury

We marched and groaned beneath our load,
Whilst Jerry bombed us off the road,
He chased us here, he chased us there,
The bastards chased us everywhere.
And whilst he dropped his load of death,
We cursed the bloody RAF,
And when we heard the wireless news,
When portly Winston aired his views —
The RAF was now in Greece
Fighting hard to win the peace;
We scratched our heads and said "Pig's arse",
For this to us was just a farce,
For if in Greece the air force be —
Then where the bloody Hell are we?

Anzac doggerel: *Rare as Fairies*

*

'Nowt like Blyth, mind,' someone mourned — and it wasn't. But it *was* another bloody retreat. A wind blowing hot from somewhere even hotter (and it was very warm indeed) brought no relief. It bounced and eddied off the ring of hills and scoured the dry plateau. The air was alive with the scents of spring; broom and gorse carpeted the dun coloured ground. But nobody really noticed. Since arriving in the Mediterranean that February, which seemed like years ago, the enthusiastic young heroes of Layforce had endured weeks of confusion, rumour then more confusion and more rumour, seasoned with unending boredom.

'Never have so few been so royally buggered about by so many for so long.' Alan 'Mogga' Morrin chimed the now universal mantra. It seemed particularly true today. The bare bowl of the Askifou Plateau was surrounded by scree covered hills, soaring peaks of the White Mountains rising beyond. A few scattered goats tinkled across the steep slopes, their bells the only melody in thyme-scented air. The wind plucked eddies of dust from sparse grass and scrub.

'Who's that bugger?' Brian Bell, known as 'Bomber' on account of his general bulk and dour temper, snapped. A youth was moving among the scattered ad hoc defences, generally unnoticed. 'Well, doesn't look too much like a Jerry paratrooper does he?' Joe, as section corporal, went over to investigate. The lad was mid teens, dark, scrawny but with brilliant teeth, set it seemed in a permanent grin. He wasn't fazed by the soldiers. Archie Dunmore, Joe's best mate in the platoon, had picked up a few words of Greek.

'His name's Andreas, lives locally. He's probably fifteen or thereabouts …'

'Does he know there's a bloody war on and we'll get Boche planes any minute?'

'Yep, he knows about the war and he's out collecting. That's what he's picking up, bits of kit an' stuff.' The boy was carrying a webbing haversack and was hung around with stray remnants of gear, pockets seemingly full of spent .303 cases. 'He says that, after the war, he's going to open a museum in the town here or maybe on the coast, with a café and flog souvenirs to the tourists ...'

'Enterprising little bastard then, all he's got to do now is survive the next couple of hours. Tell him to bugger off and take cover, he can count his cartridges while we try and hold his bloody village.'

The settlement was a raggedy patchwork of squat, stone walled houses clustered around a small white painted church, postcard picturesque with its distinctive onion dome, small dirt fields and rows of gnarled vines. Jerry was never far behind, but straggling over the scruffy road the detritus of defeat still came stumbling on. Dirty, weary, hungry and beaten, men without officers, a jumble of units, RAF and army joined by clumps of leaden-faced refugees, carts piled high with children and livestock. 'What a bloody mess,' Archie exhaled. These men and women looked neither left nor right. All had trudged up the hairpin road to the plateau and now faced the nightmare descent through the Imbros Gorge down to the port at Sphakia.

'Be worse than Whitley Bay on a bank holiday, down there like,' one of the Geordies joked.

Joe wondered idly if they'd ever see the south coast and, courtesy of the navy, their salvation. His own unit, the commandos, comprised what was left of Layforce, named after its commander Bob Laycock, of whom little had been seen of late, and was dug in around the village, safe enough for the moment in slit trenches and behind thick masonry. Aussies held one flank and Kiwis the other. Askifou was the cork in the bottle. If Jerry wanted to mop up what was left of the Allied forces, he'd have to come through here. Vaguely Joe remembered hearing of the legendary stand by three hundred ancient Greeks, the Spartans, at Thermopylae in Northern Greece. The precedent wasn't encouraging.

'Here's our morning hate!' someone yelled. Bang on time, it was mid morning and already the clear bright sun was a demon. Joe's battledress was intended for northern Europe and, like everyone else's, stiff with sweat and dust. Thick serge was hardly ideal for the hot Mediterranean. The Me 109s swept in like hawks, machine guns spitting. Men huddled and cursed as rounds zipped and careened off walls, tracer bright as fireflies. The noise was terrific. 'Bastards never think about having a day off,' Archie yelled in his ear as they crouched behind a rough stone dyke. The caravaners on the road parted as though by alchemy and dived to ground as the scourge passed overhead. A lone vehicle bounced and sagged as the fusillade struck.

'And now for the main course,' Bomber Bell muttered sullenly. Ju 87s, the notorious Stukas, followed the fighters. 'Apparently, they're obsolete, easy meat, so where's the bleedin' RAF?' Rebranded 'Rare as Fairies,' the Air Force had been conspicuously absent from Cretan skies and if there's one thing a soldier hates more than all the other things he hates, it's being exposed to enemy aircraft, 'and bugger all we can do about it.'

For most, the banshee wail of the dive bombers was worse than the bombs. Explosions crumped on barren ground or thrashed the ancient vines. No buildings were hit as far as Joe could see, though dust in great eddying wafts billowed and drifted. A lone Bren clattered in defiance and others picked up the refrain. 'Save the bloody ammo, you daft bastards,' Joe yelled, more in frustration than hope of being heard.

There was no sign of either the lieutenant or the CSM. Joe's platoon was dug in on the west side of the houses, only a couple of Brens between them. 'Now why did we have to dump all our bloody kit at Suda?' Archie complained. 'Be far nicer drivin' than bloody walkin,' an' we might have had a few bleedin' mortars.'

'Well Jerry's got plenty,' Tom Common replied, 'might lend us a few, be fairer.'

Joe glanced at Archie; he was a spare, wiry bloke who looked somehow older than twenty-three. The only Londoner in the section, the rest often had difficulty understanding him. He had the raffish good looks often associated with the lesser brand of Hollywood actor, mildly chiselled with high cheekbones, spoiled by a rash of ginger freckles. But for the colouring, he looked a bit like George Raft and both shared the taint of criminality. Archie was always clean and shaved, quick witted and equally quick on his feet. He'd had years of practice, running from coppers.

Squatting in the shale dust, Joe idly picked up a piece of pot, the worn ribbed fragment of a pottery jug handle. 'That's Minoan, I'm pretty sure,' he motioned to Archie. 'Been here God knows how long, thousands of years.'

'Not much chance of putting it back together then. God knows what those old folk would make of this bloody mess, be more than a few pots getting broke ...'

As the dust settled so did a brief calm. Everybody knew it wouldn't last, so they were working rifle bolts and checking Brens for clogging dirt. Joe moved along the section position. Doug Hall, a thickset, sandy haired ex-navvy was sharing a sangar with Dickie Bird, undertaker's apprentice. 'An I shagged his sister an' all...' Hall was recounting. Women, alcohol and cigarettes were his three principal tactical aims in war, generally, if not exclusively, in that order.

The trainee undertaker seemed unimpressed. 'Could never shag a lass as fat as that, like humping next door's heifer ...'

'Gi't manka' [huge] tits tho,' Christ an' ah'm borstin' of a shite, fokken Jerries ...'

Joe jogged into the small village. It was bare of locals. War was nothing new here, most inhabitants had rifles and as a rule they were none too keen on Germans. Just by the church, he spotted a Standard 12, one of the tillies used in large numbers by the army, just a civilian pickup given a brief War Department makeover. An officer stood nearby, reading a map. 'There's nothing more dangerous than an officer with a map,' he remembered. He wasn't too impressed with this one. The man's pips pronounced him a major, staff wallah, shiny Sam Browne, neat moustache and stiff upper lip — except his was wobbling.

'Did you see that?' the pop-eyed major expostulated. 'Bloody Messerschmitts! Where the bloody hell's the RA-bloody-F?' He glared at Joe as though expecting him to explain. 'Got to get going,' the perspiring major continued, not waiting for a response, 'important divisional papers.' He gestured at the truck, clearly his own evacuation was more pressing than any use the commandos might have. 'Can't stop — driver, start up. You, Corporal, fasten the back flap.'

Joe felt resentment bubbling; lack of sleep, lack of food and plenty of stress had shortened a fuse that had never been over-long, anyway. Muttering, he moved to the rear of the van, began fastening the canvas straps. The officer had one hand on the door handle as though somehow undecided. Glancing across the street, Joe saw a local family watching from their doorway, a man, woman, teenage girl and young boy, all muffled in the shapeless black of the island.

Then, very suddenly, somebody opened the furnace door and a white heat sent him tumbling down the dusty street. He sensed there was tremendous noise, but he couldn't hear. The force of his fall had winded him. He could taste the salt of his own blood. Time seemed slowed, random thoughts jumbled. He found himself thinking of his last school assembly at Bedlington Grammar, dark leaden cloud and scrubbed faces for the ritual photo.

'Y'alreet man?' Dickie Bird was hauling him to his feet. 'Are ye hurt?' It seemed, bizarrely, that he was not. He felt briefly nauseous then steadied, swallowing back the bile. Bird's voice was coming from a long way off, down a long tunnel somewhere.

'Christ man, you're fuckin' lucky there mind.'

'Aye, bloody lucky,' Hall echoed.

Others were not. The Standard was a shattered wreck, collapsed upon its twisted wheels, tattered canvas smouldering; division would be missing some paperwork. There was no sign of the driver, but a piece of skull was hanging from the line overhead which Joe took to be his, and a single leg — still with polished brogue — was resting on the far side of the street.

Then he saw the family. The mother and father were plainly gone, smashed and shorn of limb, the rough wooden doors behind buckled and sprayed with their blood. Of the girl there was no sign. They boy lay beside, a glistening slew of entrails spilling. Joe felt his nausea return.

'Any more casualties?' he queried.

'Nah, none, far as I can see,' Bird reported.

'Nobody's going to miss another staff-wanker; we coulda' have used his bloody van, though …'

Suddenly, the boy stood up, staring for a moment at the trailing mess of his burst insides. Then he began to run, tripping in pointless circles and screaming, a high pitched inhuman wailing that cut through to the soul. For a horrified moment the Tommies watched, utterly helpless. The lad was beyond any help. Joe raised his rifle, not thinking really, a reflex, chambered a round and shot the poor kid through the head.

'Best thing really,' Bird nodded. 'I could start me own funeral business, right here.'

The steady thumping of the German mortars had marched off

eastwards, and other villagers emerged to clear up the carnage. Milburn, Hall and Bird scuttled back to their positions. As they moved down past the houses, a couple of which were sagging like split sacks, thickening palls of dust everywhere, Joe spotted the girl. Miraculously, she appeared completely unhurt, helping to tend others who were injured. Her face was completely blank.

'Must be in shock,' he muttered, half to himself.

'Tough little bastards, these,' Hall concluded. 'They've seen it all before.'

'You OK, Corp? Archie queried. 'You look like shit ...' More helpful observations were drowned out by the racket of small arms fire. Boche MG 34s, their rapid, tearing rattle unmistakable. Joe steadied his rather fine Zeiss binoculars, formerly the property of a Fallschirmjäger officer, since deceased. Through the wonderful lenses, he could make out a steady massing of feldgrau in the distance. 'Alpine troops,' he confirmed, 'not paratroops, more of their reinforcements.' A different breed of elite, these Gebirgsjäger with their distinctive peaked caps, trained to fight in mountainous terrain.

'Well, the bastards should feel at bleedin' 'ome 'ere then, no shortage of bloody hills here. Them kiwis gave their paras some kind of hiding at Maleme, killed thousands ...'

Archie pronounced this as 'thar-sands' but Joe was attuned to his east end twang. The New Zealanders, now dug in on their flank, had indeed exacted a heavy toll before giving up the airfield. But that had proved decisive and now the British were on the run. Most were, anyway.

'They'll try to work around our flanks, just like they did down the road, won't be so bloody easy tho' — this is a bottleneck. Everyone hold your fire,' he yelled, 'wait till I give the order and remember, bullets cost money and we ain't got too many.'

The men weren't fazed by the enemy's appearance. They'd fought a couple of successful holding actions before they started the long zigzag up to the pass, and nobody had any doubts about the Anzac units. Still, they'd nothing meatier than the Brens, and not enough of those. Most had the venerable short magazine Lee Enfield that had been used in the Great War. Joe's father had carried one. Rugged, reliable and accurate with a ten round .303 box magazine and seventeen inch bayonet, the Lee bolt designed so you could load and shoot from the shoulder without lowering the weapon, significantly increasing the rate of fire. Still, the Germans had an awful lot of those quick-firing MG34s.

'I doubt we'll be needing these.' Archie was caressing his commando style knuckleduster dagger, a six inch flattened diamond section double edged blade and needle point with a brass knuckled grip, known for whatever reason as 'fannies'.

'Apparently, the Boche don't like 'em, consider it unsporting, not like shootin' women an' kids.' At least one commando battalion included a fair sprinkling of dubious types who'd escaped from Spain at the end of the civil war. They'd been on the wrong side then, but had joined up for another go and three square meals a day. 'Our Spanish heroes didn't do too well down below,' Archie went on. 'You could see why they lost first time round.'

A loud hailer cackled in staccato bursts, clipped Germanic and sneering, calling on them to surrender, that they'd been betrayed by Jewish officers. 'Had-away an' shite,' someone yelled back.

Rifle fire began pinging around them as the Axis inched closer. On their left, a heavy burst of firing erupted. 'Here we go,' Joe intoned. 'Right, mark your targets, fire at will.'

'Shouldn't that be *Wilhelm*?' some wag suggested. Then they were shooting, rifles spitting and kicking. Most had stuffed towels or rags under their battledress to soak up some of the ferocity of the SMLEs' kick. The noise was terrific, drowning out all senses, the hot tang of burnt cordite filling the air, mocking those subtle scents of spring.

'Clever bastards, these,' someone yelled above the din. The Jerries were indeed smart, trying to feel their way around the flanks. But this time it wasn't working, the narrow funnel of the pass effectively prevented any artful manoeuvring. Joe saw grey-coated figures ducking and firing in the scrub. He steadied his rifle, aimed down the ladder sight; 150 yards. The weapon banged and kicked. Did one of them go down? It was impossible to say.

He had time to glance to his right, the section line was holding nicely. He noticed a gaggle of locals had joined in, baggy-trousered, moustachioed palikari, curved yatagan daggers in bright sashes, equipped with a bewildering collection of ancient firearms. Some had enterprisingly lashed daggers, even bread knives, to their barrels as impromptu bayonets. He really hoped it wouldn't come to that.

The noise of battle ebbed like a receding tide and spluttered out. The Germans fell back. They could afford to. Time was another commodity they possessed. 'Everyone OK?' Joe called, his ears still ringing, a chorus of muttered assents while local women brought water. They were all parched and slurped gratefully. He noticed the dark haired survivor among the women. Was that only half an hour ago? Mid-teens he guessed, lithe and slender, a pale oval face, framed in jet curls. She *must* be in shock he thought — but she gave no sign of it.

'How are we doing, we happy few?' Lieutenant Blenkinsopp-Smythe was the platoon commander. Most of the men in the section were drawn from mining stock, strong and wiry but rarely above five foot six. Their officer was from a mine-owning and public school background, so seemed to have arrived from an altogether different country. He was much taller, over six feet. Joe was the only squaddie who came near. Fair-haired and well built, he'd have played rugby not soccer, and though his family money came from coal, he'd never seen the inside of a mine. Their name was originally plain Smith, but they'd married into decayed gentry and weren't about to let anyone forget it.

'See that bloody pimple?' the officer squatted beside Joe's sangar. 'Jerry's got his mortars there. God knows why we let them have the bloody place, but now brigade wants it back.'

'Our blokes call it the 'tit' sir, on account of its anatomical likeness. Have you seen the brigadier, sir?'

'Can't say I have, and you're not the only one who's been asking, seems the top brass all have pressing engagements nearer the south coast.'

'Are they perhaps looking for a Mediterranean cruise, sir?'

'You may think that, Corporal, but I'd better not comment. Fact is we want that bloody tit as you so aptly describe it, and B Platoon has been given the signal honour, alongside our Kiwi friends on the left, of wresting it back from Hitler. And we'd like it in time for breakfast tomorrow before Jerry gets his big guns up there and dug in.'

'Will they wait that long, sir?'

'Seems so, this lot are mostly Bavarians and Austrians, first class mountain troops but not necessarily your raving Nazi types. Their commander, a General Ringel, apparently believes "sweat saves blood." That's the kind of general I prefer, by and large; he'll take his time which means we have time. We'll move up, fighting order only, after midnight; be prepared to attack at first light.'

*

The earth was dry, unyielding, carpeted with small stones and rocks. Once through the canopy of vines it was pretty much bare. Wafts of thyme and broom came strongly through warm evening air. The wind had dropped to a whisper. Even in deep night it was mild and balmy. It would be perfect to sip beer and overlook one of the dazzling white-washed harbours, but instead they crawled forwards, inching over the exposed ground, sweat running freely in a hum of hungry mosquitoes.

Aside from zip and zing of the mossies, the constant chatter of cicadas, all was silent. The knoll loomed indistinct ahead. They inched forward, spread out in loose formation, Hall with the Bren in front. The ground began to rise. New Zealanders were supposedly on their left but it was impossible to tell. Time had no meaning. Suddenly a flare went up. 'Shit,' Joe moaned and shit it was, the whole stark plain lit up in clear white light. Voices rang out, screaming orders, and the hideous barking of MG34s ripped the night air.

'Fucking go,' he yelled, 'just fucking go!'

And go they did, most already risen, the Bren banging out. Up the tussocky slope which seemed farther than Everest. More flares went up. He briefly glimpsed bulky figures to his left — Maoris, by God. They stormed over the lip straight into German slit trenches. Rifles were spitting. A hefty Boche was directly in front, tugging on the stiff bolt of his Mauser. He swung towards Joe, who lunged with his bayonet driving the needle sharp point into the man's fat gut. He wheezed like a winded steer, eyes bulging impossibly, then spewed out a torrent of blood, black in the harsh magnesium glare, and went down. Joe twisted the blade sharply and dragged it free. The dead man still flapped like a stranded haddock. Hall raked the shallow pit. More Germans went down, the rest just bolted.

The Maoris were the biggest blokes any of them had ever seen. 'Fucking hell, I hope these buggers are on our side!'

'So much for the master race, run away from a bunch of Abos, have that one on New Zealand Adolf!

41

'They're Maoris you prick, not bleedin' Aborigines, *they're* from Oz. Maoris is much more civilised, like proper soldiers.'

The knoll was theirs, alongside two MGs and several mortars. 'Dig in, you idle bastards,' Blenkinsopp-Smythe ordered. 'How are we doing, Corporal?'

Joe did a quick head count; nobody missing and, astonishingly, no-one wounded. 'Here you are,' Mogga the section's star pillager, handed Joe the loot from his dead Boche, a half decent watch and some issue fags. Also the man's wallet — he could see it contained photos but he didn't want to look, chucked it back beside the body.

'Get digging,' he ordered. 'Come first light and we'll cop it for sure.' The platoon didn't need much encouragement. No need for a tactical genius to work out what would happen next. 'Jerry will be seriously pissed off, he lost this bleedin' hill an' he'll give us hell.'

It was a couple of hours till dawn and already long range MG fire was tearing up what was left of the night. They gulped their scanty rations, plus whatever the Germans had left. There was very little water, though one dead Boche had yielded a flask of pilfered Greek brandy and became the only casualty to be toasted. Perhaps half an hour later the Maoris were withdrawn, cheerful, as ever. The knoll was suddenly a lonely place.

'Change of orders,' Blenkinsopp-Smythe confided. 'In recognition of our sterling achievement taking this place, we're now going to give it back and bugger off.'

Joe was beyond being surprised. The commandos' experience of the campaign on Crete since their much delayed arrival had been full of surprises and all of them, as far as he could recall, unpleasant. 'Well, can't say we'll miss this place. It'll be bloody hot when Jerry gets going.' Contrary and often pointless orders were a feature the platoon had grown accustomed to and nobody had been looking forward to the morning. Mortars, artillery, strafing; they were in for a regular treat.

Almost as silently as they'd come, they filtered back over the scrubby plain to the village. Joe had assumed they'd be back on the defensive, but pulling out meant more retreating, covering the disappearing back of the shambles that had been the Allied army. 'Get your buckets and spades out lads,' Blenkinsopp-Smythe ordered. 'We're all going to the seaside and hopefully, the navy boys will pull us out of the shit like they did in France and Greece. They've had loads of practice. We only take what we can carry an' don't leave a single bloody round behind.'

Dawn's pink glow was spreading across the ancient landscape. Some of the Cretans watched them go, silently, no cheers or drums in this war — yet seemingly no recriminations either. He couldn't see the girl. Adam Hepburn, youngest in the section, so thin and weedy he looked as if he should still be in school, asked Joe, 'what will happen to them Corp, the locals I mean?'

He'd been wondering that himself. There were plenty of stories about how the enemy dealt with civilians. 'God knows,' he muttered. 'Hopefully, they'll ignore the place and take after us.' The lad didn't look convinced and neither was he. As they trudged wearily off across the sparse valley, Jerry mortars opened up on the knoll. 'Bang on time again,' someone commented, 'you can set your watch by the bastards.'

Together with Aussies and Kiwis, they marched forward over the scorched expanse as the sun rose and the dust came up. Light brought relief from mosquitoes, but the glare was just as relentless. He looked back at the company, practically all that was left of their battalion, shrunk dramatically since Suda. Archie had 'borrowed' some discarded tropical kit and now wore khaki shirt and shorts, 'unconsidered trifles' as he described the looting — but only an experienced thief could have pilfered kit that fitted perfectly.

All in all, they didn't look too impressive. Their serge uniforms were in sodden tatters, their boots were falling apart. Joe, like several others, had helped himself to smarter footwear donated by dead or captured Germans. More than a few were laden with Axis weapons, the MP 40 sub-machine gun a preferred accessory. Several aped their Cretan allies, improvised sashes bristling with a lethal assortment of blades. Others had abandoned their tin hats and wore improvised kepis, fashioned from ladies' underwear liberated from washing lines.

'What bloody day is it?' someone asked.

'Tuesday,' someone suggested.

'I mean the bleedin' date!'

'It's the twenty-ninth of May,' Joe decided. His captured watch handily had a date counter. 'German timepieces are never wrong.'

Now was the time of the usual morning hate. Ever predictable, Me109s came blitzing from the azure skies. 'Off the fucking road!' he bellowed. It was an unnecessary order, as most were already diving for cover. The planes came in low, very low, treetop height if there'd been any trees. He could clearly read the decals, even glimpse the pilots. Machine guns raked and hammered the track, kicking up spurts of dust, scattering stones like grape-shot. Men hugged the almost non-existent cover, tried to burrow into the baked earth, willed themselves smaller, hunched, foetal and helpless.

A few Brens barked in reply but ammunition was short. The Luftwaffe was having fun and nobody appeared to spoil it. Everyone had given up wondering where the RAF might be. The MEs made one slow, almost languorous, pass and then another.

Joe glanced back along the rutted surface, watching in mounting horror as the fighters casually pounced on a straggle of refugees tramping lost and laden behind the Tommies. Old carts piled high, hand-barrows and villagers staggering under sacks. 'They're not fucking soldiers you bastards!' he heard himself screaming. That didn't matter. The jumbled crowd attempted to get off the road but far, far too late ... and besides, there was nowhere to run. The stacked wagons burst apart, torn by 20 mm cannon. People running like terrified rabbits caught in the lights were mown down — or just blown apart.

Their final pass complete, the Messerschmitts roared off. There'd been no Stukas this time but nobody thought that odd. No-one on that blasted road was privy to Hitler's master plan. He'd pretty much done with Greece and Crete and was looking eastwards, siphoning off aircraft for the defining campaign against his ally Stalin.

From Joe's section, David Horne was hit. 'Probably a ricochet.' Archie doubled as medic. The round had torn a gaping hole in the man's left calf below the knee, strings of tendon hung from the wound. Archie was trying to get a field dressing on. There was an awful lot of blood. Horne was already grey, eyes glazing in shock and pain, the morphine hadn't kicked in.

'Do what you can,' Joe said limply. Archie and he exchanged looks. The wounded man would have to be left.

'He'd not survive the bloody climb down the other side,' Archie confirmed. 'Jerry's his best hope, sorry mate.'

Blenkinsopp-Smythe had doubled back. 'Leave him, give him some water and try and find some shade, the Boche will take care of him.'

'What will me mam say?' Horne queried feebly.

'You're the lucky one mate, POW camp's the best place, least you get looked after an' fed and no bugger shooting at you no more.'

There was little more to be done, the column was already trudging off, though a few had gone back to the smashed refugees to do whatever they could. Joe went too. It wasn't pretty. A score or more were dead, some unrecognisable. Loads more injured; some of them children. There was no screaming, the survivors bore their losses and their wounds with a kind of shocked stoicism. Tommies were doing basic first aid, but there wasn't enough of anything to go round.

He found the girl beside an upturned cart, flung carelessly and draped over a shapeless bundle of clothes and linen. Her tight skirt had ridden up in a cruel parody. Her dark eyes were wide open but with no flicker of life. He forced them shut and looked away. The war had already moved on.

*

Later that afternoon, just as the shadows began to lengthen, drenching the rugged hills in golden light, they reached the southern rim.

'Blimey,' someone exhaled. As well they might. Nobody from the southeast Northumberland coalfield had ever beheld such a view. The gorge was a narrow, precipitous canyon of broken rock and scrub, opening like an abyss, hot as a flaming cauldron, dry as sandpaper. It swooped down two and a half thousand feet to the white dots of distant Sphakia, the port, the place of refuge. It looked a very long way off.

'Look at all those useless bastards, like bleedin' ants.' Hundreds of tiny figures were labouring to descend the gorge. There was no road, scarcely a goat track. Around them lay the waste of a beaten army; uniform, webbing, even rifles and ammo, all of which they scooped up.

'We hold here, boys; keep Jerry off the backs of our heroic comrades running for their miserable lives below.'

'Any grub?' was the Tommies' universal cry.

'Not a chance, dig in.'

'Reminds me of that film, can't remember the name but it was Joel McCrea, hiding up in some canyon, looked a bit like this, natural fortress,' Archie commented.

The place did have a bit of a wild west look. Jumbled boulders, some glacial dumping ground, were scattered like sentinels at the head of the pass, a superb defensive position. 'They got him, anyway,' Archie grimly concluded. The battalion, what remained of it, was spread out amongst the rocks. Afternoon darkened into evening and the Germans didn't come. Men huddled against the smooth stone, ate what little they had, made a brew, smoked a few of the fags they'd hoarded.

'Bastards are being cautious,' Blenkinsopp-Smythe mused. 'Probably think they've got us trapped.'

'Could they be right, sir?' The shared experience of war had eased the social barrier between junior officers and other ranks, to some limited degree anyway.

'Not at all, Corporal, I'm sure brigade even now are planning a decisive counterstroke and no doubt they'll get round to telling us sometime soon. In the meantime they want some intelligence, how many Jerries, how many guns et cetera. I need you to volunteer for a recce.'

Joe groaned silently. 'Couldn't think of a better way to spend my evening, sir.'

'Good man, this could get you a mention in dispatches — or a first class obituary, of course. Perhaps both. But do not despair; you shan't be alone. Let me introduce one of our chaps from D Company, Angel Otaegui. He's got form for killing Boche, been at it longer than the rest of us.'

Joe and the other squaddies had been wondering about the dark, stocky bloke with their officer. Thickset and pretty much inscrutable, the Spaniard gave off a sense of great physical strength and endurance. He had a mass of luxurious dark curls that even an army barber couldn't subdue, not a bad face and jet black eyes. 'Basque,' the man corrected, 'not Spanish. It was them I was fighting against.'

The distinction was pretty much lost on the rest of the section, but the ripe garlic sausage he produced struck exactly the right note. The republican survivors had a reputation for scavenging. Even Archie looked impressed.

'Where are you from then, mate?' asked Doug Hall.

'A place called Guernica. I was a teacher there and lived with my family.' It seemed that nobody but Joe had heard of Guernica.

'Hang on,' Archie interjected, I have. Didn't some weird bloke paint a picture of the place, some Dago? No disrespect, mate.'

Joe didn't probe further. Guernica was one of the Luftwaffe's earlier sorties, an inoffensive and strategically insignificant market town. They'd levelled the place, and most of the people in it, just to prove they could. He and Angel (the squad could never grapple with Basque surnames) with Mogga and Dickie Bird would make up the recce patrol, slipping off into the cool night air, just carrying weapons and basic kit. They were going to look, and not to fight.

Back they crept, over the dismal plain they'd trudged across just a few hours earlier, hungry, short of sleep, aware of their own stink. The Basque was a natural, an eye and feel for ground like few Joe had ever met. Joe himself was pretty good, a farm boy who'd grown up stalking rabbits and pigeons over the fields, hedgerows and densely packed woods of his native Northumberland. Angel led them unerringly towards the German positions. Joe estimated they'd be about two miles north of the gorge and they certainly didn't seem to be in any great hurry. *Sweat saves blood*; their commander would make sure he had his guns brought well forward. It did seem the Brits weren't really going anywhere soon.

That didn't stop the Germans being cautious. Losing the knoll, however temporarily, would remind them the rearguard still had teeth, even if the rest of the army had scarpered. Angel halted them just beyond the ring of sentries. Fires burned in the camp, voices and tantalising wafts of cooking drifted over. The wind had dropped and the night was calm, just that incessant chatter of cicadas and the damned mossies, nature's Luftwaffe.

They crawled inside the ring, slithering over rocky ground, tensed against the sudden rush of flares. None came. Angel stopped at around thirty yards or so from the fires. The Germans were vigilant but clearly not expecting an attack. Joe scanned the lines, trying to get a feel for numbers. At least one, possibly two battalions, plenty of mortars and MGs. *We'd cop it in the morning, short of ammo and just about everything else.* On the extreme left, set apart, he could see what he took to be a radio pavilion with a fire outside and a small tableau — one man, clearly a German officer, standing over another who was slumped in a camp chair.

Joe signalled to the rest to sit tight and inched forward. There wasn't much moonlight and enough background noise to cloak his approach. He was probably no more than ten yards away. The man on the seat was Private Horne, Joe could see the blood-soaked bandages. The man looking down on him was tall, slender, possibly a major and dark haired, pressed and groomed, pretty too; almost effeminate. He was speaking to the injured soldier in English, good English at that; his tone calm, reassuring, almost conversational. He obviously wanted to know about the commandos; how many were they, who was in command …

Horne was shaking his head, clearly near delirious with pain and blood loss. Joe felt his spine tighten. Behind the German officer the tent flap opened and an NCO called out, 'Herr Oberst…' A colonel then … Joe knew enough about the Axis to identify this one as pretty senior, probably military intelligence or Abwehr. The man acknowledged the summons and, still all conversational, clapped a hand on Horne's shoulder, passing behind the chair. In a single fluid motion he drew his semi-automatic pistol and shot the injured man through the back of the neck. Nobody seemed to notice or care.

Joe's fingers were on the cool brass hilt of his fighting knife. He intended to kill the German, but a strong hand clamped his wrist. He'd not detected the Basque coming up behind him. 'Fuck off,' he breathed.

The man gripped harder, a steel vice. 'You won't bring your friend again alive by getting yourself killed too. Come away now.' Joe allowed himself to be pulled back, slithering back to the others and safely down to the pass.

Miraculously, Angel produced more sausage. 'He must keep this stuff up his arse,' Archie muttered, 'still, who cares?' Joe had told the rest of the section what he'd seen. Their mood was grim.

The Basque watched them through his unfathomable eyes. 'When the Boche killed my family, buried them in the rubble of what had been our home, I was like you. I just wanted to find as many as I could — but then, we say that revenge is a dish best served cold. It's probably bullshit but maybe not altogether. And now you know why you fight, the evil that these people bring. Keep this memory in your hearts and whenever you have a Boche in your sights think of your comrade they have murdered, so you are never tempted to hesitate. Just shoot the bastard.'

No-one was minded to disagree.

*

They'd long since stopped singing *Oh I do like to be beside the seaside*. For one thing there was no ice cream or anything else for that matter. Those British and imperial forces crammed like badly turned out sardines on the beach at Sphakia universally wished themselves elsewhere. However, the only elsewhere that seemed likely was a POW compound, and most didn't fancy that either.

'Look 'ere,' Archie began. 'I may have knocked the navy in the past, I admit it but bugger me, they're not doing badly. If by some bloody miracle they do get the rest of us, I'll only smoke Navy Cut for the rest of me life.'

Thousands had been lifted, thousands more remained, dirty, demoralised and supine. Of senior officers there was no sign. Bob Laycock and his aide Evelyn Waugh appeared to have wangled their free passage fairly early on. The commandos had struggled in last, and so stood at the back of the queue. It was a very long queue.

'Shame about what's his name Smythe,' Archie continued. 'All officers are bastards, goes with the job, but he was a decent bastard, all told.' Joe had really quite liked their platoon officer, who'd gone down to a sniper's bullet as they were half way down that bloody gorge. They'd had to leave him, 'a bloody long way from Northumberland,' Joe concluded.

Angel had become a fixture. Anybody who could produce supplies the way he could was worth having around. The Basque had picked up various bits of local gear, and now wore a nicely embroidered waistcoat set off with a red sash, giving him a suitably piratical look.

'God, this stuff is piss,' Tom Common complained cheerfully. 'It's called retsina, contains pine resin, gives it that distinctive taste. The locals can't get enough of it.'

'Hopefully, it'll poison a few bloody Jerries.'

They were squatting in caves, just behind the overcrowded beach, carpeted with the lost and the listless. 'Look at 'em,' Hall sneered, 'what a bleedin' shower, makes you bloody ashamed.'

'It's the face of defeat,' Angel confirmed. 'Trust me on that one. I've seen it before, when we were all fleeing through the Pyrenees to escape the Fascists. Fear is like a disease, it spreads by touch, pretty soon it's become a plague and you can't stop it.'

'What happens to us now?' someone asked plaintively.

'Simple,' Joe answered. 'We get out or end up in the bag. And before anyone asks I'm for getting out. Just as a precaution though, dump your fannies. Nazis get annoyed by 'em, an' Angel, if anybody asks, you're a volunteer from Gibraltar, makes you one of us, not just a renegade Republican on the run.'

'I am feeling happier already.'

'It's odd, you know,' Joe told Archie as they sat through the long, hot afternoon. 'When I was a kid I always wanted to come to Greece. I used to read a lot. One of my favourites was an old story called *The Iliad*, written by a Greek called Homer, all about a ten year war, thousands of years ago. Great warriors, great heroes, men like Hector and Achilles.'

'Well, if neither of them ever played for Tottenham, I'm not likely to have 'eard of 'em.'

Joe persevered, 'these men, so long ago, they looked out over the same water — "his wine dark sea", Homer called it, and now it's us.'

'Well, those blighters probably didn't have bleedin' Jerry half way up their arses or maybe they had generals who knew what the fuck they were doing.'

That night, they huddled in the caves. Ships came and went. The supine hordes on the beach eddied and flowed. Many were taken off; many more remained. Like a vacuum, as soon as part of the shore emptied it instantly re-filled. He slept fitfully and it was just before dawn's first creeping light that he was shaken roughly awake.

'Come now, all of you.' It was Angel.

'What's up mate? Don't tell me Jerry's invaded.' The unwashed, unshaved, ragged wraiths did not appreciate the early morning call.

'A boat,' the Spaniard hissed, 'and we go now.'

They went, along the rim of the crowded shore, past the huddled, shuttered settlement. It was another perfect dawn, light and rising heat washing over. Beyond Sphakia, the beach was largely deserted, narrow and bisected by a confusion of coves and inlets. *Good smuggling country*, Joe thought idly. Angel set a fast pace, the men near jogging over uneven ground.

In one of the diminutive bays, screened by low cliffs, they saw the boat. A motor launch guarded by two more ruffianly looking Basque types. Angel didn't waste time on introductions.

She was a sleek sturdy craft, one of those launched from *Glengyle* a few nights before, somehow adrift and abandoned. Cream and Hepburn were both fishermen from Amble. 'It's kosher,' Hepburn confirmed, 'there's even fuel in the tank.' Despite his boyish looks, he knew boats, generations of fisher-folk in his genes.

'Enough to get us to Alexandria?' Joe queried.

'Dunno, but enough to get us pretty bloody far from here, an' we can jury-rig a sail I reckon. We just keep heading south and we're bound to hit bloody Egypt.

Heaving, they manoeuvred the heavy craft into the water. Angel's mates had even found some abandoned spars for makeshift oars. Nobody hesitated, just to be free of that accursed shore and with hope re-kindled was enough. They'd little water, next to no food and could expect the predatory attentions of the Luftwaffe at any moment. They'd have to dump the Bren and much of whatever personal kit they still had — but for once there were no grousers.

'Steward,' Archie chimed, 'that's a large pink gin and the bosun's daughter for me, if you please and smartish.'

'Save your breath, you'll need it for rowing.'

Chapter Three

Gaberdine Swine!

We had to join,
We had to join,
We had to join Belisha's army
Fourteen bob a week and FA to eat,
Hob-nailed boots and blisters on your feet
If it wasn't for the war
*We'd have f****d off long ago*
Belisha you're boring...
   Anon: *Belisha's Army*

*

Now I want you to remember that no bastard ever won a war by
dying for his country. He won it by making the other poor dumb
bastard die for his country.
   Patton (1970)

*

'So how come a grammar school lad like you didn't get a commission straight off?' Archie sucked the pale froth from his upper lip, immaculately shaved as ever. 'It should 'ave been easy.'

'It was all a bloody shambles after Dunkirk. They'd made us into an MG battalion, part of 50 Div, tho' we didn't have too many Vickers. By the time we got off the bloody beaches, those of us who did, we'd nowt left. Afterwards, we were just hung out to dry really, sort of re-formed then posted to Home Forces. So I got bored and joined the Commandos that October. I'd seen what Jerry got up to in Belgium and I just wanted another crack. Besides, a lot of the officers I'd seen were total wankers,' Joe said.

'Well we got to 'ave a go at Jerry alright, 800 of us went to Crete. Less than a quarter got back,' said Archie.

They'd been at sea for twelve days; food gone, water gone. The fuel had run out half way and they'd had to rely on the makeshift sail.

'We were bloody lucky.'

'That we were; shame about the beer 'ere tho.' It *was* pretty awful, a thin local brew from a scruffy back street bar much frequented by Allied servicemen. 'Sellin' this cheap piss for a fortune, your Gyppo is 'avin a bloody good war. He's probably learning German as well.'

After the crushing, furnace heat of the crowded streets, the bar was at least a tolerably cool cavern, a riot of uniforms; British, Aussies, Kiwis and more colourful Greeks, the last probably the noisiest.

'What do you reckon then, for us lot I mean? Think we're for the chop?'

'Most likely, Crete wasn't exactly glorious and top brass don't like commandos, too much enterprise and free thinking.'

The survivors of Layforce, burnt black, hollow-eyed and emaciated, were housed in the Abbassia barracks, a filthy fly-infested maze that resembled the badly thrown up set for an *Arabian Nights* movie. Vast, sprawling and malodorous, it had been their home for the past month since escaping the island.

'I almost envy the blokes in Syria, can't think the French will be much cop, if they run from us like they ran from Jerry an' that was in their own backyard.'

Part of what remained of Layforce had been dispatched to the Levant where Vichy was being uncooperative. That aside, the future looked bleak.

'What happened to your mate, the one you used to hang out with back 'ome, isn't he a staff wallah out here or summat?' Joe had not seen Neville since he'd volunteered for the Commandos. They'd both got off from Dunkirk. Quite a few of the platoon didn't. He'd last seen Hinckley being stretchered off after they'd brushed the Boche on the Ypres-Comines Canal, his left arm shattered by shrapnel. 'It's so bloody unfair,' was his last recorded moan, ashen-faced. He'd ended up a POW. Dodds, amazingly, had wangled some cushy billet with the Ministry of Information and missed the whole mess.

'I think he is here in Cairo. I'm going to try and look him up.' In fact, Joe *knew* Neville was here. He'd had a letter from Evelyn. It was dated March and had taken two months to find him. He wasn't going to tell Archie that, though.

Once outside the relative haven of the basement bar, heat and noise struck them like a tornado. The sun bounced off white painted walls, no breath of wind, already their uniforms, tropical khaki and shorts at last, seemed to stick to them in a miasma of cloying sweat.

'Not even Elephant and Castle was ever as bad as this.'

In this world, strange tongues competed. Stocky Egyptian traders, Arabs, Jews, dark-skinned Bedouins, semi-mythical in their coloured robes, and strong faced Sudanese. The Souq was ablaze with colour, exotic fruits and strange wafts of scent, evocative of that deep and alien continent which stretched endlessly south-wards. Red-faced squaddies fresh from English shires wandered, swaggering or bewildered, even the powder blue of RAF uniform could occasionally be seen.

'So the Brylcreem Boys do exist then,' Archie noted sourly. 'A lot more of 'em here than we ever saw in Greece.'

For an instant, Joe was struck by a vision of home that past autumn, less than a year before and already another world, just before he joined up. Then it had been richly autumnal, hints of summer warmth not quite gone, just that edge to the east wind whipping in off a gunmetal sea. That timeless smell of rich earth coming from dark brown fields, rooks raucous in the trees, each gust leaving a fresh scatter of leaves … he had always thought it a sad time. Summer was gone and winter just around the corner, no more larking in the dunes till spring. It was the last time he'd seen Evelyn.

'Right laddie, you're in demand,' the duty sergeant bawled as they returned to barracks. 'At ten o'clock tomorrow, you're to report to a Captain Ferguson, some I-Corps Johnny at HQ.'

'Bloody hell, bin' after the crown jewels, has he?' Archie spluttered.

'None of your business cocker, and Corporal Milburn — while you're there, get a bleedin' haircut, bad enough you're consorting wi' bandits an' heathens never mind lookin' like one.'

Angel was still with them, completing an unlikely triumvirate.

A summons to Middle East Headquarters was a strange and mysterious thing. The privileged fiefdom of staff officers, HQ was situated in a large complex of apartments that, pre-war, had housed some of the city's better-off inhabitants. Now it was roped off, behind coils of barbed wire and cordons of sentries with fixed bayonets.

Garden City was very different to the native districts, an up-market English suburb adrift in the Orient. Planned by some long dead khedive who wanted to make his city look more European, it boasted lengthy tree-lined boulevards, immaculately manicured gardens and opulent villas. It was a very far cry from the crowded streets and souqs of the old city. A light breeze coming off the great placid sweep of the Nile knocked a few degrees off the broiling glare. It seemed the war, any war, was a long way off. Gleaming cars and obsequious servants attended on smart and fragrant women.

'Fourth floor Corp, second door on the right,' a Jock sentry instructed him, the man's Glaswegian accent so thick Joe practically needed an interpreter. Straightening his creases, Joe jogged up the steps and into a marble foyer which would have been more in keeping with the better class of bordello. Any number of the smart looking secretaries would have fitted in quite nicely too, though none spared him as much as a glance. Probably didn't smile at anyone below the rank of brigadier.

Captain R Ferguson of 21 Field Security Section still wore the cutaway doublet and tartan trews of the King's Own Scottish Borderers, his public school drawl just edged with a hint of lowland Scots. He was a tall, spare young man, older than Joe, mid twenties he guessed, bright auburn hair and a pale, now pinkish, complexion. He had very clear and clever blue eyes.

'At ease, Corporal,' he waved away Joe's stiff salute. 'We're not doing formal today, have a seat.'

Yet another well groomed young woman brought tea while the captain made small talk. Joe felt as though he was applying to be a member of some obscure gentlemen's club. Cigarettes were handed round. 'Place looks a bit like a harlot's boudoir you'll be thinking, still more comfortable than the barracks. I'll guess the old place is still as rat infested as ever?'

Without waiting for an answer he pushed a photo, extracted from the single manila file on his desk, across. 'Recognise the bloke on the right, the far right that is, by any chance?'

Joe felt himself stiffening; while grainy, the image was quite clear enough.

'Yes sir, for sure, I saw this bastard on Crete, watched him murder one of my section in cold blood.'

'You're sure?'

'As sure as sure can be, his isn't a face I'm going to forget. Besides, he doesn't look like your typical storm trooper type.'

'He doesn't and indeed, he's not. Your man here is Oberst Erich Hahnemann, a Bavarian, native of Regensburg. He studied history there and, for a while, at Oxford; star student all round it seems.'

'But that's not why you're interested in him?'

'Dear me no, our chappie here is quite a big fish and a very nasty one. A thinking man's Nazi. You've heard of the Abwehr?'

'Military Intelligence?'

'That's them, run by a rum character called Canaris, queer fish, not really your Third Reich type, more of a traditionalist. But our boy here signed up in 1938 as they were expanding, obvious candidate; academically gifted, keen sportsman and a crack shot. He joined their economic intelligence section, was mixed up in Spain and possibly with various agitators in India.'

'Sir, can I ask why we're specifically interested in him? I know why *I'm* interested…'

'Well it seems Hahnemann has links to the Sicherheitsdienst — the SD, they're the intelligence wing of the SS, a fellow called Reinhard Heydrich runs the show. Fancies himself as a more intellectual breed of Nazi — Canaris chucked him out of the navy for getting some girl up the duff — ungentlemanly conduct and all that — and he's been determined to prove himself a proper gentleman ever since, particularly nasty piece of work.

'The brain of this outfit is an ex-lawyer called Schellenberg, now he is a very switched-on bastard. In November '39 he ran rings round SIS and kidnapped a couple of their more inept players, happened near a place called Venlo in Holland. The perfect ambush, but it got a bit messy, a Dutch police agent was gunned down and we think your man here pulled the trigger.

'You're the only one who spotted him on Crete, but we're pretty sure he killed another of our chaps, bloke called Pendlebury, during the invasion. We're damn near certain in fact, cold blooded execution of a wounded man — sound familiar?'

'It was pretty plain my mate wasn't his first kill, he's obviously got form.'

'I, that is *we*, think he's probably in North Africa now. Rommel, bless him, doesn't much care for Nazi thugs but Hahnemann's Abwehr and we know they're active.'

'Active, how? We're a long way from the front line.'

'Depends where you draw that line, and it's been see-sawing since last December when we bounced the Eyeties. It's no secret our Egyptian friends don't really like us. There's a very active nationalist movement wants us out and we're pretty sure they're talking to the Boche. You've heard of the LRDG of course?'

'The Long Range Desert Group, sir? Yes I have, our saboteurs, they're pretty famous; half the lads would like to join up.'

'Quite so, well, when Colonel Bagnold was doing his explorer bit in the desert during the thirties, he teamed up with a Hungarian bloke — Count Lazlo Almasy, pretty colourful character to say the least. He was a flying ace in the Great War and knows the Western Sahara as well as LRDG, has an affinity with the desert *and* with Arab boys, if half the stories are true. He offered his services to Rommel, who wasn't that keen to begin with but it seems he's been persuaded to let Almasy run agents into the Delta. Hahnemann is very likely his controller.'

'What can I do?'

'Good question.' The captain puffed out his cheeks. 'I'm not sure, not yet anyway, but you've seen the man, you'd know him…'

At that point the door swung open and an impossibly tall and gangling officer, propelled on crutches but beaming widely, burst in. 'Ah, might be the wrong room,' he breezed. 'I'm looking for the general.' Uninvited, he nevertheless closed the door behind him.

'Stirling, for God's sake,' Ferguson blazed. 'What in the pluperfect hell are you doing here? Don't tell me they let you in?'

'Well no, not really, not at all. In fact they were damned rude and I had to make me own way inside through a window, not easy on these, I can tell you.'

'Need I remind you, this is a high security area and you've no authorization?'

'That's what that chump over the corridor said, the Adjutant. Hated me since I was a cadet but I do urgently need to speak to Ritchie. So, if the mountain won't come to Mohammed, then Mohammed has to pick up his crutches and hobble to the mountain.'

'Get out before I have you arrested.'

'Well, that's part of the problem, old fellow, I've a posse on my tail already, so need to lie low for a moment or two. I say, is there any tea in that pot? I'm parched.'

The tall man helped himself to a chair and to a cup. Ferguson looked ready to explode.

'You must be one of those commando types,' he said to Joe. 'Just got back from the shambles on Crete, I'll guess?'

Joe had no idea what to answer, or whether he should answer at all, so the captain helped him out. 'Lieutenant Stirling here has ideas about how he, and he alone, can win the war, indeed he's already tried — which is why he's presently incapacitated. Some would say he's a damned fool.'

'Oh I don't know. Bagnold's doing a pretty good job and nobody would listen to *him* at the start.'

'That's the LRDG, sir?' Joe felt confident enough to query.

'Those are the chaps, laddie, kicking Rommel's fat Boche arse while most here are sitting on theirs, the freemasonry of mediocrity. Wars aren't won by fossilized shit in luxury offices, no offence Fergie, obviously…'

'None taken, now drink up and bugger off.'

'We might just talk again,' the tall man confided to Joe as he left. 'Looks like I've given the dogs the slip. Thanks for the tea.'

'Sorry about that,' his host apologized. 'The fellow's a lunatic when he's not being a sloth, not sure if he's more irritating when he's comatose or manic.'

'Can I ask what he actually wants, sir?'

'What he wants is his own private army, a bunch of desperadoes who will rampage behind enemy lines blowing things up and slitting throats.'

'Couldn't that be useful, sir?'

'If it's done the way LRDG do it, of course. And Bagnold did run into a lot of opposition till he got in front of Wavell. Since then he's more than proved his point. The LRDG are our eyes and ears. Much of what we know about enemy numbers comes from them. Intelligence gathering and the odd bit of sabotage is fine, but Stirling is going beyond the pale. He's irresponsible enough in barracks, so God knows what would happen if we ever let him loose in the field.'

With that, the interview appeared to be over. As he walked back along the well carpeted corridors, past rows of neat, well painted doors, Joe couldn't help wondering about Stirling. He was clearly the maverick type, but he might also be right. The war wasn't going to be won by men sitting behind typewriters. As he descended into the opulent foyer he was stopped by a nicely groomed blonde in a well cut ATS battledress and trousers, nicely titted out, too.

'Ah, you must be Milburn?' She had the clipped, rather affected accent he associated with the home counties and ladies' colleges.

'I was told to ambush you here. Would you mind awfully waiting a couple of ticks in one of our very comfy armchairs here? Someone wants to see you.'

With that and a tantalizing whiff of some unidentifiable but probably expensive scent, she was gone, leaving him none the wiser.'

'Christ, Neville!'

'That's Christ Neville *sir*, to you, boyo!' His friend laughed at his astonishment. 'I know, never thought I'd end up as a staff wallah.'

'Or as an officer, as I recall.' Neville had changed, though in some subtle way that he couldn't quite pin down. Less relaxed, more edgy perhaps. 'Though I did say you'd always end up as one.'

'Has its perks, lunch for us both at Shepheards for one.'

'I didn't think they let ORs through the door?'

'Normally they wouldn't, but you're with me and as I'm staff, I get to invite who I want.'

Shepheards was legendary, strictly off limits to the hoi-polloi. The place looked like a proper film set, hard to reconcile with any vision of conflict. There were no shortages here, of food, drink or, as it seemed, women. Gorgeously dressed, immaculately coiffed ladies floated in and out, generally on the arms of much fatter, older and seedier males of indeterminate nationality but all, as his father would have said, with 'a touch of the tar-brush.' Universally, they ignored him.

Wide, beckoning terraces fronted the street, beautifully tended and perfectly shaded. At the rear, through the palatial interior, groaning with marble and gilt, were more gardens, the place even had its own zoo. An ordered confusion of palms, creeping vines, evergreen jasmine, agapanthus and oleander, clipped and pampered grass, the gardens seemed like some mythical Shangri-la.

'Haven't seen bleedin' lions since the circus came round when we were kids.'

They were sipping cocktails. He'd never had one before. Neville, who appeared to have acquired a taste, ordered him a gimlet. Joe had no idea what was in it, he suspected gin, and it was sweet, probably a lot more potent than it seemed. Neville definitely had a taste. In the past he'd never been a drinker; that was what being on the staff probably did for you.

'You must think this is all pretty surreal, after Crete and real fighting?'

'The grub's a whole lot better and we didn't do cocktails as a rule. Does anyone here realise there's a war going on a hundred miles or so away?'

'You'd be bloody amazed. This place is a hot-house; every spy, spiv and chancer turns up here. Everyone is selling. The girls are selling themselves, the men everything else. This is the free market economy with a capital 'F.' The Gyppos think we may be losing, so they're brushing up on their German, or their Italian or both. There isn't anything you can't buy here. The whole Delta is becoming not just a marketplace; it's always been that, but a vast factory. They're quick learners and they're making everything the army needs, from bedpans to the General's best china.'

Neville was certainly different. Leaner, the lines of his aquiline features more etched, more defined but perhaps exuding a kind of wariness, too. Joe remembered what Evelyn had said in her letter, posted in February but he'd not got it till last week, a miracle it had ever found him. At least the army postal service seemed efficient. Something she'd hinted at

suggested Neville's translation to Middle East HQ wasn't entirely volun-
tary. She was too diplomatic for specifics, perhaps she didn't know …
but there seemed to be a whiff of *something* 'not quite right.'

'You met this Stirling bloke, like I did this morning?'

'Not met him, heard a bit about him. Most seem to think he's a bit
of a joke but he's certainly persistent. Behind the lines stuff, why not?
Jerry's given us some stick alright but his supply lines and his aerodromes
might be vulnerable. Every plane he loses will cost him. Whether Stirling
is the right man or not, I can't say. Why, do you fancy it?'

'I've thought about the LRDG. We took some shit on Crete and
we owe Jerry a pasting or two. The commandos here look pretty much
buggered, no future and I don't fancy line infantry much, not anymore.'

'You've become quite the warrior haven't you? Just think, all you
wanted to be was a solicitor and join the middle classes. Have you heard
from Evelyn? She did get very worried when your lot washed up on Crete.
Papers put a gloss on it, of course, but we both know we got our arses
kicked again. Not your fault of course, you blokes held the bastards off.'

'Fat lot of good it did us; half dead, most of the other half in the
bag. It was a total bloody shambles from start to finish. What about
you though, how do you fit into the grand plan at HQ? If you can tell
me, that is?'

'Well, I work with Ferguson, the chap you just met. In fact I suggested
he debrief you. As he probably said, we're mainly worried about Jerry
sending people in to stir the pot here. The nationalists would stab us in
the back, soon as break wind. How's your meal by the way?'

Joe had been informed he was eating a local dish of fried liver, heavily
seasoned … or so it seemed to his untutored palate. Spicy it might be,
but it beat bully beef for sure.

'It's not haddock and chips, but I'm enjoying it.'

'It's called kebda, this other one is minced meat with their own personal sauce. They use spices a lot of course; it would never catch on in Ashington. Tommy generally won't touch the local food; one of the many reasons, I guess, why they don't like us.'

Now they were drinking wine, another novelty. Aside from that amorous fling with his buxom landlady, fuelled by the loot from her dead husband's cellar, he'd never drunk much wine. Asking for a glass of wine in any of the pubs he knew was like broadcasting you'd turned queer. This one was North African from the look of the bottle, probably from Tunisia. Presumably the hotel had filled its cellars before the war. Neville was drinking far faster.

'A hell of a lot of boozing out here,' he confirmed. 'It's cheap as chips and nobody cares. Intelligence work, or what passes for it, gives you carte blanche and a decent expense account. You can thank Middle East HQ for this lunch. If it was on me we'd be in the NAAFI.'

Their talk wandered on. The drowsy heat was seductive. He'd been careful with the vino but was beginning to feel its effects; even the strong sweet coffee laced with cardamom lacked a fully reviving kick. They parted as they had always done, on one level it was as though they'd done this every week, yet he was aware of some subtle shift. It wasn't about rank. Neville had changed, in some imperceptible but profound way.

Joe supposed he must have quarters or even a flat in the city, but that wasn't mentioned. After all Joe was just a corporal. Still, he treated himself to an ornate silver cigarette case from the enterprising Greek in the checking room, who appeared to run his own thriving business there without any interference or comment from management.

Neville did invite him to a party that weekend at another fashionable address, 13 Sharia Naguib Pasha. 'Bring a couple of your pals if you like, nobody will mind.'

Aren't these do's just for officers and toffs — no offence!'

'Probably be plenty of both, but women too and besides, it'll do 'em all good to see what *real* soldiers look like.'

*

He had no trouble persuading Archie and Angel. The well-worn trawl of local bars and bordellos had soon paled; far too many social diseases, fights and redcaps, too much watery beer and pungency of sewage. He knew the address was in the far more fragrant Garden City, another sleek, anonymous block, close to the embassies and trendy watering holes.

'A bit better than barracks,' Archie quipped. 'I used to rob places like this back 'ome.'

Neville was already there, not that anybody seemed to be bothered. They were washed, shaved, brushed and burnished, but still looked like the hired help. In fact the fawning waiters were considerably better turned out, in pristine white mess jackets and jaunty fezzes, suitably exotic and comfortingly servile. Drink flowed in abundance. Champagne seemed the favourite, though Joe and the other two played safe with beer. Thank God, this stuff wasn't watered and it was ice cold.

''Ere we go then,' Archie breezed. He had the knack of insinuating himself into any company. Joe hoped they'd locked up the silver.

The crowd was fashionably bohemian. Apparently the gaff belonged to a bloke called Watson, something top end at the embassy, but he'd lent it to a couple of academic types who'd had to get out of Greece. That, at least, was something they had in common. Reggie was their host, a large untidy man with an air of perpetual bonhomie and the place was full of arty types, at least one well known novelist and a poet of some renown. Joe had never heard of any of them, though all were set to make the most of their trials by sea, fleeing the Nazi hordes.

He found himself talking to a distracted young woman, probably, he guessed, in her early thirties. Moon faced, small mouthed, nervy and with very wide eyes. She was called Olivia and married to Reggie, which was probably why she looked so nervous. Escape by water was pretty much all they had in common.

'It was *terrifying*,' she confided, 'first Bucharest, then Athens. I'm still bloody windy, don't mind admitting it.' She took nervous puffs of her cigarette, one of those strong black Balkan or Turkish jobbies, even offered him one — which he dutifully coughed his way through.

'Not my idea of a Mediterranean jaunt,' he added, 'not much food or water an' only the Luftwaffe for company.' He was usually conscious of his flat northern 'a' but the range of dialects in the room was pretty cosmopolitan, so nobody seemed to be sneering.

'Will they get this far, do you think?' she continued. Her agitated manner suggested that she thought they might.

'I'd say not, not that I'm privy to anyone's grand strategy. But the desert isn't like Greece or Crete, it's infinite. Ground doesn't mean that much, but the further you advance, the more bother with supplies you've got. My pal there,' he gestured at Neville, deep in earnest conversation with another, and very decorative, young officer, 'who's on the staff, no less, calls it the pendulum effect. We got overstretched when we chased the Eyeties into Cyrenaica and Rommel's in the same boat chasing us back.'

'And we all know the staff can't ever be wrong?' They both laughed.

'Ah, there you are,' the extended and unexpected figure of David Stirling, still beaming, appeared in front of them as though by magic. 'Olivia my dear, I regret that I must steal this young man from your embraces, important military matters and all that.' It occurred to Joe that while he was wonderfully ebullient and utterly charming, you wouldn't dream of not doing what he told you. It also struck him that this invitation wasn't really social at all. Neville had engineered the meeting; or someone had, through him.

Stirling guided him through the thick miasma of tobacco and, as his untutored senses guessed, other more dubious substances. The Scot was walking with a stick, freed from his crutches. 'Blighters said I might not walk for months, if ever. Shows you what doctors know.' Joe was guided into a smaller room, probably a study of sorts, the walls lined with an eclectic range of books most of which, appropriately, seemed to do with archaeology.

'Watson's batty about the New Kingdom, or maybe it's the middle one, never can quite remember which is which. Paddy, a beer for our guest.'

The other man in the room was tall and well built. Not as elongated as Stirling, but immensely broad in the shoulders. He didn't speak, just produced an already opened bottle which he plonked in front of Joe. With practised ease he drained his own in a couple of swigs.

'Another,' he barked, more of an order than an invitation. Joe thought he detected a twang of Northern Ireland. The man was built like a rugby forward and had the restless air of a caged tiger — except he wasn't in a cage.

'Don't mind Paddy,' Stirling soothed. 'He's a bit short on social graces but he likes killing Germans. How about you, laddie?'

Joe had come to realise that nothing about this Scottish officer was ever accidental. The urbane exterior masked real purpose and he presumed he hadn't been invited into this peculiar sanctum just for a drinking contest, but if that's what Paddy wanted … He took a long swig and drained the bottle. It was immediately replaced.

'I want to kill Boche too sir, lots of them.'

The Irishman seemed, at least briefly, to brighten.

'What do you intend to do now though, Corporal?' Stirling continued.

His relationship with the Irishman reminded Joe of a man with a very dangerous dog only partially on its leash. 'The future for you chaps doesn't look too bright. I say "you chaps" but I was attached to Layforce myself, just the reserves mind you, not the sharp end like you fellows. And trust me, I know how these staff Johnnies think, as far as they think at all. They want to fight like gentlemen. They think Rommel is a gentleman. He's not, none of them are, they're out to win and they're not bothered how they do it. Full of noble sentiments as our comrades may be, they just don't get it and he *is* winning, we're not.'

'I don't suppose you did manage to get in front of General Ritchie, sir, the other day I mean?'

'Matter of fact, I did,' Stirling beamed. 'Once I'd skulked about with you and Ferguson for long enough, the goons had wandered off so I was able to find the right office. The general's family shoots over our moors, you know. There are times when privilege has its uses.'

The big Irishman snorted but said nothing. 'The thing is, when I did get sat in front of Ritchie and gave him my notes which, if I say so myself, were a masterpiece of precision and brevity, not to say total obfuscation, he decided he *liked* my ideas. Even summoned that great booby of a fat adjutant and told him to give me whatever I wanted, thought the beastly fellow would have apoplexy there and then. Yesterday I saw no lesser person than the Auk himself, on Richie's say so.

'Don't tell me,' Paddy interjected, 'he shoots with your folks too?'

'Of course he does,' Stirling continued smoothly. 'I saw him and Dorman-Smith together with Ritchie and now I'm authorized to raise a company of six officers and sixty men. We're to be called 'L Detachment' though for the moment I've forgotten why. Thing is, laddie, do you want to join us?'

'Yes sir.' He answered almost without thinking. He could feel the excitement building. 'And there's two more blokes outside who'd jump at the same chance, sir.'

'And they are?'

'One's a Londoner sir, may have had some brushes with the law, but rock solid in a fight, good at scrounging. The other one's a Spanish republican. He's good at most things and bloody hates fascists more than any of us. They killed his wife and bairns. With him, it's personal.'

'So, a cockney thief and a Dago cut-throat, just what I'm looking for,' he grinned again. Paddy gave Joe another beer.

*

'L Detachment' was scrawled on a wooden sign beneath a clear sky and burning sun that battered them like hammers on an anvil. Joe, Archie and Angel stood by the side of the dusty track as their transport from Cairo disappeared in a choking cloud of the stuff. This was Kabrit, east of the metropolis, windswept, fly-blown and empty, about as bare as it gets. If that was depressing, the camp itself was worse: a trio of tattered tents, survivors from Gordon's last expedition by the look of 'em, a venerable truck of uncertain vintage that might or might not be capable of moving under its own steam … and that was about it.

'Special Forces,' Archie commented, 'more like special needs…'

'Welcome to our desert caravanserai,' Stirling greeted. He was seated on one of the two rickety old office chairs that made up the entire furnishings. Paddy Mayne was sprawled in the other, already with a beer bottle in his hand. It was ten in the morning and this one probably wasn't his first. His expression dared anyone to comment.

'It's not much, I know, but you'd be bloody amazed at the battles I had to wage with those bloody staff Johnnies, Gaberdine Swine I call 'em, just to prise this crap out of them.' Stirling grinned again. 'Still, there is comfort in store. As we're to be brigands, we shall resort to brigandage. A battalion of those awfully nice New Zealanders is parked just a few miles up the road. They're deployed for training, bless 'em, and they've left their lovely orderly camp, packed with essentials, pretty much unguarded.'

The trio must have looked blank.

'Tonight,' Mayne wearily explained, 'you'll take the truck. And yes it does run, sort of runs anyway. Go down to their camp, nick whatever we need and bring it back here. It'll need more than one trip.'

'Thing is sir,' Archie piped up, 'they'll know it was us like, I mean we'll have all their gear and we're practically next door. Could it be they may be pissed off with us a bit, sir?'

'Spoken like a true professional,' Stirling enthused. 'Yes, we'll have to disguise the stuff somewhat, use some camouflage netting and you Private Dunmore shall be our master of deception. You, Sergeant Milburn, will lead the mission.'

'Me sir? Well ... I'm only a corporal.'

'Not any more, I've just promoted you. Besides you can't expect any of us officers to be seen behaving like that, it's decidedly ungentlemanly.'

As the hot, dry day wore on more recruits came in. One was a tall, fair-haired officer, sportsman's build and, unlike most of the others, immaculately turned out. He had the kind of fresh, wholesome looks that went with a stiff upper lip and a handshake that would have worried King Kong.

'Jock Lewes, from the Welsh Guards no less,' Stirling introduced him. 'Had a hell of a job to convince him to join us, finally captured him in a hospital bed, one of the real heroes of heroic Tobruk. Now he really likes killing Boche, don't you Jock?'

Lewes fixed them all with a manly stare. 'I'll be in charge of training and those of you who don't know me will soon come to hate me. It will be that type of training. Pretty soon you'll think taking on Jerry is a doddle by comparison.'

Some officers could have made that sound quite funny. Lewes didn't do funny, and the blokes he'd brought with him clearly knew that already.

'He's half a bloody Nazi himself,' Mayne confided as they drove the old boneshaker, thumping down the rutted track that evening as, by the mysterious alchemy of the desert, day turned abruptly to night. Despite being an officer he'd come along. Joe guessed the Irishman just couldn't bear to miss out on any available mayhem.

'Flirted with them before the war, was even going to marry some gargantuan Brunhilde, swastika tattoos and all, before he saw the light. Now, after his epiphany, he's out to make amends.' Mayne was unusually talkative. Joe would come to realise this was the convivial stage between sober melancholia and drunken fury. 'I'm not saying he's not the right chap for the job — he is — I couldn't be arsed with training.'

The third man in the reeking old cab where ancient sweat, stale oil and God knows what else competed to form a cloying foulness, was a junior officer, Eoin McGonigal. Of the same country as Paddy Mayne but bog-Irish from the south, dark, wiry and intense; you'd think he and the big Ulsterman would be opposites. And they were … yet there was a particular camaraderie between them and McGonigal seemed to be one of the very few who wasn't frightened of Mayne. Joe sensed that even Stirling was wary of him.

'Why did any of us volunteer for this?' McGonigal queried. 'I was just bored hanging about bloody barracks, tired of all the bull and sick of being called a fucking taig; how about you sergeant?'

Joe wasn't used to being addressed by his newly exalted rank. 'Bit the same, sir. After Crete an' what we saw there.'

'Now Paddy here,' McGonigal went on, smiling to avoid giving offence, 'was found in the glasshouse, there on account of his famous sense of high good humour, not always shared by his brother officers, nor indeed his superiors.'

'That supercilious wanker was just asking to be thumped.'

'And you just had to oblige, him and the four redcaps who came to arrest you.'

'It was for their own good. Anyone without any sense of humour needs the odd pointer. That poxy bar needed re-decorating, anyway.'

*

The Kiwis' camp, when they got there, was eerily deserted, row upon row of beautifully spruce and correctly spaced tents, new and untarnished, almost glowing in the soft moonlight.

'Right lads, let's have half a dozen of these down and stowed. We need chairs, beds, blankets, cooking gear and whatever else takes your fancy.' They set to with gusto. To the haul of essentials they added a gramophone, numerous records and some additional kit that had just been lying about.

'No,' Joe heard Reg Seekings snarl at someone, probably the dapper Johnny Cooper. Already there was tension between the two men. Seekings was a successful amateur boxer, generally with a grudge against the world and looking for a fight. He was good at fighting; a working class Paddy Mayne who could easily be roused to murderous rage before he'd even had a drink.

'You're not taking any fucker's socks.'

'Why, in God's name not? We've nicked everything else.' Cooper was as different to Reg as chalk was to cheese, slight and almost effeminate, once a star of school pantos who'd followed Stirling in from the Guards.

'Socks is personal like, could be his mam knitted those special and sent 'em all the way from NZ. Lifting War Department stuff is one thing, this is stealing.'

Joe decreed they leave the hand knitted socks and compensated Cooper with a couple of spare blankets, standard issue.

In all they made four trips and pretty much helped themselves to whatever they wanted. Archie supervised the re-erection of the pilfered canvas and with the use of paint and brushes miraculously aged the new to appear to match the old. The transformation was remarkable and the blokes were dead impressed.

'Genius,' Stirling grinned, 'pure genius, this is real talent but we'd best keep it to ourselves for the moment.'

On the final raid, Mayne, who'd been drinking steadily throughout, insisted on the removal of an upright piano from the Kiwi officers' mess. At least it wasn't a grand. This was plain daft but nobody was ready to argue the toss with the orangeman, so they heaved and sweated till the thing was humped onto the back of the truck. Joe half expected the wheezing antique vehicle to collapse under the weight, but somehow they made it back.

'Splendid,' was Stirling's only comment. 'Just the right touch, provided we remember not to ask any of our Antipodean neighbours around for a sing-song.'

It was now four in the morning and they'd spent a profitable evening. 'Right then,' Lewes still looked like he'd stepped off a parade. 'I'm being generous tonight as you've all had a busy evening. Reveille isn't till six o'clock, so that's two hours kip. Make the most of it. If any of you thinks he's been to war already, he hasn't been on one of my training courses.'

This time he did sort of smile, but it wasn't at all reassuring.

Chapter Four

The Blue

Of all the desert flowers known.
For you no seed is ever sown
Yet you are the one that has most fame,
O Desert Rose – for that's your name.
There's thousands of you scattered around,
O Desert Rose, some square, some round,
Though different in variety,
At night you're all damned hard to see.
Although you're watered very well
You have a most unfragrant smell;
And just in case you do not know,
O Desert Rose, you'll never grow.
For you are not a desert flower,
Growing wilder every hour;
You're just a bloomin' petrol tin,
Used for doing most things in.
    Anon: *Ode to a Desert Flower*

*

Joe hit the ground, 'like a sack of fucking potatoes,' Lewes' voice carried above the grinding of the truck's clattering gears. He was winded, tumbling over the abrasive surface of the pitted sand, thousands of shards, keen as razors scoring against his bruised flesh. 'This is nothing, this is fuck all, this is a walk in the fucking park,' the instructor hammered on. 'You have just dropped from six feet. Imagine you'd just come down from six thousand ...'

Coughing the foul dust, Joe struggled to his feet. The only good thing, as far as he could see, was that everyone else looked just as bad, everyone except Lewes, resident demon in this over-heated corner of hell. *He* still looked perfect, creases straight, unblemished, pristine. Damn the bastard.

'If I can do it, you can do it,' he'd begun. And do it he did. The lorry rattled along at fifteen miles per hour, with Lewes coming off forwards and backwards, each time a perfect roll and no, he'd never done parachute training before.

'All we need is aeroplanes and parachutes,' Archie had quipped before they began. In fact they had neither. This was 'make do and mend' and most would certainly need mending. The tally of cuts, bruises, black eyes and in some cases breakages, was impressive. Stirling's buccaneers looked like riot victims though most had padded out their gear with odds and ends of cricket kit or whatever else they could scrounge. He couldn't imagine the Germans being very afraid.

'Now we're going up to thirty miles an hour,' Lewes announced with savage exultation. 'At last we're getting somewhere. Sometime, maybe, you'll be fit to be let out on your own.' Meanwhile it was back aboard the Skylark for another circuit. The ancient vehicle groaned and wheezed, coaxed up to speed, spewing recruits like some mad confetti, the men smacking, bouncing and spinning over the unforgiving ground. Mayne was the only one who seemed to relish it. He took each bone shaking, muscle wrenching drop as a challenge. Frequently bloodied, he never flinched. Anybody could see how he'd succeeded as a rugby international. You couldn't help feeling sorry for the other side.

Now Joe's shoulder tensed to absorb the thumping recoil of the M1928 Thompson, hot air infused with cordite. He was firing five shot bursts from the twenty-round box magazine. The short, heavy weapon was very different to his SMLE, designed far more for close contact. The .45 calibre bullets punished the crude wooden targets they were blazing at, Hitler's grinning caricature obliterated. Lewes expected them to be familiar with a whole range of weapons, Joe liked the captured nine mm Beretta MAB 38, beautifully crafted and nicely balanced, the Thompson seeming heavy and crude by comparison.

'Now then,' Lewes enthused, in a makeshift classroom thrown up from spare canvas, open on all sides. 'What we need, what we really, *really* need, is a nice little bomb that both explodes and ignites. Blowing up a plane's not as easy as you might imagine.'

They'd all been aware of a regular series of detonations on the periphery of their makeshift camp, Jock Lewes at play. 'So I've been experimenting and now, I'm pleased to say, we have this little beauty here. A bit Heath Robinson, I know, but it should do the trick quite nicely.'

His device didn't look too impressive but they listened intently. If you couldn't exactly like Lewes, his single-mindedness and dedication at least commanded respect. 'What we've got is a pound of plastic explosive rolled in with a quarter of Thermite and a dose of motor oil — cheap as chips and easy as pie. All you need to set her off is a pencil detonator and up she goes, you can give yourself twelve seconds or two hours, depending on circumstances.'

'Pretty bloody brilliant,' Stirling cheered, even the taciturn Mayne looked impressed. 'I never knew you'd studied explosives.'

'Never did, in fact,' Lewes confirmed. 'Just used to mess about with me brother's chemistry set a bit when I was a kid, soon got the hang of it. I'm not one to boast but I'm going to call this the Lewes bomb. Can't wait to try her out…'

Angel had been selected to teach them knife fighting. 'He doesn't just look like a bandit; he's done this for real.' Most of them had killed enemy in battle, usually at a distance, very few had ever had to get this personal. Angel never said much about the war in Spain but Joe knew he'd been adept at leading night raids and killing fascist sentries. He wasn't generally much of a talker, but this was clearly a subject dear to his heart.

'You don't just slice; you are no cutting off a piece of bacon… To kill quick and quiet, you stab, so …' Cooper had been selected as intended victim and Angel grabbed him from behind, demonstrating the thrust with a practised lunge. The dapper young guardsman looked worried, as well he might. They were using live blades.

'You cut down thro' the big vein, so. You go clean through both sides. Keep good hold on your handle and now you punch forward and down. He lose much blood and he no speak, not ever,' he added unnecessarily. 'So you just kill this bastard and there is no noise, you make sure he go quiet and he give you no trouble. Move on to the next.'

Angel now duelled with Seekings. The big man moved with surprising speed and some dexterity, even though he'd never really handled a knife before. When he ended up flat on his broad back with the Basque's knife at his throat, he looked characteristically apoplectic. 'You sneaky little Dago bastard,' he exhaled admiringly; 'never saw that one coming.'

They weren't done. Mayne had a copy of 'Buster' Fairbairn's *All in Fighting*. 'Just my cup of grog,' he'd decided. The former Shanghai copper was a native of Northumberland and had perfected assorted nastiness over several decades in China. They learned blows, releases, holds, the use of everyday objects as lethal weapons, choking, deafening, blinding, castrating; a cornucopia of ungentlemanly tricks.

'Killing Jerry is one thing,' Lewes, seemingly master of all desert trades was teaching them about navigation. 'Now, your Boche and the Wops don't much care for our vast and unfriendly desert. For them it's a place of terror, surreal and threatening, one big bloody wilderness the size of India. They tend to stick to the coastal strip. There are those who liken the western desert to an ocean. If so, then we're the sailors and the baddies are just landlubbers. Most of whatever maps we've got are pretty much useless. Bagnold and Clayton, the two blokes who set up LRDG, stole a few marches all round, not just because of the topography they charted, but on account of the specialist kit that they created. Major Bagnold has also developed the sun-compass. Now *this* is pure creative genius.'

Joe found himself enthralled. He'd always liked maps, had spent much of his boyhood exploring the lanes and moors of his native county. The idea of navigating a path over the vast, trackless immensity of the Sahara was as exciting as it was daunting.

Lewes went on. 'The principle can be briefly described as keeping the shadow from the sun of a vertical needle, like so, which projects from the centre of a small circular table graduated into 360 degrees on to the appropriate reading in order to maintain the direction required. Sounds tricky I know, but it's not as hard as it seems. If you're forced off this bearing it's still possible to read the direction in which you're travelling. There's a few problems connected with the sun's azimuth at various times of day and depending on the season, but Bagnold thought of a way around these too, clever bugger.'

Joe showed aptitude. 'We might just make a navigator out of you yet, laddie.' It wasn't that often Lewes was so optimistic.

That evening, in the solitude of his recently pilfered tent (as an NCO he had his own, one careful New Zealand owner), he re-read Evelyn's letter. Theirs was an odd romance, if indeed it was a romance at all. She wrote as she talked, carefully and precisely, words on the page not giving anything away. As befitted a landowner's daughter, she'd been educated at one of the top end Newcastle girls' schools.

The male equivalent, where Neville had gone, was the Royal Grammar School, founded on the carpet-bagging proceeds of the Reformation which had prised the coal trade away from the clutches of Rome and into the ambitious grasp of aspiring local merchants. Joe's teacher had once told him, 'you've the wit to get into RGS, but not the connection. It's no place for oiks.'

Her hand was well formed and flowing, giving a hint of a young woman not entirely defined by her background. In Northumberland they lived quite close, but the social gulf was far wider. Her father's house was Geordie-done-good Palladian pastiche overlooking the coastal plain, an elevated site just in case you hadn't got the message. Joe's people were tenant farmers, had been for generations, their farm was set rather lower, four square Northumbrian sandstone and soft red pan-tiled roofs.

As children, they'd been allowed to play together. He and Neville were pretty much of an age, Evelyn a couple of years younger, just a rather gawky girl with long coltish legs who didn't mind playing cowboys and Indians so invariably on the losing side. Their playground was the big house's park and woodlands, then beyond to the lordly fringe of great sweeping dunes and pale, yielding sand that seemed to stretch into infinity, just the tantalising bulk of Dunstanburgh castle standing sentinel to the north. Hemmed in by the sea but with all its backs turned inland was the pit village, an industrial scar, crowded rows of sagging back to backs, half sinking into the maze of lost galleries below, the pit heap and winding gear as stark and ugly as it gets.

In her letter, she'd hinted that Neville's ostensible elevation to staff had been at least partly forced. She was discreet, possibly she didn't know, had only gone so far as saying 'daddy pulled some strings, like he always does.' Joe wondered what strings had needed to be pulled. When they were younger he couldn't recall Neville ever having had a girlfriend, nor did he share in all their usual ribald fantasising.

Podgy Hinckley, he remembered, had put it more crudely, 'he's a poof you know, your posh mate.'

'Don't be daft.'

'He is. I can tell, most of his sort is — all those cold showers at posh schools an' stuff. Arse-bandits, they're all the same.'

'He's not queer.'

'How can you say, I've nowt against 'em meself, live an' let live an' all, but I seen the way he looks at you.'

Joe had continued to defend his friend's presumed heterosexuality but the worm of doubt had begun to niggle. He'd seen Neville in deep conversation with that pretty young officer at the party where he'd been recruited, and his doubts had begun to harden into certainty. He couldn't see that the limited stresses of general staff work would account for Neville's edginess, or his drinking. So what; did it matter if he was queer?

Now he'd written a reply to Evelyn. It wasn't, he had to concede, a literary masterpiece. At school, he'd done well in English, was something of a star pupil and nursed inchoate ambition to write seriously at some point. All he could really say now was that he was well, enjoying life in the forces and engaged upon 'important' work which he wasn't allowed to enlarge upon.

Vital work my arse, he mused looking out at the flyblown, ragged base, a bunch of unemployed miscreants and vagabonds squatting in the desert.

*

It was difficult to be enthralled by the Bristol Bombay. Joe recalled how he'd been uplifted by the sight of Spitfires and Hurricanes, swift and sleek, but the Bombay, with its high fixed wings and rather clumsy twin engines, looked like some ungainly form of prehistoric bird unconvinced of its own ability to fly.

'I can see why blokes want to jump out of 'em.'

But jumping out was just what they'd be doing. Today, their parachute training became real. All the leaping off trucks and flinging themselves from makeshift platforms would finally pay off, hopefully anyway. Onboard, the stifling fuselage was heated to furnace levels. They were in sticks of ten, linked to a static line which would jerk their 'chutes open as they jumped.

'Glad I had a piss first,' Archie confided, 'knew I should 'ave joined the catering corps.'

It was certainly too late, however dry-mouthed and weak-bladdered they might feel, you couldn't be the one who bottled it now. So up they went, the elderly plane struggling to clamber into the perfect blue sky. Joe and Archie were in the first stick. 'Get ready,' the dispatcher yelled, and suddenly the moment had come. Joe's tongue felt like a slab of ancient leather, impossibly dry and swollen, but out he went into the sucking air, so much cooler.

He felt his stomach tear free and float somewhere behind him, for sure he'd be splattered across the barren rocks below, just a smear. Then the 'chute opened, jerking him upwards into an impossible feeling of lightness. He was a celestial being, drifting above earth, the wide

83

expanse of Delta, Gulf of Suez and dry Bitter Lake his fiefdom. He drifted downwards and then, when he looked, the ground was rushing up at an alarming rate.

Instantly Joe remembered all the persistent teaching, all the bumps and bruises, he braced and landed lightly in soft sand — a lot easier than jumping off a moving truck. He was an Olympian, that suffusing calm and elation persisting as he struggled clear of his harness.

'Fuck!' someone was yelling, 'Oh bloody Christ.' A small knot of men was gathered over something on the sand. As he got closer he was able to recognise the mortal remains of Ken Warburton. He'd barely known the Mancunian, even though he'd been a dab hand on the keys of their liberated piano. Now his playing days were over. 'Fucking clips,' someone else was shouting. 'Fucking things sheared off. I heard their fucking screams, man; all the fucking way down.' Another poor sod, a Jock named Duffy, had gone the same way. These were their first fatalities, and not a Boche in sight.

Lewes paraded them. 'What happened was bloody awful. It shouldn't have happened but these things do. Two chaps died as a result of a faulty static line. That has now been fixed and it won't ever happen again. You'll be going up again tomorrow.' That was as near to a eulogy as any of L Detachment would ever get.

*

A hot dry summer passed into a warm dry autumn. They trained and trained and then they trained. Lewes was a tyrant. They jumped, they marched, endless gruelling treks over that hateful ground. The desert conferred no favours, had no pity and was without end. They marched a score of miles, twice that, then a hundred. They became familiar with explosives, with every type of weapon. They could snap necks and break spines. Joe came on in leaps and bounds in the science of navigation.

They even staged a mock raid on an RAF base nearly a hundred miles away for a bet and won, much to the fury of the Brylcreem Boys.

Then it was October, and something was in the air. Rumour, like some mystical current, whispered of a grand Allied offensive. Everywhere security was tighter. There was a distinct hum. New and outwardly impressive armour was heard revving in multiplying leaguers, 'now Jerry's for it.'

'Operation Squatter,' Stirling began, one wild and drizzling afternoon in November, 'will be our coming of age. Been a while, I know, and you've all trained bloody hard, the froth has all been spooned off and we few, we happy few, are the chosen ones. Now, at last, you get the chance to show Jerry and Benito what you've been learning. Fifty five of you, just over half of us, will take off and be flown across into enemy territory. We'll jump about a dozen miles from the coast then have some sport with their aerodromes at Timimi and Gazala. We hit them hard, we blow up as many planes as we can and bugger off home before they know what's hit 'em. We go in with five teams of eleven. Are we ready?'

They were.

'Each team will have threescore of Jock's nasty little devices and when we've had our fun it's just a short jaunty hike, fifty miles or so to the RV where our good friends of LRDG will kindly be providing us with a free taxi service, God bless 'em.'

This time, the Brylcreem Boys seemed to have forgotten their earlier rancour. The tables in Bagush airfield's mess tent groaned with sumptuous delights; eggs, bacon, toast, real butter, real jam. They fell to with a will, 'condemned men's last supper,' Mayne cheerfully broadcast as he tucked in, washing down these treats with copious swigs of beer. Outside, the wind howled, gusting they were told up to thirty knots. Joe couldn't remember what the safe limit for parachuting was, but he'd a nasty feeling it was a great deal less.

Stirling was all bonhomie: if he was nervous, it didn't show. This mission would be the acid test not just of his leadership but of the whole concept. It was pretty obvious that the Big Push was about to kick off so, if they were going to get the first punch in, then tonight was really the night.

'And what a bleedin' night,' Archie groused, 'you'd be lucky to get me as far as the local, night like this back 'ome.'

They'd jump with Mayne, Angel would be with Lewes. 'The wind is getting up,' one of the aircrew advised unnecessarily as they clambered aboard, weighed down with kit, the fuselage stuffed with canisters containing more explosives, extra weapons and ammo. 'Could be a rough flight, no trolley service I'm afraid.' Sand whipped in their faces as they'd shuffled across the landing strip, the wind if anything seemed to have risen, a shrieking banshee. Joe really hoped it wasn't an omen.

This time his descent was rather less sublime. The furious wind snatched him from the door like a giant hand and buffeted him mercilessly. Dust whirled everywhere in a dervish dance and he knew he'd reached ground when he hit it. It was not soft sand, but a torture chamber of broken and jagged stones. His chute whipped him over the tearing surface. Finally, his desperate fingers found the release catch and, once free, his canopy was immediately snatched away into the enveloping murk. His fatigues and webbing were pretty much trashed, as was he.

Everyone was supposed to land in a nice orderly pattern, but Joe found himself totally disorientated and very much alone. Only one assumption was safe, that there'd be no Boche patrols around, so he switched on his torch and began yelling. Even his loudest bellow seemed infinitely feeble set against the invincible might of the storm.

It took them three hours in all. He found Mayne, who'd found Archie, and they found the others including Seekings, who'd suffered even more than Joe, his hands and knees streaked with blood. The experience hadn't improved his temper. 'Fucking bastard fucking thorns and this fucking bloody wind, who's fucking daft idea was this anyway?' It didn't seem a good time to remind him he'd volunteered, but it turned out he'd got off lightly. Dave Kershaw, a veteran of Angel's war where he'd fought as a member of the International Brigades, had fractured an arm and become one of the walking wounded. Two other blokes were incapacitated with broken legs.

'Sorry, lads, you know the rules,' Mayne confirmed after they'd made the badly injured as comfortable as possible. Their faces showed that they did. They didn't pack stretchers.

'So what have we got, kit wise?'

Joe did a quick inventory. 'We've only found two canisters sir, which makes a grand total of two Thompsons, half a dozen blankets, eight water bottles, a few rations and some spare explosives.'

'And where the bloody hell are we exactly, or even approximately?'

'I make it around a dozen miles east of the intended drop zone, sir, give or take a mile or two.'

'Right then, north it is.' Mayne had no intention of giving up. The badly hurt would be left with whatever water and rations could be spared. They were also left a pistol each, just in case.

And then it rained. The keening wind had dropped but the downpour was unlike anything they'd ever seen. This wasn't just wet, it was biblical. Great sheets of water cascaded through dawn's grey filter. The arid landscape seemed to change in front of their eyes. The deep dry wadis became fast flowing streams then raging rivers, spelling death for anyone caught in the flood.

'Well, looks like we won't die of thirst,' Archie chirped. Water, giver of life in the desert, had now become a killer. They were utterly soaked and all their gear was soaked, dragging leaden.

As the sodden dawn finally emerged, it showed a weird, transformed, landscape that a few hours earlier would have seemed impossible. Mayne found a lying up place on the upper slope of a deep wadi. The rain abated marginally as he and Joe went forward to work out their location. They agreed they were about five miles south of Timini airfield.

'We'll go in at dusk, get whatever rest you can.'

Easier said than done, and the rain came back with a vengeance. There was no respite. It hammered down in bucketfuls, remorseless, they were freezing and had nowhere to go. Even their smokes were ruined.

'Bastard, fuck and shite,' Seekings exploded. 'The fucking time pencils are knackered, bloody fuses are kaput too, we couldn't blow up our own arses.'

'We'll just have to use grenades, then,' Mayne snarled. 'I'll be damned if I'm bottling out.' He and Seekings had a brief glaring contest that took in Joe, Archie and the rest.'

'We've had it, sir,' Joe calmed. 'No point in trying. We'd just get ourselves killed or captured and that would be an even bigger waste of time.'

Mayne kept glaring, but even he had no taste for suicide. Finally, he just nodded and that was it, 'bugger,' was all he said. It seemed to pretty much sum things up. They spent a shivering, miserable day with a handful of dry rations and never a fag. That next evening, they set off on the thirty-five mile tab to the RV.

They were aiming for the Trig al Abd, an ancient desert crossing, rather incongruously signed by Il Duce's engineers, complete with fascist symbols and a helpful marker pointing towards Egypt. Trudging west along the ribbon of track, lit by a fitful moon, Joe spotted the pinprick light of hurricane lamps posted on shallow rises.

The password they'd been given was 'roll out the barrel' which seemed altogether too jolly and upbeat, but it was answered and they found themselves in the midst of their deliverers, a Kiwi patrol of LRDG. Their hot, sweet tea tasted better than any brew Joe had ever drunk, their bully beef finer than any fillet.

Fed, warmed, watered and resting they huddled beneath the stars in borrowed blankets. Despite their universal exhaustion, Mayne went round among them. The mad Irishman's quantum of stamina seemed bottomless. He was surprisingly upbeat. In fairness, the Kiwis had donated a nearly full bottle of Johnny Walker and this may have helped.

'It wasn't Jerry who beat us. It was just the bloody weather and no, whoever said we shouldn't have jumped in that wind was dead right but here we are some of us anyway. We achieved damn all but I fully intend to be back!'

Next morning, with the rain cleared and the desert once again drained, the lanky figure of David Stirling came in 'Has anyone here seen any of my boys?' Nobody had, nor would they. His fellows were gone; more than half the group was gone, only twenty-one mustered, the rest were dead or prisoners. They hadn't fired a single shot nor planted a single bomb. Two dozen men had been lost and they'd nothing to show for it.

Stirling was trying and failing to hide his despair as the LRDG prepared to break camp. 'Bit of a bloody mess I fear, all those chaps gone — just what my enemies at GHQ are waiting to hear, I'm sure. It seems we may be buggered before we start.'

'Not necessarily, sir.' The Kiwi's officer was an Englishman, David Lloyd Owen. Slim and wiry he looked ludicrously young, but the casual professionalism of LRDG was tangible. 'We've heard on the radio that things aren't going altogether to plan with the Auk's offensive, huge tank brawl at Sidi Rezegh.' They all knew that 'not going entirely to plan' was shorthand for 'totally fucked up.' They also knew that tank scrapping with the Afrika Korps was usually pretty one sided.

'Our tanks are mostly pretty crap,' Lloyd Owen went on, 'under-armoured, under-gunned and totally un-bloody-reliable. Jerry's A/T guns can knock us off at 2,000 yards. Ours couldn't penetrate a Mark IV Panzer even if you're half way up his arse.'

'I'm not sure that makes me feel a whole lot better…'

'No, sir, but the point is HQ has more to worry about than L Detachment or LRDG for that matter. To them the stuff we all do is pretty small beer. If we get a result they pat us on the back and forget about us. If we lose out they barely notice.'

Joe was looking around the camp. The patrol's thirty cwt Chevy trucks were spread out and camouflaged, barely recognisable from their civilian counterparts. Stripped, customised and loaded with every manner of gear. Fat desert tyres, sand channels, bristling with firepower, Brens, Lewis Guns, the awesome twin Vickers K and even a captured Italian 20 mm Breda cannon. Each one a mobile oasis for its crew, even piled high like a gypsy's caravan, these were still precision kit.

'I never do seem to have any luck with parachutes,' Stirling lamented.

Joe couldn't imagine any circumstance where an NCO like himself would be able to freely express ideas in a line regiment but now he had one, so sod protocol.

'Sir,' he addressed Lloyd Owen, 'LRDG is kind enough to get us out of here, but suppose you'd also brought us in. We'd not need parachutes then and we'd be pretty sure of getting close to the target?'

The LRDG officer didn't reply, just smiled noncommittally.

'You know,' Stirling answered, glancing at Lloyd Owen, 'this laddie's not half so daft as he looks. I may have to promote him again.'

Chapter Five

Piracy in the High Desert

I hear we'll soon be going
To Cairo for a thrill
There to rest our weary bones
And frolic with Tiger Lil
Of course it's just a rumour
So please don't pay much heed
The cook overheard the CO say
Soon to Cairo we'll proceed.

    J. Campbell: *Tobruk Heroes Dream*

*

And what are you? So full of hate you want to go out and fight
everybody! Because you've been whipped and chased by hounds,
well that might not be living, but it sure as hell ain't dying. And
dying's been what these boys have been doing for going on three
years now! Dying by the thousands! Dying for you, fool! I know,
'cause I dug the graves. And all this time I keep askin' myself,
when, O Lord, when it's gonna be our time?

    Glory (1989)

'Proper Gary-fucking-Cooper, or what?

It was, or at least seemed like it. Jalo Oasis lies around 150 miles south east of Sirte, just west of that empty expanse of the Grand Sand Sea. The place did look very *Beau Geste*. An old timber fort painted white, huddle of mud-brick dwellings, loads of palm trees and waters that sparkled in the brightness, a picture postcard view, 'welcome to Libya.' Like many desert halts it looked better than it tasted, mercilessly hot, fly-infested, the water brackish, undrinkable and generally scrofulous.

'You can thank old Erwin for this chance,' Joe informed Archie. 'Operation Crusader's gone off the boil. In fact we're getting a real pasting but now Ritchie's running the show, he wants us bashing Jerry, blowing up his planes.'

'Christ, I couldn't stand another caper like the last one, promised me gran, no more bleedin' parachutes.'

'This time we're going in the civilised way, by vehicle.'

Joe's light bulb moment had clearly infected Stirling, who'd been locked in earnest discourse with Lloyd Owen most of the way back from their earlier debacle. Freshly inspired, he'd sloughed off the cloak of despair and was breeding plans afresh. The LRDG officer had been right about HQ, so tied up with the scrapping around Tobruk, they'd barely registered the disaster which had all but engulfed L Detachment. Ironically, it was the worsening situation that had opened up fresh vistas of mayhem.

'How come we got the job then and not LRDG? Let's face it, their track record is a wee bit more impressive.'

'Seems Lloyd Owen spoke to his CO who volunteered us for the task; we might be crap parachutists but they still think we can blow stuff up.'

'Or they think it's a suicide mission?'

'There's that, too.'

A short time past, the Italians had held Jalo. To their surprise a British column had come whirling out of the desert and dispossessed them. This meant Eighth Army now had a forward base that brought Axis airfields on or near the coast well within range. It might be those aerodromes at Sirte, Agheila and Agedabia that L Detachment would be going for. The regulars who'd stormed the place were commanded by a Brigadier Reid who, unusually for a proper soldier, was happy to welcome the saboteurs. Stirling had been allotted a rather ramshackle warehouse as his CP, to which the faithful, including Joe, were duly summoned.

'Not quite the Ritz, but t'will do, t'will serve. As you chaps know, Jerry has set up his airfields in all these little coastal towns. They used to just fish for tuna I believe, but it's Eighth Army who's catch of the day, us and Malta. Poor old Maltesers are copping it pretty badly. The Auk has pushed Rommel back to Gazala, but the Fox won't be too concerned, his airfields are still a long way back.

'Now our intelligence sources, upon whom we can, I'm sure, rely absolutely — there's a first time for everything — tell us the fields are very lightly guarded and mainly by Eyeties. So, a trip to the seaside is in order. Paddy and I with our merry men will go for Sirte; probably the fattest target, and we'll aim to hit them on the night of fourteenth December. Jock, you and your boys will duff up Agheila, nice short drive for you. On the twenty-first you, Bill, will blitz Agedabia to oblige our hosts here who will be doing some blitzing of their own.'

Bill Fraser was a bit of an oddball so he should have fitted in perfectly, but he rarely emerged from solitude other than to dish out a few orders. Mayne seemed convinced he was queer and clearly enjoyed winding him up. It was hard to say, really, as Fraser so seldom communicated. He mostly seemed to talk to his terrier Withers, which had become the unit's unofficial mascot. Most found speaking to the dog easier.

Joe irritatingly discovered the war against Rommel was briefly postponed while Seekings and Cooper pursued their own vendettas. Hostilities we re-ignited over a missing blanket. Red faced Reg had been the victim of alleged theft. 'Which of you fuckers has nicked my blanket? C'mon, own up. I'll find out anyway then I'll do you over so even your old woman wouldn't recognise you.'

'Pipe down, for God's sake,' Cooper rejoined. 'Big fat baby's lost his favourite blanket. Get real.'

'That's it, bloody well stand up you posh twat, I'm going to knock your fucking head off!'

Joe had intervened to prevent an outbreak of civil strife but found, to his dismay, that he was lumbered with both seething antagonists when they set off next day, each still sending murderous glances. There were fourteen of them, being taxied in by the Rhodesians. They had 350 miles of open desert to cover.

The Chevies roared off in that blissful hour before dawn when the air was a cool benison, trucks piled high with gear, fitted as ever with a dazzling potency of armament. Living conditions in the desert waste varied radically from day to night, from stifling, almost crushing heat to stark, penetrating cold. Joe marvelled at the eclectic displays of kit. Standard battledress with heavy serge greatcoats alternated with KD shirts and shorts, with most personal gear carried in customized 37 pattern canvas webbing.

Peculiar to LRDG was the kapok lined 'Tropal' coat. This was very heavy and equally stiff, completely unsuitable when moving about but very warm for static or sentry work. Leather sandals, or chaplis, made walking over soft sand much easier and often replaced standard infantry boots. Both Joe and Archie had each acquired a pair. The South Africans had also introduced a lightweight durable form of footwear, descended from their Voortrekker ancestors' design, the 'desert boot' — increasingly popular with all ranks.

'Now, in the movies, the bleedin' desert is always flat as a pancake and just lots and lots of nice, soft sand,' Archie lamented as they sweated and heaved to dig out one of the trucks.

'No such thing as typical desert, mate,' one of the Rhodesians grinningly confirmed, 'goes from bad to worse, then worse again and finally to bloody awful, which is pretty much where we're at.'

Dunes reared up like primeval cliffs, constantly shifting beneath endless winds. The trick was to gun the vehicle up the slope but time it just right so you didn't shoot over the dizzying knife edged crest and plummet down the far side. If your vehicle was wrecked, so were you. Despite the skills of the LRDG drivers, trucks were constantly getting bogged; it was hard hot labouring to dig them out and jam the heavy sand channels beneath spinning wheels. Dunes alternated with seemingly limitless plains of flat hard going, though the surface of broken stones took a fearsome toll on tyres.

Heat was a physical presence. There was no escape, and those vast clouds of hot dust flung up by the vehicles meant each man was coated in his very own cloying shroud, soon mixed with sweat. A hot, enervating qibli whispered distractingly from the deep, empty expanses, sapping energy, draining the will to continue. As their hosts cheerfully informed them, Libya also hosted any amount of local wildlife that was apt to do you harm, a whole encyclopaedia of insect varieties, harbingers of many ills, poisonous snakes and scorpions; unwelcome and very dangerous bedfellows. Desert sores and the spectre of cafard lurked in the shadows.

On their first day out, just to add to these normal discomforts, a sudden sandstorm blew up, seemingly from nowhere and blotting out the world in a frenzied, abrasive whirlwind. There was no choice but to leaguer up and sit it out. 'No wonder blokes go bloody bonkers out here.'

In this environment LRDG were the natives and L Detachment the tourists. Joe had noted how patrols had to be wholly self-sufficient and every item of equipment, every drop of fuel and water, was measured. As the vehicles moved out, a lighter command car probed ahead, choosing routes and keeping a trained eye open for unwelcome visitors. Flags were used for communicating changes of plan or alterations to route.

Trucks would always attempt to remain within eyesight of each other. Behind the command vehicle came the radio truck, (which couldn't operate its wireless on the move). Then the rest of the patrol in three troops, each having a trio of vehicles, travelling in as wide dispersion as the ground would permit. As a rule, the heavily laden mechanic's or fitter's vehicle drove with the rear troop, ready to scoop up stragglers or breakdowns.

'Beware the hun in the sun,' they'd been cautioned at the start. 'They know we're here and they've constant eyes in the sky. It's a big desert but if they do spot us, we're in for an exciting ride.' So somebody was always on the lookout for prowling planes. Patrols threw out great plumes and swathes of dust, unavoidable and yet horribly visible from the air.

'It's often possible for us simply to brazen it out,' the LRDG officer instructed. 'We can sometimes just masquerade as 'friendlies' when the unfriendly are overhead. If we spot any one of the bastards you'll hear trucks' horns so we'll halt and scatter the vehicles over a wide area, try to get at least a hundred yards between each. If it comes to a fight we give 'em all we've got.'

'Often it works, clever dispersal using whatever natural cover we can find, spruced up with camouflage. If our visitors prove persistent and aggressive, we bugger off sharpish, make a run for it. Generally, they can only go after one truck at any one time. We don't make it too easy for 'em; 'jink' and swerve to confuse the fighter's aim, give 'em a few Monza turns and all that. Over hard going the vehicles can crack along at a fair rate, perhaps as fast as fifty mph, makes us a very tricky target. It's surprising how fast a frightened truck can move.'

Such adrenalin pumping moments were apparently mercifully rare and on this trip, they were spared. Their day started early, before first light, as cooks toiled over an open fire to get a brew and breakfast on. Though LRDG generally fared better than their regular army comrades, water was strictly rationed to six pints per man, per day. The first of these was served as a mug of hot tea, Tommy's universal balm. He might also begin his day with porridge, bacon fried from the tin, biscuits with marge or jam. Working off excess calories was never likely to be a problem.

'This is more like it,' the blokes approved, 'bloody good scran, here's to Rommel.' Despite being newbies, members of L Detachment were expected to pull their weight, both on stag duty and with all the general chores.

There was nothing to be gained by moving off before the sun had climbed to at least twenty degrees above the horizon, sufficient to activate a sun compass. Everyone packed stores and kit, vehicles, gear and weapons had to be checked. Guns, constantly getting fouled by blown sand, would have to have been stripped and cleaned the night before; a blockage could easily become a death sentence. This was the time for the W/O to radio HQ, for the commander to brief all troopers on the intended day's travel plus RV's in case of dispersal. On sensitive ground or near the coast, all traces of the overnight camp would be systematically eliminated.

'Attention to detail is the measure of survival.' Bill Kennedy-Shaw, leading the patrol, was an old Libyan hand. He'd explored with Bagnold before the war. He was forty, blackened and toughened by the sun to the extent he seemed to be carved from gnarled teak. His relatively advanced age and renown as both botanist and archaeologist had landed him a cushy billet in I Corps, but Bagnold had seduced him with the mystical lure of the sands. Even Stirling and Mayne were slightly in awe.

As the sun climbed, heat building to a crescendo and filling the noon sky, a halt was called. Navigation using the sun compass, and driving generally, became near impossible. The blinding white glare flattened the ground, hiding a multitude of evils. Men lolled beneath the shelter of their trucks, metal so hot it would burn the fingers, a cold, sparse meal of cheese and biscuits, another precious pint of warm water, barely enough to replace sweat. The signaller would be busy with his midday call. Heat was everywhere, a molten universe; colour drowned out by the harsh, unyielding, unwavering light, no dark, no contrast, no shadow. As the afternoon began to wane, heat moving from unbearable to just manageable, the patrol would move off again.

'We tend to select our place of repose before dusk, Kennedy-Shaw went on. 'We're looking for easy concealment, all round defence and with good fields of fire. Bit like a cowboy wagon train, we laager around the hub of the comms truck; circled and parked up for a fast getaway should any inconsiderate foe appear to disrupt a night's well-earned kip.' Joe had earlier impressed his hosts by shooting a Gazelle with his SMLE. At a good couple of hundred yards, the animal on the move, this was a canny shot. It also meant they'd dine well that evening.

Even as the abrupt desert night came in, the trooper's working day was far from over. As cavalry looked after their mounts, so the LRDG cosseted their vehicles. The ground was murderously hard on the trucks. Jerry cans that held 4.4 gallons or twenty litres of fuel, previously the property of the Afrika Korps, were used for re-fuelling. Oil, hydraulics and tyre pressures checked and, if necessary, adjusted. Stores were counted, loads sorted. There was no scope for waste or sloppiness.

'The ubiquitous jerry can is a gift from Rommel,' Kennedy-Shaw explained, 'far superior in robustness and design to our two gallon tins. You might wonder at our chosen colour scheme, the pink is particularly fetching. Fact is, the pattern aids camouflage when we're parked up — not so good on the move, though.'

Time for an evening brew, over an open fire built with used packing cases, a primus or improvised stove, the evening meal was served hot and the daily tot of grog given out. This was the social highlight and could be swilled neat or diluted in tea to suit. The Rhodesians had created a cocktail variant, mixing the raw spirit with Rose's Lime Juice, the 'sundowner' or 'anti-qibli pick-me-up.

'Bugger the Carlton,' Archie enthused, 'this is the life, fresh game, not too overdone and a sparkling cocktail, what more could a bloke ask for. Now bring on the dancing girls.' They got on well with the Rhodesians. LRDG tended to recruit from blokes who, in civvy street, had spent their working lives outdoors. Once you got used to their accent, they were a pretty decent crew. Lean as whipcord, they just got on with the job, even when they groused, they didn't stop working. Any of the Gaberdine Swine, as Stirling called 'em, at GHQ, would have recoiled just at the sight.

Men bedded down in improvised pits, shovelled from soft sand, nastily reminiscent of shallow graves. Those on sentry duty stayed awake, as would the W/O and navigator. He had to finish up his dead reckoning which was checked by an understudy. He'd then use his theodolite for an astrofix, again checked by his junior, so an exact location for the camp could be determined and agreed. Joe was still fascinated by the semi-mystical arts of desert navigation and spent as much time as he could with Mike Sadler, LRDG's whizz kid.

Sadler, a good natured enthusiast, was only too happy to have an able pupil. Stirling approved. 'Come the day, laddie,' he confided, 'we'll be making our own travelling arrangements. Look and learn, that goes for everybody, there's bugger all about desert travel these chaps don't know and while it's awfully decent of them to drive us about, I don't intend to be a dependant relative forever and ever. This is all part of your training, don't waste it.'

This crash course in the practicalities of desert survival went on for three days, bruising, exhausting and mostly monotonous. Sadler had reckoned, abetted now by his rapt pupil, that they were only seventy miles from Sirte. Officially, this was now bandit country. They were within range of the coastal airstrips and could expect enemy activity.

'An, fuck me, here they come.' A lone Italian reconnaissance plane had appeared overhead, just a speck in the endless blue. It loomed larger and came in low, planting a pair of bombs that exploded with dramatic flourish in an earthquake of sand and rock but missed by a mile.

'There'll be more,' someone grimly predicted, and he was right. Like startled Wildebeest, they scattered across the plain, making for whatever cover the thin, baking scrub could offer. Vehicles were dispersed, nets were thrown over; men grabbed whatever sparse shelter they could find. Paddy Mayne retrieved a well worn paperback novel and calmly began reading in the lee of one of the trucks.

'Now, he's a cool blighter,' Sadler confirmed admiringly to Joe, 'big bugger too, glad he's on our side.'

'Aren't we all …'

Regia Aeronautica didn't keep them waiting. Two fast Macchi fighters came sweeping in, blasting with MG and cannon fire. The British clung to the dry, baked earth. Noise filled their senses. For Joe, this was a repeat of Crete, except here he felt even more exposed. Rounds ripped into the sand, shards of stone spinning lethal as shrapnel, a shower of spent cases falling like hailstones seasoned with stench of cordite. The storm passed and, miraculously as it seemed, neither man nor truck had been hit.

That night, having passed their first human settlement since setting out, a miserable huddle of moth eaten tents and half tumbledown mud brick buildings, they again drew halt. Mike Sadler confirmed they were just over a dozen miles short of Sirte. Their taxi ride was very nearly over.

'Listen up,' Stirling ordered, though as ever; it seemed like a polite request. 'Bit of a change of plan. Our Italian friends may not have unduly inconvenienced us but they'll have grassed us up to their German masters. They know we're here and they'll be certain our intentions aren't honourable. So Paddy, you and ten of your merry men will drive a further thirty miles out to Tamet while I take a small recce party to Sirte. We check out the lie of the land and, if we like what we see, we'll launch simultaneous attacks tomorrow night at 22.00 hours. Even if one of us fails, the other might get lucky.'

Joe, Archie and the other eight commandos prepared to go in with Mayne. The Rhodesians drove them to within five miles of the aerodrome and it was a fairly easy trek towards the coast, even though their packs were loaded with Lewes bombs and they were weighed down heavy with grenades and spare ammo. Joe was packing the Thompson, probably better for close quarter fighting which seemed far more likely, especially with Mayne leading.

'Hi ho, hi ho, it's off to war we go, to bomb and burn and kill and pillage.' The Irishman was in high good humour and, as far as Joe could tell, pretty much sober. Sadler had put them on exactly the right bearing and Joe's burgeoning skills ensured they arrived bang on the target.

And what a target; the airfield was lit up like a funfair, rows of shining arc lights illuminating rank upon rank of parked aircraft. Stukas, looking both predatory and prehistoric with their slanted wings jostled with fat bellied Ju 88s. There was no sign of any security, not even a wire fence.

'Christ it's like bleedin' Blackpool illuminations.'

'Hopefully,' Mayne enthused; 'by the time we're done it'll be more like Guy Fawkes Night.'

Silently, choosing their every footfall, they moved carefully forward, Indian file, each man with his weapon cocked and ready. Before they reached the dirt runways, they'd have to pass a large wooden structure, probably a mess hall of some sort, judging by the amount of noise. Lights blazed from windows and beneath the doors.

'Right-ho,' Paddy continued. 'Here's the plan. Before we rig up the planes we're going to pay our friends inside a visit, one they'll not be likely to forget. The blokes in there will be pilots, navigators, air and ground crew. Beating up planes isn't half as damaging as bumping off the fellows who fly them. Milburn, Dunmore, you're with me, four of you fan out on the left, rest on the right. When we're clear, you make bloody sure nobody comes after us. If they're daft enough to try or we've missed a few — kill 'em.'

It was ridiculously easy. The three of them strolled over to the hut and Mayne just walked in, Joe and Archie on either side, just like Henry Fonda in *Gunfight at the OK Corral*. The results were very similar. For a moment nobody moved, a total silence descended. One youngish chap nearest the open door stood up and began to shuffle backwards.

'Good evening,' Mayne said conversationally, and shot him with his .45 pistol. He then blasted the one next to him. Joe and Archie opened up with their Thompsons, shockingly loud. Joe would recall men stumbling, jerking and screaming, one bloke's head exploded like an over-ripe melon. They were firing dum-dum bullets that spread on impact. Men were being thrown in all directions. Mayne chucked a grenade. 'Out!' he bellowed. And out they went, into the cool evening air. Blood sloshed around their boots and spread in bright rivulets over the wooden boards. He glanced back, one man, still seated, shook his bloody head then slid wearily dead to the floor, another remained stock still, staring uncomprehendingly at the jetting stump of an arm.

Afterwards, he'd remember a scene from a painting by George de la Tour he'd been taken to see as a kid, pride and joy of one of the town's museums. A group of dark figures at night, from a long ago war intent upon a game of dice, their faces lit by the glow of candles. Bizarrely, he'd recall the scene he'd just witnessed in an oddly similar way; the figure of the maimed man, his shocked, ashen face lit by hurricane lamps.

Picking up four of the team, they pelted towards the parked array of aircraft. Behind them more firing broke out as a few survivors attempted to exit. This was even easier. They moved from plane to plane, a drill they'd practised a hundred times, planting bombs and leaving the timers set at half an hour, petrol bowsers and an ammo dump included. When they'd used up their supply they jumped aboard the three-engined transports with their corrugated fuselages and shot up their instrument panels. Using his knife and astounding physical strength, Mayne ripped out an entire panel. He handed the trophy to Archie. 'There's one for the collection. If we can't take scalps, at least we'll have dashboards.'

Nobody had been hurt, any Jerry who'd survived the shooting spree was keeping his head down and they got clean away. There was no sign of any pursuit. Dead on the appointed time, the empty, starlit sky was lit up by a dull thump and a bright fireball blossoming over the trashed airfield. 'Roll on fourth of July,' someone intoned, and it *was* spectacular.

Explosion after explosion rocked the night, spilled fuel ignited and blazed high into the heavens, tracer rounds whizzed off chaotically. It was all most gratifying.

'Bloody hell,' Mike Sadler grinned as they swaggered back to the RV. 'If you imagine we're going to be impressed, you're not wrong. I'll bet that lot's given old Erwin a headache.'

Stirling attempted to be equally excited but his reaction was tinged with jealousy. He tried but couldn't hide it. 'We got there alright, lots of lovely planes like banks of willing virgins, just waiting for us. Dug in, decided we'd jump 'em at night. Then, would you believe it, they started taking off, by tea time the place was bare and we were all dressed up with nowhere to go, downright unsporting.' He was attempting to put a gloss on his own failure but it rankled.

Paddy didn't do tact, this competition between him and his commanding officer was always part of the dynamic. He was brandishing his pilfered instrument panel, wires hanging like the tendrils of a severed limb. After Mayne had drafted a brief after action summary, Stirling summoned him and Joe to his derelict oven of an office that evening.

'Now look here,' he began, affable as ever but clearly wary of how he needed to tread lightly around his volatile subordinate who'd already been drinking. 'About these Boche you slew in righteous anger, they were unarmed?'

'How the bloody hell do I know? We didn't stop to ask.'

'There are some amongst our legion of foes at GHQ, and do remember we've as many enemies behind us as in front, who would happily label this massacre as a war crime.'

'Oh, for God's sake, they're the fucking enemy. They're the enemy who fly the planes we're busy blowing up. I only regret there weren't more of the bastards.'

'How about you Sergeant, how did you feel?'

'They had it coming, sir,' Joe responded without missing a beat. 'And with respect, just look where fighting by the Queensberry Rules has got us.'

'Talking about war crimes here is a bit like handing out parking fines during an air raid,' Mayne continued. 'It's not relevant. If those fat staff wallahs back in Cairo want to keep their cushy billets and drink pink gins, then they'd better just let us get on with the job of fighting their bloody war for them and that, until somebody convinces me otherwise, primarily involves killing Germans.'

'You're both right, of course, but please bear in mind, I've got to fight these GHQ gauleiters practically on a daily basis just to stop them shutting us down. This type of show would give them all the ammunition they needed — proof we're nothing but a crew of ruffians.'

'I'm more than happy with that description,' Mayne took a celebratory swig.

'That's fine, and I can't say I mind, but let's just keep this to ourselves shall we, I don't want the papers getting wind of it.' The Ulsterman just snorted.

'They won't get a squeak from me,' Joe promised.

'I'd hope not, Sergeant, in fact by the time we get back to Jalo I suspect you'll have forgotten all about it.'

'Forgotten all about what, sir?'

'That's the ticket.'

Mayne chucked him a beer.

Chapter Six

In the Souq

We were told to go to Libya, one December afternoon
After ice-cream merchants, the fighting fifth did run
Engineers, infantry and Tank Corps chaps as well
Graziani and his crowd, they ran like blinkin' 'ell.
Chorus:
Oh me lads you should have seen us gangin'
Past the Eyeties on the road, with their hands up they were standing
Their officers wore posh uniforms; the rank and file wore rags
But every prisoner we did see was sporting large, white flags.

    R.J. Luke 1 Royal Northumberland Fusiliers: *Libyan Handicap*
    (sung to the tune of Blaydon Races)

*

He was, he remembered sixteen; Evelyn would have been barely fifteen.
They had been wandering in the dunes. It was late May, early June, one
of those rare weeks when the chill of the North Sea coast was transformed
by sun. Northumbria's beaches glowed in the unaccustomed light, the
gunmetal harshness of the cold waters transfigured in blue.

Neville wasn't with them, he couldn't recall why. She was wearing a thin floral dress, which the omnipresent breeze flattened against her emerging figure. With a start he realised she wasn't a child anymore but had joined the mysterious cohort of girls who had become interesting in a wholly new way. She looked different too, as though from another country, taller, slimmer, fairer than the generally more homely variety he saw in school. Her hair was loose, a deep rich gold that tumbled to her shoulders, her face a near perfect oval with a well sculpted generous mouth and commanding bones. The realisation dawned upon him that his childhood friend was actually quite beautiful.

More than once, Neville had sort of sneered at lumpen proles. Now he felt like one, in his worn Aertex shirt, frayed at the neck, his baggy, shapeless shorts and school plimsolls. They were in the dunes, harsh marram and the ceaseless crying of gulls. It was really quite warm. The sand was soft and dragging underfoot as they went up the steep sides. He gave her a hand up; not that she needed it, but she took it anyway.

'Would you kiss me?' she suddenly asked. 'I mean would you want to? Lots of boys seem to want to.'

He stumbled and mumbled. Who the hell were all these boys?

'I thought your school was just for girls?'

'Well, it is, but girls have brothers and their brothers have friends. You know.'

He didn't really know at all. He'd sort of assumed he was her only male friend, though he'd not really thought about it in terms of exclusivity. Now he had, now she'd introduced the possibility, he was irrationally jealous.

'Well are you going to kiss me or just gawp?'

He just gawped.

'Oh, for God's sake!' She leant forward and took his astonished face between her supple hands and kissed him full on the lips. Actually, it wasn't too bad and he soon got the hang of it. To his alarm and embarrassment, other parts of his anatomy were reacting too, entirely of their own volition it seemed. Happily, Evelyn didn't seem to mind.

'When we were very young, you said you'd marry me,' she reminded him.

'I would, will, even,' he found himself promising.

'The old man would never allow it. He's getting ready to set me up with some chinless wonder, a kennel full of hounds and pots of cash.'

'Is that what you want?' Somehow, they'd gone from vertical to reclining on the soft sand of their enclosed world, their hands continuing a separate journey of exploration. 'God no, not at all, breeding dogs and kids and playing whist or bridge or whatever, I'd rather join a convent.'

'I don't think you'd pass the entrance exam. What do you *want* to do?'

'Me? Become a doctor,' she instantly confirmed, 'I'm pretty sure I can pull it off, too.'

'You bandaged my finger when I snagged it on barbed wire last year, remember? You did a pretty good job too, so I guess you're cut out for it.' Her eyes, steady and blue-grey, were on his. She did have fine eyes, in fact she was pretty fine all round. The bulge in his shorts was becoming insistent.

'Well, you're the first one who hasn't laughed at me. Mater and Pater think it's a joke, Neville makes the right noises but I'm not sure he's convinced.' Her fingers briefly brushed the ascendant organ which seemed to swell to impossible heights.

'We'd better deal with this,' she suggested.

*

And now, in his tent, it was just the same, except there were no supple fingers to provide ecstatic release, just 'Lady Palm and her five daughters,' Tommy's inevitable substitute.

Thank God his buttons were still fastened when Stirling barged in. Joe shot stiffly, in every sense, to attention.

His CO grinned wryly. 'At ease man, you're not on parade here.' They both sat.

'Now then, I've had an unusual request. It seems the cloak and dagger boys have need of your services. Can't say I like their bloody high handed tone, but I don't need any more enemies at GHQ.'

'They want me, sir?'

'Apparently so, don't ask me why, I'm too lowly to be in the loop but I'd bet it's to do with that business on Crete, that rather nasty Boche you uncovered. Anyway, you're to report to a Captain Ferguson, you already know him I think, at ten o'clock tomorrow. They keep gentlemanly hours, these I Corps johnnies.'

Joe was silent. This summons could only mean Hahnemann was here, in the Delta, in Cairo.

'Could be murky waters, laddie,' Stirling divined. 'Keep your wits about you. I wouldn't trust any of these buggers further than I could throw 'em. Fellows in regular khaki like us are just cannon fodder to them. Trust me; I went to school with these people.'

'Especially as a mere NCO,' Joe joked.

'Ah well, glad you mentioned that, time for a further elevation. When you're in the big city, get yourself kitted out as a Second Lieutenant, decent duds, new webbing, all that gear.'

Joe floundered. 'Yes, you're an officer now. Paddy and I had a chat about it last night.'

'Don't I need an actual commission, sir?'

'On paper I suppose, yes, but you can be commissioned in the field and once you've got all the right kit you'll look the part. That's what mainly counts.' He beamed characteristically.

Joe was vaguely dizzy. He'd never really expected to become an officer, certainly not on the whim of his CO, but why not? The idea began to appeal.

'You'll get most of what you need in the bazaar, keep away from the military tailors, they'll rob you blind. Anything you can't find on the cheap, keep a look out and nick what you fancy at HQ. That lot has more kit than you could count and it's not as if they've any intention of using it.'

Was it really this easy, his elevation to gentlemanly status? His father wouldn't be pleased but Evelyn would be; no more tradesmen's entrances for *Lieutenant* Joseph Milburn.

'And I looked these out, should be your size, well in fact Paddy did. He seems to like you, which immediately sets you apart from the rest of humanity. Try em on.' The boots were Italian, their previous owner presumably having no further need. Beautifully supple, they fitted a treat.

'As an officer, you need decent footwear. Cheap khaki you can get away with but boots are the true mark of a gentleman, even a temporary one. Oh and you might as well take my car — show 'em a bit of style.'

Joe was clearly favoured. The 'Blitz Buggy' was a fast Ford V8, of the sort much favoured by American gangsters, heavily customized, stripped and painted Wehrmacht grey, it could and did pass for a German staff car. Joe had sort of learned to drive in his TA days, but the Buggy was a different league of transport. The gears were smooth and fully synchro-mesh, no noisy double-declutching. Blasting along the straight roads to Cairo, he got the car up to an undreamed of seventy mph.

First stop the bazaar where, as Stirling predicted, he picked up the uniform he needed, including rank badges, for considerably less than any official tailor would demand. He already had the newly issued tan beret with its dramatic winged dagger badge, almost *felt* like an officer. His reception at Abbassia Barracks was rather different to before. He'd quickly adopted a suitable swagger to go with his elevated status and personalised transport, the resident NCOs were obsequious, his quarters, if rickety, still a big improvement. Even the sentries outside GHQ snapped smartly to attention, and he was afforded his own parking space.

He was offered coffee freshly ground, the real thing, not your squaddie's thick, strong tea, and ushered into the same sanctum as before.

'Bloody hell!' Neville exploded. He and the Scotsman were wreathed in dense tobacco smoke, even the air conditioning, privilege of the few, was struggling. '*Now* we're a bloody officer.'

'God knows what this war is coming too,' Ferguson commented drily.

'Corporal to lieutenant in a single bound!' Neville continued. 'Are you really an officer?'

'Well, Major Stirling says I am and I've bought all the gear.'

Ferguson groaned, 'David-bloody-Stirling, I might have guessed. A law unto him-bloody-self, no doubt the King's commission will follow along shortly. Still, makes life easier and I dare say you've earned it.' He quickly noted Ferguson has risen to major himself and Neville to a captaincy, promotion was in the wind.

That was the end of frivolity.

'You recall Count Almasy, whom I mentioned last time we talked?'

'Indeed I do, sir.'

'Well it seems his ideas have found an ear, a powerful ear at that, your friend Colonel Hahnemann of the Abwehr. He's taken over from a fellow called Ritter who happily buggered himself trying to parachute people into Egypt.'

'I know all about parachutes, sir.'

'Yes,' he laughed without mirth. 'As I recall you do. Well Hahnemann, like you winged dagger boys, prefers to cross deserts by vehicle, and why not? That's what Almasy does best. They're calling it Operation SALAM.'

'Can I ask how we know this, sir?'

'No you can't, strictly hush-hush. Almasy rigged up a convoy of captured Allied trucks and tried his hand, after all he's got plenty form. Didn't work out to start with, south of Jalo they hit bad ground. That's what happens when you rely on Eyetie maps. Vehicles were damaged and he gave that one up as a bad job.'

'And now?' Joe queried.

'If at first you don't succeed,' Neville chimed this time, 'you find another way and we rather fear he has. He's dodged your pals in LRDG, not their fault; it's a bloody big desert and he seems to have come around south towards Kufra then over the Gilf Kebir. He's done that route before.'

'What exactly was his plan though, bringing in agents I assume?'

'Spot on Lieutenant, you're earning your pips. He blagged his way through at Kharga and deposited his undesirables in the vicinity of Asyut. We have to assume they're now here in Cairo preparing to spin their wicked web. There are three of them and we're pretty sure Hahnemann is one.'

'And we can assume he's not come just to see the pyramids.'

'Oh no, very much not, he intends to see the swastika flying over 'em sometime soon. We know that SALAM, the infiltration phase, is complete, so he's moving on to Operation CONDOR, phase two if you like. Fact is we dropped a goolie with our wireless intercepts, too busy listening in on tank movements and he's stolen a march on us. Idea was to nab him and his evil minions, Almasy too, before they ever bloody got here. Now it's harder, needle in a haystack job and we don't underestimate Herr Hahnemann or the damage he can do.'

'What's his actual game, then?'

'Various and nefarious, intelligence gathering on troop movements, supply situation and what have you. We know how effective this can be thanks to LRDG. We know more about Rommel's logistics than he does, and he knows bugger all about ours. Hahnemann's team will have access to a radio; we know old Erwin's got a first class listening team parked up on the coast.'

'I know Hahnemann of course, but what about the other two?'

'A brace of interesting characters.' Neville was reading from a manila file, a thick one. 'We've one Johannes Eppler, German origin of course but grew up in the Delta, fluent in English and Egyptian, sometimes goes by the name of Hussein Gaffar — his mam remarried a rich Gyppo. Hans Gerd Sandstede poses as a Yank, uses the cover Peter Monkaster, he worked in the oil business so can pass himself off no trouble. Your man Hahnemann is fluent of course, flawlessly so, claims to be Swedish we think.'

'And what do you want me to do? Show me Hahnemann and I'll cheerfully shoot the bastard.'

'We'd prefer to take this particular bastard alive. And what you bring to the party is simple. You've seen him, you'd recognise him, gives you and thereby us an edge he doesn't expect. Fact is we cocked up royally letting him get this far, you're our one remaining ace, if you're game that is.'

Joe doubted he had any choice. 'Well I'm up for it, naturally, but not a clue how I'm supposed to proceed.'

'Ah well,' Ferguson smoothed, 'that's where our true genius as intelligence comes into play and I'm the first to admit we've got some mileage to make up.'

Neville picked up the narrative. 'Someone like Hahnemann doesn't drop in just to spy on troop movements, he can leave that to the other two and they're completely expendable. He's after stirring up the hornets' nest. We know the Gyppos, some of them, don't really like us. Most couldn't care as long as they're making money — Sterling or Deutschmarks doesn't matter.'

'There's a group here in Cairo, call themselves the "Free Officers Movement".' They're rather more radical. They really want us out and they've chosen to see Rommel as their Prince Charming. Plain daft of course, they'd find life under the swastika a good deal less congenial, but Hahnemann, we think, has tapped into their network. We know a fair bit of currency has begun circulating, forgeries but good ones, not your back street jobbies and we're pretty sure this is our man buying up new friends.'

'How serious are these types?'

'Normally they're an annoyance, but the closer the Desert Fox gets, the more vociferous they become. Properly organised they could be an effective and, for us, dangerous fifth column, bloody dangerous in fact. You know the sort of thing, strikes, sabotage, assassinations, bomb attacks; the works. So far we've kept the lid on it but the Herr Oberst is just the man to blow it off.'

'How in God's name do I or we find him? I know bugger all about any of this.'

Neville and Ferguson exchanged looks.

'We've thought about that,' the Scot continued, 'thought about it pretty hard in fact, and as it happens, we think you're ideal.'

Joe no doubt looked surprised — he was.

'Here's what we propose. Happily, your sudden rise makes the job much easier. You see if anyone is able to check, there's no record of any commission. You arrive in new and borrowed robes, driving a posh car, of sorts, anyway, while in reality you're just a corporal as far as anyone really knows. Fact is, the city is full of deserters and now you're one of them. You stole the kit, you stole the car and you've got information to sell.'

'Have I?'

'For sure, you're sporting a Special Forces beret and Rommel is feeling the hurt from what you boys are doing. You've blown up a creditable number of his planes, massacred their crews in cold blood and yes, we know about that one and no recriminations, in fact a hearty "well done" from us.'

'So I'm a traitor?'

'A complete cad in every respect, just the sort of fellow they'll be looking out for. You've information on all of our desert buccaneers, names, methods, equipment. That's gold dust to Hahnemann. You're our bait.'

Joe thought about it. 'How would I hope to get in contact though? If I just arrive outside his front door, if we know which front door, he'll smell a rat straight off. The bloke isn't daft.'

'Far from it, very far from it; we have to find you a route in. Happily, we've got one in mind.'

Neville picked up the thread again. 'We do have an in with the Movement. One of our people, an antique dealer as it happens, of Levantine origin and wonderfully untrustworthy, poses as an agent of theirs. He probably is. His contact is an officer called Sadat, Anwar Sadat. We think Sadat and Hahnemann have probably already been in contact, and our man is your best bet. He meets you in a bar, it's clear you're a wrong 'un with stuff to sell, redcaps on your back. He passes you on to the officers; they pass you on to the Boche.'

'I suppose the redcaps really will be after me?'

'God yes, you'll have to dodge 'em. If you simply end up in the glasshouse, we're buggered.'

115

'Suppose I do get in front of Hahnemann, what do you want me to do, just shoot him?'

'Absolutely not, attractive as that option is, we very much want him and his cohorts alive and, hopefully, blabbing. Don't worry; we'll have eyes on you all the time. When you're sure, we'll just move in. It's pretty simple.'

'And foolproof?'

'I wouldn't go that far, these things never are. I don't need to tell you how dangerous it'll be. Are you armed, 'tooled up' as they say in the movies?'

'Well, I've a Tommy gun back in the car but presumably I can't walk around the streets with that, can you get me a Colt .38 say, a holster gun?'

'That we can surely do,' Ferguson confirmed, opening a draw and sliding the contents over together with two boxes of cartridges. 'A Smith and Wesson as it happens, one careful lady owner, should do you proud.'

'Thing is,' he said as he holstered the revolver, 'surely the gen I'm "selling" has to be fake though?'

'Too bloody right, but the essence of a good lie is that it sticks as close to the truth as can be, much harder to spot the flaws, easier to learn, too. So, a lot of what your mob get up to Jerry pretty much knows about already: vehicles, kit, weapons explosives, even your own rather nasty improvisations – tell 'em that. What they *will* want to know about are unit structures, command and control, that sort of stuff. They call Stirling the "Phantom Major". We called him something quite similar as a lieutenant. Now this,' he pushed another file over to Joe, 'is a regimental structure, you'll find your unit has grown considerably in size and potency.'

'I didn't know we had tanks.'

'God no, wouldn't trust you lot with anything that costs money, but Jerry likes his tanks and so you must have 'em. We've prepared a list of targets you're aiming at, you're not as it happens, but they look convincing and I cooked up a series of highly imaginative cross desert trails with Bill Kennedy Shaw. They look good but most are impassable. We know that, Jerry doesn't. Worst case then if he gets away with all this info, he's bought a pup, your gang and LRDG are still ahead in the game.'

'And best case?'

'Well that happens if you get all the way through the pipeline and they'll be bloody cautious, then we nab the key players, first prize is your pal Hahnemann. That would be a palpable hit, the others are a bonus. If we get him or even if we just derail his plans here, then we're well ahead.'

Joe was looking at the file. On first glance it was sound, what was there seemed believable.

'By the way, that doesn't leave the building, you study and memorize. And, another thing, nobody is ordering you to do this. You're strictly a volunteer. Stirling would hit the bloody roof, he's madly protective of his chaps, I'll give him that, said I wasn't to put you in harm's way but I am. This lot would cut your throat as soon as break wind and outside of this room you can't trust anyone. If you don't think you can carry this one off, finish your coffee, bugger off and we'll forget this conversation ever took place, won't affect your prospects one little bit. Oh, and if you do pull it off you'll get damn all thanks from anyone. As far as the official history is concerned, none of this ever happened.'

'Not the best job interview I've ever had but yes, I'm in,' he answered, before he gave himself a chance to think too much about it and the briefing was over.

Neville was leading him down one of the carpeted corridors. 'There's a spare office you can use here, just to study the file. It's not bad I think, holds water though, thank God Jerry's not got our version of LRDG.'

'What about Count what's-his-name?'

'I doubt they'll ask him, and most of what's in here stacks up till you try it. Kennedy Shaw is sure Almasy won't be aware either, he knows the feller after all.'

'Then what, once I'm genned up?'

'You've an assignation at the Central Station here in the city centre at 17.00 hours with our contact. He's called Spiros ali Khareef, "dealer in antiquities" — *you'd* call him a fence. He sells on nicked antiques and sits on as many fences as possible. Everyone uses him, nobody trusts him, makes him your ideal intermediary.'

'He's a Gyppo tho?'

'More what might be called "mixed race", that's to say a mix of most races; part Arab, part Greek, part Egyptian, bound to be part Jew somewhere.'

'How will I know him, will he be wearing a pink carnation or summat? Isn't that how you spooks do things?'

'Don't be daft, you watch too many films. He'll be the fattest, shiftiest bastard in the place despite the competition, and he'll be looking out for you. The station's a melting point for all sorts including plenty of deserters; you'll be among kindred spirits, if not friends.'

They passed another, brilliantined, creased and redolent. Joe recognised him as the bloke he'd seen with Neville at the party, seemed ages ago. He shot Neville a look and Joe too, the second far from welcoming. *Fuck, he thinks I'm the bloody boyfriend.*

*

In his borrowed office, dusty and stale, Joe went through the file, time and again. It did hang together and in parts, close enough to the truth. He had a cover name, George ('Geordie') Stoddard, and a set of military ID. They'd been pretty sure of him, clearly. He thought about Neville too. Any lingering doubts had disappeared. Did he mind though? He decided not. They'd grown up together and they'd formed the fairly exclusive Bedlington Buccaneers. Even Evelyn, as a mere girl, was only an associate member.

He drank more good coffee and got through half a packet of fags, the dead air mummified in clouds of tobacco fumes. 'Well?' Neville demanded when he returned, just gone four o'clock. 'Are we word perfect?'

'We are and ready for owt.'

Neville considered this, perched on a corner of the battered desk. 'You still don't have to do this, if you've any doubts I mean. Fergie's a persuasive sort of bastard, it's what he does, gets other people to do what he wants, normally his dirty work. From what I know of our friend Hahnemann, he's utterly ruthless, well you've seen that. If you're unlucky enough to end up in his clutches, he'll torture you for whatever he can get and his sort can be very persuasive, there isn't anything he won't do.'

'Me neither, especially where he's concerned ... and as we, or rather I'm, about to go over the top, can I ask if you're queer?'

Neville remained stock still for an instant, then began to shake and finally to laugh, almost convulsed.

'Christ, Joseph Milburn but you're a bloody caution, as me granny would have said. What on earth makes you ask that *now*?'

'Just stuff, I'm not as daft as you'd think.'

'No, you're not bloody daft at all, never said you were — it was me said you should go to university, remember? Why, has Eleanor been writing to you again?'

'Yes, but nothing about that, she never would, as well you know. I just saw you with that ponce in the corridor.'

'Ah well … Lieutenant Allerdyce is a *friend*, can I say. But would it bother you if I *was* a poof?'

'Not in the bloody slightest mate, and it's mates we are.'

'How long, can I ask, have you been wondering?'

'Not really sure, but was there some business in the regiment, the Fusiliers, I mean?'

'I'm rather afraid there was. This was after you'd left to seek fame and glory with the commandos. Well, it was pretty tedious on home service after all the fun we'd had in France, and for people like me, war's a pretty good cover. I made a fool of myself with some pretty lad in the ranks. Very silly, and while not quite caught in the act, that would have been a hanging matter, court martial … anyway I was, as we say, *compromised*.

'Bit of a bugger, you could say.'

'Plenty did, and were happy to go on saying it. Pater came to my rescue; well to salvage the family name. He pulled strings, twiddled dials, the stuff he does and I was shipped out over here. Let's face it; old style regiments like the Fusiliers assume all staff wallahs are bent, automatically. Quite a few of us are; end of confessional and you've an appointment. Better get going and remember we'll have eyes on you all the time but if it gets hairy, get the fuck out and bugger official secrets.'

Down the long silent corridor he trudged, noise soaking into thick pile, the unaccustomed weight of the revolver dragging on his hip. He had left Neville in the dowdy cupboard to take charge of the precious file. It was nearly a mile walk to the station, past the museum and along the main thoroughfare, Shana Ramses. The station was named after the New Kingdom pharaoh, too.

Elegant Lieutenant Allerdyce was coming towards him. Was that all the damn fellow did, stalk the bloody corridors? Joe would have ignored him, but he passed with a sneer and that was too much provocation. There was nobody else about. He shouldered the slim officer against the wall, slammed him about a bit and pinned him by the throat. He felt much more relaxed for this.

'Right, you horrible little cunt,' he snarled. 'I don't know you, but already I really dislike you. If I should ever see you with my friend again, in any circumstances, I'll rip your fucking goolies off, if you've got any that is, and make you eat 'em.'

He threw the smaller man down onto the pile carpet and kicked him in the arse, which felt good too, so he did it again. His victim scuttled off, still on all fours. Joe didn't look back.

Chapter Seven

Peace and War

We had French wines, grapes, melons, steaks, cigarettes, beer, whisky and an abundance of all things that seemed to belong to rich, idle peace.

Alan Moorhead

*

At the next war let all the Kaisers, presidents and generals and diplomats go into a big field and fight it out first among themselves.

All Quiet on the Western Front (1930)

*

The station was a palace of elegant glass and iron, the modern Egypt. He'd slogged up from Garden City in late afternoon, heat still bouncing from the paving, the warren of the old city on his right, mystery and monuments of the Islamic quarter to the east. Still, you didn't have to be Howard Carter to realise Ramses II had been a pretty big cheese round here, though probably never thought he'd have a station named after him. Joe had always liked the idea of Egypt, had read with awe about the discovery of Tutankhamen's tomb, had ploughed through

Bram Stoker's *Jewel of Seven Stars*. The broad boulevard had been packed with all manner of transport, plenty army but ancient trucks, bullock carts, loaded donkeys, even camels. The whole wide delta was open for business.

The merits and traces of Ancient Egyptian culture were duly lauded in *The Services Guide to Cairo*, a handy and infinitely worthy gazetteer which reminded its readers to *remember you are representing your unit in the capital city of Egypt*. Here, in the station, was the information bureau, the very heart of forces life in this dazzling jewel of the orient. As the guide enthused, you could find accommodation, clean and inexpensive, there was a list of respectable clubs and cafés and a gushing summary of the pyramids which in fairness many Tommies, most of whom had never left Britain before, were keen to see. Those other hundreds of distinctly disreputable bars, brothels and the range of perversions amply catered for, well, Tommy had to discover those for himself. Usually, he managed.

Christ, the place was busy, a sea of khaki and much else besides, a heaving scrum of young soldiers released, however briefly, from the imminent possibility of violent death or maiming. Idly, he wondered how many of them were deserters — as he now ostensibly was. He'd been staggered when Ferguson told him, no wonder Eighth Army kept that one secret.

He paused to pull out a tab, but before he could strike the match a hand, complete with gold lighter, came to his service. He'd not seen the bloke approach which, given his bulk, was remarkable.

The Levantine looked like a cross between Sidney Greenstreet and Akim Tamiroff, a mix of sleaze and menace, everything smiling but his impenetrable eyes. He wore a cream linen suit that had seen better days but was at least clean, the gold cufflinks and watch chain were certainly real and if his ebony cane concealed a long stiletto blade, Joe wouldn't have been at all surprised.

'This is just for walking with,' the spy, if he *was* a spy, had divined his thoughts. Joe guessed he'd be very good at that, his life might often have depended on it. 'Should I call you corporal or lieutenant, as you are both and yet neither?' His English was good, a richly practised baritone and only the hint of an indefinable accent. He didn't wait for an answer. 'And now I think we should walk, a man in your position would not linger too long with so many police around. Let us repair to the Empire Club, no great distance from here, where we will take coffee.'

In the rooftop bar with its fantastic panorama of the old city and the river looking over to the manicured sanctuary of the Gezira Club, they drank the strong black coffee flavoured with harsh hints of cardamom. Joe hadn't quite got used to the stuff yet, and was spooning the sugar in. The place was packed, a sprawling complex of cafés and bars with a full sized cinema — they were showing Bogart and Bergman in *Casablanca*. He half felt he was in some kind of movie anyway; but then he remembered Hahnemann.

'Most English find our coffee here bitter.'

'How about the Germans?'

'I couldn't say, the Italians brew fine coffee if they're good for little else. I'm told in 1940 Il Duce had his white charger and resplendent new uniform all ready for his triumphal entry, silly little fellow. He thought your empire was finished and now he depends on Rommel, the bulldog he's been lent by his ally. The man is truly a fool, Hitler too perhaps.'

'Good, you're on our side.'

'My dear young fellow, I'm on nobody's side. I learnt all I need to know about war and glory in Smyrna in 1922. Turks killed Greeks and Greeks killed Turks, all pretty stupid and neither showed any mercy, so now I just buy and sell and you, I am informed, are selling.'

'I've information, yes, and I'm pretty sure Jerry would pay for it.'

'Well I know nothing of any Germans here but it may be I do know people who might know other people who might be in the market.'

'How will I know who to speak to?'

'You don't need to. I will speak to someone and the message will be carried on and on again, so it goes here. There are many who would sell, but perhaps fewer who will buy. Tonight at ten you will be at the Luxor Club on Shana Dahsur. The place will be heaving, that I can guarantee, our famous Sultana of Romance is dancing; she always pulls a good crowd.'

'Will you be there?'

'Lord no, I'm far too old to be aping belly dancers, however voluptuous, and I find crowds irritating. Besides, who you may meet there is none of my affair. If you have not been contacted by midnight then I fear your merchandise has failed to excite any potential purchaser. The market as we say is fickle and trust, like truth, remarkably rare.'

*

The Luxor Club was pretty much what you'd expect, a vaulted basement bar in the Old Town, cleaner than most though the discreet and far from reliable light cast merciful shadows. The war had boosted the city's less salubrious economy no end. The place was thronged much as the fat man had predicted, a *Who's Who* of allied servicemen, civvies and spivs, good looking women exuding cheap scent, trying unsuccessfully to compete with a pungent tide of sweat, tobacco and testosterone. A jazz quartet, immaculate in evening dress, was playing, almost audible above the row which billowed and eddied like the restless tide. He managed to squeeze into the one empty booth. He was ostensibly alone but probably not. God knows how many men Ferguson had inside the place.

Star turn that night was Hekmet Fahmy, a celebrity belly dancer of legendary status. Joe had not seen belly dancing. He'd imagined it was something akin to strip tease. From the expressions on the flushed faces of the sea of squaddies, they had similar hopes. They were to be disappointed. The dancer was a Juno-esque young woman, long limbed and graceful. Her costume, while eminently suggestive, allowed no excess of bare flesh, her toned midriff enclosed in a tight body stocking with a strategically placed jewel to mask her navel. None of it came off, either.

Her dance was both restrained yet seriously sensual — if rather more sophisticated than her enthusiastic audience might have looked forward to. She moved with easy, practised grace, sweeping sinuous movements, the music vaguely rustic but with what must be European influences. Preoccupied as he was, he found her fascinating. It was rumoured numerous high ranking officers were similarly impressed.

'She's very good, isn't she?' A man slid into the booth, rather closer than he'd have liked though, from his face, he wasn't that keen either. An officer in the Egyptian Army, signals by his badges, and a Second Lieutenant.

'She's not really classical, of course.' The man's English was accented but precise. 'Our ambitious choreographers developed a new, well, hybrid style in the twenties. Took the more traditional, tribal dances and blended in western ballet and ballroom. A re-packaging you might say, aimed at a western imperialist clientele.' He spoke evenly but clearly with some disapproval; western imperialists were not really his type.

Joe thought he was probably Sudanese, dark skinned with high, almost Asian bones, and rather narrow, devious eyes. He had the buttoned up look of a righteous zealot. This he supposed was the Lt. Anwar Sadat whom Ferguson had mentioned.

'Have we met?' Joe asked politely.

'I doubt it, my knowledge of you British mainly relates to the inside of your gaols.'

'Well, I'm sure Rommel will be more welcoming. What's your name and why are you here?'

'We'll skip names for now if you don't mind. Mine is too well known to your people already, suffice to say I'm here as a result of a conversation you had earlier and ...' he held up a well manicured hand, 'I don't believe a word of it.'

Joe's instinctive dislike of the bloke hardened. 'Then just fuck off Abdul and stop spoiling my view.'

'You're in no position to bandy insults, if you are who you claim.'

'And I've no time for time wasters, either. It's really very simple. I have goods to sell. I'm looking for a willing buyer. If you're in the market, fine, if not then piss off and go back to shagging camels.'

The other man's narrow eyes hardened still further. Joe could sense this wasn't going to be a lasting relationship. There was a staring contest as the hubbub continued without anybody noticing.

'Let me be plain,' the Egyptian continued. 'I've no time for your squalid little treacheries, your greed and betrayal. But, it may be there are those that would listen to you. Who knows, they might even pay you. My job is just to find out if you can be trusted.'

Joe laughed openly. 'Can you, can any of your kind, be "trusted"? Look, this is just business. Once it's done I'm out of here. It needs to be quick as the bloody redcaps are on my tail. I don't care about you, about Jerry or any bugger else. Get your people to check me out, there's probably a warrant with my name on it by now.'

'There is, so you best go carefully *Mr* Stoddard. Where are you staying, which hole are you hiding in?'

'Like I'm going to tell you...'

'No matter; at the end of this glittering performance whilst your fellow soldiers are jeering and cheering their own pathetic excitement, you will go backstage. It will be arranged and you will talk with the lady herself. Certain other arrangements may then be made and you will comply with them, is that clear enough?'

'As crystal mate, now bugger off and give my regards to the camel.'

He eased his way towards the stage, trying to look anonymous though there wasn't a redcap in the place as far as he could see. The rear area was cordoned off and a pair of hulking bouncers with rather silly fezzes perched on bullet heads kept watch. They didn't give him a second glance as he stepped through the curtained arch. The joint was more squalid backstage than front, a row of scruffy cubicles which passed as dressing rooms. One door only was open, nobody was in sight. He knocked.

Even close up, Hekmet Fahmy didn't disappoint. She had a good oval face with suitably generous lips and very wide, dark eyes. She'd thrown a robe on over her outfit and an open tin of potent Egyptian fags stood open on the dressing table. Their strong exotic fug filled the small space.

'I get these made up especially by a fellow in Alexandria, stronger than is good for you I expect.' She extended the tin and he lit them both up, getting out would require a machete just to hack through the atmosphere. 'You're not bad looking,' she started, her English excellent with a suitably beguiling accent. 'My friend wasn't too flattering. I suspect you didn't get on.'

'I may have insulted his camel.'

'He's a bit of a stuffed shirt, most of his kind are. They see themselves as successors to the pharaohs, they really hate you Brits.'

'How about you?'

'Why would I care? It's the British who are paying my rent at present, people here are doing pretty well out of this war as long as it doesn't get too close. Do you think the Germans will win? Is that why you're running away? Not that I blame you.'

'Let's say I've done my bit, done it several times over and I'm sick of being treated like dirt and I've decided I don't want to die to keep a few chinless wonders in caviar.'

'Do they really eat caviar here?'

'No, I doubt it. But my father was in the last war, it made him into a socialist. I thought that stuff was all bollocks, but turns out he was right.'

'Not that easy I'd have thought, getting out. Where do you go, over to the Boche?'

'Not likely, out means out. With a few bob in me pocket I can hitch a ride on some nice neutral freighter and sail off somewhere quiet, keep me head down till it's over.'

She thought about it.

'If you have information, *good* information, then of course there are buyers. You'd better be sure, though. If you try and sell these people a dud, then the nearest to the sea you'll get is a Nile cruise in cement overshoes.'

'If I wasn't kosher I wouldn't take the risk.'

'How do you know such people just wouldn't torture you for what you know then dump you in the Nile anyway? Much easier for them, and no loose ends as they say.'

'They could, but I'm trained to resist interrogation and, even if they broke me, by then the information would be out of date. Cheaper and easier just to pay me off. They get to sample the goods and don't buy unless they're satisfied.'

'It's your neck,' she shrugged. 'There's a coffee shop down the street on the right. It's pretty busy during the day, be there at eleven tomorrow and you'll be contacted.' She saw his look. 'You can't blame people for being careful. There're so many in this city spying on each other it's practically an industry.'

*

Ferguson had arranged a dingy flat on the fringes of Garden City, bland and anonymous, just the sort of place you might hide out. The rent was cheap and strictly cash, a seedy janitor asked no questions. Joe's hobnail ammo boots had long since been replaced, first by sandals and now suede desert boots, reassuringly quiet. He walked in what he hoped was a suitably insouciant way and just prayed he'd not run into any redcaps. A jeep full of them roared past as he was passing the suburb of Bab-al-Luq but didn't even slow down, probably the Aussies beating up town somewhere or the Jocks, or both. Perhaps Mayne was on leave?

He spent an uneasy night in the sagging armchair, dozing on and off, revolver in his lap. Jerked awake by the dawn chorus of the Muezzin, summoning the faithful to prayer and a new day, he felt weary and generally dirty. Not the sweat and grime of the desert, but ingrained dirt you seemed to pick up from the streets, or possibly it was the company he was keeping.

Ferguson had furnished him with a parting gift, a supple chamois ankle holster, something he'd not seen before, and a neat Walther 7.65 mm PPK pistol. The seven round magazine was fully loaded and he had a spare. His Smith and Wesson held six cartridges and he'd a dozen more in his webbing pouch.

It was early and there was only ersatz coffee in the dingy flat though, as outlaw hideouts went, it wasn't too bad. At least the wheezing shower did produce water and the lights worked. There was no telephone. As he sipped his insipid brew, he reviewed his cover story. Ferguson had okayed using details of past raids. The Boche would be aware of what had happened, of course, but he'd still know stuff only a player could know.

He went over the mental script he'd cooked up. It seemed watertight, unless they did get the thumbscrews out. He was at the café by the appointed hour, slightly early in fact. Again he'd walked, enjoying the breeze that wafted in from the great river, bringing hints of the limitless continent that stretched forever south. The café was painted light blue with a jolly striped awning, the sort of thing you'd see on Tynemouth beach on a sunny day before the barbed wire. Inside was cool and cavernous, neatly pressed newspapers racked and ready.

Joe was on his second cup of the strong Turkish coffee that he feared he was getting addicted to, black and viscous — though he gave in to the westerner's penchant for loads of sugar. The man who came in was Eppler. He recognised him from the photos. Not bad looking really, about Joe's height and build, hair oiled slick and a pencil moustache, just a hint of Clark Gable.

'Herr Stoddard, I assume. Allow me to buy you another coffee.' Joe did allow him.

'Like most Tommies, I imagine you are unfamiliar with our great city?' Joe shrugged as he went on. 'It's quite an experience, this place. I myself was brought up here, my name is Hussein Gaffar.'

'You don't *look* very Egyptian.'

'We must be the biggest race of mongrels on the planet I suppose, but, as a matter of fact, I'm not.' He didn't elaborate. 'I'm given to understand you have certain information, that you wish to sell, and that you are a deserter from the Special Air Service as your unit is now called, I believe.'

'It is and I do.'

'If I or certain associates of mine were to be interested in such information, might I enquire as to your asking price?'

'I'm asking for two thousand pounds and preferably in gold.'

Eppler hesitated for a moment, his amiable expression staying in place. 'That is rather a lot of money; it *is* a lot of money. Even if my associates had access to those kinds of funds, they would require, as you say, proof of good intentions.'

'Yes, I can see that. I'd give them a taster, all verifiable, and they give me a deposit of five hundred, the balance on completion.'

'You're a confident young man Herr Stoddard. One might think you had done this all before.'

'Once is enough, but I have had months in that stinking desert to think about it. I just want out, clean away and then I'm gone for good and you can enjoy your war. I'm done with it.'

Eppler nodded sagely. 'Well then, while we enjoy this excellent local coffee, could I entreat you just to give me something I can take back? People are deeply suspicious, as you know. They might just think you're a plant foisted on us by British military intelligence.'

'Look mate, unless you went to Eton or fucking Harrow or some other factory for inbred wankers, you wouldn't even get through the door. People like me don't exist — or if we do it's as cannon fodder for their fucking armies. So it's dead easy Mr Gaffer or whoever you really are, you give me money, I give you gen that you can use and you don't have. Trust me, it's value for money.'

Eppler was still smiling. 'Tempt me.'

So Joe told him about the raid on the airfield. A lot of it was true. He omitted the LRDG role and awarded L Detachment its own specialised vehicles and startling navigation skills (thanks to him). He described the Lewes bombs, their weapons and kit. When it came to details of the raid itself, he was unsparing, covering every shot of the mess hall massacre. He'd changed names but not facts. The other man seemed impressed.

'Well, that is enlightening for sure. Not all of you English play cricket it seems. But as you are a navigator perhaps you could tell me how a sun compass works? It's just curiosity on my part, I've heard of them, it seems a most ingenious device.'

No Official Secrets Act there, just a simple test. He described the compass in detail.

'And, of course, there is more?'

'A helluva lot, yes, I can tell you how we're organised, units' strengths, the routes we use, how we select targets and what the next ones are likely to be. You're not going to get that from anyone else and you can forget any of the tossers at GHQ, they've no idea what we do.'

Eppler nodded sagely. Outside the midday sun was broiling, though the café stayed cool. The place was pretty busy, nobody looking their way. If Ferguson did have people around, they were bloody good.

'You will understand,' Eppler began, 'I'm no expert in these matters, I'm a businessman not a soldier, but it may be that what you have to say will be of interest to others, and they may well be tempted to buy … or at least be ready to treat.'

Joe shrugged, 'I can't afford to hang around mate, not with the redcaps on my tail and my lot doesn't take to kindly to desertion. I've spent time in the glasshouse, didn't much care for it. Deal or no deal. I need out, and pronto.'

'I understand your difficulties, trust me; that's a sensation I've experienced myself. So, look here, I'm going to speak to people and I'll suggest a further meet later this afternoon, somewhere open and public for everyone's ease. Remain here for one hour and I'll send a message. The baklava here is quite good too.'

He did try the sweet dessert, quite liked it, drank more coffee — *be buzzing soon*, he thought. What the fuck did he do now? He had to play the game their way, any wrong move and he'd frighten them off.

He had to assume Ferguson was on the case, if not he was on a very sticky wicket. The hour dragged by, he read the starched papers. The Russians were doing well, it seemed, well, anything was better than losing millions like they'd done the year before, and the more left leaning papers were all over Joe Stalin. Funny thing that, before the war they'd branded him a monster.

An Arab boy, anonymous in a flowing white jalabiyyah, brought him a handwritten message. 'Meet at the Egyptian Museum entrance 16.30 hours.' It wasn't signed but he assumed this was from Eppler. The museum wasn't far, he had plenty of time.

It was still hot when he left the café, that oppressive blanket of late afternoon when the stones seemed to radiate heat, the breeze had dropped and he could feel sweat pricking as soon as he abandoned the shaded interior. The city seemed to have surrendered to heat, retreated indoors until the shadows lengthened. He had one bad moment when he spied a couple of redcaps ahead but he got to the museum plaza without any bother.

Tahrir Square backed onto the Nile, a leafy, well kept park fronting the great pile of the museum building, loudly confident in red sandstone, a statement of Edwardian solidity and permanence, home to all the fabulous treasures of the pharaohs. There were very few people around and he'd arrived with ten minutes to spare. He liked museums, had spent hours in Newcastle's science and engineering display on the city's Town Moor. He decided if he survived the next few hours he'd like to look in this one.

A car rolled up the boulevard, one of those black Citroen Tractions, a lean racy model, well known for speed. The paintwork gleamed as the car abruptly pulled up and the back door opened. Joe had released the flap of his holster with one hand on the butt.

'No need for that,' Eppler was inscrutably reassuring. 'It seems your prayers have been answered, get in.'

'Where are we going?'

'Somewhere safe and yes, public, we wouldn't be going to this trouble just to bump you off but we do need to know you've no unwanted baggage.'

Bugger all choice really, it was that or a runner and he knew he was too hooked on the game.

The car moved off smoothly; no fuss, no squealing tyres like in the movies. The driver was a thickset bloke with very little neck but considerable bulk, probably local hired muscle. He drove well though, confident through the smooth synchromesh gears, Citroen's moncoque design and superb suspension coping with everything Cairo's variable street surfaces could throw up.

He knew they were heading south and east through Bab-al-Luq, a neat grid of streets, crossing the main Port Said road at Al Helmiya. Here, they branched east towards the majesty of the ancient citadel. He guessed that was their likely destination and while he'd dearly love to look back and see if they were being followed, he dared not. Their silent chauffeur drove calmly and unhurriedly, which clearly suggested they weren't. Eppler was relaxed and engaging, pointing out anything vaguely interesting as they swept by. As far as Joe could see he wasn't armed, he assumed the driver probably was.

'And behold, the Citadel,' Eppler purred on. 'Built by Saladin himself, trying to keep you English out, I imagine.'

Despite his preoccupation with life expectancy, Joe was impressed. The great cream coloured walls soared above them as the road swung around the north flank. They drove through a heavily fortified gateway, its mute towers standing sentinel as they'd done for nearly a thousand years. 'Not too many tourists, this season,' his guide continued, 'blame Rommel, I suppose.' The place had an impenetrable, shut in feeling. Once through the heavily studded timber gates, he sensed they were entering a closed world.

'Like a city within a city,' Eppler confirmed, 'used to be the centre of government, was so for centuries, till you English rather rudely took over.'

'I wouldn't have taken you for a patriot,' Joe snapped.

'God no, none of that flag waving stuff for me. You met one of our more zealous contacts last evening, a mix of piety and pomposity; no sense of humour whatsoever.'

Their car swept up through an inner bailey into the northern wing of the complex, the Egyptian army museum on their left. 'Big place for an army that's never won a battle.' Across an open sun swept courtyard, broad and empty, to a much smaller building, garnished with Ottoman frets and domes. 'Suleiman Pasha's Museum, and all ours for today, impressive in its way, don't you think?' The Citroen came sedately to a halt. They got out, their burly driver making a show of pocketing the keys.

'I could ask you to surrender your firearm but I suspect you may be reluctant.'

'I will if you will, *all* of you.'

Eppler merely smiled and indicated the front door . 'Shall we?'

Inside, the place seemed to have come straight out of *Arabian Nights*. Coloured tiles, lofty ceilings and casual opulence. No great throng of tourists either. An octagonal marble topped table was placed centrally in the main hall, four elegant columns held up the roof, walls hung with armour, spiked Mameluke helmets and elegant, long hafted lances. Their driver, who'd not spoken, stayed with his back to the door and another couple of heavies, anonymous in ill fitting suits, were trying to look casual at a smaller table some distance away. He guessed this was normally a kind of café/shop area in the museum. Another hulking brute was busy at the counter, rather incongruously making coffee.

He and Eppler sat at the larger table. Joe positioned himself so he could see each of the hired helps, although killing them all would need some pretty impressive shooting. Large bevelled edged and gilt framed mirrors hung on the walls, giving the place a far more extended feel. A cumbrously ornate brass chandelier hung low from the high coffered ceiling. The air was cool and still, no sound from outside intruded, quiet as the grave, as his gran might have said.

Coffee was served in silence. Even Eppler was quiet, he seemed more nervous now. The flap of Joe's holster stayed undone and he'd previously cocked the Walther, snug in its concealed harness. A man walked through the beaded curtain behind the counter. Joe recognised him instantly, an electric shock running up his spine. Erich Hahnemann sat down opposite.

His linen suit was pale blue, crisp and unblemished, only a German officer could make a civvy suit look like uniform, though this one hadn't come from any bazaar. He wore a cream silk shirt and paisley cravat, quite the gentleman. He looked relaxed. Joe knew the man couldn't possibly recognise him. The dark eyes were vaguely humorous.

'Herr Stoddard,' he began conversationally in precise, almost accentless English. 'I must apologize for the rather theatrical nature of our surroundings, but it is at least both quiet and discreet.'

The tone was affable, the threat implicit. Joe decided this was going to end badly and did a quick calculation on lines of fire.

'My colleague, indeed various colleagues and associates,' just the right hint of scorn, 'have given me to understand you have information which may be of value to me. Indeed,' he gestured at Eppler,' you come with high commendations.'

'And I told your pal the terms.' Joe was struggling to sound as casual. Firstly he was shit-scared, and secondly he really, really wanted to kill this man *right now*. He reined himself in, this was the organ grinder and so far he'd just seen monkeys. Hahnemann was the consummate professional, he'd see straight through any bullshit and he'd be finely attuned to body language.

'And what has persuaded you, an elite soldier, with a good record, to betray your country?'

'I need the money.'

'No sudden conversion to national socialism, no idealism, just money?'

'Oh no,' he said conversationally, 'I still think you Nazis are a bunch of cunts who need to be exterminated, just that I'm leaving that to others. And they will, you know. You can't fight us all, the Yanks and the Russians and given what you've done to *them*, I can't see much of your precious fatherland being left standing.'

Hahnemann seemed unperturbed. 'Well, we'll see shall we, and I don't think we're here to discuss grand strategy, certainly not with you, Herr Gefreiter.'

'Same rank as your precious, fuckwit Fuhrer.' This was reckless, but he was enjoying the needling.

Eppler wasn't. 'Can we just get on with business?'

His boss smiled, a mirthless grimace. 'Thank you Johannes and yes, let's proceed. I've a gold bar here worth five hundred pounds sterling. As a gesture of our bonafides, that's yours if I like what you tell me now; yours to keep regardless. If I *really* like what you're telling me and you've got more, then I will pay you more, is that acceptable?'

The fact they were offering to pay him in gold rather than their dodgy fivers was a sure sign he wouldn't be around to collect the prize. If Hahnemann was undecided before, he'd made his mind up. Joe decided that whoever got out of this place alive, it wouldn't be the man opposite.

'Let's see the bullion.'

Hahnemann clicked his fingers and the hefty brute behind the counter reverently laid a slim gold bar in the centre of the table.

'Gold,' Eppler exclaimed cheerfully, 'always makes me feel happy, so wonderfully reassuring. That, Corporal, is your passport to freedom.' The bloody stuff was hypnotic for sure, only Hahnemann seemed uninterested.

'So,' he continued brusquely, 'what do you have to tell me?'

He could feel the weight of the Walther dragging on his ankle, as though begging to be used. *Your time will come*, he thought. 'I enlisted with the Northumberland Fusiliers September 1939 and transferred to the Commandos in October 1940. I served on Crete,' no reaction from Hahnemann, 'and once I'd got to Egypt, was recruited into L Detachment.'

He went through his carefully remembered script, vehicles, weapons, explosives– generic stuff, but traceable. He'd already expanded L Detachment into a full regiment with transport, signals and even the mythical tanks.

'I'm most intrigued about your supporting panzers. How can Eighth Army spare any of these for your little adventures when we are destroying so many in battle?'

Neville and Joe had thought of this. 'We've just got light tanks, Honeys, Yanks call 'em Stuarts, thirty-seven mm gun not much use for anything but recce.'

'Ah yes, I've come across them, quite agile I think, good for running away.'

The questioning continued. He talked up an imaginary command and control structure, logistics and commissariat — he almost believed it himself.

'And you were one of those who murdered our airmen in cold blood, or so you boasted?'

'Yes, I particularly enjoyed that one. You should've heard your blokes screaming, not much sign of the master race, more like a bunch of frightened schoolgirls.'

Hahnemann was careful not to rise to the bait, throwing in the odd random question.

'And what is your view of General Auchinleck, the 'Auk' I think you call him?'

Joe shrugged, 'never met him, as a rule my sort never meets his sort, be some posh public school bastard, probably queer to boot.'

'Your family is socialist, I believe you said, perhaps we have more in common than you might imagine?'

'Yeah, socialist but not National Socialist, we tend not to murder people just because they disagree with us.'

'And this part of England you are from, Northumberland I believe. It is in the north of course and I have not been there. My time in England was spent studying in Oxford, a most beautiful place, not unlike my native city Regensburg in Bavaria. Do you know Oxford?'

'You've got to be joking, never been south of the Tyne in me life, not till now anyway.'

'Of course, the north/south divide I think you call it, very much the same in Germany. Do you support football?'

'We all do up north, an' before you ask me to recite the names of all the players in Newcastle's front row to see if I'm kosher, well yes I can, so no need to bother.'

'I don't doubt you, Corporal. Not for one moment, and what you have told me checks out and yes, it's of interest to us. I believe we are making good progress, you will leave here a much richer man I think.'

He gestured to the café/bar heavy who dutifully brought over a bottle and three glasses. 'A small toast is in order,' Hahnemann seemed in good spirits. 'I've not been to Scotland either but I'm a great admirer of their malt whiskies, not the cheap blended stuff they export, mind you.'

He sloshed the enticing amber liquid into the three glasses. Eppler took his without a comment. Joe quite liked whisky but hesitated.

'Ah, don't worry about the Scotch. It contains neither poison nor sedatives. Even an out and out Nazi like me wouldn't adulterate a twelve year old Glenlivet. If I intended to do away with you, I'd have offered Schnapps.'

For a surreal moment, they just sat and savoured the malt. It tasted bloody good. Joe made a mental note that if he survived the next few minutes, he'd never drink anything else. Hahnemann however, now only had one hand visible, the other was beneath the table. Joe was very similar, the wrap around butt of the small pistol comfortable in his hand.

'You'll need to take the safety off first,' he cautioned the German, I already have,' he lied. If Hahnemann was nervous he didn't show it. Eppler looked ready to piss his pants. The heavies were all on full alert though none had moved.

'Major Ferguson is to be congratulated,' Hahnemann continued, still outwardly relaxed. 'You spin a good yarn, just enough truth to make it convincing, I'd have done it much the same. You certainly fooled my friend here and our dumbkopf Egyptian zealot.'

Joe just looked at him. The others wouldn't move until he did. Eppler would be off with the first shot.

'It was the girl who swayed me, you see. Women are very good at this; far more subtle I'd say. If it matters she rather liked you but she had you down for a soldier not a traitor, so do I.'

Joe still didn't move.

'Besides,' Hahnemann conceded, 'we have other sources and you chose to play the hero, you're way out of your depth.'

His thumb was clearly on the safety, his black eyes looking straight at Joe.

'But that's not the reason I'm here.'

He could sense the German's hesitation

'I'm here on account of Dave Horne, a mate of mine you murdered on Crete.'

For that instant, Hahnemann was confused. The table seemed quite heavy but Joe was very fit and had desperation on his side. In one movement he heaved it over, priceless scotch smashing against the floor tiles. Hahnemann was flung back and his shot, shockingly loud, only wounded the chandelier which merely danced a bit.

Covered by the table and the moment of confusion, Joe shot left handed at the heavy by the door. He missed but the bloke was already halfway out — he'd hung onto the car keys for a reason. Eppler was scrabbling left, Hahnemann was scrabbling right. The two heavies were half on their flat feet but way, way too slow. He aimed to double tap both. One went down, the other reeled and stumbled clear, retaliation didn't seem like an immediate priority.

He ducked around the stone column behind his seat, just as well — a burst of nine mm sub machine gun fire chewed lumps out of the upturned table, flinging marble chips like shrapnel. He had already guessed what the other heavy had under the counter. Eppler was now beneath the same counter too but entirely in the spirit of self preservation. Hahnemann was behind another pillar, a round from him cracked the stone above Joe's head.

Joe ducked and ran to the next pillar, the Bergmann followed then jammed, bloody things always did. He shot the shooter twice with his .38. One round went through the barman's head, smashing the mirror behind which came down in a crashing waterfall of glass. Hahnemann fired again, breaking another mirror behind him, glass shards flew. Joe had a couple of rounds left in the Walther, four in the S andW, a gun in either hand, regular Wyatt Earp. He gave Hahnemann the two in the automatic, missed by a mile but kept him penned. Crouching, he ejected the spent mag, rammed home the other — seven more shots.

It was now only the two of them. He couldn't see Hahnemann just giving in, somehow. In the movies the cops always yelled 'come out with your hands in the air, the game's up.' No such thing as a fair cop in this game. But time was now on his side. If they stayed put the cavalry would arrive at some point, ours not theirs. The German had a limited range of options.

Hahnemann chose flight. Pumping wild rounds from his P38, the heavy pistol bucking even in his experienced hand, he bolted for the archway. Joe sent a couple of bullets after him but they were wasted, he made it through the curtain almost certainly unscathed. Joe had no choice but to follow.

This was not any part the public saw, an anarchic store room, worryingly dark, narrow corridor lined with barrels, it didn't invite reckless pursuit. He ducked behind the nearest barrel; standing still in doorways got you killed. He briefly recalled that Geoffrey Keyes had won a VC that way. A round, louder than ever in the narrow vaulted chamber, plugged the barrel, spilling a gush of strong red wine, nastily like haemorrhaging blood in the poor light. Shame he hadn't brought a grenade. There was a door at the far end but he'd have a clear shot, Hahnemann wasn't about to play jack rabbit. Conversely, charging down the line of barrels was a Light Brigade job.

Something struck the hard stone floor and rolled ominously towards him. Fuck, Hahnemann *did* have a grenade. He flung himself bodily back through the arch. The blast followed him, chucking him carelessly, flailing over the tiles, slick with the blood of those he'd already killed. Of the other survivors there was no sign, Eppler and the wounded heavy had cleared off.

The vaulted store was a no-man's-land of busted staves, swimming in their own wine lake with enough smoke to cover his stumbling charge. He still had the .38, must have dropped the automatic. Hahnemann was half way over the cobbled plaza, moving fast, zigzagging to spoil his aim. Feverishly, Joe crammed fresh cartridges into the revolver as he half ran, half stumbled after.

It was at least two to three hundred yards over the uneven surface and his quarry had a good head start. Another fortified arch led out back into the sprawling city, narrower than the one they'd entered through. He glanced back towards the main entrance, vehicles and men in khaki were spilling out; the belated cavalry charge.

Hahnemann was almost at the gate, Joe could hear engines revving over the cobbles. *Outrun this lot you bastard*, he thought. The Abwehr man was beneath the vault, swallowed by the blank light. Joe pelted after. He barrelled through the arch to see his enemy now about fifty yards ahead. Christ! The sod had a second car, a low slung open tourer had swerved alongside. Hahnemann reached for the door. 'Bastard,' Joe yelled and took a shot from thirty yards. Not a chance. The German ducked and levelled his own weapon. Joe could hear the empty click. *Got you now*, he thought, the gap was twenty yards, the car door open.

He stopped to take aim. The German was a dead man for sure. Just vaguely, almost peripherally, he saw the driver of the car lean across the windscreen over the open roof, something metallic glinted in his hand. Joe made to turn, switch his aim just that fraction too late. Something struck his chest like a sledgehammer, throwing him back. His head struck the hard pavement surface with sickening force and he remembered no more.

Chapter Eight

Out From Battle

Send out the Army and the Navy,
Send out the rank and file,
Send out the brave Territorials,
They'll face the danger with a smile
(I don't think).
Send out my mother,
Send out my sister and brother,
But for Gawd's sake don't send me!
   Tommy doggerel

*

The words of the music hall tune kept filtering though his mind as Joe attempted to concentrate on the letter to his mum, mindful both of the censor's keen pen and his own shortcomings; 'Dearest Mother,' he began. So far so good but, not for the first time, he was struck by the sheer impossibility of communicating to someone 'back there,' what it was like to be 'over here.' These were two entirely different and parallel worlds; home, solid and tangible, had somehow become distant, almost unreal, seen through a mist, or fine muslin, like the sort his mother used to strain her preserves. Here was now the reality, a regular and unending shop of horrors. He strove to continue:

I am well and in good heart, despite my injury, which is healing well. I cannot say too much of what has passed at the front but it will be enough to say that we gave a very good account of ourselves and all at home should be proud of us and know we have not let you or the regiment down.

What stupid, meaningless bollocks. What he meant was more along the lines of:

I cannot describe to you the reality of this place, so far different from Northumberland, you can't think it's on the same planet. Just a little while ago, I murdered men who were eating their dinners in cold blood. I could bathe in fresh waters every day and still fail to wash away the blood and pain, the filth, degradation and randomness of war. A place where the men and boys I grew up with have come to die, to choke out their uncomprehending lives in places whose names mean nothing and which they cannot pronounce…

No, that wouldn't do at all.

The bloke in the next bed began to scream again, a now familiar pattern, a low whistling howl, whispering though broken lungs, building to a steady crescendo of agony, the stick-thin figure beneath the blanket rigid and juddering. 'Shut up,' someone else yelled, again not for the first time and with predictable effect. Nurse Fleming hurried down the line of cots, her apron dazzlingly white, bending and soothing, easing the dying man's protests.

'You're looking grim today,' she told Joe with the merest hint of a smile.

'Writing to my mother,' he confided, 'always find that a bit of a trial.' This time she did manage a smile, and it transformed her, removed the starched severity of expression and showed the young woman beneath.

'You'll think of something cheering, don't fret, I'm sure she'll be very worried about you.'

Nurse Alice Fleming was a tall young woman with capable and rather lovely hands. Her face was on the classical side of long and her skin fair, she was perhaps not beautiful, her mouth too generous and chin too square, dark hair caught in a severe bun beneath her cap. Joe had wondered what it would be like to unpin her rich brown tresses and see them tumble around her shoulders. She seemed slightly angular, almost boyish in shape beneath the regulation uniform, but with that subtle, tantalizing hint of roundness. He had no idea whether she noticed him or not. After all, there was no shortage of candidates for her affections and she, like the other nurses, seemed perpetually in motion, almost always exhausted yet never distracted.

Along the ward, somebody else began to sing, not as bad as the screaming, but a pretty fair second, the song wasn't even from this war, something he must have learned from his father.

Far, far from Ypres I long to be/ Where German snipers can't snipe at me/ Damp is my dug-out/ Cold are my feet/ Waiting for whizz-bangs/ To send me to sleep.

'It's Marie, bleedin' Lloyd again,' someone yelled.

The singer's efforts were drowned in howls of derision, an uproar swiftly silenced by a stern look from Nurse Fleming, who surveyed her charges with a firm and matronly eye, though she was probably younger than most there. She turned back to Joe. 'In fact you're looking much better, Lieutenant Milburn, I can see we'll have you back on your feet in no time.'

'Where are you from?' he enquired, the question blurting unheralded from his lips as though delivered by a stranger, amazed at his own temerity. 'If you don't mind me asking,' he hurriedly added, desperate to sheer away from giving offence.

For an instant she did hesitate, then decided. 'From Devon, a place called Ottery St Mary, I doubt you've heard of it.'

He hadn't, he had a vague notion of Devon as a county in the south-west of England, rich pastures, many cows and famous for cream treas. 'Where the cream teas come from?'

This time she did smile and it seemed to Joe she lit up the whole of the abattoir they were in. 'Yes, cream teas and croquet on the lawn, have you ever played croquet?'

He was already floundering, assuming this was some genteel sport but could venture no further. She saved him from further confusion. 'And where is your home?'

'A village named Nedderton, in Northumberland. It's a mining village, though we're not, miners I mean, my family farms.' She asked him if he was fond of his home, which confirmed his suspicion she'd no idea about mining villages in Northumberland. And then she was summoned away, some other poor sod gearing up for the pearly gates, and he was alone again, or as alone as you can be in a ward full of the broken, damaged and demented.

His own damage didn't seem too bad. He remembered the gunfight and the twat in Hahnemann's second car; should have seen that one coming. Ferguson had confirmed on his one visit that this was Hans Sandstede. He was in the bag along with Eppler, Fahmy and the Gyppo Sadat. He'd the impression Ferguson was quite pleased, hard to say as he'd still been woozy. The bullet had missed his heart and he'd mild concussion from the fall. Ironic that he'd survived France, Crete and the desert, Saturday nights in Ashington … just to get shot up on a bloody main street in Cairo.

'Fifteen aimed shots a minute,' cackled Sergeant Hayes in the next bed, 'doubt you bloody Terriers could manage that.' Joe listened politely, his neighbour was an old time regular, started his wars against Germany fighting the Kaiser, wizened and wiry, his savage face pockmarked with acne and a fearsome moustache.

The sergeant's thick cockney accent was unfamiliar, even though he'd become attuned to Archie's, and his one good eye blinked continuously, the other, or whatever remained, swathed in a thick bandage that gave the wearer a vaguely Indian look. '"Contemptible Little Army", that's what they called us, contemptible, well we gave 'em contempt, come to the First Royal West Kents my lads we'll show you contempt, fifteen rounds a minute, we 'eard prisoners said we all must've 'ad machine guns, we dropped the swine in scores.' Hayes was heavily flushed and vaguely feverish, Joe had heard this tale from the 1914 Battle of Mons before, from his father in fact.

Fifteenth General hospital was in Alexandria, that fabled city by the Nile, a long two storey building in rather rigid classical style, surrounded by its own gardens. Cool and airy, the wards belonged to another age, Kipling and Kitchener, a statement of imperial ease and certainty. Nobody then had quite anticipated Rommel.

'Coming along quite nicely,' commented Dr. Harding, grey wisp of a man with a precise sandy tash and immaculately scrubbed nails, yet one who always vaguely smelt of disinfectant, as though no amount of scrubbing could quite get rid of death. 'Won't need the chest tube for much longer, that lung seems to be recovering and we've no sign of infection, thank God. How does your head feel? Funny feller concussion, all that banging about of the brains, not at all good for you. No more nausea or dizziness? Yours is relatively mild, though you'll find the symptoms may recur, some irritability too, you may start to resent our Teutonic friends when they persist in long bursts of shelling.'

'I'm not over-keen at present,' Joe answered.

He was doing rather better than his companion Sgt. Hayes who, in the next cot, was in the midst of his final battle. 'Shock, I'm afraid,' confided the doctor, 'often the case where there's a wound to the thigh – gunshot wound to the femur, poor fellow.' His head wound was now the least of Sgt. Hayes concerns, he had become very pale, pupils clearly dilated, skin looking clammy, beaded with perspiration. Nurse Fleming and another of her colleagues were shrouding the desperately sick man in additional blankets. 'They call that rechauffment,' Harding continued, 'keeping the patient warm is the thing, you see.'

His tone was brisk, professional but overlaid with resignation. Shock was a thief, it stole away men whose wounds should not have proved fatal. Many who congratulated themselves on a Blighty one, a bonne blessure, were ambushed, their ticket home heralding an altogether longer journey. By that evening the sergeant had joined them and his bed was eagerly filled by another.

After a week the dizziness and nausea had passed and Joe was able to sit up, it was then, sound of mind if not entirely of body, that he continually noticed Nurse Fleming. The cool swish of her skirts and the glimpse of light that played across the planes of her face began increasingly to occupy his thoughts, embarrassingly so, for whilst his lung was affected, other parts were not.

He wondered if she noticed him. Why should she? He was but one of thousands who passed through the hospital, the mangled and bewildered arrived in droves and only the fortunate left on their feet. Some, damaged beyond repair, were evacuated to base hospitals in England, grey pyjamas sewn over empty sleeve or leg, others contributed to the rapidly expanding, makeshift cemeteries outside. Some, whose bodies might be preserved had mislaid their minds; the worst afflicted had suffered trauma to both.

Their daily exchanges increased. Fraternization with nurses was strictly forbidden, the army was painfully aware of the effect such visions of feminine grace might have upon young men, very far from home and exposed to all the rigours of war. Walking out, even with officers, or indulging in such dangerous pursuits as dancing was stiffly proscribed and so their conversation was essentially formal, exchanges on his progress, that of other patients and the great battles raging in the desert.

'You are on the mend,' she informed him a few days later, 'almost healed, no sign of infection.' For Joe this was very good news, every wounded man dreaded gas gangrene; muck driven into wounds. It paid to get shot in clean kit. 'There's no mistaking that smell,' she confided, 'it's awful, you never get used to it, the sight of men's limbs swollen up like that, dreadful. I think it's one of the worst sights.' She had been nursing at Alexandria for less than four months but, even in his own relatively short sojourn, Joe had seen sights he could never, in his worst nightmares, have anticipated.

'I tell them lies,' she confessed; one boy about to lose his leg, his face so wasted and thin, his nostrils working like a rabbit, tongue darting over dry, gluey lips. She'd told him about men she'd heard of who could do almost anything with an artificial leg. It didn't matter in the end, he died anyway.

Joe's walks grew longer and he could feel his strength returning, shortness of breath and the occasional dizziness no longer troubling. To be free of the confines of the hospital was undiluted relief. Grossly overcrowded, the place stank, reeked of hopelessness and death. In his time there he had witnessed plenty of both. Joe had chanced one day by the entrance to be confronted by several wicker panniers, filled with amputated limbs, some swollen and black with gangrene, others oddly intact and healthy looking, blood, fresh or darkly clotted.

A northerly wind blew in off the Med, easing scorching temperatures. The ancient port stretched out along the coast, a city of legend. Founded by Alexander, once home to Cleopatra and now the Navy's Mediterranean Fleet. Mighty battle-cruisers, leviathans with their great guns reaching skyward, nimble destroyers and a host of transports jostled. The British Empire seemed invincible except that, just a few months earlier, Italian frogmen had got through the defences and damaged a pair of capital ships. The city was vast, somehow less crowded than Cairo, marginally less frenetic.

Dr Harding had established his office in the former superintendant's panelled haven, which also doubled as a storeroom, the great mass of bundled dressings, boxes of medications, splints, lotions and the whole plethora encroaching so the physician's desk appeared framed in supplies. He was a precise, sere man, one who, if Joe was any judge, from time to time, found solace in alcohol.

One evening in May as the spring shadows were lengthening Joe passed, returning from an evening stroll into town. Harding was at his desk and looked up as his patient approached. A bottle of spirits in plain view upon the desk had clearly taken a hit. 'Young Milburn,' the doctor intoned, his speech showing perhaps just the very merest hint of slurring, 'approach and let me look at you.' Joe did as he was told.

'You seem a lot better,' he continued, 'sit down and let me gaze on one of my successes.'

'I'm sure there are many, sir,' Joe dutifully responded, though they both knew the mortality rate to be shockingly high.

'You are very kind, and such charity deserves reward. Have a drink, lad.' This was as much an order as a suggestion and Joe did not demur, merely nodded his thanks as the doctor sloshed spirit into a reasonably clean tumbler.

'That is a single malt whisky lad, so I'll thank you to drink with respect; such brief glimpses of a civilised world are rare in these quarters.' Harding had clearly been showing respect for some time, and though his hand was rock steady, his eyes were bloodshot, gaze uncertain. This was the second time Joe had been offered malt whisky in a short time, hopefully he wouldn't have to shoot his way out again.

'What's your opinion of the war?'

Joe's antennae were on full alert, before he could frame a suitably non-committal reply, his host continued.

'For myself, I find it perfectly horrid, abominable; hideous beyond all measure.' Joe did not immediately respond. 'We doctors, you see, are always perfectly geared to deal with the casualties of the previous war. Was this the field of Waterloo or even Ypres our modern medicines would cope, our surgery be effective. The devil of it is that war ain't what it was, and we ain't caught up. We're a bit like the generals, completely out of our depth.'

'They do say commanders are very good at fighting the last war,' Joe chanced. 'But not the one we're in. Fact is Jerry was ready, been planning this little show since 1933. He's got better planes, better tanks, better guns and more of all of 'em. He kicked our arses in France, I know, I was there, next in Greece, then Crete and now here.'

'How then, does it end?'

'It ends when we win, sir. Can't be any other way, it could just be Adolf's bitten off more than he can chew taking on the Russkies as well as us. Rommel might seem to have the upper hand but his line is stretched awfully thin. If we can muster a big enough punch we'll send him reeling back to Tunis.'

'And all of us here just pick up the broken pieces and try to put 'em back together?'

'Nowt else we can do, just do our bit and hurt the bastards as best we can. Every one of us you patch up and get back in the fight is a loss for Jerry.'

'You should be working for Churchill, son.'

'I am sir, so are we all.'

*

He had visitors. First up were Archie and Angel, on furlough. Blackened and hawkish, they looked more like remote tribesmen than British soldiers. The Basque was sporting Arab headdress, a keffiyeh, and Archie a black tankie's beret that he had no conceivable right to wear.

'Been bloody busy since you bin' away, can't have all of us lolling round the fleshpots and eyeing up the nurses.'

Angel glanced at Archie. 'We lost Jock Lewes, him get himself killed.'

'Jock was bloody unlucky,' Archie corrected. 'We'd been bashing up Nofilia Aerodrome when Messerschmitts bounced us. We gave 'em hell I can tell you and saw 'em off.'

'Then there was the Stukas.'

'Yeah, and not 'arf, they give us a right good seein' to. Only when they'd gone we noticed Jock wasn't around. Found him in one of the trucks, he wasn't going to leave kit behind for them to shoot up but they shot 'im up instead. We buried the poor bastard out in the blue. Damndest thing was when we got back Stirling found a letter waitin' for 'im from his girl like, accepting an offer of marriage; fucking Boche cunts.'

'You need get back soon,' Angel advised. 'All this dagger and cloak stuff is no good for you.'

Next up was Neville, bringing grapes and discreet spirits. 'You gave me a bit of a bloody fright, you know. God knows what I'd have said to Evelyn if I got you killed. She'd do me in for sure.'

'Hahnemann?' Joe asked, 'Tell me you got the bastard.'

'No such luck, but no fault of yours. He got clean away. I've no doubt we'll be hearing of him again.'

'I'd look forward to that.'

'Not just yet though, I'm under strict instructions both from Eighth Army, and more frighteningly from my beloved sister, to take very good care of you. I'll report faithfully on your excellent progress and I won't say a word about the way you're looking at that pretty nurse.'

'Well, there isn't a great deal else to look at in here,' he pleaded lamely.

'Don't blame you for a moment old fellow, and she is quite fine but the queue I suspect could be quite lengthy. Ferguson's all for getting you a medal, except we can't actually admit to what went on, strictly hush-hush, Official Secrets and all that. Last thing we want is folks getting the notion Jerry's got people in the Delta and largely thanks to you, we think we've pretty much scotched that particular snake.'

'Speaking of snakes, what will happen to the ones we caught?'

'Rather less than you might think. Eppler and Sandstede will likely escape the hangman though they'll be old men before they get out, and the lovely Ms Fakmy will get off with a slapped wrist, suspended sentence most likely — HQ doesn't want to risk offending our Gyppo friends too much.'

'I'm sure she'll soon be back on her knees again.'

Mayne also stopped by. He brought whisky, most of which he drank himself, oblivious to disapproving glares and blind to 'No Smoking' signs. 'He's gone and promoted you again; seems the undercover johnnies aren't keen to broadcast your heroics but at least we can. So you're now a full lieutenant. Let's see, that's from corporal in about four months. At this rate you'll be a brigadier by Christmas. I might even have to be civil to you.' The thought was so alarming he took a hefty gulp.

'This is Glen Grant by the way, ten year old malt. We shouldn't really be swigging it like this.' The bottle was already half empty. Nurse Fleming was not amused, and if she was impressed by the Irishman's Herculean build and steely good looks, she didn't let it show. Meanwhile, Joe was getting an increasing taste for decent whisky.

'Do you think it's a good idea, plying him with alcohol with his chest still not fully healed?' she admonished, trying to look stern and matronly.

'I'm convinced it'll do him the world of good and, if you'd sit down and join us, he'd feel even better, I know *I* will.' This was Mayne at his most charming, but Nurse Fleming wasn't about to be seduced. She flounced off, though Joe felt, or at least hoped, that her strop was largely theatre.

'He,' (by this he meant Stirling), 'has put me in charge of training now we've lost poor old Jock. Can't say I ever liked him, bit too much of a stuffed shirt, but he was one hell of a soldier.'

'Are you OK with that?'

'Not bloody likely, oh I don't mind a spot of instruction and stuff like that, but full time? Give me a break. No, I want to be out there, in the blue. Just 'cos I didn't like Jock Lewes that much, doesn't mean I'm not going to make Jerry pay for his death and for the other poor bastards we've lost. I expect you to be with me.'

'You can count on it, soon as I'm out of here. Besides, I feel safer out in the desert, at least you can generally see who's shooting at you.'

*

There was to be a concert, 151 Brigade had acquired the use of a palatial hall in the heart of the Old City, surrounded by history, most of it forged in past wars. Joe, pretty much fully mobile went with Angel, Archie and Mike Sadler of LRDG. The air was warm, the space gaily decorated with flags and bunting. 'Regular music-hall,' Archie observed, knowing the show off by heart.

The performers, all from the brigade, knew it too. Some had been professionals, others inspired amateurs, but the majority just amateurs. It didn't really matter, there was better end local beer good and strong, robust red wine flowed. Harry Oldenshaw, who'd trodden the boards in Newcastle's Haymarket, told jokes they'd all heard before and sang *Never Trust a Sailor*; *If it be a daughter/ Bounce her on your knee/ If it be a son/ Send the bastard out to sea*.

Dear Mother, the Army's a bugger: sell the pig and buy me out, your loving son John

Dear John, pig's gone: soldier on.

After the comic, several section sized choir groups each sang well known north-country songs — *Lambton Worm* and *Keep Your Feet Still Geordie Hinnie*, finishing with a platoon-sized rendition of *Blaydon Races*. The audience joined in with each chorus, growing more raucous as the evening progressed. Several of the officers gamely tried to up the cultural tempo with violin pieces and poetry which, though politely applauded, failed to reach the mark.

Hitler has only got one ball,
Goering's got two but very small,
Himmler is very similar,
And poor old Goebbels' got no balls at all.

The blokes were not in search of culture, merely escape, though a spirited recital of *Gunga Din* from Sixth Battalion CO Colonel Turnbull went down well enough. Captains Stevens and Bradford sang *Ching Chong Chinaman* in easy harmony which was well received, the explosion of applause as much a testament to a pair of officers who'd performed such prodigies of valour in the desert fighting. For a finale there would be a version of *East Lynn* with the elfin Corporal Patterson as the doomed heroine, destined to expire with the immortal line *Dead, dead and never called me mother…*

More ale was drunk. The air was now heavy and thick, sweat and the heady aroma of strong tobacco, mingling with the harsh Delta beer. Corporal Patterson, whom Joe had last seen shearing the thick neck of a muscular German with his entrenching tool on Crete, performed his part admirably, wildly camp in an electric blue satin gown. Corporal Ruddick, a burly farm labourer with the ruddy features and strong hands of the Cheviots, did sterling if unimaginative service as the prissy Archibald.

Joe felt weary and vaguely light-headed, he had consumed a fair amount of vin rouge and the thundering choruses still sounded in his head as he trudged back. He was due to be released from the hospital. He should be thinking about Evelyn but his mind, once again, turned to thoughts of Nurse Fleming. She was doing night-duty when he returned, a makeshift desk behind an equally makeshift screen at the head of the long ward, a single bulb for illumination.

'Somebody looks like they've had a good time,' she observed, pale light from the uncertain lamp gilding her strong cheekbones, the wide and generous mouth. He very much wanted to kiss her.

'Went to a concert,' he mumbled, floundering, 'same old songs, just a good few less familiar faces.' She did not immediately reply but continued looking at him. She possessed a quality of stillness, her look direct, yet unfathomable, her eyes luminous. They did not speak but she leant forward slightly and placed her hand upon his sleeve. He was instantly electrified, but then some stupid bastard down the ward started yelling and she hurried away, the moment lost. Fuck.

Secure in the relative sanctuary of his cot, despite his exhaustion, sleep eluded him. The ward was never truly quiet, when there was no fine performance of terror-filled screams, there was a steady undertone of whimpering, muttering, laboured breathing and, now and then, the final signing off of another poor sod who'd found the whole business just too much. Joe had other concerns that night, he thought that if, when her shift was finished and she walked back to her nurse's billet, he chanced to be walking at the same time and, by happenstance, in the same direction, then surely it would be normal they might speak. This could never be deemed an assignation, surely, a violation of the golden rule, merely fortuitous coincidence?

Morning was barely formed when he was up and about. He knew her shift finished at eight, so, cleaned and brushed, polished and gleaming, looking like a proper officer, he was ready, their meeting in the cavernous foyer seemingly devoid of artfulness. She looked unutterably weary, a hint of dark smudges beneath the eyes, face pale, yet she did manage a smile. 'You are bright and early,' she noticed, 'and fit for parade, is there one?'

He ignored the irony, he knew the ground, had spied out the defences and his attack was fully rehearsed. 'No, just going into town,' God, even he could sense the lameness, but it was she who came to the rescue.

'Well, we might as well walk together, it seems a pleasant morning.' And indeed it was, warm but not stifling, just enough breeze. So they walked, along the straight, tree-lined road that led from the hospital into the Old Town. At first they didn't speak, it was clear she was very tired but when she did break the silence, she took him partly by surprise.

'Tell me about your home, what is it like, do you miss your family?'

'You'd think it a pretty miserable place, like I said, mining country mainly, small villages dotted between the workings, rows of red-brick houses, church, chapel, public houses, allotments and pigeons, little enough to recommend any of it.'

'And what about your family, they're farmers aren't they?'

'There's not a great deal to say; my old man has farmed all his life, active in the Peace Pledge Union, and my mother was in service at the Big House. I have a younger brother and two older sisters, both wed, both their men now in khaki. Northumberland, the southern bit anyway, is very much a close-knit mining region, most of us in the Fusiliers originally. I got into the Commandos pretty much by accident. And your own family, down in deepest Devon?' he prompted.

'Father a clergyman, mother a clergyman's wife, one brother destined for the clergy, God help him,' she paused, 'it all seems a million miles away from this.' A hint of bare trembling in her voice, she was, of course, exhausted, the ward was not a restful place. 'Well, I longed for escape, and now I am here.' She smiled without rancour. 'We cast off one burden to pick up another. No use in complaining of course, besides, what have I to complain of? I witness what comes through these wards every day. I wonder if there'll ever be an end to it.'

He realised she was expecting him to answer. What to say? Clearly there was no end in sight.

She saved him with another question. 'Why did you join the Commandos?'

'Well I was already in the Terriers, Territorial Army, and it seemed natural, going to France I mean. I'm not sure if I really thought it through, besides it promised to be an adventure. After Dunkirk, my battalion was pretty much put out to grass, what was left of us.'

'Has it been a great adventure?'

'Not exactly.' They both smiled. 'I'd no idea what war would be like, none of us had. Oh, we'd talked to old sweats who'd fought in the Great War. Me dad served on the Somme and then in the big battles of 1918, he hardly ever mentioned it, though he hated war in general ever after. For me it promised to beat normal life in Nedderton.'

An officer of engineers walked past them, his uniform crisp, boots polished to a high gloss, pink and shaven, he gave Joe a look but said nothing.

'And now, life at home seems rosy?'

'Not quite that,' he answered, with perhaps a touch more hardness than he might have intended, her look cool and appraising. 'I was determined to escape Northumberland, in fact I was serving my articles to become a solicitor and now, well the more of this you see, however bad, makes it that much harder to go back.'

'Why? I don't get it.'

'You didn't see the look that sapper just gave me, if I'd been a squaddie he'd have had a go at me for walking out with a nurse which is strictly verboten. But now I'm an officer and, don't get me wrong, I quite like it. And that's the problem, becoming a gentleman, even a temporary one, is something you can get used to.'

'I suppose life in the army teaches you these things.' It was then she slid her hand into his and he felt as though another jolt was passing through him. He managed to continue. 'It's just like home only more so, makes you a social climber or a socialist.'

'Like your father?'

'Well, he's a good socialist for sure.'

'So, you're the climber then, I guess you don't see eye to eye with him.' There was no note of accusation.

'That's something of an understatement. The plain fact of life in the coal field is that you're likely dead at fifty. Your lungs done in, that is if a roof hasn't fallen in on you, or someone hasn't lit a match down below at the wrong moment and you're blown sky high, or as high as can be several hundred feet down. It's a grim place, with a grim life. My father and the other reforming types are dreadfully worthy but they won't succeed in changing the system, far as I can see. I can't hang around waiting for Utopia.'

'My father would heartily approve,' she endorsed. 'He believes in self-help, pulling yourself up by your boot straps. Being born with a healthy fixed income helps, of course.'

'Does he approve of the war?'

'Oh God yes, couldn't wait to rush into the pulpit and deliver some pro patria sermon on the just war, the moral crusade, getting young men to join up straightaway, muscular Christianity.'

'I take it you no longer support the war?'

He meant the question to be wittily ironic but he could feel her stiffen, he had not sensed the depth of her anger. 'How could I?' she implored. 'Doing what I do every day, watching all those young men, without arms, without legs, shorn of faces, ripped and torn.' She was suddenly almost tearful.

'Damn,' she said, 'I did not mean to give in.' He squeezed her hand, feeling the thrill. 'It is when I see our young men, like you, ready to go back and do it all over again, seems such a stupid waste.'

They'd arrived. Her accommodation was in a smart modern block just this side of the ancient heart, Delta art deco, lots of glass and steel, rather grander than he'd expected if not quite Garden City standards. 'Daddy pays the rent,' she smiled.

He had absolutely no idea what he might do next. It was she who rose to the challenge by kissing him fully and firmly on the lips. Her taste was wondrous, the softness of her lips, the hint of a subtle but heady perfume (strictly forbidden), set his already heated blood fully on fire. He was, of course, still pretty inexperienced, but youth, instinct and the restorative effect of several weeks of convalescence came immediately to his aid. If he was embarrassed by the painfully obvious fact of his tumescence, she quite plainly was not. Was kissing a nurse in public a court-martial offence? Very probably, and the only mitigation was that he no longer cared.

Now she drew him down the short gravel path, toward what appeared to be a side door, perhaps he was delirious and the concussion had returned, she was flushed, the motion of her breast against him. She was trying to retrieve her key, an ecstasy of fumbling — then they half tumbled through the oaken portal, into a shadowed hallway, heavy with dark wood and dour furnishings. Here their exertions intensified, his hands moving at will over her firm contours, down the curve of her spine to the resplendent swell of her taut buttocks.

Even beneath the obligatory layers he could feel the response of her swelling nipples as he caressed the full, firm orbs. She was strong and supple, both tender and urgent, leading him up the narrow flight to another landing. Providentially, the place seemed deserted. And now to her flat, bright modernistic if a bit Spartan, beige coloured furniture straight from the showroom and carpet to match. Except for a handful of family photos, the place was pretty anonymous. It did, of course, have a bed.

She began to undress them both, a clean, businesslike economy of motion that caused his already very considerable excitement to soar to unimaginable heights. Her body was a marvel, in the first, full flush of womanhood, girlish traces banished, long limbed, her skin as pale and smooth as alabaster, inviting and guiding his touch. They had not spoken since that first kiss. His lips worshipped at the temple of her breasts, licked the smooth, flat plain of her belly and explored the sacred swell of her mound. He slid his questing fingers over the answering wetness and allowed them to probe. She gasped slightly and arched her back.

When she was quite ready, she took him in hand, her touch sensuous as silk; she lay back and parted her thighs, leading him on till his swollen cap was brushing against the lips of her womanhood. For a moment they remained thus then, as her hand pressed upon his buttock, he drove deep into her warm and velvet elasticity. He was moving within her, she responding, careful and deliberate at first then with the increasing tempo of rising abandon.

Somehow, she succeeded in flipping them over so she straddled him, riding him like a destrier, her fine breasts swinging wildly, the dark curtain of her hair tumultuously unbound. He decided he was in love. For a moment they paused, like the attacker before the breach, gathering strength and then were off again, straining toward the final victory, her orgasm like an electric current pulsing though her limbs, even as the dam finally burst and he was gloriously released, spurting like a geyser.

Then they lay spent, like athletes after the race, he pillowed on her breast, loose limbed and sprawling. He remained in awe.

'Do you love me, Joe?' she asked at length. 'Just tell me so, you do not particularly have to mean it.'

He said he did and it was no lie, he believed himself in love, this strange, dark, marvellous girl had him now in thrall — in truth had held him since they first met.

'Have you no sweetheart at home?' she pressed, stroking his damp and unruly hair. 'One who waits by the fire for you?'

'No, not really that is, well … I'm not sure.' He felt a twinge of guilt even if it was rather too late.

'If I were she, I'd keep tight hold,' she smiled.

'What about you?'

'Well I was engaged to be married, an officer naturally, not just some

165

ragamuffin Tommy.' She laughed and pulled his hot face closer to her breast, 'someone my father approved of.'

'And you didn't?'

'Not really, he was a reasonable enough sort, good, solid husband material, respectable family, some money, of course, even if it came from trade. A decent type you'd say but scarcely exciting in any way. Not like you my wild, northern savage.'

'You broke off the engagement?'

'No need, Hitler obliged, right at the very start, before Dunkirk. But sometime you'll go home on leave and forget me.' She said it lightly but he sensed she was afraid and so desperately lonely. 'I pronounce you fully recovered.'

'I will write,' he said and meant it, 'I will write every day.'

'See that you bloody well do, too,' she commanded.

Chapter Nine

Over the Hills and Far Away

Courage, boys, 'tis one to ten,
That we return all gentlemen,
While conquering colours we display,
Over the hills and far away
    Redcoat marching song

*

War isn't hell at all. It's man at his best, the highest morality he's
capable of. It's not war that's insane, you see. It's the morality of
it. It's not greed or ambition that makes war: It's goodness. Wars
are always fought for the best of reasons — for liberation or mani-
fest destiny. Always against tyranny and always in the interest of
humanity; so far this war, we've managed to butcher some ten
million humans in the interest of humanity. Next war it seems
we'll have to destroy all of man in order to preserve his damn
dignity. It's not war that's unnatural to us, it's virtue. As long
as valour remains a virtue, we shall have soldiers. So, I preach
cowardice. Through cowardice, we shall all be saved.

    The Americanization of Emily (1964)

We're now the Special Air Service, SAS for short, has a kind of ring to it, don't you think? More dashing than plain L Detachment, can't see that really putting the wind up Jerry — and it seems we have.'

Stirling, newly promoted and Mayne, also newly promoted, were holding court in Peter Stirling's Cairo flat, another smart billet in Garden City. An estate agent would have quailed at the sight of the place now, festooned with assorted kit, a plethora of various small arms half looted from the Axis, a profusion of maps and a distillery's worth of empty bottles.

'Bob Tait, you remember him of course, well he's designed us a new cap badge, Excalibur surrounded by flames and we've chosen 'Who Dares Wins' as our motto. Paddy wanted 'Strike and Destroy' but that seemed a bit ungallant. 'Descend to Ascend' was another one, but given our experience with parachutes, we thought it best to forget. Good to have you back, laddie.'

Joe was indeed back in the fold, fully recovered and a full lieutenant. 'And you're entitled to a set of these operational wings, one of poor old Jock's legacies. You can sew 'em onto your breast pocket as well, shows you've completed three combat missions. And yes we'll include your foray into the dark side as one of them, though I'll personally throttle that bastard Ferguson when I see him next. Typical of these intelligence Johnnies; using my chaps as expendables.'

He'd not been asked to explain what had happened, but Stirling clearly knew. Security, he was coming to realise, was a pretty elastic concept around GHQ. Meanwhile, there were new faces. The unit was expanding. Rommel seemed to be caged at least for the moment, Tobruk relieved and the Auk in high good humour. Despite the ceaseless tide of hostile mutterings, Stirling's stock continued to soar.

'Ah, and here's Maclean, the newest star in our firmament and a proper gentleman too, not some nasty oik on the make like some.'

Only Stirling could heap insults with such innocuous humour but the newcomer certainly looked the part, tall, immaculate and pure Hollywood to look at. He seemed pretty affable though.

'Now we've been bloody lucky,' the CO went on. 'Fitzroy here is quite a catch, why he's done exploration, diplomacy, journalism and all sorts, covered old Uncle Joe Stalin's show trials back before the war, though now we're on the same side I doubt we're allowed to talk too much about those, are we?'

'No idea,' Maclean smiled. He had the look of a warrior no doubt, reminded Joe of the pictures he used to look at of Greek heroes such as Achilles or Perseus, full of strong bones and powerful hands. 'I couldn't wait to get out of the FO, especially as it counted as a reserved occupation, cushy billet of course, if you're that way inclined.' Clearly, he wasn't.

'Got himself bloody elected didn't he?' Mayne picked up the story. He'd been drinking steadily but, as ever, the booze had no discernible effect. 'As an MP you've got to resign from the diplomatic service, joined up with the Jocks till we ran into him.' Even the taciturn Ulsterman seemed impressed with the new arrival. Joe vaguely thought Maclean might be Mayne's ideal, a formed version of his own unfinished and incomplete myth.

'When I got to Kabrit,' Maclean went on, 'got to me tent, seemed alright and the NCO who showed me around was adamant the previous owner had no further use. Well blow me, a day or so later, this wild figure clutching a dog barges in, looked like Moses with a hangover and asks me what the bloody hell I think I'm doing in his digs.'

'Ah yes, Bill Fraser. We'd sort of written poor Bill off on account of his being lost out in the blue. But he's only crossed several hundred miles and got back, eating locusts and drinking his own piss, all that stuff. Bit of a downer finding your mates have decided you're a goner and divvied up your kit.' Stirling waved at two other officers, both rather formal and wearing Free French badges. 'And we've got our own Froggies too, Colonel Georges Berge and Lieutenant Jordan.' The Frenchmen nodded gravely and politely. Both were impressively turned out, courteous and precise. They were probably wondering just what kind of cowboy outfit they'd landed in.

'Now the colonel here does know how to parachute, dropped back onto his home turf last March with murder on his mind. Paddy and Milburn, you'd have thoroughly approved. He was planning to ambush a busload of Boche airmen. What went wrong, Georges?'

Berge gave a classic Gallic shrug. This wasn't the first time he'd been ribbed. 'The bus was late,' he explained in perfect English.'

'Late?' Stirling queried.

'Well OK, it didn't turn up at all. It seems the driver was sick.'

'Ha, been out on the vin blanc more like. But we've fifty odd of our allies with us now and Paddy's going to be training 'em up.'

Mayne looked thunderous but said nothing. Being Jock Lewes' replacement was not an ideal posting. Joe could see he was seething with resentment. The germ of paranoia, always just below the surface, was ready to erupt. He thought, as Joe would come to understand, that he was being sidelined out of jealousy. He feared that Stirling, who'd not yet been able to claim a single enemy aircraft destroyed, wanted to skew the odds so he could catch up.

'And you, young Joseph Milburn, will assist,' Stirling pronounced, 'just till we're sure you're fully battle ready again.' Joe wasn't happy, either. The rest of the unit would hit the Axis port of Bouerat, beating up shipping and harbour installations. Mike Sadler, who was contemplating defecting from LRDG, would be navigating. That was a job Joe coveted. He didn't take to training by and large but then somebody had to. Mayne produced a massive sulk and retreated to his tent, oblivious in a whisky induced, verse-fuelled haze, while Joe at least tried.

Despite his newly elevated status, he was as pally as ever with Archie and Angel. Rank counted for much less in the regiment and both the Basque and the Londoner were now famed for their skills at scrounging. Both had taken the idea that 'God helps those who help themselves' and honed it into a distinct art form. Joe harnessed Angel's skills in close combat to impress his eager Frenchmen, while Archie taught explosives. He'd no previous experience that he could openly refer to but was plainly at home with gelignite. If the Free French were wondering why the unit CO was never seen but could, now and then, be heard singing, they were far too polite to ask.

*

'Well that was a bit of a waste of bloody time,' Mike Sadler confirmed when the raiders, dusty, unshaven and generally dishevelled, limped back into camp. 'Not a bloody ship in sight, five hundred miles of desert and the damn place was empty. We blew up some workshops and the like, torched some of Rommel's bowsers, but that was pretty much it. We were shot at on the way in and shot up on the way back, lucky we had some heavy firepower with us or we'd have been stuffed.' The LRDG navigator didn't criticise Stirling directly but was obviously not overly impressed. He didn't say 'Paddy would have done better' — but the suggestion hung in the air.

That wasn't all that was in the air. Stirling and Mayne were having their own highly voluble war. For once the Major's equable temper ran out. Mayne's was running out all the time. The row was pretty biblical. Stirling chose to confide in Joe later. The social gulf between them made this easier — confessing to a temporary gentleman could be classed as a wartime expedient. Once peace broke out, the gulf would be instantly reinstated.

'He's an odd bugger, stubborn as a mule but immensely gifted. Once we'd stopped yelling we began to talk seriously. He's both a loner and lonely, hasn't recovered from losing poor old McGonigal, went down on our first shout, you'll recall. Not that he's queer or anything like that, he just finds it difficult to get close to people. Saw this training caper as some kind of rejection. You'd not think he was the sensitive sort. He likes the idea of women but is terrified of them. God knows what he'll do after the war. God knows what *any* of us will do, assuming we survive. What about you young Milburn? Can't see you going down a pit or chasing sheep, whatever it is you Geordie types normally do.'

It was a polite question. Joe sensed Stirling wasn't really interested. Like Paddy Mayne, he had enough demons on his own back.

'Not sure sir. I'd possibly like to write I think, the law doesn't appeal that much anymore.'

'Well, you could try writing this lot up but I doubt you'd get anyone to believe you. Now that everyone's friends again and I did cock it up making Paddy training officer, he's about as suited to that as I am to being Pope, we're off to pastures new.'

'Jalo's gone of course, back under old Benito's flag.'

'God yes, the Desert Fox has rather caught us running round the hen coop. We've been kicked pretty much back to where we started from and he's not done yet, not by a long chalk.'

'Then where to, sir?'

'Siwa Oasis this time, just inside Egypt but a good springboard for having another crack at Libya, an ancient place and quite convivial, certainly compared to Jalo, flea ridden pit that it is. They say Cleopatra herself swam in the pool there, though I doubt *we'll* find any such exotic or obliging company.'

*

He was right, Siwa Oasis didn't disappoint. 'The Gyppos called this place the field of trees,' Maclean enthusiastically explained. Its remote allure drew out the explorer in him. 'Been inhabited for at least twelve thousand years or so, it's vast isn't it? You can't see clear across. It housed the great temple of Amun and even Alexander passed through. Not much left of the fort,' he pointed to a rumbling outcrop, 'oh and that big mound over there is a Roman necropolis.'

Maclean's obvious fascination had transmitted itself to Joe, who was entranced. Most of the blokes were not. 'Place is full of poofs,' Archie smirked, 'or so I hear. Buggery is pretty much normal apparently, queers can even get married here, well bollocks to all that, if you'll pardon the pun.'

To many, the place did look like something from *Arabian Nights*. The mud brick walls glanced bright in the sun. There was no sign of the twentieth century, men still wore traditional white robes and glimpses of the heavily veiled women were rare, donkeys and camels competed for space in the narrow thoroughfares. Beau Geste would have felt completely at home. Their HQ, in the cavernous, relatively cool hall of the old Egyptian administration, all peeling whitewash and gambolling cockroaches, certainly fitted the bill.

'Rommel has us pretty much on the ropes,' Stirling confided. 'Which as serendipity would have it isn't necessarily such a bad thing for us ruffian types. The crisis means our legions of adversaries at GHQ are temporarily silenced and our ideas for bold and daring deeds fall on more fertile soil. Malta is threatened. If it falls, we're buggered, and the war's pretty much buggered too. Both Winston and Erwin agree on that.

'But we few, we hopefully happy few, can make a difference, a palpable difference, which is why we're looking at Benghazi. Quite a nice place, the Eyeties gave the port a full makeover before the war. As long as we've got Tobruk, whatever supplies are coming in pass mainly through Benghazi and the airfields there can be used for bashing Malta and that wee island is indeed taking a beating and a half. We'll clobber both docks and aerodromes. The place will be packed with Axis ships and we're going to sink a few of 'em. How do we like that idea?'

They liked it very much.

Joe was to drive the Blitz Buggy and the taking up of Benghazi would involve little more than a car load of commandos who would simply drive into the port, passing themselves off as Axis. The big charabanc in its stripped and painted form did resemble some breed of German staff car. Next to him would sit no lesser person than the Prime Minister's son. Joe hadn't even met his local MP, never mind anyone as exalted as Captain Randolph Fredrick Edward Spencer-Churchill.

Bellicose, loud and one who made Mayne seem like a teetotaller, Randolph Churchill was far too fat and had far too many opinions on too many subjects. He'd been with Layforce, so Joe was vaguely aware of him, and was now foisted on the SAS because no-one else would have him. He was as ardent for glory as desperate gets, and it was drink-fuelled desperation at that.

'Randolph Hope and bleedin' Glory, who'd have thought it?' Archie chimed. 'Like going about wi' royalty, even if he is a knacker.' Stirling, however liked him, even Jock Lewes had been impressed by his courage — though not by Churchill's fitness or aptitude. His oversized bulk didn't made for a soft parachute landing.

'It's a bloody risk, I know,' Stirling had admitted to Joe and Maclean. 'God help us if he gets himself killed or captured, we'd better not come back alive. On the other hand, if he sends glowing reports then we've an ear at court.'

'If you're sure, sir,' Maclean cautioned. 'He's not a bad fellow, once you get to know him, and the brandy fumes aren't too heavy. He's brave enough, just like Old Winston himself, but I'm not sure he's too well designed for covert operations. Stealth and secrecy isn't really his sort of thing.'

'Well, I'm not proposing to have him anywhere near the firing line. He can bide with the escort when we go in.'

Stirling's plan for Benghazi was simple and audacious. He intended to cripple two ships by the harbour entrance, putting the port temporarily out of business. This would not only damage Rommel's supplies, it would force him to divert more troops to defend his bases. Maclean had been tasked to find some reliable dinghies and had conjured up a pair of small rubber inflatables. There'd be a round half dozen of them in the Buggy; Stirling, Joe, Archie, Angel, Seekings and Cooper now, and through the weird chemistry of war, best buddies.

It was four hundred desert miles to the port. They were all old hands by now, familiar with the practicalities. Still hosted by the LRDG, they felt they'd soon be fully independent, all round desert warriors in their own right. Sometimes Joe drove, sometimes Stirling himself whose technique was modelled on one of the more stylish Italian drivers in the mille miglia — pipe in one hand and attention for everywhere but the track. Joe had the feeling the others felt safer with him, he being more familiar with sedate and lumbering three-tonners.

For all its vast emptiness, the desert houses many ghosts. 'It's said King Cambyses, the second I think, disappeared around here some five centuries BC, him and a whole army of fifty thousand. Nobody ever found a trace.' Maclean knew his history.

'Probably had Joe's granddad navigating for 'em, poor bastards.'

Skeletal tanks, blasted by high explosive, scoured by sands, still guarded the rutted tracks. Joe supposed they'd be here in a thousand years time, burnt out trucks, the ripped remains of a fuel tanker, tomorrow's legends, maybe. Pieces of scorched kit, broken tin hats, British and Axis, stocks of rusted rifles, here and there the odd crude cross.

That night they leaguered up in the lee of the Jebel, safe from enemy eyes if not from the watchful Senussi who always magically appeared, looking to trade; sometimes eggs, sometimes information, sometimes both. They probably kept up the same commerce with the Axis. Joe and Maclean, warmed by grog, watched the aerial display over the port, a softening up raid, courtesy of the RAF.

'You never did find Jock Lewes?' he asked Joe, no accusation, just fact. 'No, and he'll probably not be the last of us to leave his bones out here. It shouldn't matter really, I mean, you're dead anyway — but it'll matter to families. They like to think we've at least got a proper grave somewhere.'

'I'll tell you a story about that if you like', Maclean went on. 'Just before I signed up with David I was working with a bunch of sappers based at Kufra. We were surveying in the Fezzan. I was in charge of logistics. During one, otherwise unremarkable, run we'd hoped to get back to Kufra before dark but found we'd be spending a night in the open. The ground was broken, low indistinct hills, traversed by narrow wadis. I'd never been there before, obviously.

'Our existing maps were pretty poor and the wadi we drove down proved tricky, we got bogged several times and we decided to call it a day under the lee of some rock buttresses. Now, as I stepped out in the dark after a cold supper, for the purposes of nature, I distinctly heard a voice. It was clear if indistinct, I mean I couldn't quite make out what was being said. None of the crew had called out it seemed, so I just turned in, thinking the sound a trick of the wind.

'Next morning, I woke up to the same internal imperative and stepped out a few paces from the camp. It was just before dawn and a dull half light was sharpening outlines. This was when I saw the truck. The ragged, wrecked but recognisable shape of an LRDG vehicle, the carcass surrounded by the detritus of battle, spent cases, ammo cases, rifle parts and all that.

'Daylight showed us a vehicle graveyard; the shells of more blitzed trucks littered the wadi. High up, almost hidden amongst the stones, we found a Pattern 37 canvas haversack, a Kodak camera and a pile of spent .303 cartridges. I was sure this was the remains of Pat Clayton's patrol, jumped by the Italian Air Force and Auto Saharan Patrol back in early '41. We also found the remains of two graves, marked by simple wooden crosses, presumably those men the survivors had buried.'

'What did you do?'

'Well, we just tidied up the graves, saluted, held a moment's silence then drove away back into the present — but I never found out who it was had spoken to me that night. Odd business though, I could really feel someone else's presence.'

Had that unsettled him? Despite being utterly knackered Joe didn't sleep well. Long after the fireworks stopped he lay, the cold at bay outside his kapok filled cocoon, night stars brilliant in the flawless sky above. Mentally, he was composing a letter to Evelyn, long overdue, and one to Alice Fleming. For economy and tidiness he was going to keep the same content and just change the names, it would be a right bugger if he got the envelopes mixed up.

Did he feel guilty? He should, but he could always conjure up the war as a convenient excuse. For a long while he'd thought, if not actually planned, that he might marry Evelyn. The social gulf was their main impediment but now he was an officer and nearly gentleman his prospects had improved. Then there was the wonderfully enigmatic nurse Fleming and the pleasingly stiff erection he got every time he thought about her.

'Fuck, bugger, bollocks, shite.' Dawn had broken with a bang and a string of random curses. It had to be Reg Seekings. 'Raggedy arsed, fucking, twat cheap detonator. The cunt nearly took me fingers off.' His language was worse than the injury which, though it could have cost him a hand, had just scored some deep lacerations and surface burns, bloody painful but not disabling.

'Shit,' chimed Stirling, not a habitual swearer. 'Randolph, you're with us,' he continued without any discernible zeal.

'Oh huzzah,' the fat man chirruped, immediately stripping and cleaning his weapons like the good soldier, 'I get to party after all.'

'Look here,' Stirling drew Joe aside. 'Seekings is no good for now. He'll have to sit this one out. I'm none too keen on taking Randolph, I'm not sure the car's suspension can take much more, but I want you and Maclean to keep an eye out for him. For God's sake stop him doing anything vaguely heroic. If he tries, knock him out, PM's son or not — tie him up and gag him if you have to but *do not* let the fat lump get himself killed. If bullets *are* flying, kindly place yourselves between them and him and we'll make sure you get a top notch obituary.'

'Christ what a bloody racket; must have woken up every bloody Wop in Benghazi.' The Blitz Buggy was protesting loudly at the distortion of its track rods after the long, grating descent from the ridge down to the coast road. Smooth asphalt humming below, the drive would have been almost luxurious aside from the mechanical wailing. With sparkling stars and wonderful rushing of the adjacent sea, it was almost possible to forget you were deep inside enemy territory and about to insert yourself up his fortified rectum.

'Good thing about being Germans for the night is we can be as rude as we like to the Italians. If we were being British and polite, they'd smell a rat straight off, so we'll just bullshit our way in.' That was Stirling's operational briefing as they approached their first road block, the car's angry protests dying away like a banshee's chorus as they slowed to a halt.

The Italians, perhaps half a dozen of them, not overly tidy but well enough armed, seemed pretty disinterested. Maclean used his limited grasp of the language to be haughtily dismissive. Had the guards looked inside, they might have been less indifferent. The Buggy was fitted up for light machine guns and two Brens were stowed on the floor. Each passenger had a weapon to hand and even Maclean in front beside Joe had a hefty wrench in one hand in case the conversation turned less cordial.

But they were waved straight through, headlights ablaze and contrary to all blackout regulations. The Italians had just missed a potential opportunity to capture the Phantom Major, a serving MP and Winston Churchill's son. As well as its cache of weapons, the car also held Maclean's two folded up dinghies. 'Clear and away,' Stirling yelled above the swelling racket, 'seaside, here we come.'

Not quite. They were barely through the checkpoint when they met headlights coming the other way — and these weren't Italians.

'Bollocks,' mouthed Maclean. 'Shoot 'em up time?'

Randolph Churchill was enjoying himself immensely. He was out of cotton wool and into the field and in a very unsafe corner. 'Can't wait to bag a Boche or two!' The fat man didn't lack guts and his audacity levels were frequently topped up from whatever was in his canteen.

The Axis cars passed but then could be seen reversing and turning to come back. If we slowed they slowed, if we picked up speed they conformed. Bugger. 'Right, young Joseph,' Stirling ordered from the back. 'Best Jimmy Cagney style and lose 'em. Burn rubber, as they say.'

Despite its tortured wailings, the Buggy still had poke. Joe banged his foot hard down and the V8 roared appreciatively. Off she hurtled, leaving the startled Boche trailing. They bowled into the outskirts still doing seventy, neat pre-war Italian style villas with well tended plots and wide boulevards. As they swept deeper and downhill, moving towards the ancient core and harbour, the streets narrowed, scruffy mud brick buildings and a maze of ramshackle workshops.

Joe swept blindly round a turning, off the main thoroughfare into the maze of dark alleys, careering around blind corners, screaming track rods protesting loudly. Now there was more noise, the insistent dirge of an air raid siren, the refrain soon picked up by others, a dismal choir of alarm. That helped drown the sound. Joe reversed sharply into a handy cul-de-sac and cut the engine. 'No RAF tonight,' Maclean observed, 'must be us they're worried about.'

'Right then,' Stirling took command. 'Fitzroy, let's get one of your rubber jobbies packed into a kitbag, we'll need all guns and ammo. Time to ditch the car I fear, they'll be looking out for her. I'm damned sorry to say goodbye to the old girl, I'll miss her and it's a bloody long walk back. Still, can't be helped.'

A Lewes bomb, set for thirty minutes, was left in the vehicle. The six commandos, heavily laden, set off in the dark, heading towards the harbour and suitable prey. Churchill was bubbling with joy. For the first time in his frustrated life he was off the leash, experiencing the kind of madcap adventure his father had so loved. For once he was almost on a par with the old man. The streets were empty, except for the sole Eyetie copper they encountered, lounging under a street light, apparently unaffected by the raging sirens.

'Are we under attack?' Maclean enquired in his best pidgin Italian.

'No, no,' the policeman responded, 'just a false alarm.'

That rather changed things, the motorised patrol that had been after them were probably just air raid wardens, their own presence undreamed of and undetected.

'Cooper, get back to the Buggy and defuse that bloody explosive. We'll de driving out of here after all, hurrah. Randolph, Dunmore, go back with Cooper and get the car safely stowed out of sight somewhere.'

The remaining four, Stirling, Joe, Maclean and Angel, continued down to the port. The wire fencing proved pretty feeble and they worked their way down to the narrower strip of shingle beach below the harbour wall. Numerous fat-bellied merchantmen lurked temptingly, unsuspecting. While Stirling and Angel set off to identify potential targets, Joe and Maclean were left to inflate the dinghy.

Manfully they puffed on the inflator but very little appeared to be happening. 'Bloody hell, the damn thing's got a puncture, about as much use as a chocolate fireguard.'

'We'd best dump it and retrieve the other one — bollocks.'

The heady drama of the raid was fast sinking into light comedy. When they got back to the cul-de-sac, Archie was manoeuvring the car into a tumbledown garage space. ''Ome from 'ome, just like the old days, feels like I just blagged some posh geezer's motor.'

They hauled out the second boat and lugged it back to the beach, still undisturbed by any vigilant sentry. A few watchmen on board the crowded freighters called out half heartedly — grunting 'Fuck off' generally seemed to work.

'I don't bloody believe it. This blighter is holed too.' And so it was, and so their amphibious larks seemed increasingly unlikely. By now they'd also lost Stirling and Angel, presumably still selecting targets they'd now no means of engaging. Worse, daylight was approaching and the sentries were perking up. Challenges from the boats rang out more regularly. Finally they re-assembled, a forlorn little group huddled on the dirty streak of shingle.

'Best bugger off.'

So bugger off they did, laboriously packing the unsullied or unserviceable kit. Getting out proved a wee bit trickier; Maclean found himself confronted by a very large African sentry with a fixed bayonet. He looked keen to use it.

'Fuck off out of my way,' he said in passable Italian, but the solder just grunted and hefted his rifle.

'Fuck off, I said, you dumb bastard,' this time much louder and with expansive, suitably theatrical waving of hands. Finally, the sentry sulkily let them pass.

'It's odd,' Archie muttered to Joe. 'I'd 'ave sworn there was only half a dozen of us?'

'We have two extra Italians with us,' Angel confirmed.

'Now it's a bloody parade.'

Stirling was equal to the situation. Despite being in British uniform he marched his tiny column up to the harbour guardhouse and laid into the bored looking NCO like the wrath of the Wehrmacht unleashed.

'A bloody shambles, call yourselves security? We've paraded round your precious docks all night, humping these great sacks of good Afrika Korps supplies. Nobody challenged us; in fact there was nobody *to* challenge us. This will reach the highest levels of Comando Supremo, you can be sure. My God man, we could have been British saboteurs!'

As they all walked stiffly on, the Italians stayed rooted in near panic.

*

'Welcome to Downing Street,' Churchill greeted them as they climbed up to the shabby little apartment above their makeshift garage. 'Doesn't look like anybody lives here.'

It didn't, the place had a long abandoned air. 'Probably they buggered off for the duration.' After the excitement in the streets and harbour, the tatty flat seemed like an oasis, tension draining like a receding tide. Only Churchill was still hyped up, fortified by the happy succour of a reserve canteen. They slept on the scruffy carpets.

Joe woke with a start late morning, sun was streaming in through the narrow windows, plenty of street noises audible from beyond the thin partitions. Disquietingly, much of this seemed to be in German or Italian. Angel, with Maclean, was discreetly studying street life. 'Desirable bedsit in West Benghazi, all mod-cons and industrious overseas neighbours, it seems we're opposite some form of Axis hub, Eyeties and Boche, lots of comings and goings.' Even their little courtyard at the rear was busy, unsuspecting Arab neighbours preparing food. That made them hungry; they'd no rations with them and precious little water.

Stirling awoke, announced he was going for a swim and with draped towel, the epitome of an Englishman abroad, off he went in broad daylight. 'This is a very mad fellow,' Angel said admiringly. The long, drowsy day drew on into the basking, somnolent heat of afternoon. They read or dozed, movement was impossible until dark.

At around two, footsteps suddenly sounded on the feeble stairs. 'Shit, we've got a visitor.' Churchill was beside himself with glee. Whatever fortification he was relying on, it was good stuff. The steps stopped and the handle turned. They stared hypnotised, weapons cocked and ready. After an endless moment the door opened and a clearly very pissed Italian matelot stumbled in. The man stared goggle eyed at the hideous, bearded figures brandishing weapons and then left, rather more rapidly than he'd arrived, pelting off down the street with arms flapping. He could have just gone across into the HQ set up opposite but, mercifully, chose panicky flight.

Stirling returned refreshed and unscathed. 'Wasn't just enjoying meself you know, did some recce as well and there's a brace of E-boats down in the harbour we could deal with as we leave.' Archie had also spent a productive afternoon, trying to fix the howling track rods. He thought he'd succeeded but they'd barely piled aboard and got onto the main drag when the whining broke out again. Despite his best roadside efforts and many curses, the problem refused to go away.

Accompanied by the continuing racket, they parked up near the waterfront like regular tourists and strolled nonchalantly towards their targets, their webbing full of devilish instruments.

'Looks like your earlier talking to did the trick,' Maclean whispered to Stirling.

Indeed, having been so thoroughly dressed down by a German officer that very morning, the Italians had got their act together. More sentries guarded the dock and crew on the two E-boats began to show interest as they got closer.

'Well that's bloody annoying. God, I hate to go home empty handed.'

But home they went, the screaming Blitz Buggy barging though the same checkpoint as before with scarcely any more difficulty, along the smooth tarmac then up into the hills and away.

Chapter Ten

Lions of Judah

Of course, the super-saboteurs were our long range desert patrols.
These were the super 'Desert Rats'. Stories were legion about their
exploits ... No men were braver or fitter than those in these groups.
Occasionally we actually saw them move out into 'the blue', but
mostly they were as legendary as Lawrence of Arabia. They stayed
out behind enemy lines for months at a time ... They were led by
men of unrivalled knowledge of the desert, and did untold mate-
rial damage to German supplies, but their main contribution was
in boosting our morale and lowering the German morale corre-
spondingly. Whenever news came round of their exploits, our tails
went up like anything.

Driver Crawford

*

Every man who wages war believes God is on his side. I'll warrant
God should often wonder who is on his.

Cromwell (1970)

*

Her skin, he decided, was flawless, the most perfect thing he'd seen. Joe was back at Shepheards, this time as a proper officer and with Alice Fleming. The room was crowded with exotic women but, at least in his bedazzled eyes, she was by far the most exquisite.

'You're looking pretty perky,' she said.

'I've only really ever seen you in uniform.'

'And out of it,' she countered.

Barely an hour before, they'd been frantic in Peter Stirling's ever handy apartment. They both had twenty-four hours leave and he'd collected her from the hospital.

'This is new,' she said of his near pristine jeep. The ubiquitous four wheel drive light cars had come in from America, rugged, nippy and ideal for the desert. Spartan they might be, but he enjoyed driving his. True it had the springs of a medieval cart and stuttered judderingly even on best asphalt, but it could still manage a decent turn of speed with your foot hard down.

'What happened to your posh limo then?'

'I'm afraid my CO pranged her a bit.' More than a bit; Stirling's kamikaze driving had caused more casualties than the Benghazi raid. He'd rolled the Blitz Buggy at seventy mph, killing one passenger and injuring the rest. He, Maclean and Churchill had all ended up in hospital in varying states of disrepair.

'Bizarrely, the convalescence has inspired portly Randolph to write up an account of our and his heroism and send it directly off to the old man, that's a hotline to God in effect.'

'Not everybody gets to serve with Winston Churchill's son, what's he like?'

'Alright bloke really, talks too much, drinks too much.'

'Sounds like most of the men I know then,' she said, laughing.

All the hot dusty way from Alexandria to Cairo, the tension between them flared. He could barely keep his hands off her but manfully focused on keeping the jeep on the tarmac. Once inside the flat, (happily theirs and theirs alone for the day), they were at liberty to explode freely. And they did. He had been a long time in the desert and she on the wards. They had both seen far too much of death and needed the reaffirmation of life and of each other. Neither was disappointed.

Now, refreshed, coiffed and with just the right amount of makeup, she sat coolly opposite him as they sipped daiquiris, another US import it seemed. It might as well have been Irn-Bru, his veins were still so charged. She wore a cream silk dress; the cocktail variety apparently, it went with the drink he assumed. The fabric clung tastefully but alluringly, her curves neatly suggested. Most of the other women were in evening dresses that left little to the imagination. He decided that she was a goddess.

'I'm impressed by your choice of wines,' she commented. 'Being an officer suits you.'

'I'm still a salt of the earth sweaty oik underneath though, and I'd better fess up the wine was Neville's recommendation. He wangled this table, too.'

'Aren't you supposed to be marrying his sister sometime?' She wasn't accusing and he did feel the odd twinge of guilt, although it was pretty rare and easily suppressed. 'Presumably he knows we're not just here to see the pyramids?'

'Neville doesn't judge, his own position's a bit ambiguous I think you'd say, besides, it's wartime.'

'That's all right then.'

'Alice,' he stumbled. 'I think I'm in love with you.'

'Then no more daiquiris for you my lad, next thing you'll be proposing.'

'Suppose I did?'

'Then I'd probably do something truly stupid and say yes. Entirely on the basis you're not bad looking, can order decent claret and are one hell of a rousing shag. As I desperately need both the alcohol and the sex, I'm maybe not completely rational … so best not ask me just yet.'

'When, then?' he blundered on.

'Probably not too long ahead but when we're sober and not just post-coital.'

'But how do I know you'll say yes, then? You might change your mind.'

'I might, we girls do, but then again I might not. If it helps, the odds are leaning pretty much in your favour. God knows what daddy will say. If you were still a corporal, he'd be apoplectic but as you're an officer and from a distant county, we can extend your farming credentials by a few hundred acres, so he'll probably come round.'

'Can I have a whisky then?'

'Yes, but just one and then it's straight to bed with you.'

*

'Captain Herbert Cecil Buck MC of 3/1 Punjabis and Scots Guards, now there's an interesting character. He's so bonkers he makes most of us lot look pretty normal and, if you think about it, that's quite something.'

Stirling's left wrist was still in plaster but he'd not spoken of the car accident. Joe could guess it weighed pretty heavily, the dreadful irony that his first 'kill' was a civilian passenger in his own vehicle.

'I'll tell you the story,' the Scot went on. 'Buck comes from impeccable imperial stock, fluent in German, was educated there in those heady, hedonistic days of the Weimar Republic. His battalion, part of Fourth Indian Division, trained in troubled Palestine where he developed a kind of understanding with our friends of the Hebrew persuasion. It's an odd thing that, as most of your upper crust tend to prefer Arabs, sweaty and sleazy as they are.'

'And so it came to pass that whilst commanding a truckload of his Muslim soldiers, driving on the hot and dusty road between Tel Aviv and Haifa, he ordered his driver to stop and make room for two young female hitchhikers. One of them, Leah Schlossberg, was only thirteen at the time, but she and Buck chatted amiably about the delights of peace and culture. Buck missed the opera but burgeoning Tel Aviv had claims to refinement. Bertie was invited home for tea.'

'Now, before you make any lewd assumptions, he's not, as far as I'm aware, interested in chasing under-age girls, but he'd come to the realization that German speakers could be found in Palestine which sparked the idea that would become what's called Special Interrogation Group. The Haganah, no friends of ours, already possess a German-speaking section within their more militant wing. You can see where this is going. Even the most zealous of Zealots realises Hitler's the worse enemy.'

'So he wants to form a unit of German-speaking Jews to fight for us?'

'That's it and, if you think about it, not such a bad idea. If you can bluff your way in and out of Benghazi with bad Italian just imagine what you might achieve with perfect German. His plans might have been a bit derailed when he was captured at Gazala late last year. But despite being wounded and a long way behind enemy lines, he escaped, stripped the uniform from an Axis officer he'd throttled and made his way back.'

'So he intends on deploying German-speaking Jews, dressed as Axis soldiers, operating deep behind enemy lines. Describing that as high risk could be something of an understatement. A firing squad might be the least of their worries.'

'Oh God yes, you'd need pretty determined types. We're pretty sure old Adolf has set up death camps in the east to help get rid of his Jewish obsession. And now we've got Jock Haselden, decent sort of chap, keen as mustard to have a crack at Jerry, bloody good on the intelligence front but does have some daft ideas at times.'

'Is he the bloke who was leading 'D' Squadron at Siwi?'

'That's him, made up to lieutenant-colonel and now elevated to some kind of staff johnny. He thinks we could dress Buckie's chaps up in full Boche rig and sort of prowl about in trucks, shooting up whatever they fancy.'

'How are we involved, sir?'

'Well we, that is *you*, are going to be their liaison with us. Your fame as a trainer and leader of men has spread as far as the other side of Kabrit, that's damn near a dozen miles. Take your cockney and Dago chappies with you, main job is to try and stop them getting killed on their first day out and, who knows, they may just come in handy.'

*

'This shithole,' Angel sighed, 'reminds me where those Frenchies dumped us after we got over the Pyrenees; not a happy place.'

The SIG base was as flyblown as flyblown gets and as far away from anywhere. It made their original camp at Kabrit seem inviting.

At first, as he switched off the jeep's ignition, the metal dashboard hot from the high sun, Joe nearly panicked, thinking they'd somehow stumbled into an Axis outpost. Commands uttered in harsh, braying German rang out over the baked parade ground. Men were in full Afrika Korps kit with their distinctive peaked caps, KAR rifles and MP40 sub-machine guns.

'They are looking the part I think, like proper fascistas.'

They did. Most of them were ethnic Germans who'd fled to Palestine to escape the Nazis, their fellow countrymen who they'd soon be fighting.

'Big cojones. Fascistas will cut them off if we are being caught.'

Buck was pretty much what he'd expected, a toff he'd once have called him, before becoming a provisional toff himself. He had the same easy public school charm as Stirling, the same high enthusiasm which, however hard you tried to resist, was contagious. He was no bloody fool either.

'Now let me introduce David Russell, my second in command.' The spruce lieutenant was Scots Guards who always looked like guardsmen, particularly when they attempted to look like anything else. This one was tall, very, slightly gangling and vaguely melancholic. He appeared to be quite shy.

'He's not as daft as he looks,' Buck enthused. 'Fluent in God knows how many languages and prefers cognac in his foot baths, probably because he went to Harrow.' Joe was aware Harrow was a public school and that there was rivalry with Eton, another public school whose alumni seemed to consider themselves a cut above. Then there were the Wykehamists (whoever they were), who considered themselves a cut above everyone. Bedlington Grammar didn't feature anywhere in the ratings.

'I struck gold,' Buck went on. 'It's one thing speaking German, it's one thing *being* one, but you've got to know just how the Afrika Korps move, just how they carry their kit, what the in jokes are, all that sort of insider stuff. They don't dish out handbooks.' He gestured towards a thickset, square-headed type, obviously a junior NCO, bawling out orders on the parade ground as the SIG sweated through Axis drill. 'That's Bruckner; I chanced on him and Essner, the sandy-haired fellow there, in a POW camp. Both had been with Jerry, ex legionnaires, but no Nazis.'

'Isn't that a bit of a gamble, sir? I'd tell you pretty much anything to get out of a POW laager. Couldn't they equally be Abwehr plants or just plain opportunists who'll jump ship at the first chance and spill the beans?'

'I did think of that. Tiffen here,' he pointed at a sharp looking corporal, another likely lad east ender, (he and Archie had already compared notes), 'isn't happy. Are you, my cockney sparrow?' Tiffen shrugged. He had the look of a bloke who'd seen most things and didn't believe any of them, wiry and dark, his eyes gleamed with intelligence.

'He's not quite right. He's nearly right, but not quite.' Tiffen had confided to Archie that he had deep doubts about Bruckner in particular. A survivor's instinct, he called it. Both Archie and Joe believed in survivor's instinct. Herr Bruckner would stand watching.

'We're Jews,' Tiffen went on. 'It's a different kind of war. Rommel calls it "Krieg ohne hass". Well not for us, we fucking hate them. Hitler wants to destroy us, wipe us from the planet. We either win this one or we and our children all die, that kind of clears up any ambiguities. And once we've finished with Adolf, we'll presumably have to fight you Brits for Palestine.'

'I know about the civil wars,' Angel confirmed. 'It is worse than this, very much and the Arabs no much like the Jews I think?'

'Not much, their Grand Mufti talks to the SS, you know. That's quite a partnership. The master race making common cause with Muslims and *he*, the high and mighty Mufti, makes your average Nazi look like the bloke next door.'

Even if Buck was overly optimistic with his Afrika Korps recruits, every aspect of their training was immensely thorough. The men lived, trained, slept and thought as Germans. Their conversations were entirely in the language, orders were given in German; notices were pinned in German. They had photos of blond Brunhildes in their wallets, they even wrote to gushing buxom madchen back in the fatherland, who were blissfully unaware that their men were serving the Allied cause.

They were an odd assortment. Tiffen a tough Londoner, Israel Carmi had served with the Brits in Palestine, had won his spurs under that very strange eccentric genius, Order Wingate. Ariyeh Shai had, like Buck, come from Layforce. Tailors, cobblers, clerks and terrorists all rubbed shoulders. Joe, Archie and Angel were accepted, but apart. The Basque was more accepted as an exile from a losing cause, crushed by fascists, something they understood.

Lack of attention wasn't a problem. These men understood how much their lives depended on training. Surrender was out of the question and they were keen, most of above-average intelligence. Even if he didn't speak the lingo, Joe was aware of an undercurrent of distrust.

'They have a traitor, they are convinced.' Angel knew a thing or two about paranoia. 'With such people it is always so and usually they are right,' he concluded, depressingly.

Joe found the whole experience oddly surreal. Of a morning he awoke to the martial blare of Kompagnie Anfsteher, PT in staccato German and an intensity of training even the SAS would have doffed their berets to. He taught navigation and weapons drill. Angel instructed in unarmed combat and general thievery, Archie played with explosives. All their vehicles were Axis and lusty renditions of *Wenne die Soldaten*, *Lili Marlene* and such other DAK favourites were both encouraged and practiced.

'Got to give 'em their due, haven't you?' The high and rakish Russell indicated to Bruckner and Essner, both of whom looked more Afrika Korps than most. 'They do know their stuff.' Joe grunted in agreement. They were bloody proficient and the SIG gained enormously from their instruction. That didn't mean they wouldn't stand watching. He'd already briefed Angel to keep an eye out if and when they were deployed and not to be shy if it came to necessary decision making. The Basque hardly needed telling.

'We've done bits and bobs,' Buck was briefing them. 'Haven't we, David?'

'Sort of cutting your teeth stuff, testing our disguises really, we set up dummy roadblocks and it's bloody amazing what bored drivers will tell you. We strike up chats with chaps queuing for grub, just having a smoke and what have you. It worked a treat and the gen was worth having, but we haven't really struck a blow so to speak. Not like your lot, of course.'

'You've been saying nice things about us,' Buck went on, 'just the ticket — and now the good major is letting us in on the action.' This was no surprise. SAS could certainly use a German speaking section and more strikes were in the offing.

'Stirling's going to bash Derna and Martuba aerodromes. We'll RV at Siwa and pick up your French section, you know them of course. Not too many of us, say eight of my chaps, you three and a dozen or more Free French. We'll be going after at least two fields near Derna.'

*

It was a five day trek from Siwa up towards the coast. The French, crammed into a beaten-up three-tonner and all rather serious looking characters, were kitted out, as were Joe and Angel, in suitably distressed Tommy kit, looking like disgruntled POWs while the SIG, once they were well clear of Siwa, changed into full Axis rig. Archie had stayed to keep up with the bangs and flashes. Despite the fact this was all bluff, it had the effect of totally segregating the two groups. Uniforms made it very much 'them' and 'us.' Joe, as an officer captive, rode in the captured Kubelwagen with Buck, Bruckner and Essner crammed in along with Shai. They bristled with weapons and the three-tonner was crammed with hidden guns and explosives.

As Brits were in something of a minority, Tiffen was allowed to chat with Joe in English. He liked the ebullient but intense little cockney. 'If you don't mind me sayin' sir, you don't seem like the same sort of officer as Captain Buck there. He and the lieutenant are more what we're used to.'

'Proper officers you mean,' Joe laughed. 'No, I'm not quite one of those. I don't really fit; wrong class, wrong school, wrong accent. My old man was in the last show, made it up to sergeant, one of the youngest ever RSMs in the battalion, won the MM and all that. He once told me, his company officer, bloke he'd shared a trench with for months, once passed him in the street in Newcastle and never even registered, not a flicker. So I'm an outsider and only to be tolerated for the duration.'

'Well, we know all about *that*.'

'Don't be daft, you're as east end as Bow Bells.'

'Born there, for sure, but not really one, none of us is, never can be, comes down to it we're still Kikes and Jew-boys. Oh, *you're* not burning down synagogues or putting us on cattle trucks — but there's plenty who would. My war started back in '36, when Mosley and his gang were on the go. I know he's banged up now but plenty agreed with him at the time, probably still do.'

'I remember that, he had a few supporters even up north.'

'This was Cable Street. There was about twenty thousand of us, outnumbered the black shirts by ten to one, 'cept they had the coppers on their side. We'd barricaded off the east end but the rozzers moved our barriers. We gave the fascists a good hiding, sent 'em running tho' we suffered for it in the cells afterwards.' Tiffen stroked his crooked nose, 'courtesy of the Metropolitan Police.'

'Are you sure the police were on their side, then?'

'Not altogether, but some, yes. A lot of Mosley's gang were ex-soldiers, as were many coppers, and nobody much likes Jews.'

'And now you're in uniform?'

'Sure. Mosley's a rank amateur compared to Hitler. We know what's going on in Germany and in the east. It's not just deportations and ghettoes. We've met people who got out. They're systematically murdering all the Jews. They've set up special camps just for that purpose. Sometimes they use bullets, but we think they're using chemicals too, carbon monoxide and poison gas. This isn't just a pogrom; it's a fucking nationalised industry. They work us like slaves and then we're got rid of, free labour and genocide. Welcome to the Thousand Year Reich.'

Not much you could say about that, only Angel commented that it was 'same in Spain.'

Next day they struck the coast road then ran into their first road block. The three-tonner was struggling and the engine had died, necessitating a tow from the already overloaded VW. The guards here were Italians, but smarter looking than the average.

The barrier was firmly down and a password demanded. Buck was all reason and smiles. 'Look,' he began in pretty fair Italian, 'we've got to get this lot of Tommies through to the coast, we've been out in the desert for the last couple of days and our radio's buggered.'

The Italian sentry, now joined by an NCO, was all smiles but adamant, no password, no further, someone would have to come and vouch for them. Just when it seemed like they'd have to shoot their way through, bad from every perspective, the burly Bruckner launched into the Italians with a flurry of Wagnerian fury, cursing them for dullards and slackers while others had been doing the real fighting. It was a star performance and by way of applause, the barrier went up.

So far, so good, but the road was getting busier and the next hurdle was another road block — but this time manned by Germans. Oddly, this proved easier. Their cover story went by without comment and nobody demanded passwords. The portly, sweating gefreiter even offered some helpful advice, that they should laager up at a roadhouse nearby. 'You can't be too careful, Tommy commandos have even got this far before.'

Nobody laughed.

The transit camp was wonderfully anonymous. Nobody paid them any heed and Tiffen worked on the ailing truck. They fuelled up, courtesy of Rommel, and queued for their ration of lentils and dumplings, nothing special but filling and probably better than they'd have got back at Kabrit. With tanks and bellies full they discreetly moved off a few miles down the road, to laager more anonymously. No point pushing your luck.

Derna was close and they cruised quietly into a good lying up place, camouflaging the vehicles. Joe scouted forward with Bruckner, Jordan and a trio of the Free French, yomping over four miles of coastal scrub to overlook the aerodromes. There were two, and fat, inviting targets they looked. The first strip was home to a Jasta of Bf 110s, heavy twin-engined fighters, the other to more of the predatory Stukas. Like most Tommies who'd been on the receiving end, Joe had a particular hatred of the screaming dive bombers, sky-birds of serious ill-omen. Blowing a few more of them up seemed a very good idea. They didn't hang around too long, but the nearby strips at Martuba looked equally busy. Even better, security was pretty minimal.

Buck was delighted. 'So we didn't all get dressed up for nothing. Tonight's the night. I'll have a crack at Martuba with, say, half the team and I'll borrow your Spanish gentleman, if I may. Milburn, you and

Jordan with Bruckner here will visit our friends at Derna and make sure some harm comes to them.'

'The password,' Bruckner grunted, 'we'll be needing it.' Joe had taken a dislike to the thickset Jerry, couldn't say just why, but there was *something*. Still, the man had done well so far.

'Right ho,' Buck replied, 'you're right. Tell you what we'll do. You and Essner go back to that last roadblock where we met our portly benefactor. Ask him. You know the story; we've been out in the desert, radio bust, etc.' Joe suggested Tiffen should go too, Bruckner stiffened at that, the slur was implicit. Tough, the Londoner went along anyway and Joe made sure Angel trailed them at a careful distance. The Spaniard was good at not being seen and very good at killing quietly, should the need arise.

It didn't. The trio came back in the Kubelwagen and their friendly corporal had been as obliging as ever, even if he couldn't quite remember the right words. An Italian officer who was passing was consulted and obligingly checked his codebook. 'Siesta' was the challenge and 'Eldorado' the response.

By 21.00 hours Joe was crammed into the front passenger bench of the labouring three-tonner with Bruckner driving and another SIG, Hass, between them. Jordan, with four other Frenchmen, sat in the back, this time they were fully loaded and ready. Their slitted lights danced fitfully over smooth asphalt, marred here and there with potholes, some of them deep enough to damage the aged vehicle's fragile suspension. Even on good bits the hard springs jarred and bounced. Long-eared bats flitted by, lit briefly in the feeble light. Nobody spoke. Not much traffic either, just the odd flock of Axis trucks, shapeless and unconcerned.

Derna reminded him of Benghazi, new, neat and colonial on the outside, scruffy and native at the core, a ribbon settlement stretched along both sides of the coastal highway. No sign of blackout, plenty of lights, though mostly fairly dim. The streets looked pretty deserted. They were passing what seemed to be the local cinema, with some stirring epic of the new Roman Empire showing. Joe doubted the place was packed.

Bruckner started swearing, German's a good language for guttural oaths.

'What's up with him?' Joe asked Hass, who spoke English.

'He thinks the truck is overheating, same problem as before. He's going to stop here, there's a garage.' And it seemed there was, just next to the cinema, a set of rusting pumps and the place looked shuttered. Joe's alarm bells were starting to ping as the bulky NCO slid, surprisingly agile, from the cab and disappeared into the shadows.

'*Fuck,*' Joe exhaled to nobody in particular. He was suddenly very aware of being banged up in a buggered-up truck in the middle of an enemy garrison and with no sign of the cavalry.

'Qu'est-ce qui se passe?' Jordan demanded huskily from the back.

'Be on the bloody qui vive,' he snapped back, no mastery of language but the urgency was clear. He distinctly heard the drawing of bolts and snapping of safety catches. Hass next to him cocked the MP40 he was carrying. Joe hefted the bulk of a Colt .45 in his right hand. He could clearly hear the sound of the film projector whirring noisily through makeshift walls. Otherwise the place was dead quiet — bad pun.

The Germans appeared from nowhere. *Shite*, looked like a couple of full sections, twenty men or more. The truck, sat stolidly by the broken curb, was completely surrounded, no lights thank God. Orders were being screamed at them. The enemy had rifles and SMGs, all were levelled in their direction.

'Raus, raus,' Christ, you normally only heard that in movies but this lot definitely weren't acting. Hass was swearing steadily and calmly in the same language, 'we're fucked,' he concluded helpfully, in English. As a comprehensive analysis this was hard to fault. 'Raus!' The command was screamed again, louder than before if that was possible.

The side door of the truck was yanked open. Joe found himself looking at a tanned, blue eyed face of classic Teutonic squared symmetry — and the stubby, business end of a Bergmann nine mm. The Hun had his finger very much on the trigger.

'Haftling,' prisoner, Joe improvised sounding suitably cowed, no acting skills required. The Jerry grimaced, grabbing his left arm to drag him out. He could hear the rest were trying to haul the Frenchmen out of the back. He was aware another Boche was struggling with the driver's door, he could have told them it was buckled and chronically unreliable.

Joe tried to look engaging, allowing the German to half pull him towards the passenger door before shooting him in the face, the bang shockingly loud in the thin night air. The German's head was flung back, a mess of bloodied bone and brain spraying. Next to him Hass opened up with his MP 40, shattering glass. And the French were shooting.

He thudded onto the dusty asphalt. His victim was sprawled in the unmistakable sack-like posture of the very dead indeed. He grabbed the SMG, as bullets were smacking into the cab above his head. He loosed a couple of rounds from his pistol at the nearest German, who stumbled against the next. Others were more interested in finding cover.

'Ici!' Jordan was pulling him beneath the truck. The French seemed to have escaped certain death in the canvas tilt. He fired a short burst from the Bergmann; rounds were pinging off the steel panels above their heads and kicking up dust. Theirs was not a happy position. The Boche would be shifting and assessing, ready to move in for the kill.

'We'll make a break; get across the street, darker on the far side, looks like plenty of alleyways.' As impromptu planning went this was pretty crap, but options were in short supply, time even more pressing. A grenade exploded in front of them, Hass was still in the game up front. The blast probably didn't nail any Germans but it stirred up a cloud of dust, filming the darkness, and the noise was disorientating.

Jordan and the Free French didn't need telling. They slid out, straightened and sprinted for the far side. Hass was by the front of the truck, still chucking bombs, which punctuated their flight. For a few blissful seconds he thought they'd get clear … then the shooting started. He saw one of their blokes go down, sensed Jordan stumble. He grabbed the French officer and half dragged him into the lee of a blank faced alley, reassuringly black as sin. Bullets were pock-marking the mud brick around them but they had shelter. For the moment, at least.

He risked a glance back. Hass had thrown his last grenade it seemed, and was slumped by the riddled bonnet. Germans cautiously closed in but the SIG hadn't quite done and still had a final pin to pull.

Joe promoted Bruckner to second place in his 'must-kill' list, after Hahnemann.

Half dragging the Frenchman he jogged down the alley, a labyrinth of foul smelling lanes that seemed to lead everywhere and nowhere. He didn't stop for a good few moments then they halted, gasping against rough masonry. There was no pursuit and the shooting had stopped. He and Jordan seemed to be the only survivors. Amazingly, Joe was unscathed, the Frenchman more shop worn. Jordan had a shoulder wound — a nine mm, he guessed, it had passed clean through and though bleeding profusely, there was no massive exit wound.

Swearing in French seemed somehow less uncouth than doing the same in German. 'Save your breath,' Joe cautioned. Using the field dressing from his pocket and an improvised sling from his ripped off shirt sleeve; Joe applied some basic first aid. 'You're the ugliest nurse I've ever met,' the Frenchman gasped, 'and the most cack-handed.'

'Right now, I'm your new mother,' Joe answered, 'let's get out of here.' It was five miles back to the RV and they kept to the side of the road, pushing through scrub and bushes as carefully as they could, risking the tarmac only when long, clear stretches beckoned. Frequently, they had to duck or lie prone as Axis vehicles passed. There was a red glow in the sky to the west suggesting Buck's group had torched at least a few planes. Nobody seemed to be looking for them.

Tiffen found them, thank God, or they'd have missed the RV. Both were knackered and Jordan was now almost delirious from pain and blood loss. With a hot brew inside him, Joe recounted the dismal tale. Tiffen wasn't surprised. 'I knew that bastard was wrong, the pair of bastards in fact.' No more of them came in, not until Buck's team fetched up, cock-a-hoop with their success in taking out a score of aircraft. Joe soon punctured that happy mood. By now it was nearly dawn and they'd have to lie up that day. Angel had repossessed a jeep from Martuba aerodrome, so they'd not be short of transport. Essner, sullen and resigned, was put under arrest. Angel was all for cutting his throat there and then.

Buck's brief moment of triumph had evaporated. It seemed he'd fully vindicated the whole concept, that SIG had proved itself and come of age. The survivors weren't in an understanding mood. 'I thought the risk was worthwhile, I really did. They seemed like manna from heaven, those two. Too good to be true of course, I realise that now it's too late.'

Joe wasn't in sympathetic mode, either. He'd come to realise that part of the class difference between him and regular officers like Buck and Stirling, from public school backgrounds, was their assumption of privilege, a casual acceptance that things would go right just because they willed it so. Those like Joe, clawing their way up, rung by rung, had no such expectations. They knew from experience that life was basically shit, and anything which came right was a bonus.

That night they set off, Joe with Angel driving took the jeep, morose Essner sandwiched between Shai and Tiffen in the back, Buck with the rest took the lead. Once they were into deeper desert, clear of the coastal strip, Joe indicated to stop. Angel halted and the SIGs bundled Essner out.

He was too experienced not to know what was coming, damned by association. If he wasn't a wrong 'un himself he must have known about Bruckner. He didn't speak, just turned away before Joe pulled the trigger. They left his body there. Joe briefly reflected that three years ago he'd still been singing in the church choir and couldn't have imagined he'd ever shoot a man through the head in cold blood. What *should* have bothered him, was that it didn't really bother him at all.

'Shot while trying to escape?' Buck asked later.

He was beginning to learn.

Chapter Eleven

What did I see in the desert today?

What did I see in the desert today?
If you can wait and never get tired of waiting
For mail that never seems to come
If you can face the desert heat each morning
And never let your thoughts stray back to home
If you can play your fiddle as good as Nero
And never swear or curse when things go wrong
Then, all I can say is you're a blinkin' hero
And, what is more, you'll be the only one!

    J. Campbell: *If*

*

'Now then. *This great collection of ancient monuments includes the three pyramid complexes known as the Great pyramids, the massive sculpture known as the Great Sphinx, several cemeteries, a workers' village and an industrial complex. The pyramids, which have historically loomed large as emblems of ancient Egypt in the western imagination, were popularised in Hellenistic times, when the Great Pyramid was listed by Antipater of*

Sidon as one of the Seven Wonders of the World. It is by far the oldest of the ancient wonders, and the only one still in existence. So there you have it. Anyway, so says Sir Gardner Wilkinson, though his book is nearly a hundred years old and I imagine the place was less of a tip then.'

A fitful wind was blowing Alice's hair over her face so she kept having to brush it impatiently back as she read from the guide book. He was more interested in her than the pyramids. He'd not often seen her with her hair down, not when clothed, anyway, and she wore loose cotton trousers that the breeze obligingly billowed, moulding her long, firm legs.

'I always wanted to see them,' he enthused, 'I was gobsmacked by the photos when I was a kid; obviously, they cropped out the slums.' And he was enthusiastic, being there with her lifted his excitement towards ecstasy.

On one elevation the whole range of iconic monuments stood proud and enigmatic, looking older than time, sculpted by the gods and aeons of desert storms. That was the good side. On the other, filth, degradation and squalor as the city's sprawling mess expanded, unplanned, unchecked and seemingly un-drained. This unholy rookery crept up to the sagging perimeter fence. They were early, it was just past dawn, but already the army of touts was stirring like locusts.

'Is it always like this?'

'Pretty much, I guess, well I've just driven past before not really stopped, not ever. Place is usually crawling with hawkers but I'd guess the 1942 visitor season won't be a bumper year, not with Rommel only sixty miles away. A lot of these chaps will have taken the day off to brush up on their German.'

Nonetheless, as soon as they stopped, they were surrounded, lean, hungry, chattering faces, proffering all manner of stuff. 'If this crap was genuine, you could probably fill London Underground with Egyptology.'

The morning sun was rising; they'd seen its red glow light up the great silent masses of stone. Even aged, denuded and degraded, it seemed almost impossible that these structures had been built by men.

'*The Great Pyramid, or the Pyramid of Khufu, is the oldest and the tallest of the three pyramids towering over Giza. Constructed circa 2551–2528 BC, it originally stood at 481.4 feet (147 meters), or about forty-five stories. Its immense size makes it a marvel to behold, but the Great Pyramid, and its neighbours, the Pyramids of Khafre and Menkaure, are mostly just solid masses of stone — 2.3 million blocks of cut limestone, to be more precise, which is the approximate number making up the Great Pyramid. All three pyramids would originally have had an outer casing of lighter limestone, as seen on the cap of Khafre's pyramid.* Alice read diligently, ignoring the press of sweaty humanity surging around.

'They say Napoleon spent some time contemplating stuff inside the King's Chamber, in the Great Pyramid. Went in alone and came out pretty shaken.'

'Somebody must have mentioned Nelson. But the French got their revenge; one of their blokes just blasted the present entrance, apparently. That's what passed for archaeology then.'

'You love it don't you? The archaeological stuff, I mean. You should have been one. You still can be.'

'Well, there aren't too many openings for archaeologists where I come from, though mind you we've got Hadrian's Wall and some serious blokes like Richmond and Birley. Still they're toffs; us oiks only get to dig turnips.'

He gave one of the meaner looking touts a few bob to make sure the jeep still had wheels on when they got back, having briefly outlined in general terms what would happen if it didn't.

'Your language skills are improving, I see.'

'It helps when you're in uniform and carrying a gun.'

'Don't you ever wear civvies, or are you just trying to impress me?'

'You'd bloody better be impressed, I got these duds made up by a proper tailor, cost a small fortune and, now you mention it, I'm not sure I've *got* any civvy gear, been in uniform for so long. And besides, whatever I do possess was designed to be worn in Northern England where the temperature's a tad cooler.' Already the heat was rising like the tide; soon it would reach the level of a baking oven.

The pyramids rose ahead like a range of steep-sided, conical hills, the great ancient city of the dead. A rather sad looking older man offered, in excellent English, to show them around, seeing off their milling followers with a few choice expressions and judicious raps from his cane.

'I am Demetrius Kostantopolous, lecturer in Ancient Egyptian history, at your service.'

'Your English is very good.'

'I venture to say I am passably fluent in a number of languages, before this unfortunate business of the present war, I met tourists and visitors here from many countries.'

'Fewer Germans and Italians this year, I'd guess.'

'Just so,' the old man smiled. He was one of those indeterminate Levantine types, stocky and stooped, probably in his sixties, good teeth with a flash of gold and, regardless of the heat, wearing a heavy tweed suit that had definitely seen better days. 'My students at the university dwindle also. War does not much benefit the humanities.'

'Well, if Rommel gets his way you might be getting a good few more.'

The old man smiled his kindly, knowing smile. His hooded eyes still had a sparkle. They both decided they liked him, as the dark blue flies buzzed excitedly amid the offal and muck all around. 'I think perhaps the Germans have, as you say, shot their bolt. I offer this not just because you are British and may like to hear such things, but this land has seen many conquerors come and go. Persians, Macedonians, Romans, Arabs, French and British. When Alexander came here, these pyramids were already as old to him as he is to us.'

For whatever reason, an incident on Crete came suddenly and vividly to mind. In the early hours of the fighting as Fallschirmj*ä*ger were tumbling from the skies, many of them, obligingly, onto the sharp points of the commandos' sword bayonets, one of his blokes had brought him a dead Boche officer's notebook. Amazingly, it was in German — so he'd taken it to their intelligence bod, who spoke the language. Waugh, the fellow was called, and a would-be literary type. Well, he read some passages aloud. Joe had expected the stereotypical Nazi type diatribes but instead the bloke's jottings were all about how he loved Greece, the sights and scents. 'in the footsteps of Schliemann.' Waugh had been impressed that Joe knew who the father of archaeology was — stuck up little twat.

'One of your fellows, an officer called Douglas, came here,' the Greek went on. 'Keith, I think is his Christian name. He is a poet I believe?' Joe hadn't a clue, Wordsworth he could just about remember from school, 'trailing clouds of glory' and that was about it. 'Well, he told me Wilfred Owen, one of your very famous poets, wrote that "poetry is in the pity" but that was in another war. I know about that one, I spent a couple of years in your uniform at Salonika. Quite what we did there I was never entirely sure.'

'My old man, my father, was in that one too, didn't much enjoy it either.'

'This war, your man Douglas told me, is one of great distances and rapid movement and for him the poetry comes when least expected, *in the interstices of a generally agitated existence, in the rush of sudden contrasts, and the recognition that, whatever else changes, one's own mortality does not.* I rather liked that. He is right too, of course, if nothing else war does reminds one of one's own short span and how fragile that is.'

Joe quite liked it too — memo to self, read more poetry, Alice was bound to be impressed. Paddy Mayne carried a travelling library of verse; he would ask to borrow some, choosing his moment with care, obviously, just in case Paddy was at the bellicose stage and thought he was taking the piss.

They took refuge, briefly, in their guide's on site 'office', a quite precarious lean-to, tacked onto ancient masonry. He made coffee for them, fussing over the obligatory ritual. Just the precise amount of water poured into the cezve, adding the requisite quantity of sugar, then coffee and bringing the mix carefully to boil both times, the strong, reassuring smell filling the small space and temporarily overpowering the general stink. Joe did his bit by proffering a tin of Kyriazi Frères. He'd come to prefer the harsh bite of Egyptian tobacco over Woodbines or even Player's Navy Cut, his father's favourite. The Greek professor took one gratefully, Alice declined. Unusually, she didn't smoke much.

'It is to be regretted,' the old man went on, as they sipped the sweet, viscous coffee, 'that you young people can only see these places in wartime, your minds clouded by conflict and the roles you must play, yet the British Empire is only one of many who have occupied us, even if almost certainly the most benign.'

'I was never quite sure why we did, in the first place,' Joe confessed.

'It's probably not best to set an old man off on history when he's starved of students, but Britain's interest in Egypt stems primarily from her need to safeguard the vital passage of the Suez Canal. This got you involved as far back as 1882, when nationalist sentiment in the Egyptian army simmered. After you'd suitably chastised our forces, such as they were, at Tel-el-Kebir, you became the dominant force. Resentment has lingered of course and, over time, increased.'

'People here would prefer the Boches? They'd pretty soon regret it. We might be annoying but they'd sharp find Jerry a thousand times worse.'

'Oh, that I do not doubt, one only has to see how they behave everywhere else they've conquered. We Greeks have no love for them and at least you tried to help us.' He was diplomatic enough not to mention what a sad farce that intervention had been.

'Now though, there's a host of divergent political and religious groups from fledgling communists to the Muslim Brotherhood all sharing anti-British sentiment. They see that your enemies must be their friends, stupid and short sighted as that may be.'

'Our rather vapid and indolent King Farouk was minded to enter into the Anglo-Egyptian Treaty, especially as you were good enough to install him. You did agree that you'd withdraw from Egypt, leaving only a modest garrison who'd remain for a certain period to defend the Canal. Fear of Italian aggression following Mussolini's invasion and grabbing of Abyssinia was an influential factor. But when war came, Egypt once again assumed a key strategic role. At that time and indeed even now, many in the opposition would not be unhappy to see the Axis victorious. Being both Greek and Jewish, I prefer things the way they are.'

The old man's office was furnished with a rough trestle on which a whole slew of artefacts were laid out, private collection for admiration or simply merchandise, Joe couldn't determine. As they rose to leave, he was ready to proffer some cash but the professor politely declined. 'If it wasn't for you brave young fellows, I'd be on my way to one of their camps by now. Besides, I see little enough of Homeric youth and,' bobbing towards Alice, 'such great beauty.' He gave her a parting gift from his collection, Middle Kingdom he said, a miniature blue pottery hippo, painted with black-leaf designs. She was entranced. Joe was delighted for her, though his cynical half suspected the Greek had a cupboard full of these things, mostly made last week.

The entrance into the Great Pyramid resembled a direct hit from an eighty-eight, smashed into the masonry, now just a stepped core, all the smooth ashlar facings long since recycled by locals. They had to be helped up by those who eked their living by helping tourists up to the mouth of the passage. They seemed to be the only visitors, aside from some groups of Tommies milling about uncomprehendingly just 'doing' the sights. There were no lights and Joe was glad he'd brought his torch, good solid Wehrmacht issue with its set of coloured lenses; the previous owner had even contributed a new battery.

At first the stone passageway declined sharply, proceeding into the vast unfathomable bowels of the monument. But soon they were going up just as steeply, the tunnel beautifully constructed from smooth limestone blocks, looming whitely as his torch glanced off the imperturbable stone. They seemed to be climbing for quite a while though time and distance meant little. He was acutely aware of the pressure of Alice's hand in his.

'Don't tell me you're claustrophobic, or you don't like enclosed spaces?'

'God no,' she whispered back, 'I'm loving it. Blame Enid Blyton. Why are we whispering, do we think they can hear us?'

They reached the entrance to the Grand Gallery; here their beam showed the high almost cathedral-like vault, way above their heads. The space wasn't much wider and the gradient just as severe but the great mass around and above them, the vast age of the structure pressed down on them. At least the air was cooler. They were still the only visitors, 'courtesy of General Rommel.'

Access to the King's Chamber, so called anyway, was through a very tight gallery, so constricted they had to bend and kind of shuffle through, 'eat your hearts out *Famous Five*,' Alice joked. 'Tintin for me,' Joe responded, *Cigars of the Pharaoh.*' The tomb itself was really not that big and quite plain. He'd expected lively frescoes of darkly tantalising Egyptian priestesses in gauzy dresses that left very little to the imagination. Alice reverted to their guidebook:

'*Like its neighbours, the Great Pyramid has very little open space inside its hulking mass. Napoleon would have reached the King's Chamber through a very tight ascending passageway, past the Queen's Chamber (a misnomer), and then through a taller corbelled passageway called the Grand Gallery. Once inside the King's Chamber, Napoleon would have seen that it was small and lined, like other kings' chambers, with thick granite blocks. The space would have been very austere, as Egyptians only began decorating burial chambers with hieroglyphic texts in later pyramids. Moreover, by the time of Napoleon's Egyptian Campaign at the end of the eighteenth century, the pyramids would have long been plundered. He would not have found any rumoured treasures in the chamber, only the enormous granite sarcophagus, once containing the king's mummy, set firmly in the floor.* I wonder what he thought.'

'Who?'

'The Corsican gentleman, what was he expecting? If indeed he *was* expecting some kind of light-bulb moment. Probably someone had carved 'Nelson was here.' The place seems to have spooked him, anyway.'

'Possibly one of those *Ozymandias* moments, when you realise how insignificant you are and despite how many monuments you build, history might just forget you after all.'

'Well, I'm certainly not going to forget you,' he ploughed ahead with plodding gallantry. The matter of matrimony hadn't been raised this leave, not yet. Her slender back was firm and beautifully sculpted beneath a thin, silky blouse, the smooth planes of her delicate but strong shoulder-blades prominent and infinitely tactile.

He pressed close, anticipation already tenting his natty new KD shorts, palms cupping the delightful globes of her taut buttocks. She resisted firmly. 'These bloody trousers cost a fortune and they're clean so you needn't think you're going to do a Mark Anthony in here.'

'You'd be spot on for Cleo.'

'I once played her in school, loved it, I fancied dying naked, sprawled on a couch, just my jewelled collar and other vulgarities.'

'Bet that went down well.'

'The headmistress wouldn't hear of it. I *did* sprawl, pretty immodestly, but in full kit only.' Her fingers were breaking her own rules at this point and his manhood was demonstrating its ardent appreciation.

He wasn't sure if now was the right time to press his suite and formalise the marriage question. His head rushed at the thought but there was always that argument for pressing ahead while the iron was warming nicely.

'Don't,' she warned, divining his thoughts. 'Not just yet, we'll get back to that once we've seen to the more immediate stuff.'

'What about your trousers?'

'They're washable, that's nursing training for you, always think tactically.'

*

Earlier, he'd received a long letter from Evelyn; this by courtesy of Neville who had ways of avoiding the censor, presumably pulled strings, fiddled knobs and all manner of clandestine ruses. On the one hand this was welcome, on the other he'd have to reply at length — 'by the way darling, I met this absolutely spiffing nurse and now I'm shagging her senseless at every opportunity — yes, war is hell.' Well, that wouldn't quite do now, would it?

Her letter was full of local news and gossip. She was now a full time medical student and the war seemed far away, though much of the farm work was being done by young women, Land Girls. His father complained much about them, and most other things. This war made him increasingly more morose just as the last one had made him fairly morose beforehand. He was sure this was all the work of international capitalists and profiteering upper crust spivs as a plot to diminish the oppressed workers: Nothing new there, then.

Pater got himself a position as captain of the local Home Guard unit, he loves parading in the uniform and chucking his weight about, even though he's rather too short for proper officer material (not like some). And, as we're pretty sure we're not likely to be invaded it's pretty safe. If Jerry did invade he could try the Queen's Head, catch the lot of them in one go.

It's a pretty safe way to go to war. Recently, the Bedlington Platoon had to take the Battalion HQ at Nedderton Colliery. The Nedderton and Morpeth lads dutifully manned their lookout posts protecting every approach to the old colliery, that big sprawling place, the manager's house was the HQ, (we used to raid their orchard, remember) but these cunning attackers chose a rather unorthodox route – they hung on to a rather slow-moving coal train at Ashington, jumped off at Nedderton and strolled into the HQ without ever meeting a defender. Daddy then foolishly accused them of cheating (you know what a bad loser he tends to be) and was promptly inverted; his head ended up in the wastepaper basket!

But then Bedlington platoon scored a pretty spectacular own-goal during one such exercise. They were part of the force defending their HQ at Tranwell. The 'enemy' were from Whalton and Morpeth Platoons and to add a touch of realism they were dressed in German uniforms. During the exercise our brave defenders captured one of the opposition and took him to their HQ for questioning. Unfortunately they'd forgotten to search him and, when

he produced a 'hand grenade,' the umpire declared the HQ blown up. The
excitement wasn't over. As the attackers made their way home they caused
quite a stir among the residents of Morpeth — a crowd of German soldiers
casually walking across the golf course, laughing and joking as they went,
not an everyday sight in these parts, thank God.

We did get some proper excitement a few weeks ago. A Wellington bomber
crash landed in one of old Atkinson's fields. They'd been shot up over Germany
I think and their instruments were out. The plane got down safely, even if
it was pretty much a write off and the crew all got out. The Home Guard
were on the job soon as you like and rounded them up. The thing was they
were Polish and our lads got the idea they were German and were all for
a quick firing squad job, till one of the fliers, a football fanatic, showed he
could recite the names of the whole Magpie's first team. Well that did it;
no Jerry would ever know that so the Poles were taken home for tea and
cakes — fortunes of war, eh!

It would soon be two years since he'd seen home, whatever that now
meant. It seemed increasingly remote, well remembered but disconnected
as though the umbilical that bound him to everything he'd known was
gradually being severed. How could he really explain what this war in
the desert was like, in a place so distant from Northumberland it might
as well be in a separate solar system? He had changed more in those two
years than in the previous twenty, had seen and done things he could
never have imagined and wondered if he could ever describe. Well, he
was the one who had wanted to write.

*

Neville looked decidedly louche, sufficiently so to be instantly recognisable as a staff officer, and Joe was past being overawed by Shepheards,
after all he was practically a regular. His friend had taken to smoking
a pipe, presumably that made him look more like a spook, just in

case everyone in the place didn't already know. If they all drank like Neville the war effort must be draining the taxpayers' coffers at a truly Olympian rate.

'I ought to be annoyed with you, putting the wind up Jimmy Allerdyce like that, the poor dear's not used to being rudely confronted and duffed up by hirsute northern barbarians.'

'Then he won't be surprised that I didn't lose any sleep, sleazy little tosser if you don't mind my saying.'

'I don't,' Neville shook his head amid a cloud of billowing Mellow Virginia. 'Nasty little prig as it turned out, been spreading his favours over half of GHQ, probably most of Cairo, too. For an ill-educated peasant, you've got good character insight.'

It always struck Joe — the clashing discordance between the realities of life and death in the bare crucible of the desert and the casual opulence of the Delta, as though the war was just an insignificant skirmish on some distant frontier, very far away. He imagined Rome was a bit like this when his painted ancestors got restless.

'Do any of this lot know Jerry's just three score miles west of us?'

'Well I imagine there's been a run on Italian and German phrase books, but most don't really care. They'll make money, whoever's in the driving seat. Besides, things are starting to look up for us.'

'Are they? The Auk saw Rommel off at El Alamein but he's still sitting there, just waiting for another crack at the line and our track record's none too good of late, he got past Gazala and Mersa Matruh without too much bother. I can't think the Yanks are very impressed.'

'That situation's better than it was. Colonel Fellers, their attaché here, was no friend of ours and since the Axis had cracked his codes, a first rate source for them, he became a proper loon. But he got the shove and the tide is beginning to turn.'

'I've heard that one before. We've been up and down this coast a few times.'

'And you more than most,' Neville smiled. 'We've knocked hell out of Rommel's supplies, he's shackled to the Italians who are no more enthusiastic and who resent him bossing them about. We've got new kit too,' he did lower his voice to a suitably conspiratorial tone, though the ambient chatter and clatter was loud enough to drown most conversations.

'What, we've got tanks that don't break down every five minutes?' Joe had once been in a tank, only on manoeuvres, a great lumbering Matilda, regular dinosaur. Like most infantrymen he'd imagined being in the belly of the steel monster would be reassuring. It wasn't. The immense noise and near total lack of vision scared him half to death. The idea of being immured in a blazing hull had haunted him since.

Once, while they were patrolling and the great tank melee at Sidi Rezegh was raging, they'd picked up a seemingly random transmission from one of our Valentines. The commander was clearly very young and the first panzer round had killed his driver and smashed the officer's left hand. The thing brewed up and he yelled for them to get out, but the hatches jammed and all they heard then were the dreadful mounting screams as the men burned to death. The lifeless driver's foot was still rammed on the gas so Joe could imagine the flaming tomb still racing over the desert as the poor bastards inside incinerated.

He dragged himself back to Neville, too much vino collapso.

'The Americans are sending us Shermans,' his friend was explaining, 'big improvement on the Grant, bigger gun, faster, more reliable, can take on a Mark IV Panzer on pretty equal terms, or less unequal anyway. *And* our six-pounder A/T guns can actually knock 'em out. Shame about the Auk of course, I respected him. Most of us did.'

217

'What's the new boy, Monty, like, any good?'

'Too soon to say. The Auk didn't make much headway after he'd stopped Jerry. Our counter-attacks were pretty shambolic, just didn't cut the mustard. Winston was looking for an excuse to get rid of him and Dorman-Smith, "Chink".' The Auk hadn't delivered and Chink has rogered too many other officers' wives. "Strafer" Gott, who was first choice, got strafed himself before he even had his bum on the seat. Not too many tears about that.'

'So Monty's the man?'

'He's an odd little fellow, full of himself, right bantam cock, you'd think he might be ridiculous but he's so full of confidence it sort of rubs off. Ruthless too, there'll be a few heads rolling, new brooms and all that. He's a tortoise to Rommel's hare.

'And we know who wins the race.'

Neville had made it up to senior captain. 'Fergie's a lieutenant-colonel now,' he confirmed, 'got the rise largely on the back of your antics.'

'I'm delighted for him. All I got was a bullet.'

'And you met your rather lovely nurse Fleming, well worth losing the odd pint of blood for?'

This was tricky. 'Oh and mum's the word,' Neville went on, 'what goes on in the trenches stays there and all that, though I suppose I should ask if you want to marry her?'

Here was the crunch. 'Well ... we've sort of talked around it, just recently in fact.'

'And what form did this conversation take? I'm just asking as a friend, not a potential brother-in-law.'

'Er well, I sort of asked and she sort of said yes.'

'Sort of said yes, or actually uttered the word while sober and not under torture?'

'Pretty much yes, it just sort of happened.'

'As these things do. Well she does seem like a jolly nice girl, good family, no skeletons in any closets, no unsuitable friends from college days, you know the sort of thing. If it wasn't for the war, I'd say she was far too good for the likes of you.'

'Christ, you bloody well checked her out.'

'Course I did, can't have you running off with some Mata Hari type and making fools of us all.'

'Who the bloody hell is *us*? I'm the only one marrying her.'

'Ah well, the wider *we* is your military family, more particularly in this case, the narrower *us* is Military Intelligence.'

'I'm not sure I want to be related to your boss, he's careless with his relatives.'

'He refers to us as "assets", I believe, and you're one of his better bets. The way you dealt with the opposition last time was bloody impressive and we hear rumours you've been ridding us of enemy agents in the field, those unfortunate enough to be "shot while trying to escape," as a few of them invariably are.'

'Operational necessity,' Joe said flatly.

'Oh, quite so, you'll get no complaints from this end. Least said, soonest mended and all that. By the way we got corroboration of Bruckner's treachery from a couple of downed Luftwaffe pilots, a Leutnant Friederich Korner and Oberleutnant Ernest Klager. Both claimed that DAK already knew of the planned raid and were on high alert. We're not so sure about that, though.'

'What seems to have happened is that when Bruckner got out of the truck he found and saluted a Jerry NCO, claimed he was an Afrika Korps soldier acting as driver of a lorry containing a party of heavily armed English troops in Axis gear, loaded up with explosives.

'The officer summoned was rather suspicious at first but Bruckner pressed him to organize as many men as possible to disarm the raiding party. He apparently used the story he'd been recruited as a POW, true enough of course, but that he'd just gone along with Buck so he could get a chance to escape and strike a solid blow for the good old fatherland. Whether this is anywhere near true, or whether he simply suffered a crisis of nerves in Derna and bottled out you can't really say, seems they're going to give the bastard a medal anyway.'

'I almost feel sorry for Buck. His idea's a bloody good one and we came close to carrying it off.'

'Well you might get a chance to work with SIG again,' Neville hinted, enigmatically.

'Ah, no such thing as a free lunch, are you trying to get me hammered so I volunteer for some other crazy op?'

'No need to fret about that, I've already volunteered you.'

'Better get another bottle in then.'

*

'That's bloody Tobruk.' Stirling was studying the map on Ferguson's wall.

'And everyone told me you were a complete duffer at school, David,' Ferguson drawled.

'At least I went to a decent school, not some Scottish hovel, where you just ate porridge and learnt how to chuck cabers.'

'You get a proper education at Fettes, not just arse-banditry and needlework, besides we didn't *always* have porridge and, for the record, I can't stand the bloody stuff.'

Joe was beginning to learn that insults were par for the course among the upper strata. The more they casually chucked random abuse at each other, the better they were getting on. When they were at odds, an icy politeness descended.

'Don't tell me you're expecting us to take this damn town back? We lost what, thirty thousand in the bag, last time we mislaid it?'

'That's classified.'

'Ah, you just want us to biff the place?'

'That's even more classified.'

It was an elite kind of gathering in Ferguson's impressive pad at GHQ. Joe, Neville, Stirling, Buck and another character Joe hadn't met but had often heard about. John 'Jock' Haselden was hard to miss; a tall, well built bloke with a well defined bone structure and an air of considerable physical strength. Joe knew he wasn't regular army, a successful cotton-trader with a lifetime's experience in Egypt. He looked older than his late thirties, burnt by desert sun. He'd been running agents in and out of Axis strongholds with the connivance and conveyance of LRDG.

'And, representing the Senior Service Lieutenant Denis Jermain, commanding Fifteenth MTB Flotilla,' the naval officer, impeccable in whites, looked on the one hand very young to be commanding anything. but at the same time savvy and experienced.

'Ah, so we're going in by boat,' Stirling suggested. 'Don't tell me, that's classified too. Well at least the boats will be more watertight than security around here.'

Ferguson grimaced but said nothing. Not much he could say, Joe reflected sourly, GHQ leaked like a sieve and everyone knew it.

'"We" aren't going anywhere mob-handed.' Ferguson wrested back control. The room already filling with the comforting fug of tobacco, Joe lit up in sympathy.

'All of you know,' Ferguson continued, 'how vital Tobruk is, perhaps now more than ever. A big chunk of Rommel's supplies come in through the port. You probably know the stats, too. There's no better harbour along eight hundred miles of coast, two and a half miles long, not quite half that in width. Mostly built by our Eyetie friends of course and re-modelled by both Luftwaffe and Desert Air Force several times since 1940.'

Haselden took over the briefing. 'You'd think there wasn't much we *don't* know about the place, a few of us have spent a fair amount of time there and there're thousands of fellows in the bag who could tell you all about it. What we're unsure of is how well the place is now defended, where the coastal batteries are, how strong, who's manning 'em, Fritz or the Eyeties, makes a difference of course.'

He tapped the map with his cane. 'The port itself is here, on both sides of the basin, mostly what you'd expect, all a bit knocked about but still working. Behind the town, the ground rises up to the escarpment and we suspect Rommel's fuel dumps are here, and perhaps here. Fuel is his lifeblood, he's perennially short and our Navy colleagues here have proved very adept at sinking much of what tries to cross the Med.'

'He's got coastal defences here,' he indicated west, 'and there,' gesturing east. 'The entrance is protected by a hefty boom and we think there are POW camps just down from the ridge, possibly as many as ten thousand men in the cages at any one time. What we really need now is exact detail on all this, ideally with troop numbers, unit identification, shipping; all that sort of thing.'

'What about the air force?' Stirling asked. 'Can't we do this by aerial reconnaissance?'

'Good point, David.' Ferguson took over again. 'But that's not always as easy or as useful as you might think. Plus our airborne friends aren't being entirely helpful; too busy elsewhere, they assure me.'

Joe, despite being the most junior officer, felt it might be time to show keen wit and observation. 'You want us to do a full recce then, going in by MTB?'

'And out again,' Stirling added.

'That's about it,' Haselden confirmed. 'We need good, up to date intel from reliable operatives. It's one thing sending in a few spivs and chancers after a quick buck, but we need trained eyes on this, a thorough and completely reliable analysis.'

He didn't say a great deal might be riding on it, it was hardly necessary. HQ clearly had Tobruk in its sights, which meant a major offensive pretty much had to be in the offing.

'And it's back along the bloody coast we go,' Stirling chimed. 'I know, don't tell me, that's classified. You know I'm always ready to have a go but won't Jerry be expecting stuff like this? He knows we strolled into Benghazi without much bother and Tobruk's a much bigger fish.'

'He won't know we've been. This is strictly eyes and ears, not smash and grab. We go in, look around and get out again.'

'How?' Joe queried. He'd guessed he was here because he'd be the silly sod doing the actual going in.

Lieutenant Jermain spoke, and he wasn't as upper crust as Joe might have expected. He assumed all RN were toffs by definition, but the man's flat northern vowels suggested he was from further down the social pyramid, not as far down as Joe perhaps, but probably another grammar school type.

'We'll leave Alex late afternoon and cruise along the coast by night — we drop the party off east of the port at a handy cove known as Mersa es Sciausc and return the following night. If nobody's there we'll come back further east for three nights running.'

'The inlet's here,' Haselden pointed. 'We're pretty sure it's undefended and it seems coastal patrols are pretty lax. This part of the shore is held by the Eyeties, well prepared coastal batteries, numerous bunker complexes and here,' he tracked further east, 'Jerry has a nice rest camp by the sea. From there we track along the coast, size up the port and see if we can get a glimpse west over on the far side of the town. We think Jerry's in charge here.'

'Who, precisely, is *we*?' Joe asked .

'Jock here will lead, he's got plenty form, then you, Lieutenant Milburn and two of Bertie's SIG, you'll all be kitted out as Afrika Korps. Three out of four will have fluent German.'

'What about him?' Stirling gestured at Joe. 'He's a Geordie for God's sake, barely speaks English, he'll be rumbled straight off and we know Jerry doesn't take kindly to us dressing up in his clobber.'

Ferguson and Neville exchanged glances and it was Neville who spoke.

'You chaps do need to be aware that we've heard rumblings from Berlin. Nothing official yet but it seems Adolf *is* pretty pissed off by some of our commando operations. We know Jerry tends to deal with any partisans pretty summarily and you fellows are at risk of being put in the same category.'

'My men were born in that category,' Buck spoke for the first time. 'It makes no odds to us.'

'The Wehrmacht are getting orders that any commandos, even if they're in Allied uniform, are to be handed over to the local SD for special treatment, special as in expect to be shot out of hand.'

'I thought Rommel didn't allow any SS thugs onto his patch?'

'He doesn't but he's got Abwehr and I think we can rely on Herr Oberst Hahnemann to oblige. Besides, he and young Milburn here have prior acquaintance. So no illusions gentlemen, this one is strictly volunteers only and if anyone demurs then that's it and it won't be held against him, not even by me.'

'So,' Joe ventured to sum up. 'Four of us in enemy uniform are landed by dinghy on the most heavily defended coast in the Mediterranean, under the noses of the Boches at their most sensitive spot. We are there to spy out and record their defences in detail without being observed and make our escape the same way, quiet as church mice with bed socks on.'

'That's about it. Can you do it?'

'Piece of cake.'

Chapter Twelve

Across the wine-dark sea

Across the wine-dark sea
To sun one's bones beside the
Explosive, crushed-blue, nostril opening sea
(The weaving sea, splintered with sails and foam,
Familiar of famous and deserted harbours,
Of coins with dolphins on and fallen pillars)
   Bernard Spencer

*

I just know that every man I kill the further away from home
I feel.
   Saving Private Ryan (1998)

*

Evening sun gilded the calm surface of a glittering sea as they surged out from Alexandria. Joe allowed himself a brief reflection that Alice was working just a few blocks away from the harbour, with no inkling he was so near. This op was very much top secret, which meant only the more attentive half of the bazaar was aware.

He had little or no experience of boats, aside from sluggish troop ships and dinghies on Paddy Freeman's Lake in Newcastle but, as Mediterranean cruises in wartime went, he was quite enjoying this one. The boat sloshed around a fair bit and the engine noise was pretty intense, yet still oddly comforting, and they had the sea to themselves. Little or no chance enemy planes could spot them in the dark. It seemed they, like Odysseus, were alone in a limitless ocean.

The four commandos, Joe, Haselden, Tiffen and Shai, were excess baggage aboard Jermain's motor torpedo boat. As their naval host explained, MTBs were from a British design but built by the Electric Boat Company at their Bayonne Plant in New Jersey. 'Optional' extras included power-operated .50 calibre turrets and a 20 mm Oerlikon cannon. The seventy-seven feet 'Elcos,' as they were known, were fitted with British torpedo tubes, self-sealing fuel tanks and additional bridge armour. As ever, the imperative for protection and firepower came at a cost of decreased performance, but the boats could still hammer along at an impressive forty knots.

All in all, these were excellent craft. They were sound, fast, highly manoeuvrable and apparently a pleasure to sail. What they were not, was troop transports. Even four extra hands were encumbering but the great thrust from those powerful engines spurring their sea passage was impressive.

'*I am the son of a clever father,*' Haselden quoted. '*I have come here now with ship and crew, voyaging over the dark face of the sea to places where they speak other languages than ours…*' Somehow, a cotton trader turned spook and now masquerading as an Axis officer quoting Homer in an MTB off Alex seemed quite fitting.

'*Well, now, I will play the prophet, and tell you what is in the mind of the immortals, and what I think will come to pass,*' Joe continued, just to show at least some northern lads from sooty coalfields had read Homer. He was kitted out in similar style though temporarily reduced to the ranks, short waisted tunic, fitted up with badges and even a fake iron cross (second class), leather KAR webbing, bleached out shorts and peaked cap.

'You don't make such a bad looking Hun,' Tiffen grudgingly observed, 'just work on the arrogant sneer and keep the sunglasses on.' Joe's pilfered Axis watch and desert boots completed the image. He'd fired the 7.92 mm KAR in the past so the weapon was familiar, even if the stiffer Mauser bolt inhibited rapid fire.

The sea stayed calm and the sudden shift to night dimmed the frothing water, leaving just their furious white wake spitting out behind. They were heading west and to Tobruk. Haselden carried out a briefing in the little ship's narrow wardroom, enamel mugs and a strong brew laced with grog vibrating on the table, air thickening with smoke from standard issue Wehrmacht fags. 'Smelling right is as important as looking right, if Fritz detects the old familiar baccy scent, he's halfway to being convinced we're all batting for Adolf.'

Haselden knew his stuff; he'd been in and out of the Axis held port a dozen times. 'I'm not trying to sound like a travel agent, but Tobruk constitutes the finest natural harbour in North Africa, nearly three hundred miles from Benghazi to the west and further still from Alex and the Delta in the east. It's almost a coastal oasis, the higher ground behind being pretty bloody bare, home only to our Bedouin friend who can be trusted as far as you could chuck his mangy camel.'

'During the nineteenth century the town was an important bastion of the Senussi sect. The Italians claimed to act as liberators in North Africa, freeing folk from the Ottomans, but the people soon found their new masters equally tyrannical. From the outset the Senussi fought the invaders and though King Idris was forced into exile, armed resistance under Omar Mukhtar prolonged a bitter war throughout the 1920s … till they hanged him, that is.

'Murder, mass deportations and the establishment of concentration camps were usual orders of the day. Up to 80,000 Libyans died, they say. In tandem with this ungentlemanly repression, something like 150,000 native Italians were settled in Libya. In 1937 pouting Benito himself came on a state visit, to celebrate the opening of his spanking new arterial highway, the Via Balbia. We've found that pretty useful since, chasing the Eyeties along the coast.'

'The prize, as you gents know, is the harbour. The town itself isn't much, never that extensive, just a few streets of white-walled Mediterranean-style buildings, facing the highway of the sea rather than the inhospitable expanses inland. Most of what's still standing was built by the Eyeties; an outpost of empire. It's more Europe than Africa.' Haselden, who was enjoying himself as self-appointed expert, indicated on the map. 'The port nestles in the curve of a natural amphitheatre bounded, both east and west, by steep-sided wadis. Nearest to Tripoli is the Wadi Sehel, while towards Alex run the wadis Zeitun and Belgassem. These features are natural anchors for the defensive circuit and that's what we've come to see.

'Inside this ring, two shallow escarpments rise like natural shelving, the first's only fifty feet or so in height, the next one double that. Along the southern flank a third level butts in, reaches away and then swings back again south-westwards. The scrub beyond stays relatively flat and open then southwards the real desert begins. Access to the escarpments is by a series of tracks leading up from the port. These are unmetalled and connected the outpost lines. Then you've got the old defensive line, sixteen miles of it. That's where we were all fighting for so bloody long.'

'Didn't do us much good last time,' Shai commented dourly.

'Nope, and 30,000 went into the bag but we're not going in to storm the place, just look and learn.'

'Do we have any contacts?'

'We do indeed. I've ferried agents in and out like a London cabbie since it all went tits up, and we'll be seeing *Signor* Garibaldi, one of my more reliable regulars. Like his illustrious forbear, he's a good patriot but hates Mussolini and his bully-boys, fought in the Izonzo battles during the last war and doesn't much like what the fascists made of that. He works in the post office so picks up quite a lot of gen, even if most of it is just tittle tattle.'

Joe had decided he liked Jock Haselden. He had that same infectious enthusiasm that drove Stirling and Buck though perhaps, and like them, he carried a fair streak of romanticism. Perhaps you needed that, as long as it didn't create blinkers.

'Remember what we're here for,' he went on. 'We need to assess just how strong the coastal batteries are, both east and west, what size garrison, where the fuel dumps are, what's in the harbour and how many POW compounds there are.'

'This bloody coast is a nightmare,' Jermain told them from the wheelhouse in the dark hour before dawn. 'Last time we were here, we had plenty of light. This was when it all went pear-shaped last time. There we were bobbing happily in the port while you Tommies were holding the ring. Next thing you know, Mark IVs are shooting at us from the track, downright uncivilised. We were probably the last ones out, bit of a bloody shambles really.'

'Next time will be different.'

'I rather think we've heard that one before, but I reckon the cove you boys are wanting is pretty much dead ahead'

'Are you sure?'

'I could tell you the Royal Navy always has its bearings properly fixed but I won't insult your intelligence. Want to take a shufti?'

Their dinghy slid into the blackened inlet, hopefully the right one. Even Joe's polished navigational genius was struggling. They were in total darkness, the calm water's dull gleam disturbed by the swish of their oars though a light offshore breeze offset any noise. 'Could be half the fucking Afrika Korps lined up on the bloody beach,' Tiffen breathed. Happily, there wasn't. The boat slid onto rough shingle, they picked up their kit and stepped ashore, feet still dry. As landings on a heavily defended enemy coast went, this one was a doddle, so far at least. The boat glided away with just a muffled 'good luck,' and they were alone.

'This is Mersa es Sciausc,' Haselden predicted, with more certainty than Joe was feeling. They were badged as members of Wachbattalion Afrika with the distinctive 'W' on their shoulder-boards. Haselden knew at least two companies were attached to coastal defence in the area, so their presence wouldn't raise suspicions.

'There are shore batteries above us both left and right, probably manned by our Italian friends. I speak some of the lingo but if we generally treat them with contempt, they'll think we're kosher ... no offence, obviously.'

'Where do we meet your contact?'

'The good Signor Garibaldi will be waiting in a café opposite his place of work at 09.00 hours. A local chatting to soldiers won't draw any attention. Meantime, we just process along the coastal track, discreetly marking enemy bunkers and any big guns they've got.'

They picked their way up from the beach, the natural arena of the small bay, sand, shingle and scrub, not easy going in the dark, up narrow goat tracks. Light was beginning to streak the rising sky, cool chill of night already morphing into the furnace that would be day. The place seemed deserted, though they winced at every scattering of stones beneath their rubber soled boots. They met neither foe nor challenge, but above the raggedy rim they could discern the squat cubes of blockhouses. Joe thought it a mean, low sort of place, pungency of goat hanging in the air.

Incongruous atop the dunes, they passed what looked like a boarded-up holiday villa, crumbling and neglected, like a funfair left out on the battlefield.

'Cheap holiday let,' Tiffen quipped.

'Quite a nice location, though,' Haselden answered, 'quiet neighbours and near to the beach, besides there's an Axis rest camp just east of here, regular tourist trap.'

They continued moving west along the silent coast, its many defenders blissfully unaware.

'Tits like ripe grapefruit,' Shai was boasting, he and Tiffen began a casual conversation in rapid German, lighting up. 'Quite likes it up the arse as well but you know these Hamburg girls.' He even had a photo, real enough, some ardent fraulein who had no idea her long-distance suitor was on the other side and racially at odds with the Aryan ideal. They were marching along a broader coastal track, battered and rutted by vehicles. Closer to the bunker network Italian sentries lounged, savouring their first fag of just another fag-end day in an outpost of Benito's empire where they'd rather not be. Others were about and brewing coffee. None paid them any heed.

Haselden strode over to one of the emplacements, where a burly NCO in nondescript kit was engaged in the serious business of morning coffee. He acknowledged the arrival of the master race with a bare nod. Joe wondered if Jock spoke Italian with a German accent. Well, it worked anyway and Haselden translated later for his benefit.

'That coffee smells good, not like the ersatz shite we get.'

'Help yourselves, boys, it's Il Duce's best, nothing too good for us.' The rest of the scruffy looking crew, at best half awake, laughed at this. It was obviously an old joke and the sergeant looked the sort who'd thump anyone who didn't find it funny.

'All quiet?'

'Well, you're the ones on patrol,' a cue for more mirth, 'but it's quiet as the grave, Tommy has plenty worries besides us.'

'Ah yes, naturlich — final victory is just around the corner, or maybe the next one.' This was cause for universal tittering, they'd all heard it before, every swing of the desert pendulum.

'It's a sure thing this time. Our new caesar has even got his white horse out of the stables again for the triumphal entry into Alexandria like Benito-the-fucking-Great.'

'Right now, he's probably riding Clara, just to keep in shape.' This went down very well. The idea of the portly runt of a dictator sweatily rogering his slender young mistress had a distinct appeal.

Joe was quietly trying to assess the state of the defences, a pre-war line of pretty solid looking concrete and steel blockhouses, obviously well if not enthusiastically manned. He couldn't get in see the guns themselves which might be pushing their deception just too far. The coffee was bloody good, mind.

They trekked further along the dusty coastal path as the sun began its inexorable climb, orange glow of early morning spreading over the bare coastline. There were a lot of bunkers, most manned it seemed. Joe was making mental imprints for the sketches and plans he'd draw later. On the move, they just had to look bored. The SIGs kept up their coarse, trivial banter and nobody gave them a second glance. They were heading northwest, towards the harbour and jumbled town beyond.

Up on their left they could clearly make out heavily camouflaged compounds. These were definitely guarded by Germans, none of whom looked to be the approachable sort. Planes were lifting off beyond, cigar shaped tri-motors lumbering up into warming air. They passed one heavily watched fuel dump, then another at the T junction where the coast track joined the main road up to the escarpment.

'What you see when you've not got your Lewes bombs,' Haselden muttered. 'What a lovely blaze that lot would make.' The road into town had seen better days, taken from the Italians, held by us in a desperate siege then lost. The buildings themselves were in a similar shop-worn state. 'Distressed Italian colonial,' Tiffen suggested.

What had been a sleepy little port just looking wistfully back towards Italy had taken a fair pounding. White-walled buildings sagged and cracked, mounds of rubble where others had been, power lines hung crazily; odours of raw sewage and burnt kerosene fouled the heated air. Most structures had suffered damage, though the main harbour complex, however mauled, was going full tilt.

'Business as usual,' Haselden commented. 'You've got to hand it to Jerry, he gets things moving.'

And things were indeed moving. The docks were sandbagged and wired in, a lot more awake than Benghazi had been. Afrika Korps uniforms much in evidence, plenty of Feld-gendarmerie, more Germans wearing their own borrowed shoulder tabs, they'd have to be careful, pioneers, navy, the lot, all purposeful.

'Busy as east end docks any day,' Tiffen noted. Fat bellied, striped merchantmen, all Italian, tended squat, functional barges, dragged from Baltic ports, ack-ack guns crowded the piers and sleek E-boats stood ready as hungry sharks.

'Time for another brew,' Haselden ordered. It was nearly nine o'clock and civilians were threading their way to work in the port offices. Mostly Italians, Joe guessed, and some locals too — though clearly these were at the bottom of a precisely defined pecking order. As representatives of Rommel they were far closer to the capstone of the military/civil pyramid and had no trouble sequestering a table at the dingy café-bar opposite the post office. This once shining example of the New Order had lost its slender clock tower and its classical face looked like Rome, but only after the barbarians had passed through a couple of times.

Signor Garibaldi was a movie caricature; precisely how an Italian spy would look in any film, or the dodgy professorial type in an Agatha Christie, one of those who has a younger, none-too-bright mistress and hides a dark secret or two, bit like Il Duce himself, perhaps. He was narrow, vaguely ascetic with a finely waxed 'tash and goatee. He even wore a pince-nez, just in case you didn't get the picture. He seemed shifty rather than nervous. He naturally never even glanced in their direction, nor they in his, but Haselden contrived to be at the scarred counter at the same time.

'I'm meeting him this evening at 19.00 hours at his house,' he reported. 'Gives us the whole day to check this place out, best we may. Shai, you're with me, going to try and get as close to the escarpment as I can, see about those POWs we keep hearing about. Joe, Tiffen, scope the town and harbour, don't do anything daft of course and for God's sake don't get noticed, just lurk purposefully as though you've orders. We meet up back here at 18.00 hours.'

'We'll keep our minces peeled,' the cockney confirmed.

'Pardon?'

'Sorry sir. Mince pies equals eyes, rhyming back-slang I think it's called. You can take the lad out of the east end but...'

'Just don't try any of that out on our hosts, or you'll probably end up a very long way east of the Isle of Dogs.'

The sun climbed higher and baked the bustling port. Hiding in plain sight was easy with such an eclectic flurry of Italian and *DAK* units. They kept well clear of others in their distinctive security kit but watching and observing was easy — just keep moving and look generally businesslike. They drank more ersatz coffee and queued for rations. Tiffen spoke just enough German to avoid being noticeably silent, while Joe mapped out the town in his head.

Early afternoon, and they were chewing their way through stolid dumplings, with some kind of fish base possibly, just off the main piazza which might once have aspired to colonial chic but had since been extensively re-modelled by everyone's air force. Military HQ, judging from the comings and goings, was directly opposite, appearing through the clouds of dust chucked about by assorted trucks like a scruffy mirage. It could once have been the town hall he supposed, faded swastika flags hanging limply over the ravaged façade.

It was 14.30 hours, the high, hot sun at its late summer zenith, a veil of torpor slowing the bustle, when he saw a sand-weary Kubelwagen pull up outside and a smart looking officer, unusually cool in immaculate tropical kit, get out and trot lithely up the steps. He didn't get much of a look but it was unquestionably Oberst Erich Hahnemann. Joe could feel his blood stiffening and the itch in his chest, souvenir of their last encounter, kicked off in sympathy.

'Friend of yours?' Tiffen had picked up the vibe.

'A bastard I mean to kill, preferably very slowly.'

'Yeah, but not today laddie. Sir, I mean. We're not here for vendettas and trust me I know the feeling, I've got plenty on my list too.'

Joe brought his blood down from boiling point and added

Hahnemann's presence to the file he was composing, though now he really did wish they'd be biffing Tobruk sometime soon. Afternoon seemed like a good time to check out west of the town. Here, a well-defined circular track led to the cove at Mersa el Mreir, a wider version of the one they'd landed at. You didn't need to be a military genius to work out the possible Allied plan.

'So,' Tiffen surmised, 'let me guess. We're going to bump this place from east and west, amphibious landings on both sides, take out the guns and enjoy ourselves in the harbour while depriving old Erwin of his gas supply?'

'You may think that, but we're not supposed to know.'

'It's bleedin' obvious though, ain't it?' The more excited he got, the more Cockney he became. 'Thing is, if we can see that, maybe Jerry can as well, they're not *that* thick.'

Joe was thinking along very similar lines. If this was a raid, it was a big one. He disliked big raids. He'd seen all the things that could go wrong with a small one.

'Look how we buggered up at Derna, just a dozen or so of us and one rotten apple. GHQ leaks worse than the bleedin' *Titanic*. We'd be all over Völkischer Beobachter before we'd left Cairo.' Joe wondered if Tiffen was psychic or indeed it was all so bloody obvious. Hitting this place from the sea could be another costly Dieppe fiasco and that was really not encouraging. Ill-planned, under equipped, under supported and plain wrong.

'Best not hang about too much, either.' Nobody had showed any interest in them but they could sense these Germans were more wary than the Italians across to the west. They had much to be wary *about*; here the thirties bunkers were interspersed with camouflaged gun pits, mostly eighty-eights.

'Jerry just loves those guns, doesn't he?'

'Can you blame him? Rommel tried those out against our tanks back at Arras in 1940, their old A/T guns couldn't touch our Matildas. Great slow, stupid things they were but Rommel used eighty-eights designed as ack-ack guns, blew the tanks apart from 2,000 yards, been doing it ever since.'

'I often wondered why we didn't use our spare anti-aircraft guns the same way, would make sense.'

'To most of us yes, but not to the bloody RAF, their kit is too precious to share with Eighth Army. It all needs to be kept safe and warm somewhere where there's no risk of wear and tear and they can be rolled out intact for the victory parade — if we ever have one.'

'Sir, I'm suggesting it's time we buggered off, be easy to outstay our welcome and somebody comes along demanding you sing the Horst Wessel song with a proper Bavarian accent.'

'As long as I don't have to wear a daft trilby and start yodelling,' Joe groused.

'We'll both be yodelling for England if they catch us out.'

They decided discretion was to be preferred and retraced their dusty steps back into the town. The port, while tempting, was too heavily guarded and they'd already got a fair idea. Joe was slightly spooked from seeing Hahnemann; it wouldn't do to run into him. He very much doubted the Bavarian had forgotten him. The basement entrance to the HQ, presumably an old cellar, had been flanked by two sentries and he sort of sensed it was generally shunned; maybe people didn't know what went on there or just didn't want to ask.

The tatty bistro hadn't changed much in twelve hours, full of off-duty Eyeties and seedy locals. They ordered grappa as Haselden and Shai sauntered in, a quiet toast to a good day's work. He couldn't remember who was with Daniel, the other three in the lion's den, but he knew how they felt and right now they were still inside the cage. Jock and the two SIGs made small talk while Joe nodded and grinned, a convivial idiot.

They kept to one glass each, the fiery spirit just taking the edge off their nerves. The hour dragged till it was time to call on Signor Garibaldi. He lived just a few bomb-marked streets away in one of those many anonymous thirties villas, all of which had seen happier times. Faded bougainvillea and earthen pots of dead hopes and flowers just reinforced the overall decay.

Haselden went inside. The place was shuttered and dark. There was no surveillance and no lights. Joe and the two SIGs lurked discreetly out of sight, covering the approaches. Nothing stirred, a dog barked and truck engines sounded in the dusk but no vehicle came near. Nobody walked by.

'Quiet as the grave,' one of the others muttered, not an altogether reassuring simile.

'Right then,' Haselden seemed very pleased with himself when he emerged. 'I think we've got enough gen to keep our masters happy, time to be buggering off.'

'Right,' Joe took over, 'let's filter back to the beach, split into pairs again, RV at the abandoned villa at 23.00 hours.'

'No, I think we should go back to the bar, hide in plain sight till a bit later, less chance of arousing anyone's unwelcome attentions.'

'That's not a good idea.'

'But it is an order, and I deserve another drink.'

He could tell the SIGs were as unhappy as he was, but their CO was on a roll. There's an art to pushing your luck and once you hit the tipping point, you just keep sliding. Theirs came at ten, just as they cautiously sipped more grappa and Haselden, in what seemed like very good German, was telling a joke. It seemed to concern Goering and the RAF. Some in the bar clearly found it funny. Haselden was a consummate actor, revelling in his role, perfect, or very nearly. What followed was enacted in German, so Joe struggled to follow exactly.

'Perhaps the Herr Hauptman could satisfy my curiosity?'

The German officer who came over was a tall, sparrow hawk with the eyes of a snake, a Hauptman it appeared, same ostensible rank as Haselden and, if Joe was right, with one of the security companies. A couple of squaddies were standing close to the bar, their MP40s ready, possibly one other by the door. This was horribly déjà vu and it hadn't ended well last time. The odds were better now but they were in the middle of the most heavily defended enemy port in Africa. Joe knew he'd have to kill this man very soon, Tiffen and Shai didn't need any instructions.

'Is the Herr Hauptman an officer of the garrison here, if I may ask?' The man was professionally polite but this was still an interrogation. Haselden's acting talents were about to be subjected to a rigorous audition. Failure was a firing squad.

'Not so much 'attached,' more a supernumerary really, just passing through in fact.'

'Herr Hauptman, I know every German officer in the Tobruk Garrison, attached and visiting. I don't seem to recall *you*.'

'That's because I'm just passing through.'

'Passing through, Her Hauptman? Passing *from* where and *to* where, if I may ask?'

I think that's a matter for OKW my dear fellow, and not for local consumption.'

'Perhaps you'd be good enough to tell me anyway? I take a particular interest in such matters, a policeman's natural curiosity you might say and I believe our superiors will not be unduly alarmed. It is necessary for us to be most careful, most vigilant. I'm aware there are deserters hiding out in the town, so naturally I wish to eliminate you and your fine fellows here from any taint of suspicion.'

'Why then, that's perfectly in order. I'm coming from Derna to Tunis, liaising with our Italian allies.' Joe would have sworn Jock was enjoying himself, a regular mummer — but bullshit with confidence is still bullshit.

'And who, Herr Hauptman, commands your unit at Derna? I was pretty sure most of your complement was here, on the escarpment above us.'

'That is classified, as I'm sure your own senior officer will tell you.'

'Quite right of course, quite right, yet I'm sure you will forgive me but I cannot quite place your accent, I'm pretty good with accents usually, I'd say your stocky corporal here is from Hamburg, the thin fellow probably Dresden but you I cannot quite place nor for that matter can I place your subordinate, who has not spoken at all since you've been in here.'

'It seems my accent fools a lot of people, actually I'm from a very small place in the Bavarian Alps, place called Glockenschnadelfahrtlich — you probably won't have heard of it but we're very close to the Austrian border and we do have a very particular accent, can't seem to lose it.'

'Must be all that yodelling. Perhaps you'd kindly oblige me by handing over your documents, just to ease my conscience, naturally, that I've carried out due diligence.'

Haselden reached into his top pocket for his papers, which were pretty good forgeries. The officer's eyes followed him which was Joe's cue, while he was distracted, to draw the P38 he'd kept ready beneath the table and shoot him once through the heart and once through the head – *now the bastard's doubly dead.*

Tiffen and Shai did the same, leaving their machine-pistols on the table's flat surface and drawing Walthers. The pair at the bar weren't anywhere near ready, one sent a posthumous burst through the decayed ceiling, showering everyone in flakes of plaster. Joe shot the man by the door who was just sitting there with his mouth open, probably just some poor sod after a warm beer, hope he'd enjoyed it. The rest of the bar seemed to empty very quickly.

'What the bloody hell was that for?' Haselden gasped. 'I could have bluffed my way through.'

'Not a bloody chance,' Shai snapped back before Joe could, 'should have shot that fucker soon as he walked in.'

They were already shoving back through the door, half dragging Haselden. One stroke of luck in a luckless evening was the late captain's VW parked outside. They piled in and within thirty seconds Tiffen had the engine going and they drove off.

'If you want to get your wheels moving, find an east end lad, used to be able to get one started in half that time. So what the bloody hell do we do now?'

'Drive,' Joe commanded. He was now in charge. Nobody demurred. 'Head out towards the coast, cut your lights when we hit the path and we'll dump the car by the boarded up villa, with luck they won't find it till morning.'

'Even if we get clear,' Haselden was recovering his composure, 'they'll bloody know we've been here. Bollocks.'

'Not necessarily, your deceased acquaintance was looking for deserters remember, not spies. It was just chance I'm sure, not from any tip-off. We're hundreds of miles behind their lines so with any luck, they'll write the whole thing off as a domestic that got out of hand.'

Tiffen drove quickly but not fast, behind them was silence, no doubt temporary. The main road-blocks were all on the track leading up to the escarpment, the road towards the coast was clear. They'd got clear away from the dingy streets before the sirens went up behind them.

'It's half past ten,' Joe went on. 'Our boat is due in at midnight. We dump the jeep, get down to the shore and lie low.' Again no-one argued. Bumping along the shore path without lights was quite exciting and they had to get out and push a couple of times when the VW got bogged. 'They should really get themselves some decent four-wheel-drives,' Haselden suggested, his earlier pique forgotten.

Silence still reigned by the deserted house and they parked the car out of site at the rear. The alarm was still banging away in town but no sign of pursuit. Finding the right cove wasn't easy; the whole coastline was indented with them. In part this was reassuring; if the enemy mounted a search it would take forever to comb the whole lot.

They had an hour to go. The MTB would be offshore at midnight but would only wait for sixty minutes. They were to signal with torches just before the witching hour. This was the nervous part. If searchers were out they'd spot the flashes. It was eerily quiet just below the rim of rock and scrub.

'I still think I could have bluffed that bastard,' Haselden said, good-naturedly.

Tiffen answered on Joe's behalf. 'With respect sir, no you couldn't. You've been fighting these pricks for what, three years? Well we've had 2,000. Not the same pricks, new uniforms, same mentality. You can't bluff them, they intend to do for you whatever, just because they can, being clever just winds them up that bit faster. That tosser was only playing with us, probably hoping for reinforcements. Shooting them is the only cure.'

It occurred to Joe that Haselden had never been involved in an actual contact before, certainly not at close quarters. Spooks work in the shadows. Well he'd have done better to stay there.

Midnight approached, the chill of darkness gripping them. At five to, Joe scrambled down to the shore and began flashing his torch. He had no idea what was going to happen, a friendly light or a burst of MG fire. In fact nothing happened, just the inky blackness and slapping of the wavelets on shingle, bugger. He'd no idea how long he stood there, cold creeping into his bones. The bloody torches must be too feeble. In desperation, he got Tiffen down to join him and they sent alternative flashes. Nothing. More flashes and still nothing, batteries would be going soon.

The light, when it came, was close, very close, 'I nearly crapped myself,' Tiffen confessed. The dinghy slid out of the murk directly in front of them. 'Taxi for Colonel Haselden and friends,' the cheerful rating whispered. 'All aboard the Skylark then.' Even the sailor's irritating cheer was welcome. They didn't hang around. Dawn was only a few hours away and the further east they got before first light the better. They might just have got away with it.

Hot, darkly thick tea, Navy special generously laced with grog, served with toast and jam. Bloody marvellous. The launch was powering eastwards, her flying wake billowing white, the thrum of her twin diesels even more reassuring. Jermain seemed relaxed. 'We should be out of fighter range by dawn with any luck, glad you fellows could be so punctual. There did seem to be some activity further up towards the port. Have you been upsetting the locals?'

'Billy the Kid here,' Jock indicated Joe 'made his mark, you could say, several vacancies in Koruck Battalion. Probably my fault we had to shoot our way out, now I think about it, I was a mite cocky.'

'Not much harm done,' Joe consoled him. 'They said they were looking for deserters, nothing to suggest we were anything else. You all spoke German, you heard him say where he thought Tiffen and Shai were from, nothing to really make them start putting two and two together.'

'I hope to God you're right.'

So did Joe, but he remembered Hahnemann was in town. Tonight's fracas might just jog a few memories and he was a very hard man to fool.

*

'That's the thing about public school you see.' Ferguson was unusually expansive. Joe had a cracking malt sloshing in his glass and a decent measure too. He could feel the warm, mellow fire spreading agreeably. 'Jock's a public school product, as are most of us, not you obviously which is one reason why I sent you along. You see, to survive a decent English or, God help us, Scottish private education you need to become a proficient liar. Not just the odd fib, I mean develop an ability to lie confidently, continually and competently till it becomes a reflex.

'Compared to your average public school, war is a walkover. In school you form packs. You have to be part of the pack or you'll be torn to pieces. From time to time the pack will turn on one of its own, just because it can, and the system encourages that. It's no bloody wonder so many go on to become actors, they're probably already very good at it. The trouble is, the real weakness, you come to think you can get away with it full time. And once you start believing your own bullshit, then you're in serious bother.'

'So Jock really thought he could have talked his way out of that bloody bar?'

'God yes, still thinks he could have, still a bit peeved you took matters into your own hands, Jesse James style and thank God you did, and you were right, shouldn't ever have gone back to that fucking dive anyway. There's something to be said for you grammar school oiks after all. Jock assumes the Boche are as stupid as your average prefect, but *you* know they're not.'

'This is bloody good scotch though sir, so a privileged upper class education isn't completely wasted.'

'You're right. It is, damn good stuff in fact, from my family's distillery, so make the most of that one. I can't afford to waste it on commoners.'

Chapter Thirteen

Naming of Parts

Naming of parts
Early next morning
The sailor he awoke
Went to his pocket, took out a five pound note
Take this me darling
For the damage I have done
I'm leaving you in charge
Of a daughter or a son
If it be a daughter nurse her on your knee
If it be a boy send the bastard out to sea...
  Anon: *Then there was a Servant Girl*

*

Joe had kept a letter from a pal of his from school, Jim Ward. Now Jim was a skilled machinist, so was in a reserved occupation, a cushy billet you might say, but his letter written during the bombing spree of 1941 had always affected Joe. North Shields, a port on the Tyne, suffered one of the worst single atrocities when a single random bomb from a lone aircraft struck a civilian shelter and killed 107 people. Jim had witnessed the aftermath, searching for the bodies of his family.

The last time I saw Mrs Gibson and Ethel was in the old wash house on the corner of Church Way and Saville Street, opposite the Alnwick Castle, I was looking at their faces, but they could not look at mine; they were dead, victims of the bombing of Wilkinson's air raid shelter. The wash house was utilised for a mortuary. I was in there with my brother Bill, looking for three of our family, they were there with many more we knew.

My brother Bill and I went through the wash house, to identify our dead; we managed to get Bill's wife Lily out and their eldest daughter Lily. As we went into the mortuary, the attendant offered us a cigarette. Bill took one, I don't smoke. The attendant had a cigarette case with a lighter attached, the first that I had seen. He could not keep his hands still as he tried to light Bill's cigarette.

This man had the worst job in Shields at that moment. Bill steadied his hand and he took us around. The children and small adults were on the top bunks and the big people on the bottom bunks. It was like walking down 'Memory Lane', there was everybody I knew by name or sight, Mr Gibson and Ethel, the Broans from Tyne Street, and one woman in particular, her big black eyes used to make me uncomfortable when I was a kid, and there they were staring at me as before.

I was going to go around the back of the bunks, when the attendant said, 'Don't go around there, there is nothing there for you.'. He was wrong. I did go around and found my sister, Lizzie. She had a black eye and I think that she had been pregnant at the time. The back of the shelter was like a butcher's shop, all of the corpses were wrapped in burlap, that kind of muslin that the butchers use.

Bill had found Ann, Lizzie's daughter, but could not find Maureen, his own daughter. We climbed up the ladders to examine each child. One did look like her, but the attendant showed me, three chalk crosses on the side of the bunk. 'Three people have identified this child as their own'. It was so hard to tell the difference.

Joe had tried to imagine that. It was the saddest letter he had ever read. He had seen much of death but had never had to suffer that nightly torment so perfected by the Luftwaffe. Imagine that, night after endless night, as you crouched in your Anderson shelter — damp, claustro-phobic, a ready tomb — and listened to the wail of sirens, the steady droning of the bombers overhead as they drew ever nearer, wave after fucking wave of the bastards. Listen to the steady tattoo of the ack-ack, the beams of arcing light, bright as beams from the sun, poking the night sky, maybe capturing and holding one of the blighters in its grip like the spider and the fly. How you hoped the guns would fillet the plane, incinerating the crew, hoping they screamed all the fucking way down.

*

'It's not about what you want, or even what the enemy wants, it all comes down to what you *want* him to want.'

Joe looked blank. Dudley Clarke had the face and build of a socio-pathic cherub, a very direct gaze and a kind of sinister charm. 'I invented you lot, remember, made the Boche think you were an entire fighting brigade not just a bunch of scruffs with an antique truck and a load of knocked off tents. Good job your mate did on the camo mind, the Kiwis never rumbled you, probably just as well.'

Haselden and Joe were in Clarke's dimly-lit office, which was tactically located in the basement of one of Cairo's more flourishing brothels. 'Perfect disguise, this, Jerry would never house an intelligence outfit underneath a knocking shop, he'd be far too grand, no discount on a shag, either.'

'He's a bit of a weirdo,' Jock had confided as they'd made their way through the city's teeming warrens. 'Served as a fighter pilot towards the end of the last show; he kicked off this whole commando business. Grew up in the Transvaal on stories of those Boer raiders that caused us so much bother and nicked the name. He's a born performer but certainly an original thinker; managed to get himself arrested in Spain dressed as a woman.'

'As a form of disguise?' Joe had queried.

'Nobody's quite sure really.'

Clarke went on, 'What we, or I, call "strategic deception" is all about getting the other fellow to believe what you want him to believe. I've asked generals what they want their enemy to think and half the time they can't tell me. How about you?'

Joe answered. 'We did a recce on Tobruk, got a bit messy, we'd prefer it if Jerry forgot all about that and concentrated his attention elsewhere.'

'Well, yes, I heard about that, a touch of the OK Corral wasn't it? No matter as long as the right people get killed and Jerry writes the whole thing off as a domestic — am I right?

'Spot on. Here's what we do then. Let's assume he's thinking *Ah, Tobruk, I know what their game is* and most of the Delta knows we've our eye on the place. We need to persuade him, to make him think we're really intending to pop up somewhere else and that whatever suspicions he may have had about Tobruk were deliberately planted by us just to make him think that way.'

The "He" in question is a fellow called Hahnemann and he'll take some fooling. This "He" and I have form, and that may make it harder.'

'Ah, a personal vendetta, nothing like a bit of bloodlust to stiffen the mix. We'll simply have to find out just how clever your Herr Hahnemann actually is. We know he's a clever bugger, but I'm a clever bugger too, and you can probably help me get inside this particular bastard's head. And when we do fool him, just think of how pissed off he's going to be.'

'Yes, Dudley,' Jock cautioned, 'but just how in the pluperfect hell do we manage it?'

'Drip-feeding. We drop a series of hints through agents, wireless intercepts and a dummy trail. Not all at once, an ounce not a ton at a time. First, as I said, we decide what we want him to believe. He knows we're up to no good, he knows Rommel's supply chain is his Achilles heel and he knows we're out to biff him somewhere. Where's obvious besides Tobruk?

'Got to be Benghazi,' Joe insisted.

'And you've already visited *and* Jerry knows that. So we begin the process; dodgy info, a set of equally duff plans, a phantom order of battle. Should be easy enough. Most of what comes out of GHQ is pretty spurious at best. We'll move some non-existent ships to ferry non-existent troops and detail a plan for biffing the harbour, making it perfectly clear that any attempt on Tobruk will just be a diversion.'

'Will they buy that?'

'I'd say better than even chance, yes. Benghazi is inviting enough and we'll give the further impression we think Tobruk is too tough a nut to crack so we're looking at a softer target. Have either of you ever heard of Leo the Isaurian?'

'Eighth century Byzantine Emperor,' Haselden answered.

'That's the feller. GHQ could use someone like him; he put the Eastern Empire back together, saw off the Arabs from his front door and won a series of brilliant campaigns, many without striking a blow. He used bluff, deception and artfully constructed bullshit. He'd have been ideal in my job, lucky for me he's not around now. Leave your friend Herr Hahnemann to me.'

*

'Odd little bloke,' Haselden commented as they left the stygian basement, avoiding the special offers of the ladies who lived above. 'Clever
sod though, works with Dennis Wheatley, the chap who writes spy
novels and such.'

'Well if he can get Jerry off our case, that'll do for me.'

'I think he very well might, and we can follow that up with a very
nasty surprise.'

Jock had that fixed biblical gleam in his eyes again, a man with a
mission in mind. Joe decided this would be a good time to start worrying.

*

'What in God's name are you reading?' Archie liked a good murder
story, the bloodier the better, and always seemed to have a tattered
'true crime' paperback to accompany his leisure. 'I'd have thought that,
coming from the east end and being stuck in the middle of a world war,
you might have seen enough violent deaths to last a lifetime.'

'Nah, war's different, innit? An' back 'ome some bloke gets topped,
well, 'arf the time you know which firm done it straight off. This stuff
is different, real mysteries.'

'Don't tell me, your granddad was really Jack the Ripper.'

'Doubt it, me gran would 'ave rumbled him straight off, now if I
'ad a quid for every bloke who *might* 'ave been Jack, I'd be a bleedin'
millionaire and could 'ave bought the judge off so I wouldn't have ended
up 'ere, stuck wi' you lot. An' Joey boy, Sir I should say, this one's from
round your way, up north.'

Joe knew Archie's sense of geography became progressively shakier
once you got north of Wapping. 'Northumberland,' he went on,
pronouncing it carefully as "Norf-amber-land". 'Some place called
Otterburn, that's near you, innit?'

Even Joe thought Otterburn remote, an ancient river settlement under the humped, sullen lee of the Cheviots. 'Nobody gets bumped off in Otterburn, Archie, not since we stopped fighting the Jocks.'

Archie read from his book. '*Evelyn Foster was twenty-seven, the daughter of a garage owner in Otterburn, her family long established in the area. She drove the local taxi. On the night of the seventh, at around 9.30 pm, a bus travelling north on the A696 spotted a burning vehicle seventy yards or so off the road at a desolate spot north of Kirkwhelpington, Wolf's Nick. Evelyn was lying beside her taxi, horribly burnt but still, if only just, alive.* 'ow's that for proper drama then, poor cow?'

Joe's memory stirred. 'It was a few years back mind,' Archie went on, Twelfth Night 1931, must be bloody wild up there in winter, over ten year ago as well, you'd just 'ave been a nipper, nasty one, though ... the murder I mean, not you as a nipper.'

He kept going. '*Clearly beyond help, she was carried back to her parents' house where she died an agonising death the next day. She did manage to describe the circumstances and her final testimony sparked a controversy which has persisted ever since. An enduring mystery which attracted national interest at the time and, despite a massive manhunt which began immediately, no suspect was ever arrested.*

'*Evelyn's story was that she had taken three fares to Rochester then, returning towards Otterburn, at Elishaw she was stopped by a well dressed male, mid twenties, Tyneside accent and sporting a bowler. He wanted to be driven to Ponteland and arranged to meet her again at the hotel at 7.30 pm as he might need her services. He wasn't there but flagged her down a few moments later. He asked her to take him to Newcastle, but changed his mind as they reached Belsay and instructed her to take him back.*

'*She had become concerned but as they drove north from the village towards Kirkwhelpington, he attacked and overpowered her. She must have passed out and only came to when she felt the car bumping over uneven ground. Dazed, she recalled the smell of petrol and the distinctive sound of a lighter. The car went up with her on the back seat covered in a rug. Somehow Evelyn dragged herself out of the car, sustaining terrible burns. She could recall the sound of another car engine driving away.*

'From the start there were doubts, she hadn't been robbed or sexually assaulted, doctors found no trace of injuries sustained in the struggle. Witnesses who'd seen the car travelling, stated she appeared to be on her own. Rumour spread that this was just an insurance fraud gone wrong. At her inquest the coroner directed the jury not to return a murder verdict (they did anyway).'

'You know I do remember this, just vaguely. It was quite a sensation. Some people said she'd made the whole story up as she'd really been intending just to cheat her insurers.'

'Indeed they did, a lot didn't believe her even though she was dyin'. But, an' here's the twist, more'n a year later this geezer gets nicked in Yorkshire for a copycat crime, same MO an' everything, an' he fits her description to a T. Daft thing is nobody makes the connection, see, coppers up your way must be as slow as the Met. When this bloke's standin' before the pearly gates or leastways on the scaffold, first rung you might say, an' the vicar asks if there's anythink else 'e wants to get off his chest before old Albert pulls the lever — he just says 'Otterburn' — so 'e must've done it. Now, is that a proper crime story or wot? Not like stuff out 'ere. Everyone knows Rommel done it.'

*

If true crime was bizarre, sunbathing was verging on the surreal, yet here they were on the beach at Alex, like proper holidaymakers. One whose job was to tend the dismembered and maimed, and the other whose mission was to keep the supply topped up. Alice reclined elegantly on a towel. She was wearing a blue single piece swimsuit designed to provide some semblance of modesty. It wasn't working, just emphasised her supple curves and long shapely thighs. She had a straw hat tipped low and looked as though she was modelling for *Vogue*.

'You could be a model you know, be on the covers of magazines and stuff, after the war of course, if you wanted?'

'What about the madly possessive husband I'm hoping to have? Besides I was asked, for the forces magazine, to pose with some of the patients, the ones they'd let people see. Cheery smiling Tommies, happy in the Med with the 'pretty girl,' just the odd empty sleeve or trouser leg, a screaming sweat-soaked nightmare or two, nothing a decent cup of char won't sort out. Don't' worry mum, I'm having a fantastic time out here. Forget it.'

'That's a no, then?'

'Too bloody right, now pour me some more wine and stop winding me up.'

Though he remained firmly lost in adoration, in thrall, to this beautiful young woman who seemed to want him to marry her, he could sense she was edgy, tense. He knew her work at the hospital was no sinecure, the sights, sounds and smells she encountered daily, hour on grinding hour. He was no stranger to horror but she, on reflection, was experiencing even more of it.

'You do realise I'm going to morph from frantic lover to nagging wife, don't you? Marriage tends to do that.'

'I'm delirious to be marrying you on any terms.'

'We'll see about that my lad but now I've a seriously vested interest in you, I'd rather you didn't get yourself killed, if you don't mind. You don't have to play Lawrence of Arabia all the time.'

'I've not dressed in Arab robes like him yet and I'd not be seen dead on the back of a camel.'

'I suspect he was interested in Arabs generally and not just the robes.'

'Well, I'm definitely not turning queer anytime soon.'

'Well that's one thing I'm *not* too worried about,' she confirmed, reaching for him.

*

There was a hint of theatre. More than just a hint. Lawrence would surely have approved, as L Detachment rode forth from Eighth Army lines. Stirling's much derided vision had achieved maturity, a fleet of fairly decent three tonners and a dozen spanking new jeeps, bristling with the awesome firepower of Vickers Twin Ks. This booming ordnance was intended for aircraft not vehicles, pumping out over a thousand rounds a minute, the juddering recoil seemed set to shake the Willys to pieces. God help the target, though.

Joe was navigator and their long and happy partnership with LRDG largely redundant, SAS having come of age, Stirling's private army of desperadoes was bent on mass havoc. Our blokes cheered the commandos out. 'At least we're one bunch not bloody retreating,' Mayne muttered savagely, caught in the uncertain dawn of a fresh day's drinking and not yet topped up to near sociable levels.

'No messing about this time,' their CO had stated during their twilight briefing. 'This time, we're going to biff Jerry right between the eyes and keep on biffing him. 'And we'll be doing it from here.' He pointed to a place marked Qaret Tartura. 'Not what you'd call desirable real estate, makes most of the other shit-holes we've been in look like Monte Carlo. It's on the edge of the Qattara Depression, even Bagnold kept clear; hopefully so will Jerry. He don't much like the open desert at the best and this is very definitely the worst.'

Stirling wasn't joking. The going was a nightmare, across a vast empty bowl of nothingness that marked the edge of the desert war, southern anchor of the Alamein line. Navigation was a test of all Joe's carefully acquired and endlessly honed skills. 'Fucking *hell*,' Archie groused as another three- tonner got bogged. They all got bogged; the thin crust of hard sand fractured into a fine cloying powder that dragged the laden trucks into its maw with monotonous, sweat-soaked, endlessly cursed, predictability.

There was nothing here, only the limitless horizon, dunes like sullen breakers, salt pans, lots of flies, more heat than you could imagine.

'Christ, who's that bugger? See him?'

Joe just about could, a lone figure, long way away, like a stick in the shimmering haze, just watching them. 'A Boche, is he a Boche? Bloody hell.' Instinctively Joe decided he wasn't. Jerry had only one small listening post on the far rim of the depression and those few unhappy, endlessly bored watchers, daily reporting, day after day, that they'd nothing to report, didn't venture this far south.

'Bedouin, I'd guess. By the time he finds somebody to tell, even if he *wants* to find somebody, we'll be long gone. We're out of fighter, even bomber, range so no need to worry overmuch.'

Still, it was unnerving, that weird lone speck who soon vanished entirely from view. And on they went, the agile jeeps ranging like mechanical hussars while the much heavier trucks laboured, protesting, bogging and spinning. It was slow going and Qaret Tartura was every bit as depressing as Stirling had predicted, flyblown tip of a place, scruffy, scrofulous and remarkably uninviting.

'A mere three score miles north and opportunity beckons.' Stirling was in his element, his very own private army poised to thrust a dagger into Rommel's underbelly. 'We've lots of really tempting stuff lined up, so we'll split into three teams: George, you've got the coast road, Bill I'm giving you Fuka while you, young Milburn, will accompany Paddy and I on a visit to Bagush. Gentlemen, I rely on you all to do your very worst.'

That night, with the Blitz Buggy leading the charge, they motored the sixty miles toward the coast. It was a clear and bright night with a canopy of blazing stars, the ghostly wake thrown up by the jeeps created a gauze-like effect, the roaring vehicles in permanent soft focus. The dark ribbon of coast road was clear, their airfield lit up 'like Christmas,' Archie chortled. Parked up a mile out, they humped their sacks full of Lewes bombs and cut through the perimeter wire. If there were sentries they were astonishingly lax. Fat-bellied Ju88s loomed invitingly and they planted bombs on each, setting the fuses for thirty minutes.

'Bugger,' Stirling muttered as they watched the planes explode. It was spectacular, great tongues of fire leaping towards the heavens. 'Bloody damp fuses,' he continued, glued to his binoculars, 'half the buggers haven't gone off. If he was with us poor old Jock would have been bloody furious.' It was damned annoying, they'd probably netted a score of planes but it was still bloody frustrating.

Stirling didn't look downhearted. 'How about this?' he suggested. 'We mount up and go in all guns blazing, finish the job. These bloody Vickers were built to shoot up aircraft so let's gets some practice.' This was plain bonkers. Raiders hit and run, they don't go back for seconds. The defenders, even if dazed, would be bound to be on the qui vive.

But there was something in the air, madness was perfectly OK. Off they hurtled, Blitz Buggy still in front, Mayne next and then Joe, both in jeeps. Barging through the sagging fence, they ran the course of still intact planes like greyhounds. Bullets spewed from the Twin Vickers, a torrent of lead and destruction. Like rows of defiled virgins the planes reeled and buckled, sagged and flamed. 'Fucking hell!' someone was screaming. It was intoxicating, like assassins on speed, they zapped Bagush. Whoever was left on the field just kept a low profile as the guns chopped and burst apart the doomed transports.

Though they maintained a stately pace, a sedate caracole of destruction, the jeeps shuddered and bucked beneath the fearsome recoil. Guns glowing red in the darkness, lit up by flashes of blinding light as yet another aircraft brewed up, ruptured fuel tanks exploding. They left, tearing back into the dunes and escape. Nobody tried to stop them … and Rommel was short of another three dozen transports.

As they tore back southwards dawn began filtering in the east and brought the Regia Aeronautica up with the rising sun. Macchi fighters came in for a low pass, the raiders scattered and got free with only a single loss — and that was the faithful Blitz Buggy. The big car's raiding days were over, thanks to Benito's air force. Despite this, the night had been well spent. Neither of the other two parties had scored so spectacularly, but had certainly inflicted damage.

'Right then.' Stirling de-briefed them. 'Typical Eyetie trick, shooting up me own car, so I'll just have to nick another one. Still, we've punched well above our weight and no good reason why we shouldn't push our luck just that little bit further, not too far of course but we're on a winning streak and we're hurting Jerry pretty badly. Rommel will bloody well struggle to replace those planes and he knows nowhere's safe. He'll have to pull more chaps out of the line to beef up security.'

'What about this place sir, room service isn't up to much?'

'Well, we're not staying. It won't take Jerry too long to work out we're here and then he'll plaster the place good and proper. We're moving out and moving now. Joseph the Navigator will be guiding us to a fresh refuge, place called Bir el Quseir, an old LRDG haunt, should be safe enough if not quite five star standard.'

'I'd swear me auntie lived in a place like this,' Archie commented, 'wasn't the best.'

Bir el Quseir wasn't really a place at all, no trace of a settlement, just a long low ridge as near featureless as any kind of feature gets but slashed and studded with caves and tiny canyons, fissures and overhangs, most nigh on invisible from the air and enough to swallow up their whole caravanserai. They'd live like Bedouins in their own, idiosyncratic version of a desert halt.

No Axis planes bothered them, but they bothered the Axis with a string of raids. Their tally of destroyed aircraft mounted daily, aircraft chased them back; one popular officer was unlucky and died. That was the price of playing this kind of game and radio intercepts clearly showed they were hurting Jerry. The pendulum was all about supply, so no supply meant no movement.

'You'd think 'itler would be a bit more grateful,' Archie pondered around the camp fire. 'I mean, old Erwin's doing a pretty good job all round, led our generals a right bloody dance.'

'It seems Adolf's got his eyes firmly fixed on Russia, turned out it was bigger than he thought.'

'We had those Russians too,' Angel added. 'I no communist you see, and they were no good for us, they killed as many of us as the fascists.'

'Probably suit old Winston if Hitler and Stalin just fought it out and did for each other.' Mayne was at that expansive stage where he could charm endlessly, until he hit the maudlin phase when it was time to watch out.

'Well, it's a bloody odd life,' Archie went on, 'goin' to be interesting getting back into civvies, that's for sure.'

'What will you do? Don't tell me you're going back to thieving?'

'Nah, I'll become all respectable me, think I might open a little garage somewhere. Come the end o' the war and the army'll be sellin' off 'undreds of jeeps and trucks an' all, a bloke could do alright. 'Ow about you Angel, even if we win old Franco ain't goin' to want to see you again in an 'urry, now will he?'

'No Spain for me,' Angel confirmed. 'There is nothing left and I have a price on the head. My family is gone, my country is fucked. I go somewhere else, maybe England if you have me?'

'An' why not, there'll be bleedin' allsorts around after this lot, displaced persons an' what 'ave yer, just re-invent yourself, done that a few times meself already.'

Mayne, who had a strong, clear voice, launched into some Irish melody, a sure sign he was passing from one stage into another, sentiment and violence usually went hand in hand. Others launched into more popular tunes.

I may be right, I may be wrong,
But I'm perfectly willing to swear,
That when you turned and smiled at me,
A nightingale sang in Berkeley Square.

Grog had been passed around. The dead were commemorated in silence. Joe was slightly alarmed that he was having trouble remembering what some of them had looked like. Was he so inured, so indifferent to death, that it was now as commonplace as the common cold?

Blokes wallowed in the cloying romance of Anne Shelton's song. It went well with alcohol, easy enough to drown in either or both. Light from the fire flickered around the bare, jagged rock, impenetrable, cold and sterile. Nobody came from here; all of them, British and French, Kiwis and even Basques were aliens and united in their isolation. Something a bit more lively was needed, Joe decided.

I'm Henery the Eighth I am!
Henery the Eighth I am, I am!
I got married to the widow next door,

She'd been married seven times before.
Everyone was a Henery,
She wouldn't have a Willie or a Sam,
I'm her eighth old man named Henery
I'm Henery the Eighth I am!

'I hope whoever writes us up after the war gets it right,' Mayne went on. 'I mean, Christ just look at us, not exactly Britain's boxed tin redcoats, are we?'

Indeed they were not, their faces were blackened by the sun, bearded and unruly, shocked hair stiffened by wind and dust, their kit as eclectic as it gets, half of it Axis with enough assorted hardware to fill a medium-sized arsenal.

Yet, at that moment, they were the ones taking the fight to the enemy. Most of Eighth Army was huddled in trenches, battalion boxes and redoubts along the Alamein line, just waiting for the next push, whichever direction it came from. He remembered Neville predicting the next and decisive swing of the fickle desert pendulum but Rommel was still the one sitting only sixty miles from Alexandria.

'Ever done any Scottish dancing laddie?' Stirling asked, as he was fiddling with his pipe, that careful, neatly obsessive ritual of clearing out, re-stocking and lighting up. Joe said that he hadn't. It wasn't on the curriculum for Bedlington Grammar where they'd stumbled, clumsily and self-consciously, through the waltz, foxtrot and others he'd forgotten, all blended into a single tableau of helpless ineptitude and total boredom.

'Well then, you're bloody lucky, being a social inferior has its benefits. We did it for bloody hours at school; they tell me your pal Ferguson was pretty quick on his feet, no wonder he's a bloody spy. Well, you'll benefit from my experience and keep well away from it, and for God's sake never be tempted while you're sober.'

'Sidi Haneish,' Stirling came back to the present, pointing on the map. 'Can you get us there?

'Yes, sir,' Joe immediately responded, with far more confidence than he felt.

'Right answer laddie, but you better be bloody sure it's seventy miles away and, if we go wrong at all, we'll be buggered, right royally so.'

Joe repeated his assurances.

'Right then, well back to Scottish reels. I've a mind to create one of my own but this one will differ in that, thank God, there'll be no bloody bagpipes and our partners will be provided by Messrs Ford and Willys.

Both Paddy and Joe looked suitably nonplussed.

'Remember when we beat up Bagush? Well, we're going to do it again. Jerry is getting wise to us, reinforcing his airfields, digging trenches, anti-tank ditches, not that we've got any tanks of course. It's a kind of compliment I suppose, and any little Fritz manning said trenches isn't in the line up the road. Well, we're going to go back and do it again, brass up this particular airfield good and proper, blast our way in, shoot 'em up and, if we have to, fight our way out again. Does that idea find favour?'

The question was entirely rhetorical but the notion was still appealing. Just so they got it right on the night, everyone took his partner for the Stirling reel. Seven jeeps in two files, five yards between, their formidable fire directed outwards. Stirling, as CO, led like a centurion, his jeep in front between the two lines, those behind creating an arrowhead formation. They'd loaded up with tracer, incendiary and armour-piercing rounds.

'And,' Stirling announced as he sent a Verey light up into the night sky, 'take your partners please, and off we go.' Timing would be everything, so it had to be right. Everyone put in ear plugs — you had to, or be deafened. Jeep drivers in the left hand column had a very nervous time, the front gunner was firing from right of the driver so if he did anything inadvertent or too sudden, there was every chance he'd lose his head. In the meantime, he was constantly deluged in spent cartridges which cascaded like heavyweight confetti. It was pretty bloody impressive though. The racket, even with ear defenders, could have rivalled Krakatau in one of its more explosive moments. Tracer scudded like myriad, manic fireflies, darting over the desert darkness; rounds shredded rock and kicked up miniature sandstorms.

'Well, that was bloody good fun,' Archie commented. 'Let's 'ope Jerry enjoys it just as much.'

*

'Now, where the bloody hell are we? I see no airfield.'

It was twenty-four hours later and L Detachment was about to pounce on Sidi Haneish. At least that was the intention. By Joe's (exhaustively and exhaustingly made) calculations, they were about bang on. 'About a mile directly ahead, sir.' Joe rubbed his gritted eyes.

'Call me an unbeliever,' Stirling went on, 'but I'd expect to see a bit more activity, you can't run an airfield in the dark.'

Deus ex machina, and to Joe's inestimable relief, someone threw a switch, in this case for the landing lights, and the entire strip sprang magically to life before their eyes. He really, in his wildest dreams, couldn't have asked for more. 'Well, well, well,' Stirling exhaled, that's quite a show, well done laddie, and it's wagons roll.'

Altogether they had eighteen jeeps, each bristling with four machine guns, 'never did so few fire so many.' Stirling sent up another green Verey light and the waltz kicked off. They crashed the barrier at speed, startled guards bolting in every direction. One guard got a stray round off, the first shot of the evening, and was literally cut in half by retributive burst from a Tommy-Gun, torso ripped clear away, legs in shorts still standing for a stupid moment before folding.

Obligingly, the enemy had parked aircraft in two neat rows facing each other, planes beautifully lit up by their own lights. At an almost funeral pace, hunters closing in for the coup de grace and with almost balletic care, they stalked the lines. A hurricane of fire blazed from the jeeps, a storm of noise and flame, tracers glancing bright, red hot incendiaries spitting. Like a son et lumiere straight from Bedlam, they moved down the orderly lines. Planes groaned and crumpled, one erupted in a fireball that nearly engulfed them. Spent cases in hundreds, thousands, were scattering in their wake. Even with ear plugs, the crescendo pressed on their senses like a thunderstorm, the diabolical fury driving out consciousness. Hell on earth and whoopee.

Some poor bastard was coming in to try landing another Ju88. He came down a lot faster than he'd intended. Lines of tracers sought him out, a rabbit in his own side's headlights, too late to pull up. Bullets hammered the plane, ripping off chunks of metal, engines faltering then bursting into flaming torches, a regular Gotterdammerung. Wagner might have loved it. The stricken Junkers crashed into its parked up brethren and its fiery demise engulfed a couple more.

Joe was manning the forward Vickers in his jeep, Archie driving, Angel as tail-end Charlie. Suddenly, the vehicle stopped dead. Joe was nearly flung clear. 'What the fucking hell are you doing?' he screamed. 'Get bloody going!'

'We ain't goin' nowhere,' Archie yelled back, 'take a look.'

Somebody had been shooting back, a cannon round neatly drilling the engine, neat as a surgeon's knife. Rounds were pinging off the chassis. Folk or Volk had woken up. 'Right, let's get going,' Joe, Archie and Angel jumped clear leaving a grenade to disable the guns, and sprinted back for the next jeep, piling untidily aboard. 'Get bloody shooting!'

Joe yelled at the young rear gunner — but he had a bullet in his head so Angel took over.

They were close to outstaying their welcome but had time for a return pass along the stricken line, brassing up any planes that didn't look brassed up enough already, individual jeeps careering off to sort out the odd aircraft parked up on its own. Then Stirling sent up a red flare; time to go home and they raced back over the wasted 'drome and off into the night. Joe's job, now in his borrowed Willys, was to ensure everyone got clear and take photos of the damage, enough to keep the Gaberdine Swine happy.

Sidi Heneish was a vision of the inferno. Those once proud and ordered lines of Ju88s were reduced to debris, half of them unrecognisable, the rest on fire. There was no pursuit; shocked defenders were scurrying about looking for damage limitation. Joe calculated they'd destroyed nearly forty aircraft, a palpable hit by anyone's standards.

'Who was he?' someone asked as they dug a shallow grave in dawn's grey filter. Joe had joined Stirling at a lying up place a few miles southwest. After the raid, the column split into three smaller sections, more chance of avoiding the Hun in the sun and there'd be a few up that morning, Jerry would be after vengeance, big time. They'd kicked Fritz in the goolies and he'd be wanting to kick them back.

'A lad called Robson, just joined us.' Joe had barely registered the newcomer and now he was gone. Only in the light did he realise his fatigues were doused in the dead man's blood and brains. The rest didn't look much better, blackened, be-grimed, senses still reeling from the blast of the hurricane they'd created, sand, sweat, reek of cordite, fused into the devil's coating.

Joe's head was thumping. They dug a shallow grave, the stiffened remains of Bombardier Robson were wrapped in a blanket and lowered in and covered; only a ring of stones and a crude cross made from a discarded packing case. There was no ceremony as such. They just stood for two minutes as a desert wind plucked at the fitful sand.

This was the most any of them could expect. For them, there'd be no neatly tended plot in some tranquil Commonwealth cemetery, just sand and stones soon obscured and lost.

He realised that he couldn't recall what this lad had looked like.

Chapter Fourteen

Delta Blues

Land of soap and water,
Hitler's having a bath,
Churchill's looking through the keyhole,
Having a jolly good laugh
  Sung to the tune of Land of Hope and Glory

*

How much I missed the dead — how easily I could have replaced
the eleven living with eleven dead all of whom, or at least eight
out of the eleven — I should have loved better ...
  John Julius Norwich (editor): *The Duff Cooper Diaries*

*

'I bloody love cavalry,' Joe exhaled, his breath frosting crisp in November air. He and Neville, ostensibly on opposing sides in the social divide, had taken a joint decision to skive off school and watch the drama unfolding at Woodhorn Colliery, 'and with both our dads in action,' Neville confirmed.

'Can't see yours...'

'Oh you won't, he's far too grand to actually confront the revolting peasantry himself, that's why we've brought up the arme blanche, even if it's just the Hussars.'

'Not so much 'just,' most other regiments are converting to armoured cars and stuff, the Northumberland Hussars are retaining their mounted status through precedence.'

'And now they're about to draw swords against their own people.'

'I know, can't wait.'

It was a tense standoff. The angular iron gates of the pit, they'd have worked as well for a gaol, were closed and padlocked, this elegant line of horseman deployed to mount guard. The worn range of buildings was unusually quiet, stark winding gear silent, though everybody knew there were men working; 'blacklegs,' 'scabs' the crowd was chanting.

Ten years since the general strike and both boys were sixteen.

'Your dad's in the ILP, isn't he?'

'Yes, a leading light, well he thinks he is, mates with Manny Shinwell and Jack Sadler, even shaken hands with Maxton, the party leader. And the old man's big in the PPU too, right bunch of wankers they are an' all.'

'Now they're the ones who want universal peace throughout the world — but think old Adolf is pretty much an OK sort of bloke?'

'Appeasement they call it — give Hitler whatever he wants. This country, that one, whatever it takes to keep him happy, half of them are practically on a par with Mosley.'

'Well, your old man seems to be enjoying himself.'

'Having a go at yours keeps him happy, and it's loads more fun than chasing bloody sheep.'

They were safely hidden in a small copse about a hundred yards from the pit, black, begrimed, depressing, harsh cheap bricks and mean sheds, layered with muck. Miners got the muck; owners got the brass and weren't coughing their lungs up by fifty. His father was with the crowd, clearly a ring-leader, wiry, weary men, no colour in their drab woollen suits, flat caps pulled low, hunger on their faces, anger in their souls.

'I hope they get to charge,' Joe continued.

'Wasn't your old man in the Hussars himself during the war?'

'Yes, but hated the whole business ever since, never speaks about it.'

Not entirely true, he reflected. His father's experiences were more communicated by what he didn't say. At times, you couldn't predict when, he'd just lapse into silence, deeply withdrawn, as though comatose. It was as if, in some metaphysical way, he'd left them, going back to the horrors he'd seen, replaying the scenes time and time again in his head, perhaps hoping one day it would make some kind of sense. Plainly, it never did.

When Joe went shooting the old man would always stay indoors, said nothing and never complained, but the noise of the gun, even his poxy little .410, was too much to bear close up. Some nights Joe would hear him screaming in the grip of some dreadful nightmare, a raw inhuman sound, finally calmed by his mother's soothing. She said nowt as well, but he'd heard other kids say much the same of their fathers who'd been in the war — as if their parents' entire generation had just drawn a veil over the whole thing, bloody irritating when you really wanted to hear all about it.

'They've got full kit, too.' Neville was studying the hussars through pilfered binoculars. 'Just look at that gear.' For a self-professed cynic and almost pacifist, Neville had an eye for style. The cavalry were immaculate in khaki, their gleaming tack accoutred with spare bandolier around the horse's neck, .303 rifles in saddle buckets, all manner of blankets, ropes and pouches, their cup-hilted 1908 pattern sabres carried on the left, hung from the saddle.

'Class traitors,' the strikers were yelling, 'bloody-handed assassins of the workers,' his father chanted, straight from the party script. Joe didn't see himself as a class traitor. He wasn't exactly sure what his official social caste was. As the son of a tenant farmer, he was a damn sight better off than most pitmen's sons, better fed, better read and usually better kitted out. Those were the doughy, sallow-skinned and spotted boys he fought with at school, podgy from their potato diet. He ate better and had even been to Newcastle on the train, more than once too.

The protestors grew more vociferous, probably as the bottles went round. The silent squadron of horsemen shivered as though getting restless, their horses, sensitive creatures, picking up the hostile vibe. An order was shouted and swords, swinging up in unison were drawn, feeble autumn sun picking up the flicker of needle pointed blades.

'Here we go, getting lively.'

It didn't really. As revolutions go, this one was a bit of a non-event. Joe's vision of the people's struggle had been heavily influenced by a colour plate of Delacroix' 'Liberty at the Barricades,' some nineteenth century French do. He couldn't quite remember which revolution this was, they seemed to have them pretty regularly, but Liberty was a sturdy, bare-breasted young woman exhorting some nattily dressed Froggies to go and overthrow somebody. It looked both sensual and dramatic; he'd created some youthful sticky puddles over Liberty.

This time there weren't any barricades or half naked girls, just the steady press of the cavalry as they forced the surge back, using the weight of their horses rather than swords. The strikers were pushed aside and most just dispersed, hardly worth bunking off school for.

That evening Neville's dad hosted the officers. The men got fed too, but not this side of the servants' hall. Joe and Neville had sort of sneaked in; the colliery owner had allowed his son one friend at table though it was unlikely he'd have approved of Joe, spawn of the discontented rabble.

'Remember how to use your knife and fork,' Neville reminded, 'no farting or swearing. You're amongst the gentry now.'

Nedderton Hall was set out to impress. As its owner was really trade, barely two generations past a blacksmith's forge, he needed to try that bit harder. The long mahogany table groaned under the weight of silver and crystal, most of it paid for. Neville's mother, having come from an impoverished stratum above, knew how these events were managed.

'You look smashing,' he'd lamely complimented Evelyn, and that was an understatement. Her shining hair was up and she was encased in a shimmering, vaguely risqué frock that clearly hadn't come from the Co-op, her height and bearing belying her youth. Others noticed her too and Joe suddenly felt distinctly proprietorial. Their earlier fumble in the dunes had led to further and deepening encounters and he was self-assured enough to think of himself as potential husband material, even if both sets of parents would be rather harder to convince.

'To law, order, trade and profit,' the rubicund major, dress uniform straining over a most un-cavalier gut, was proposing. The toast was noisily applauded and sealed with fresh and lusty draughts of their host's wine. 'No beer on this table,' Neville observed, 'ale's a sight too common for cavalry,' though the ORs outside would be enthusiastically swilling. Joe was between Evelyn and Neville so was spared the need to converse with any of the uniformed guests.

'Mulligatawny,' Neville explained as Joe puzzled over the soup. 'Good choice for the Hussars, comes from the Raj, cheapskates like you would just call it curry soup.'

'I didn't know the Hussars ever served in India.'

'Probably never did, but this will make them feel like it.'

A rather porcine, pink-faced young officer with knowing eyes sat on Evelyn's other side. He was being very attentive, irritatingly so, attempting to fill her glass at every opportunity and leering closer as he emptied his own. Joe attempted to ignore him, enjoying Neville's fairly witty caricatures of the rest. Then he felt Evelyn stiffen next to him and her eyes, for a second, beseeched his. She stiffened again; the fat fucker had his podgy hand on her knee.

'I think she'd rather you didn't do that,' he spoke quietly.

The fellow turned his nasty little eyes, not yet bleary, towards Joe.

'Good Lord,' he said much more loudly, 'somebody's let the groom join us, surely a mistake, shouldn't you just be serving the soup?'

There was a silence. Evelyn's father looked as though a stroke was imminent. The portly major intervened. 'Mr Coates, I'll thank you to remember you are a guest here and that you represent the regiment, behave accordingly.'

But Coates could sense the younger bucks were with him and drink had stiffened his sinews. 'But sir, this ragamuffin was interrupting my conversation with the young lady. Surely we can't have that? Why if I wasn't being polite, I'd drag him outside for a lesson in manners.'

'And what kind of lesson do you think *you* could manage?' Joe found himself challenging. And Christ, this was really bloody stupid.

'Any sort I care to administer, and someday you'll find out.'

'How about *this* day, you fat loon?'

Joe could feel Neville exhale and Evelyn go rigid; she put a hand on his arm. Coates couldn't miss that, or the implication. On the other hand, he'd sized Joe up and was perhaps not so keen as his bluster.

'Well I'm sure a brawl would suit anyone of your type, I was thinking of a more gentlemanly affair.'

'Enough, Coates,' the officer barked, 'you will desist.'

'Swords it is then,' Joe replied, no more hope of a truce. There was a full silence. Neville's father made to intervene and say something but couldn't find the words. That's what happens when you're no better than you ought to be as his mum would say. Coates' reptile eyes flicked over the room. He was boxed in. Joe was kind of confident. He'd done a fair bit of fencing. His school, even if not for gentry, could boast of its own fencing academy run by a Belgian exile from the last war, who'd never gone back to Belgium but had been a champion swordsman. He'd told Joe he had some skill with the sabre. Joe fervently hoped he was right.

Now he could sense the excitement, Evelyn looked wretched. Well if he was prepared to fight for her, it showed he must be genuine, not that her horrified parents would think so. His heavyweight opponent looked a bit less cocky as they trooped into the yard. Neville would second Joe.

They'd fight with practice sabres, '08 Pattern but blunted, first blood from the torso. Joe took guard, right leg thrown back, blade low and to the left. His opponent's stance was similar, Joe wondered how much teaching the fat boy had had, possibly less than him, hopefully. Joe moved first, cutting upwards under his opponent's wrists, shifting grip and springing forwards. Fat boy simply stepped back then thrust, venom-ously swift, aiming for Joe's belly, now his turn to step back, parrying loudly, clang of steel on steel.

Blades touched again and broke off. Together they made six feet of steel, even when baited still capable of serious injury, controlled by mass of muscle, sinews and nerve, tight as a bowstring. They beat lightly, a dancers' step, flicked away and drew back, his slime-green eyes on Joe's.

Around them the crowd, half-glimpsed, milled and shifted, mutter-ings on form, shouted odds. Joe gathered he was ahead, guaranteed to goad his mad bull opponent even more. Joe's turn to swipe at the fat bastard's gut but he skittered back out of reach. Joe came on, aiming for his lumpen head, pivoting on his left. He side stepped also to the left, took Joe's blade on sloping parry. The swords scraped and parted.

Overhead an owl called out its harsh serenade, oblivious to the madness below. Fat boy was quick, far quicker than his bulk suggested, tremendous power in his blows, like trying to block a falling oak. That was his style, use weight and force to batter an enemy. He turned his parry into another belly-slash, forcing Joe back on his right, weapons high, balance and protection. This saved losing an arm, though his point flicked blood. A glancing cut, no damage to muscle.

Someone was yelling for a halt, nobody else took any notice.

Joe sprang back fast and low, keep this ox on his toes and make the bastard sweat, wearing him out. He parried downwards, left leg back, blade down. They closed and he sought to rearrange Joe's features with his guard, tensing his right leg for the lunge. Joe beat him back. Sweat coursed from them in rivulets, steaming like prize hunters.

No respite for Mr Coates. Joe lunged hard, opening a distance, sent him scattering back. Swords grew heavier, muscles of wrist and arm knotting against the strain. Joe feinted, Coates parried too close and Joe stabbed down into his thigh. Piggie grunted with pain, blood on his dress breeches, just a prick though.

'Finish him off,' someone exhorted, though to which of them Joe couldn't tell. Men truly enjoy others scrapping, the more gore the better. Porky came back grunting, knuckles up, passing right. Joe moved left for a circular parry, both heaving like blown nags. Joe's last parry, delivered with as much force as he could muster, spun the heavier lad round so Joe could plant his kidneys with the heavy steel guard, a rousing thump, must've bloody hurt.

He arched back, swung around, too slow, too damn slow by far and Joe lunged straight for his podgy, mottled face, pulling the blow sufficiently just to plant the guard again, squashing his nose in a pleasing bright red shower. Coates went down like a sack of spuds. It would be some time before he got up.

Joe's lungs were screaming, dragging in great gob-full's of cold evening air as two burly hussars dragged their unconscious subaltern under cover. Most were slapping Joe on the back and settling their wagers. From the amount of grinning, he must have been favourite from the start. Neville brought him water, Evelyn had disappeared, as had her father, this probably wasn't quite the level of entertainment he'd had in mind, but the cavalry loved it.

'The old man will be locking my sister up. It's one thing for her honour to be trifled with by gentry, quite another for her saviour to rise from the should-be-oppressed masses. Best come in and have some more wine while the going's good. I doubt I'll be able to wangle a return invitation.'

'Well, that was bloody good sport.' The red-faced major was redder and sweatier than ever. 'Time somebody taught young Coates a lesson in etiquette. I hear you want to be a solicitor? Well forget it I say, come and join the cavalry.'

'Thank you, sir,' he managed.

'Oh I mean it alright. I'm a tenner ahead thanks to you.'

*

Joe dragged himself back to the present, which was reclining on Alice's splendidly aroused breasts, her erect nipples wonderfully prominent. 'I thought you'd drifted off,' she said, 'thinking about other women.'

'Matter of fact, I was.' He told her the story.

'Oh I like that, fighting a duel to safeguard the maiden's honour, even if the swords weren't that sharp.'

'Quite bloody sharp enough, and I think she was more embarrassed than gratified.'

'Well, she'd only have been a kid at the time so no wonder, and I'm assuming you'd already had your wicked, working class way with her. And I'm specifically *not* asking if you've written to her with news of your engagement.'

'I have written,' he replied truthfully, 'but I did sort of dance around that subject, I confess, not bloody easy.'

'No, I do understand the whole childhood sweetheart thing and she does sound nice, so let her down gently. Mind, if she's still after you then, I'll scratch her bloody eyes out.'

He neglected to say he'd had another letter from Evelyn, in response to his own, suitably guarded on account of the censor — even if Neville had his dark paths around. He assumed his friend was reading the letters anyway. She'd talked more about conditions at home, whatever that meant now. His father was more withdrawn than ever. This war had just reinforced his obsession that the whole thing was a capitalist conspiracy, invented to thin out the masses by slaughter. Though why these scheming capitalists, most of whom (according to his dad and those of his persuasion) were Jews, would want to decimate potential workforces in battalions led by their own sons, escaped him.

The war had finally come to Bedlington-shire. An American transport, off course and with engines failing, had crashed into a farmhouse killing all four children asleep in an upstairs bedroom. Somehow this random horror was more horrifying than all the others going on — and there was a lot of competition in the atrocity stakes. Probably because he knew, or at least knew of, the family and it had happened on his home turf which he'd always thought of as being pretty much safe.

'Lost you again.' He wondered how he could ever be distracted lying on such a perfect pillow. He did quite often ponder whether he and Alice had spent more time horizontal than vertical since they met. He told her about the letter.

'Death is random,' Alice confirmed. 'I see it every day, fickle, capricious, a thief in the night. There's no reason or pattern to any of it and that won't change till this beastly war is over.'

He'd looked at himself, once he'd bathed and shaved after the last op, and he wasn't the same man he'd been a year ago; older, more lined, somehow weighed down. He saw it in all the others too: Mayne, Fraser, Mike Sadler even the ebullient Stirling, hollow-eyed, drawn and suffering from desert sores. They were becoming old men, though most were no more than half-way through their twenties. God knows what they'd look like in a couple of years if the war kept grinding on; and if any of them lived that long.

'I'm getting to be a selfish cow,' Alice continued. 'I don't want to be a war widow before I'm a war bride. I want to go home to a cottage in the country, married to a dull stick of a solicitor and raise a handful of kids, grow staid and boring tending roses and begonias or whatever.'

'Join the WI?'

'Not sure if I'm ready for that, maybe leave jam and Jerusalem until I'm really old, forty at least. God, I hope the war's over a long time before that.'

'Germany's buggered. They'll take some beating but Hitler's shackled to a corpse with Mussolini and now he's got the Russians and Yanks after him as well as us, still got the Japs of course, horrible little bastards. I'd sooner fight Rommel any day.'

'I became a nurse to tend sick people, mostly old, or ill children, not just to try and patch up fit young men who've had bits of them blown off or their intestines ripped open. You're one of my successes, yet you just go back and keep doing it all over again.'

'I'm not sure the war gives us a lot of choice.'

She sat him up to look at him. 'Some might say you've done your bit, probably more, at the sharp end … and I do know how sharp your bit of the end is. Everyone talks about your lot as though you're supermen, all derring-do and rugby jokes round the campfire.'

'What's a nice girl like you know about rugby jokes? Besides I only ever played soccer, rugby's for toffs.'

'My brother plays rugby, went to that sort of school. They sing crude songs in the showers and probably do other things as well. A good start for the army, I imagine. He loves the bloody war just like you, 'cept he's never been nearer the front line than Eastbourne.'

'Well, I can hardly turn into a conchie *now*, can I?'

'No, but your mate Neville could wangle you a job at GHQ. I know you can't stand them but I'm sure he could.'

She was, he realised, deadly serious. 'Look, that's all very feasible but recall last time I worked for those johnnies they damn near got me killed, though I did meet you, which was worth it, naturally.'

'I was thinking more some kind of desk job, strategic planning, all that sort of thing, you've got the experience and you can speak the King's English, sort of anyway. We'll have to iron out that northern twang but you do scrub up quite nicely.'

He'd have to think about this. If he asked, Ferguson might possibly take him on and he might even be useful. 'The idea of a cushy billet and a posh flat in Garden City could be appealing, you can choose the bed.'

'You just want me at your beck and call, so you can have your wanton way.'

'Dead right boyo, starting from now!'

There'd be no further conversation for a while.

*

'A defector, *you*? I'm shocked!'

Neville was enjoying himself. They were in his apartment which, while maybe not so grand as some, wasn't half bad, adorned with various scraps of antiquity he'd picked up in the bazaar and Old City. The windows were open, so a relatively fragrant breeze was drifting in from the Nile.

'I can't really understand it. Why would you want to swap sand, flies, scorpions and Nazis for this? Joining the Gaberdine Swine, what would David Stirling say?'

'It's bottling out, I know.' He shifted wretchedly, gulping more Laphroig, the dense peaty fire easing his twitching nerves. 'And I can't really see what I've got to offer …'

'I see the charming nurse Fleming's strong hand in all this, the silly girl must really be in love with you. Fixed a date yet?'

'Not exactly, and no I haven't written to Evelyn, it's unforgivable I know … and I was hoping you'd be best man.'

'I should damn well hope so, and don't worry about Evelyn. Oh, I know you two had a thing going and I daresay you're very fond of each other, but that was then, before all this, and it was a very small pool you were both swimming in back home. She's twenty now and you've not seen her, or she you, for two years. She's doing medicine and you're killing Germans, you're different people now. Keep the past for your memoirs.'

'Do I have any skills that GHQ would be interested in? I can't see it. I can strip and assemble any weapon you like, blindfolded. I can navigate most places, pretty much dead on too. I can kill people in all sorts of ways and tell you what works best, but none of that qualifies me for any kind of staff work, does it?

'Au contraire, as we say in intelligence circles, it's a perfect CV. You've actually fought the enemy at very close quarters, that's a rare distinction in the hallowed precincts of GHQ, trust me. Besides, Ferguson likes you; he's even suggested I try to recruit you — so it looks like I have, even if it wasn't my idea.'

'What the hell would I actually *do*, though?'

'God, loads of stuff, you've seen most of Rommel's rear end, none of us has. You know how to plan raids, what makes for success, even better you know what *not* to do. You know our particular enemy Herr Oberst Hahnemann; you're the one who buggered up his little game here. You understand logistics and navigation, most at GHQ couldn't find their own arse-holes. Since your last little nautical jaunt you can class yourself as an expert on amphibious landings, and Fergie has influence, so if you want in, you're in.'

'I'd feel like a total bastard, like I'm leaving L Detachment in the lurch.'

'Maybe it's just time to move on. Plenty do, Maclean's doing other stuff and nobody's complaining. You've been a commando for what now, two years? You fought at Dunkirk and before in Belgium, then Crete and now here. You've at least a dozen missions under your belt and the scars to prove it. I decided I'd had enough of being shot at once I'd got off that bloody beach, so you've no need to apologise to anyone. Besides, as a soon-to-be-married man, you'll have responsibilities.'

'I can't believe it's as easy as that.'

'Oh, nobody said anything about it being easy and before you slide seamlessly in here. You've got a prior engagement.'

Joe felt his sudden burst of near-euphoria dissipate, abruptly.

'Why is there always a catch?'

'Well you shouldn't make yourself so damned useful. Jock Haselden wants you.'

'Oh God, not bloody Tobruk again?'

'You may think that; I couldn't possibly comment. Besides, if you want top secret just pop into any café in the bazaar. Generally the waiters there know more than any of us.'

'Look, I like Jock, he's a bloody good bloke and all that, but he does have some pretty daft ideas at times.'

'This one's a peach and it's all your fault. He was impressed by the stunts you and Buck pulled with his Hebrew friends.'

'Christ, that's some kind of encore, we got completely stuffed, remember?'

'Practice makes perfect and his scheme does have a ring to it, of course *I'm* not the one going with him.'

Joe had a light bulb moment, but it was a red light — and not the sort that beckons you in for carnal release. 'Bloody hell, he's going to try and bluff his way into Tobruk, SIGs in charge and us as POWs, just blag his way through the front door. That's across 1,800 miles of enemy territory and right into his living room.'

'I did say it was ambitious.'

Alice would kill him, but the idea did have appeal. It was so bonkers it might just work. Every gun guarding Tobruk was pointing out to sea, hardly any facing inland. Even Rommel at his most creative wouldn't dream of a commando attack coming in from the desert, columns of POWs came and went all the time. Buck's SIGs were word perfect; and they all had the balls for it.

'The idea is,' Neville went on 'that LRDG will go with you and provide your taxi ride back after you've extracted, be like old times. Jock's still persuaded there are thousands of Allied POWs just waiting for you lot to come and liberate them.'

'We saw no bloody trace of any, and all that messing about in boats wasn't just for a breath of sea air, was it?

'Er no, this one is a bit like Operation Topsy. Every time somebody thinks of it, then the bigger it grows.'

'KISS,' said Joe.

'I thought you'd never ask…'

'KISS, as in "Keep it simple, stupid." The guiding principle of special ops — the more complex the plan, the more there is to go wrong, and it always does — go wrong, I mean.'

Neville was thoughtful. 'Fergie agrees with you, so do I for that matter. And complex it is, I fear. Your job, let's call you Force B, once you've got through the wire, will be to clobber those coastal guns to the east of the harbour.'

'And then?'

'The navy will, as though by magic, appear in the cove you scouted with a nice flotilla of MTBs or Fairmile launches and drop you off some infantry reinforcements, let's call this lot Force C. Meanwhile over on the west side, a couple of destroyers with landing craft will deposit a battalion of marines who will duly duff up the west side. Then you all come together and trash the port before a mass extraction. Oh and even the RAF have a role, they'll biff the place, just before you go in. Does that sound good?'

'It sounds like a prescription for total bloody chaos.'

'I've a very nasty feeling you may be right.'

Chapter Fifteen

Now We'll Show Jerry

Most secret document — only to be opened by an officer — from Supreme Command of the Army to Panzer Army Afrika. There are said to be numerous German political refugees with Free French forces in Africa. The Fuhrer has ordered that the severest measures are to be taken against those concerned. They are therefore to be immediately wiped out in battle and in cases where they escape being killed in battle, a military sentence is to be pronounced immediately by the nearest German officer and they are to be shot out of hand, unless they have to be temporarily retained for intelligence purposes. This order must NOT be forwarded in writing. Commanding officers are to be told verbally.

Afrika Corps Memorandum 1942

*

But it's "Special train for Atkins" when the trooper's on the tide
The troopship's on the tide, my boys, the troopship's on the tide,
O it's "Special train for Atkins" when the trooper's on the tide.

Rudyard Kipling: *Tommy*

Joe, Archie and Angel were with their old sparring partners from LRDG, pleasantly ensconced at Faiyum Oasis, a fertile basin scooped out of the desert just south and west of Cairo, watered by a branch of the Nile. It was here that the various elements of Force B were to gather. Joe felt a bit like Moses assembling Israelites before the flight. Pharaoh had been happy with chariots, Joe found himself burdened with their armoured descendants.

'Bleedin' tanks…'

'We were having these in Spain, Stalin he give, no he sell them to us, they were, as you say, the complete shite.'

Named after the hard-riding Confederate guerrilla of the Civil War, the Stuart was billed as a fast and versatile vehicle, armed with one thirty-seven mm cannon and numerous machine guns. They'd first appeared in North Africa in time for the Crusader battles with mixed results, handy in reconnaissance but outmoded and outgunned in tank-to-tank encounters. Light or not, tanks were not suited to LRDG-style operations and would at best be an encumbrance. The crews looked no happier than Joe and his ruffianly raiders.

'Operation Topsy,' Joe sighed. 'It just grows and bloody grows.'

'How far we goin' then mate?' one of the tankers, another estuarial type with a cavalryman's swagger chirped.

'It's how far *sir*, and I'm not your mate,' Joe corrected him. 'And the distance is classified but you'll need a full fuel tank.' This didn't make them any more cheerful.

'These old girls,' he pronounced it 'gels', 'ain't up to long journeys mind, not across desert an' stuff.'

'Tell yer what,' Archie offered, ''ow about you develop some serious mechanical fault what with them being so old like, and we 'ave to leave you all behind?'

'What, you mean sabotage our own kit so we can't bleedin' fight? Shockin' that is.'

'I'll do it for you,' Archie offered, 'a spot of inter-service co-operation.'

And that was that phase of Operation Agreement dealt with. A mere slight of mechanical hand and both the venerable light tanks were hors de combat long before they'd got close to any combat. That suited just about everybody.

'Now, if it could all be that easy,' Joe mused, a rhetorical statement. He knew it couldn't. In fact he would have trouble remembering any sortie that had worried him as much. He'd had a kind of blanket confidence that somehow he'd always get through, but this one was different. And there was Alice. A strange business, being in love, being so attuned to the soul of that significant other. Problematic, too. Worse, she was so bloody understanding, 'just one more op,' how many women must have heard that one. And, plain fact, he didn't want to go; the ease with which a new and infinitely cosseted billet at GHQ had opened up, a vista of privilege and expense accounts, had been completely seductive.

But this was how he paid for the ride.

Most of his all-too-short leave had been spent between the sheets with her, a horizontal paradise, cleansing him of the desert. She had been desperate, an intensity he could never before have even imagined, and his was a very lively imagination twinned with a fit young man's active libido. He knew she was fearful, verging on distraught — and the way she'd clung to him as they parted. She'd wept, too, and her distress had nearly unmanned him. Thank God Geordies don't cry, at least not over anything significant.

No sooner were the tanks disposed of, clanking and wheezing most convincingly, than the commandos arrived.

'God, did we used to look like that? They're all so bloody shiny.'

Even if considered irregular by more conventionally-minded officers, commandos were still very much part of the everyday army. Smartness was expected. They had no real experience of desert warfare and even less of the informal ways of LRDG/SAS, whose cavalier appearance raised more than a few eyebrows. The commandos were elite, yet these bearded banditti were *the* elite. It was now the twenty-fourth of August, the start of Operation Agreement, these hardened desert warriors first glimpsed their new charges, emerging from a shimmering, dust shrouded haze, crammed aboard a small convoy of eight three-tonners.

'I'm Colin Campbell, *Major* Campbell,' a tall, kilted officer introduced himself, elegant, rake thin, nicely chiselled. 'I'm in charge of this lot. We've got thirty-eight NCOs and ORs, plus seven officers. I'm in charge,' he added again, as if not quite sure who was.

'You're mostly from Middle East Commando, then?'

Well what's left of 'em. First Special Service Squadron, though we've not seen much service of any sort of late. Not like your lot.' He looked rather uncertainly at the untidy sprawl of bearded vaga-bonds, as if wondering if Joe and company were carrying anything contagious. 'We've got an RAF chappie along as well and a pair of navy types, there to help us guiding in boats, at least I think so, it's all pretty hush-hush.'

This told Joe that Campbell hadn't spent much time in the bazaars, or he'd probably have known every detail of the operation. 'Look,' the major continued, I'll 'fess up we're pretty much the amateurs here, you fellows have done this sort of thing before, time and again if half the stories are true. But we won't let you down.'

In a previous life, Joe might have been touched by the commando officer's earnestness, but there'd been a lot of harsh reality under the bridge since then. 'I never doubted that for a second, sir,' he dutifully replied, with his best dutiful grin, 'not for a second.' Repeating the mantra might make it come true, you could always hope so.

Combined, the two units appeared ill-matched. The SAS/LRDG lived in the desert. It had now become their natural habitat. They had developed and adapted to meet its challenges, its extremes and its demands, those demands that so hostile and unforgiving an environment naturally imposed. Physical toughness and stamina were essential, and went without saying. That much they shared with the commandos, yet Campbell's men did not know the desert; they had not yet seen its sparkling, life-enhancing dawn or the deep gilded calm of sunset. They were fit, trained and proud, but still unready.

After a brew, without which no British Army operation can possibly be undertaken, the joined up convoy moved off. The two components were not a good fit. LRDG vehicles, like their owners, were part of the desert, stripped and bristling gun buses that disposed firepower far greater than normal with any conventional soft-skinned patrol. The trucks lumbered after these trail hounds and soon fell behind.

Away from the Delta, the late summer's heat still radiated. The commandos, perched above their mountains of stowed kit, were uncomfortable and exposed, but the discomfort they felt here was only a pale shadow of that which they might expect once they left the security of the cultivated land. They had nearly 2,000 miles to cover.

Early on the road, one truck skidded over and down an embankment, cargo spilling from its ruptured bowels. Miraculously, no one was hurt. As an officer had been driving, the general view was what else could be expected?

'Bleedin' Ruperts,' Archie groused, 'can't be bloody trusted with serious stuff like driving, not even in a straight fucking line.' Crowding among the remaining seven vehicles became even more acute. Bowling along the floor of the Nile Valley, mile by mile, being progressively swallowed by the vast African continent, the force covered two hundred miles that first hot day.

The RAF bloke, pilot officer Scott, also managed to come a cropper, much to the amusement of his army colleagues whose only words of consolation were that it was a far less dramatic fall than coming down in a plane. 'That poor bastard must wonder what the hell he's got himself into,' Joe mused to David Lloyd Owen.

'Down among the riff-raff, sure to mess up his Brylcreem.'

For that night they were all billeted in a cotton mill in the small Egyptian town of El Minya. Their host was none other than John Haselden himself, who had a vast commercial stake in the country. Officers dined in his elegant villa while ice-cold beer refreshed the weary, dust-caked warriors. After the Spartan rigours of the day, it was a very relaxed evening. Joe, Campbell, Lloyd Owen and the other officers enjoyed a convivial dinner, starched linen and gleaming silverware, an imperial twilight away from the harsh realities of industrial war.

'Like Kipling,' Lloyd Owen commented. 'You'd think we were going to fight Zulus or Pathans, not Rommel.'

'Does Rommel read Kipling, do you think?'

'Hard to say, I think he might. At heart I suspect he's a bit of a romantic, doesn't let that interfere with the business of war, mind you, and he's got the Italians to contend with. Not your ideal choice of ally.'

'What about Jock, our ever attentive host?'

Lloyd Own shot him a glance. 'Very much the romantic I fancy, just look at this lot.'

The food bettered NAAFI standards by a significant margin and pristinely liveried servants kept glasses topped. European women, bright as fireflies, lent a touch of glamour and perhaps a hint of flirtation.

An orchestra played, and their host, fully at home in his wealth and taste, beamed and entertained, his eye ever attentive. It was wonderful theatre, a night to remember. Remarkably few knew this man was the inspiration behind the whole scheme; or what the final cost might be.

'I'd say,' Lloyd Owen continued, 'and not speaking out of turn, that Jock is a good leader of men, he knows the country and his ideas are bold and unexpected.'

That was a good word, *unexpected*. 'But?' Joe probed, sensing a serious 'but'.

'His planning isn't as tight as I'd like to see, strong on bold strategic moves, rather lighter on key detail. You know what the plan is for this op and it's grown and grown, like a monster out of control. What we normally do, you and I, we skulk about the sands below everyone's radar and pop up here and there to biff Rommel. That's what we do. It's *all* we do, and we've got pretty bloody good at it. The key is simplicity. Once it gets complicated I start to worry.'

'How I'd love to disagree.'

Next morning they piled southwards again, along the course of the timeless Nile, as far down as Asyut. The dirt road was no autobahn but when the LRDG vehicles peeled off, away from the road into the waiting vastness, the going got much worse. As the ride grew rougher, so the sun climbed higher. Exposed and choked by the inevitable dust cloud, the commandos began to get their first real taste, in the most literal sense, of what they'd taken on. This was just the beginning. Kufra was days away in the west, Tobruk far, far distant.

And this wasn't the worst. El Dakhla Oasis lay a couple of hundred miles south-west and there was a track of sorts, an ancient camel route that had been used for centuries, though historical connections were probably not uppermost in the men's minds as the convoy shuddered and jolted. The LRDG, sure as thoroughbreds on the home straight, knew the way, even when the ill-defined track seemed swallowed up by the shifting sands. The army drivers, however, were new to this type of treacherous, sliding and altogether unforgiving terrain. The overladen trucks frequently got bogged down and their sweating human cargo was required to dig and heave and shove the sand channels beneath stubborn, spinning wheels.

'Welcome to Professor Rommel's guided tour ...'

'Dakhla Oasis is one of the seven in Egypt's western desert, fifty miles broad east to west and a third of that in depth, an outpost of the pharaohs since 2,500 BC,' Lloyd Owen lectured. 'It's not one settlement but several, scattered along a chain of sub-oases.' And here they were, exotic to those who'd not been before. Mud-walled, silent communities, dun-coloured and labyrinthine, seemingly as ancient and enigmatic as time.

Cool waters were welcome bliss, but their lavish feasting from the night before was not to be repeated as they ate Maconochie's stew and bully beef. Moving out and still heading south-west, they faced the crushing, unpredictable jolting over rock-strewn wadis or that mad rush, scaling the great breakers of sand dunes, risking a disastrous slip over knife-edged ridges. Movement and momentum were critical to continued progress. Heat engulfed them and dust enveloped them. These 'balaklavering' rushes were a case of every truck for itself. If you got bogged down, you were on your own and it was time to dismount, unload and get digging, seared by the merciless sun.

'I'm not sure about our Scottish friend,' Joe had confided to Archie. 'He really doesn't look like he's enjoying himself.'

Major Campbell, who had now clearly contracted dysentery, was in a worse state than most. Such unrelenting hardship was bound to be pure hell for anyone exhibiting symptoms of illness. The LRDG were past masters at this crossing-the-desert game, past masters at anything to do with Sahara generally. As the professionals, they halted every hour to let the amateurs straggle in. Everyone's sense of humour began to evaporate as surely as the water boiled in radiators. 'Like a bleedin' nanny or wot? Some bugger shoulda' let these silly sods know what they were in for, maybe even though' abaht a bit o' training?'

At last they passed the brooding russet bulk of the Gilf Kebir, southern marker for the impenetrable waste of the Great Sand Sea, bigger than the whole of Ireland. Happily, this obstacle was now behind them and the way to Kufra was clear, along the old caravan trail joining the oasis to Wadi Halfa and distant Khartoum. Almost clear, anyway, since there was an alarum as the dust of another column churned in the distance. The accepted drill was that, in the event of colliding with enemy forces, which this far south would probably be Italian Auto-Saharan patrols, LRDG would form a well 'tooled-up' defensive screen while the commandos would barrel on straight for Kufra. In this case, the interlopers turned out to be friendly SAS en route to more mayhem elsewhere. Much cheering and waving, alarm over.

By the time they came into Kufra, they'd covered just under 1,000 miles in eight days. It was now the thirty-first of August and they'd have six days in Kufra, a surreal environment for those not accustomed to it. Many of the larger buildings were inherited from their Italian builders, with wonderful shade and cool, limpid waters. For the officers, there was much business to be done.

Stirling and his SAS crew were flying into Kufra aboard Hudsons while Buck, Russell and his SIG squad were delivered by Bombay aircraft. As ever, the SIG were different, apart. After all, where there was one turncoat, there could be more. Those simmering tensions between

British and Jews in Palestine didn't make for instant bonding. Haselden, the universal ringmaster, making his grand entrance, duly arrived on the fourth of September and convened a general officers' briefing.

'Reminds me o' Harry Lauder,' Archie commented sourly, 'an' I never liked him neither, too far up hisself.'

Joe felt he should stand up for their presiding genius and CO and not allow such chatter. Trouble was, he was thinking just the same.

Like Montgomery, Haselden radiated confidence. Even in its adapted form, this operation was still his child. Oozing charisma, he possessed the gift of carrying all before him, as though the effort of will could influence reality. This briefing, if high on aspiration, was rather low on realism. Haselden was convinced the port's defenders would comprise nothing more formidable than low-grade Italian units.

'Nothing more than a few bored Eyeties who are about to get the wake-up call of their lives. My sources confirm there's at least 4,000 Allied POWs incarcerated inside the perimeter, with four times as many corralled in camps south of Benghazi. We're going to hit Rommel where it really hurts, in his fuel line. The Wops can't find him enough and we're sinking a good deal of what they can scrounge up. No fuel, no tanks. I'm not saying we're going to win the war with this show but, if we get it right, we'll kick old Erwin in the goolies and that might just make a difference, might be *the* difference.'

Stirling was outwardly as ebullient as ever, though the strains of constant action were etched into his face and he looked a great deal older than twenty-five. He and Mayne, outwardly unchanged, had been as glad to see Joe as he was to see them. Christ, these men were now pretty much his family, the real kith and kin back in Northumberland seemed insubstantial by comparison, a memory from another life. And no, he hadn't written again to Evelyn. Memo to self, if you survive, do so. Mayne had crammed the ageing Bombay with his travelling supply of liquor, as ever he wasn't stingy. Spirits rose — and why not?

Again, similarly to Monty, Haselden had the ability to cascade his enthusiasm through all ranks. His briefings were the first chance the men really had to understand their target and the full and ambitious scale of this fucking operation. There were no dissenters, despite the distances, the manifold dangers, uncertainties and staggering odds. They were all up for it.

The really cunning part of Haselden's plan was the use of the SIGs. Buck's men, perfect in their role, would pose as DAK while the commandos would appear as their quiescent captives, looking suitably dejected. The fact they'd be crammed in Allied transport, suitably re-branded with Afrika Korps insignia, was immaterial as the Axis had a large stock of captured vehicles. The ruse would get them up to the wire. It *might* get them through. If the guards grew suddenly suspicious, then they'd be swiftly silenced.

'That's all splendid,' Stirling commented as he, Joe, Mayne and Lloyd Owen sipped beer in the near opulent surrounding of a deserted colonial villa, a signed photo of Il Duce still presiding. 'But I'm not sure about all these phantom POWs, did you see any?'

'Nary a one,' Joe confirmed, 'and I'm not sure about Eyeties only. We distinctly saw German security types around, had to shoot our way past 'em and I'm bloody sure there'll be more up on the escarpment. Seeing as we fully recognise the importance of Tobruk, I doubt Rommel hasn't.'

'We're going after Benghazi,' Mayne added. 'I don't like it.' He threw a glance at Stirling who could only shrug. He clearly wasn't that keen either. 'We've been once too often already and Jerry's a fast learner. He's beefing up security on all the airfields, brassing them up isn't the easy sport it used to be.'

'I like Jock, as you both know,' Stirling went on, 'bloody good bloke and brave as a lion. But, and it's a bit of a big but, he tends to believe his own bullshit and that's dangerous. It's easy enough for the Gaberdine Swine to dream away in their ivory towers, nobody's shooting at them and they've about as much grasp of reality in the desert as I have of astral physics, whatever that is.

'So look here young Milburn,' he went on. 'You might be a low life Geordie oik on the make, but you're *our* oik and nobody else's. If the shit does hit the fan — and I've a nasty feeling it will, just get the hell out, bugger off sharpish and bring those other two renegades with you. Natural born thieves, cut-throats and scoundrels aren't as easy to find as you might think.'

Later that evening, as the cool of night came down and a fire was lit in the absurdly ornamental grate, nice Carrara marble, fine veined and intricate, a memory of Rome in the reaches of a new empire, Joe and Mayne kept talking. Paddy was in that easy expansive mode halfway between dour sobriety and fighting drunk.

'Occasionally I wonder what the bloody hell any of us is going to do if we get out of this business alive and in one piece. Just go back home and pick up the threads? Not sure if I fancy being a small town solicitor. The place will seem an awful lot smaller and writing up some old dear's will isn't quite going to compare.'

'Before, well before all this, before I joined up back in '40, a lifetime ago, all I wanted to be was a solicitor, too. I wanted to be a *professional*, wear a suit, not overalls, no dirt under me fingernails, probably even own a car, marry the girl I thought I was in love with and live happily ever after with a mortgage on a four bed semi and enough to pay school fees for the kids.'

'And now?

'God knows. I'm in love with someone else and my only trade is killing.'

Kufra was at least the chance for officers and men to get to know each other. Something of a cliché, Joe reflected, but those bonds of comradeship would be the threads that could make all the difference on so complex and risky a mission, or so he profoundly hoped. The four main groups, LRDG, SAS, commandos and SIG, tended to keep apart, especially SIG — nobody wanted anything to do with them. Besides, their aloofness was a necessary part of the drama they were to enact. Joe, Archie and Angel were the exceptions; they knew Buck, Russell, Tiffin and Shai already.

Campbell, slightly older and a something of a strict disciplinarian thought of as 'old school', but a superb soldier and much respected, was now increasingly and obviously being debilitated by sapping dysentery. His second-in-command, Lieutenant Graham Taylor, had at least seen service with the New Zealand patrols of LRDG and was cast in that informally aggressive and forceful mould. Lieutenant Michael Duffy had also served a desert apprenticeship so they weren't all novices. It made a difference.

Two other officers, lieutenants Ronald Murphy and Mike Roberts, came from Joe's old outfit the Northumberland Fusiliers, now working as machine gunners for the duration of the war. Roberts also had responsibility for MT overall, as ever the desert took a high toll of vehicles designed for far less harsh terrain.

Campbell wasn't the only one sporting tartan; Lieutenant Hugh Sillito was with the Argylls and Second Lieutenant Bill MacDonald, a Kiwi, had fought in the Spanish Civil War, something he and Angel swiftly discovered they had in common. Tom Langton, also a lieutenant, was a tall, lanky officer from the Irish Guards, now adjutant, a former rowing blue with a history of surviving some risky operations already behind him.

Lieutenant George Harrison of the Royal Engineers led a section of eight sappers, keen to start blowing things up as sappers love to do. Lieutenant Henry Trollope, or 'Trolly', commanded the signallers. Unlike many of his fellow officers, Trolly did not like the desert and did his best to minimize its excesses. A hammock beneath shady palms suited him just fine. He hadn't enjoyed his trip so far and was pretty sure it was going to get far worse.

'Old' John Poynton was a gunner, possibly as ancient as thirty. He and four artillerymen were from coastal defence. Poynton, as Joe found out, had taken care to conceal the fact he had a barely healed left arm, broken only a few weeks earlier in Cyprus. Another gunner was Lieutenant Bill Barlow. He wasn't christened William, but Hugh, and for whatever reason disliked that name. He did like the desert, though, had earlier seen service at Tobruk during the siege and had fought throughout the North African War. Medical care would be provided by Canadian Captain John 'Gibby' Gibson RAMC. Joe liked him immediately, a sound MO in the desert could be a proper life-saver.

Squadron Sergeant-Major Swinburn from the Leicesters was the senior NCO and a very big man indeed. Very much the epitome of the stiff-backed professional, he commanded instant respect. Sergeant Evans came from the Welsh Guards, Jock Walsh from the Black Watch, Paddy O'Neil, unsurprisingly an Irishman, from Tipperary and the armourer Sergeant Alford RAOC out of the southwest of England. Included in the ranks was another rugby international, a delighted Mayne had someone he could converse with.

For the best part of a week, the force stayed beneath the palms of that ancient oasis, merely the most recent band of desert warriors to drink from its wells. Kufra remained timeless. Even the Italians, setting their reviled stamp, however briefly, on the necks of those they'd conquered, had made little real impact. And now they were gone, and their performance in the war didn't suggest they'd be coming back any time soon. Hasleden's arrival on the fourth had been the trigger to dispel any incipient stir-craziness.

'Got to hand it to the bugger,' Stirling pronounced, 'he's a bloody inspiration. Not many people could tell a whole bunch of chaps who are already a long way from anywhere, that they're going as far up Rommel's arse as you can get and about to take on God knows how many defenders, even if they're only the Wops, in well dug in fortified positions straddling the best defended harbour in the whole of bloody Africa and get them to like it. I almost believe him myself.'

'It's still too bloody big and too bloody complicated,' Joe groused.

'Well you're spot on there, I'm afraid. Even your pal Fergie don't much like it and if an intelligence Johnny can see something, it must be pretty bloody obvious. The Navy for God's sake and the RA-bloody-F, MTBs, marines and, oh yes, us. The only ones who've done this before and we're the sideshow for the sideshow.'

Poynton, the gunner, was equally unimpressed. 'I was supposed to have two dozen men and now I've got four. We're to man a series of Italian guns once they're taken. That's a big order for four blokes. Do we know exactly how many working guns they are, what calibres?'

It seemed 'we' didn't. Joe couldn't recall if it was Napoleon or some other bugger who'd said 'the cult of detail is the religion of success.' Even though he might, if indeed he had said that, have forgotten in the key moment down Waterloo way, it was a bloody good saying. Nobody had an answer for Poynton, except that his quartet of gunners was likely to be very busy.

Buck and his team were industrious with their artwork, giving the three-tonners an Axis makeover. The SIG were bloody thorough. Each door carried the distinctive sign of the black palm tree backed by a swastika. Written over every bonnet was the symbol Beutezeichen — 'booty,' and even the necessary divisional marker, ER 372, was added, a nice touch and a very credible detail. That last evening, everyone enjoyed a good supper, perhaps not up to the standard of Haselden's fare, but still memorable, washed down with grog and easy camaraderie. They all knew this was their Rubicon — there was no going back.

'I used to like it when there was just us, and the desert, and the odd enemy,' Lloyd Owen mused, sipping tepid ale from Paddy's inexhaustible stock. No wonder the plane seemed so nose-heavy. 'This bloody war's got too damn popular.'

'You've got to wonder,' Stirling added, 'if dear old Ralph Bagnold, Pat Clayton, even the dreaded Almasy, ever thought how their desert travels in the thirties sowed the hydra's teeth for this lot. I'm bloody glad they got the ball rolling, of course, or I'd probably be relegated to the Home Guard by now, Paddy would be banged up for sure and young Milburn here would just be an uppity squaddie somewhere very boring.'

'I'm glad you're looking forward to the next 700 miles of the worst kind of desert conditions,' Lloyd Owen smiled. 'I've got to get us through the Zighen Gap, then across two belts of sand sea. I'm aiming to slide through the next set of narrows, avoiding the Kalansho Sand Sea and we'll give Jalo a respectable berth.'

'Grand job, being a tour guide…'

'Ha, well you're not the only ones going through the wire. We're up for taking out the RDF station just inside the perimeter. GHQ, in their ancient wisdom, have equipped us with a shopping list of desirable loot they'd like us to grab and there's always a few planes we could shoot up.'

'Speaking of planes, this is a pretty big convoy?'

'The tricky part of this long haul up to the coast is passing the enemy at Jalo. I'm aiming to slip between them and the sand sea during the night. The Eyeties send up regular daily sweeps morning and evening. We need to be well clear before dawn and lie up at Hatiet Etla, that's about ninety miles south of Tobruk. I'd like us to be there by the tenth.'

Their desert journey continued through broken country split with many hills and wadis. Every time they stopped and Lloyd Owen and Joe marked progress on the map, one of the commando officers would be bound to wander over, demand to look at the map and then take bearings on the different features shown on it in order to check their position.

Joe had to keep pointing out that it was SAS/LRDG practice to rely far more on the navigator's dead reckoning than on bearings taken from anything marked on a bloody Italian map. Taking a lot of fancy bearings might have been all very well at the OCTU, but it was a waste of time, and indeed, dangerous in their situation. The difference between experience and bull, the commandos still had a lot to learn.

Hatiet Etla was a good lying-up place with plenty of scrub around to camouflage the vehicles; seven commando three-tonners and five LRDG trucks. There was time for drill and last minute rehearsal. One of the LRDG, Ken Tinckler, who spoke German, acted the German guard who became suspicious and called out to the guard commander. The dispirited British prisoners at once leapt to life, produced weapons, wiped out the guard commander and drove off. Joe and Lloyd Owen were impressed.

Angel had found common ground with Kiwi MacDonald who'd served with the International Brigaders. 'I'm lucky to be here at all. When we got back to Blighty, the few of us that did, I was treated like public enemy number one. This was about the time of Munich and appeasement was all the rage. Plenty Brits thought Hitler was a good bloke and dead cert to fight the commies. Took me six months to get back and I couldn't get a job, the union helped but even some of them were windy. I tried joining up straightaway in '39, but the army wouldn't have me. Bloody ironic. I'd spent a year fighting fascists but my country was ashamed of me.'

'Not all of us were supine back home.' Mike Roberts picked up the thread. 'I was a lad in Stockton eleven years ago. The tenth of September was a Sunday and in the early afternoon the British Union of Fascists motored up in a convoy of hired coaches, around a hundred led by their spin doctor, some twat called Collier. Their column halted by Victoria Bridge on the south side of the Tees. Some were from Manchester, others Tyneside. I remember how they looked, their bloody black shirts. They dressed ranks and marched along the High Street to just north of the Town Hall like a bunch of fucking storm troopers.

'If they'd hoped to succeed through stealth, they were going to be sadly disappointed. Some of our local activists had got wind of the planned demo and trades unions had taken up the gauntlet, organising a counter-rally with perhaps 2,000 of us shouting down Collier's shite as he tried to stir up a crowd. Even his loud-hailer couldn't help. The only people who didn't seem to be aware were the coppers.'

'I sort of remember this. Like a mini Cable Street, wasn't it?'

'Bastard Collier, realising the odds were pretty much stacked, decided on a rapid tactical withdrawal to the lee of Silver Street to regroup. Then with the river at their backs the Fash attempted a stand. I was only eleven but, like everyone else, pretty much 'tooled up.' We had pick-axe handles and other gear. We chucked rocks, half-bricks and spuds, each with a free razor-blade inside. At least one of the bastards lost an eye. A couple dozen needed hospital treatment and a whole lot more would carry the bruises for a while. The BUF didn't hurry back to Stockton. And now I'm fighting the bastards here, a bloody long way from the Tees.'

*

On the bright, hot morning of thirteenth September the combined force moved off, driving north to about forty miles from the wire. This was a sobering march. Ahead lay the enemy, secure in his fortified lair. Surprise and guile were the commandos' only advantages. If bazaar gossip had reached Tobruk, they could be pelting straight into an ambush.

Soon it would be time to part. Haselden's men with Joe, Archie and Angel were to bowl boldly down the main road, relying on their cover, with Buck, Russell and the SIG playing their allotted roles. Lloyd Owen would breach the perimeter two hours after the commandos, LRDG taking on any opposition in their path. Two trucks would be parked up to provide a rearguard and the rest of the patrol would hit the RDF station, blending vandalism with constructive larceny.

They'd then fall back to the perimeter and set up as a blocking force. At dawn, they'd attack again, this time hunting enemy aircraft. Once the attack was over, LRDG would come out via the eastern gate and hold this for the rest of the day until they were ordered back inside yet again, this time to free POWs and herd their charges to the shoreline where the navy would take them off.

'All that's a pretty tall order for a twenty-man patrol,' Joe cautioned as they sipped an evening's Sundowner; the Rhodesian cocktail had caught on. 'Can't argue with you there, any one of our precious objectives should be enough; strike hard and fast, then bugger off before the skies fill.'

'Surprise has always been our trump,' Joe continued. 'Once you've played it, it's time to go.'

Joe obliged Campbell, pinched and grey-faced, with a group photo, which was bound to be against regulations, like a university OTC. Seven young officers stared back at him, two in kilts; the rest in random khaki. Slender, bearded and confident, they stared at the camera, looking destiny in the eye. Joe had long since dumped sentiment but now; he could feel a lurking lump, a swelling of pride that he was with these men. They were all magnificent.

There wasn't much more to be said. They were just actors on the stage, not the impresario, the song not the singers. Worrying was part of their job, it had kept them alive — but this one was different. Bigger, *too* big, Joe kept coming back to the same glum conclusion, just too fucking much of it, a jigsaw with too many pieces, drop one and we're all buggered.

So, on the evening of the thirteenth the force moved once again towards Tobruk, with clouds of dust rising high in the air from the ploughed up desert which had been the scene of so much bitter fighting. They were all rather quiet and at the occasional halts conversation was a little forced. Their approach ran through the old Crusader battlefields of dismal repute. At El Duda the skeletal detritus of war surrounded them, a surreal, lunar landscape of industrialized destruction; twisted, broken barrels of abandoned guns pointing in mute supplication to an empty sky and the scorched and blackened shells of burnt-out tanks. On the far horizon there was movement, dust of other vehicles. They had caught up with the war.

It was almost the moment of parting. Joe felt an unaccustomed knot in his gut. Normally, he didn't suffer from pre-action nerves. This time was different. A big part of him — and he knew Archie and Angel felt the same — would have loved to head up from Kufra with Stirling and the rest of the SAS to biff Benghazi. It wasn't likely to be any kind of picnic but there was something frightening about Tobruk. Lloyd Owen clearly felt it too. The silence was heavy, just the smoke from their fags curling up into the cool of evening.

'A bit of a change now isn't there,' the LRDG officer noticed. 'We've been a bit bored by our commando friends, might as well admit it, and Buck's crew are decidedly strange but now, with the wire just ahead I feel pretty kindly towards us all. I don't envy you fellows your job and I think it's a damn fool idea, but I respect the sheer balls of every last man of us.' They shook hands, just like the movies, and the two columns went their separate ways. Ahead lay the enemy and just the enemy; there really wasn't a way back.

As if to offer a fanfare the night skies lit up with fingers of searchlights and then the steady, drowning drone of heavy bombers.

'Christ it's the bleedin' RAF … and bang on time for once.'

Ack-ack boomed out across the darkness puncturing the thin desert air. It felt odd to be back in the real war, even at a distance. Now the whine and crump of the bombs, gouts of flame like a diabolical fifth of November, shock waves reaching out.

'That'll shake the bastards,' an optimist observed.

'Just wake the buggers up, more like,' a pessimist replied.

Joe was with the pessimists, he could see Lloyd Owen was too. Surprise and stealth had been their constant watchwords. What was the point in a fucking air raid? Every German unit would be on alert, damage would be minimal and the whole place would be wide awake and on the qui vive. Joe just felt naked on their scrubby waste of dusty earth.

Time to go; Joe had half expected Haselden to quote the Agincourt speech or at least Tennyson, though perhaps *the Charge of the Light Brigade* didn't set quite the right note. They'd blundered into the Valley of Death by mistake. Joe and everyone else knew exactly where they were headed.

As light thickened and in their re-branded trucks, the commandos barrelled across the last ragged fringe of open desert towards the coast road, throwing out a billowing cloud of dust that marked their passage. 'Fuck,' from Archie. This wasn't a general observation, they could see the equally unmistakable haze from an enemy patrol moving along a parallel course. The setting sun was low in the west and Joe saw they'd a crucial advantage. Without waiting for instructions, he gave the order to drive fast in open formation towards the enemy. For these *had* to be the enemy. Shit, it wasn't an auspicious start.

For desert raiders, being able to dispose massive firepower in an instant conferred an immediate and enormous advantage, likely to be decisive. Convoys of Axis vehicles could very quickly be deterred from resistance by a few well-directed non-lethal bursts. Those which were made of sterner stuff would receive the full deluge. This wasn't buccaneering; rather it was a micro-version of industrial warfare. In such sharp, sudden encounters, he who shot first with accuracy and weight of fire would decimate his opponents and shred their vehicles. The commandos were very well trained, well rehearsed and possessed an awful lot of guns.

Swift as terriers, the British raced to intercept. Archie crouched over one of their machine guns, Joe hunched up against the anticipated crack and whine of enemy bullets: he felt that the radiator in front seemed very large and vulnerable. There was no fusillade as the Italians were totally surprised and disorientated, never imagining they'd encounter the Allies so far behind their own lines. There wasn't a fight; one truck load and a Fiat command car just gave up.

If this was the measure of the opposition, then Haselden's predictions were spot on. There were six of them in all, ill-armed and raggedy. Their guns joined the general cache stowed in the trucks. Half the prisoners fell to the ground in tears and screamed about their homes and families.

'What are we going to do with these fellows?' Haselden asked innocently, as his attempts to question his gibbering captives just unleashed more torrents of pleading. Campbell, grey-faced with pain and exhaustion, stayed mute.

'We have to kill them,' Joe confirmed. 'We've no room for prisoners and we can't let them go.' Haselden winced as though in pain himself, such brutal realities didn't quite fit the vision.

'He's right,' Campbell stated flatly. 'Get it done and we keep moving.'

Haselden turned away. Joe glanced at Archie and Angel, who'd already taken position behind the terrified Eyeties. Archie had a Beretta nine mm SMG, nice touch in its way, and Angel a Thompson. The staccato fusillade was drowned out by the symphony of crashing bombs, just reaching its crescendo. There was no more wailing, the Italians sack-like in death, a couple still shuddering, sand-soaking rivulets of blood, pooling in dusty puddles.

It was a moonless night as the column moved off towards the wire, driving in line astern. The distance was around fifteen miles and Joe aimed to reach the outposts at 22.00 hours. First they had to scale the escarpment, Sidi Rezegh of evil fame. This necessitated clearing rocks and half-building an accessible track. Nobody mentioned the dead Italians, tumbled into hasty graves.

'Fucking radios,' someone complained, 'can't raise LRDG, can't get any fucker.'

'Keep trying,' Campbell snapped.

'Got off to a real good start, ain't we?' Archie exhaled sourly.

You could hope things might get better but then you'd need to be a real optimist.

It had begun.

Chapter Sixteen

The Italian House

Along the twisting terraces of broken view
The silent colonnades, the shattered arch
Look down on dust-masked things that pass
Tired, waving shadows in the ghostly streets
Stumbling in rubble spewed from gaping mouths
New torn in tall, smooth walls, cool-drenched
    E. Yates: *Salerno Fragment*

*

Pfc. Al Thomas: *That's war*; Pfc. Charlie Bass: *What's war?*; Pfc.
Al Thomas: *Trading real estate for men.*
    The Sands of Iwo Jima (1949)

*

Joe was again reminded of Tennyson's poem *Charge of the Light Brigade*,
which had thrilled him at school. So had Errol Flynn in the movie even
if, for whatever bizarre reason, the action had been set nowhere near the
Crimea, but somewhere on the North West Frontier. The actual cavalry
charge had been bloody great though, even if Errol didn't make it back.

'*Into the Valley of Death rode the six hundred,*' he quoted aloud; aware this mightn't be such a good precedent.

'We ain't nowhere near six 'undred,' Archie corrected him, jolting alongside, 'an' it's the coast, innit, not a valley.' Tennyson hadn't been on the east end curriculum. 'Nah, too busy learnin' 'ow to thieve proper an' keep out the 'ands o' the peelers.'

After cleaning up their little mess, Haselden's commandos, each three-tonner holding about thirty soldiers, drove straight for the wire. One vehicle only, in approved LRDG manner, was left behind with its distributor cap removed and concealed, a last ditch insurance and getaway. They now had about four miles to go.

Buck drove the first vehicle, each of the others driven by one of the SIGs. They carried their fake passes and papers, good enough for casual scrutiny. Anyone who decided to peer too hard might find his life expectancy dramatically curtailed. Joe, with Archie and Angel, rode shotgun in the last truck.

Now and at last about to hit the main highway, they saw two German Opels motoring straight at them. These they simply ignored and were ignored in turn; so far so good. Once onto the flat, hard tarmac, the first they'd been on since leaving the Nile Valley, they simply merged with the flow. Nobody took any notice. Why would they? Such convoys were a common sight and the Axis nearly had more allied vehicles than the Allies. For the commandos, this was a moment of bliss.

'I'd forgotten what just bowling along felt like,' Haselden confided to Joe. 'The Light Brigade I heard you quoting didn't have it quite so easy.'

At the fence, Buck, the consummate actor, leaned languidly out to show his papers but the bored Italian sentries just waved them through. The bluff had worked. Their great, long, gruelling journey through the vast expanse of desert had not been wasted. Haselden was right. The

SIGs were sublime, even bandying casual insults, in best Afrika Korps mode, with their 'allies.' Joe could feel the tension of high morale; many seemed to think the hard part was the travelling. He really, *really* hoped they'd be right.

Once inside, they drove on unchallenged except for a minor road rage incident when passing a German convoy heading in the opposite direction. One vehicle, likely a staff car, struck a glancing blow off the bumper of the middle commando truck. Shai thought the car belonged to a senior officer. Wisely, nobody on our side stopped but the angry voices followed them into the gathering darkness:

'Verdammte Scheisse, du Schwachkopf! Ich fass es nicht, du blöder Idiot,' spiced with other even more colourful epithets, fading as they sped on.

They could hope the incident might be written off to the usual hazards of a busy military highway but, soon after, the raiders discovered they had an attentive escort of three motorcycles, two with 'tooled up' sidecars, sleek, very business-like MG34s, barrels gleaming. These could be, probably were, military or field police. This might not be so good. After what seemed like an eternity, as their shadows buzzed around, the bikes, apparently satisfied, sped off.

It was now nearly 21.00 hours, fully dark. What looked like a cliff-edge loomed ahead menacingly. Haselden casually confirmed, 'that's the bomb-proof oil storage depot we must destroy later tonight.' All around lay the tented camps of the enemy. Like Alfred among the Danes, they prowled un-noticed, sheer dazzling bravado was their talisman. The enemy didn't credit that the British could pull off such a stunt. The ruse was brilliant and had succeeded beyond reasonable expectation. Buck and his team played their roles to perfection. Getting out again of course, by whatever means, might not be so easy.

Bertie Buck was leading the convoy, seeking the minor junction which would access the track leading down towards the target zone and landing cove. This was where it should have been but someone had, very inconsiderately, thrown a substantial fence across. Shit. An anxious halt as Buck with Joe disappeared into the night, groping for some way through.

'It's really not on,' the SIG officer quipped. 'We come all this bloody way and they can't even offer us a decent road in.'

The delay only lasted a few moments but to the tense commandos, fingers close to gun-butts, it seemed a lot longer. There was a second lane further down; that was clear. Off they went.

For a quarter of an hour they bumped along the sandy, rutted surface, busy sweep of the highway behind and above, scent and murmur of the sea coming closer. It all seemed so calm. Not quite, the next sentry was German, clearly less lax than the Italians on the perimeter. Shai, all smiles and handshakes, offered him a tab then cut the man's throat, his weapon brought in as their first trophy. Five hundred yards further on, the small column halted.

Men got down, easing stiff limbs and breathing clear night air, a balmy late summer's night, buzz of insects chorusing around. Nearby, they could plainly see the angular, silent outlines of the coastal command centre, their first target. Not a squeak from any enemy. They got kitted up for battle as the air raid reached its crescendo, sweeping cones of light searching the black skies as bombs still fell on Tobruk.

'Jock, you're taking a detachment eastwards from the landing cove, taking out two gun emplacements on that flank, then pushing further east and repeating the joyful process, duffing up as many enemy positions you can find, as far up as Brighton Rest Camp; odd name for somewhere on the North African coast but there it is.' Campbell, despite his weakness and exhaustion, hollow-eyed yet still bright with keyed-up tension, just nodded. 'Brighton' lay two miles or more away and there'd be no rest for anybody this busy night.

The Major was clearly very drained by his debilitating condition. At that last moment, Haselden detailed Tom Langton to accompany his group as a backup. This was sound in one respect but dangerous in another. Langton's primary role was to signal to the MTBs during their crucial approach to Mersa Umm Es Sciausc. Failure here would be disastrous. Sending Tom Langton off on a separate mission east in the treacherous, uncertain dark, could easily be fatal. In fact it was pretty much certain to be so.

Ahead of them the Mediterranean, a fine glow from the water lending a kind of dim silhouette to the broken, ragged ground. Light from search beams still poked at the heavens. Shrill commands barked at sweating AA crews rang clear across sharp night air. The hornets' nest was stirring. Nobody had twigged they were in the enemy's inner sanctum but our bombers were blasting away any initial surprise. Buck checked his watch. 'For students of precise timekeeping, we're on target almost to the minute.'

'Not bad,' Haselden noted. 'We've covered the best part of 2,000 miles across the most hostile terrain on earth, a great deal of this under the noses of the Axis. I'd say we owe ourselves a pat on the back — but let's wait till we've finished the reel.'

Pilot officer Scott, perhaps wishing he was with his comrades massed overhead, was sent off to feel his way towards the cove, clutching his Aldis lamp. As it turned out, this refused to work and he spent most of the night wandering in the dark. 'Trolly' and his comms team were setting up. Graham Taylor was ready to establish a blocking force to secure the western approaches, Archie and Angel went with him. Haselden, with Joe, Buck, Russell and the SIGs, crept up on the Italian house. Tonight the place was clearly occupied. Random kit and packing detritus was stacked around, music drifted out from the half open door, something sentimental in Italian, a gondolier mourning for his lost love or perhaps just lack of trade.

They walked in unopposed. *Just like old times* Joe mused, his Beretta unslung and cocked. The dirty, drowsy garrison, half dozing, probably very bored, were rudely awoken. There was no resistance, only shock and panic. In fairness, the front line was 300 miles away to the east.

No shots were fired. Like their deceased comrades below the escarpment, they just gave up. Haselden brusquely interrogated the twitching captives. They were desperate to be amenable but had little useful information to spill. Four were trussed and left in a corner while one, an NCO, was conscripted as guide. He wasn't very enthusiastic. They left the radio on, the soulful gondolier unaware of the shift in audience.

The captured NCO blurted in fear-laced stink that there were perhaps fifty or so gunners spread across the various emplacements. He did know and was happy to blab the location of the command post. Overhead, the blazing hurricane of the bombing raid added a blasting Wagnerian flourish, the sharp retort from AA batteries stabbing flame and fury into the sky. They still hadn't been rumbled.

Haselden commandeered the villa as his command post, 'Gibbo' was soon setting up a first aid station, while Trolly lugged over his signals kit, using one of the trucks. This would now be the nerve centre. All in all, things seemed to be going well. Allied bombers were providing cover and distraction; the commandos had successfully infiltrated without giving notice.

'Right you two,' Haselden detailed Joe and Graham Taylor who'd caught up, 'let slip the dogs of war and all that, be so good as to clear our Italian hosts from their positions between here and the port.'

It was almost like a night exercise, the two officers flanked by their 'minders,' a London Scottish NCO and two squaddies, Mackay and Allardyce. The other section leaders, Sillito, MacDonald and Barlow, were strung out left and right, Poynton and his gunners kept pace on the left flank. 'Just like a rough shoot,' Taylor cheerfully suggested. Joe could have said he wouldn't know, as the only game he'd ever shot at, besides rabbits with his old .410, were the sort who shot back.

Noise from the air raid ebbed and flowed, beating in waves. They met with no challenges. These young men, each armed with his weapon of choice, were the cream of Eighth Army; immortal, Olympian. They had collectively participated in a huge gamble, embarked upon this desperate, far flung mission and yet, certainly until now, had succeeded almost beyond hope. Nothing could stop them. Nothing *would* stop them.

At this point, the Italian NCO recovered some semblance of manhood and made a dash for it. He'd been hog-tied to a commando NCO but somehow slipped the leash and took his chances. Sergeant-Major Swinburn nailed him with his bayonet; the thrashing man squealed a bit but not for long. Private McCall suddenly went down in a burst of fire — 'blue on blue' in the modern idiom. Everyone froze but there was no encore. 'You fucking idiot,' someone hissed at someone else.

Joe was already bumping the sandbagged redoubt of one of the gun emplacements. A nervous moment as, Beretta at the ready, he crept through the narrow entrance, briefly and infuriatingly snagged on cammo net. Nobody was home; the guns and two searchlights were unmanned. *This is no fun at all.*

'What about the guns?,' Joe quizzed the taciturn Poynton.

'Tip top,' the gunner advised, 'no sights, ammo or breech-blocks but if I was collecting for a museum, I'd be dead chuffed.'

Another, smaller, position loomed ahead. Graham Taylor led the way but this was when their luck ran out. The defenders here were ready and awake. A ragged chorus of shots barked as Taylor crept down the concrete steps, loose gravel giving him away. He was dragged clear and a shower of grenades killed the Italians inside, the bangs thumping dully. The screaming went on a bit longer.

Still conscious, the injured officer was left in a nearby, unoccupied hut. He was fit enough to hope he might pick up some handy booty but the Italians had left only a single Chianti bottle and that was empty. 'I could have done with a glass,' he coughed, bubbling bloody dribble. A lung wound Joe guessed, not too good but not fatal either. With David Sillito as the new 2/IC he continued, the final flourish of falling bombs had masked the sound of gunfire and grenades.

More enemy bunkers loomed, the defenders still blissfully cocooned in their bunks. Death was swift, sudden and terrible, more shattering, lethal grenades with a full accompaniment of automatic fire. Joe did his own kicking in the door routine, breaching the most imposing of the bunkers, and a whole platoon of shocked Italians would never be seeing their homeland again. Men's faces, twisted with fear, were lit by the harsh light of strong bulbs, as though drawn from a Breughel painting. Joe caught three together in a single rolling burst, noise of gunfire louder than thunder, reverberating around the concrete tomb.

This was probably these men's sudden first and final taste of war; there were no prisoners, just the huddled heaps of restless corpses. Blood in bright red streams spilled and sloshed around their boots, splattering uniforms. Outside, he could hear John Poynton, using a captured German Mauser, energetically clearing other positions on the west flank of the headland.

This bunker was the gateway to a labyrinth of underground shelters; the commandos bombed and strafed up each gallery. Shorn off body parts littered the spaces, messier than a badly managed abattoir. Like lemmings, panicked Italians were spilling into the night. None paused to pick up a rifle. They just bolted, scattering like rabbits in front of the hunters. No captives. Bursts of automatic fire spat out, men tumbled, stumbling like spinning marionettes.

Joe marvelled, not for the first time, at how difficult it is to kill a man. A few yards in front of him, a beefy squaddie was frenziedly bayoneting a prone Italian who just wouldn't die. The commando thrust and thrust, each razor edged slice drawing a spurt, drenching killer and victim like Webster unchained. The man screamed and twisted, shrieking, his flailing hands cut to shreds.

Then there were no more enemy living.

The Brits had taken the ground they'd come here to take. Tobruk's harbour installations were now dead ahead of them. They were masters of this small peninsula. All they had to do now was hold it. Joe instructed Swinburn, the four-square Geordie Sergeant, to send up the success signal. His watch told him it was midnight. All points west were now secured but what, Joe wondered, about Campbell's detachment to the east?

After the brief sound and fury of the attack, a lull descended. Joe left Sillito in charge while he worked his way back to the villa, supporting the injured Taylor. Gibson found the bullet had nicked one lung. The officer was amongst half a dozen casualties; the rest seemed to have been hit, in the confusion, by 'friendly' fire.

'We've got off pretty lightly it seems, up to now anyway,' Gibson muttered.

'Speak for yourself,' Taylor managed, resolutely cheerful, and with plenty of adrenaline still surging. 'Tel Il Duce I'm going to sue ...'

Archie and Angel with Buck, Russell and the SIGs had been off on a private foray of their own, taking out several enemy MG and AA positions. Their job was then to act as an additional blocking force against any early attempt to recapture the peninsula. Joe heard later they'd cleared all their initial objectives, but the Jerry gunners proved more resilient and they'd had to fight off four counter attacks. They were only a handful but they'd held their ground.

'We just rolled grenades, dahn the barrels,' Archie enthused, reporting back. 'Ain't no feckin' picnic though, there's more o' the bastards poppin' up all the time, an' they ain't no feckin' Wops neither.'

Italians were one thing, Germans were another. 'I've a nasty feeling you're going to get an awful lot busier,' Joe prophesied glumly to the MO. 'We've caught them on the hop but that won't last. Where the bloody hell is Campbell?'

'I was rather wondering that myself.' Haselden looked as unflappable as ever, your better kind of avuncular headmaster, but this wasn't school sports day.

'Radio's still useless,' the rubicund Trolly confirmed, 'we're fighting half blind.'

Poynton had sent Lance-Bombardier Stanton back to report, 'the boss with our gunners, all three of 'em, is holding on but only just, we're coming under increasing pressure.'

'Have you got any of the guns in action?'

'We did think of getting at least one to fire but they're all antiques, sightless and ammunition-less. As gunners without guns we're just ordinary bloody infantry, no offence sir.'

'Oh, none taken. I just wish I could spare some reinforcements but I've nobody to offer.'

A nerve shredding hour had passed and still no sign from Campbell. The MTBs would now be close, the destroyers would be closer. The RAF had stopped dropping flares. If success could not be signalled unequivocally by 02.00 hours, the raid would be called off and they'd all be stranded, their only hope being an overland breakout with half the Afrika Korps in hot pursuit. No-one fancied that too much.

'Right then,' Haselden ordered. 'Joe, get out there, find Campbell and let's know where we're at, don't spare the horses…'

Joe had time to spare a glance around the villa. It was no longer the sort of place you'd choose to holiday in. Khaki-clad figures and a confusion of gear filled the rooms, a steady stream of walking wounded were leaving bloodied trails over dusty floors, the wireless kit bristled in lordly impotence, signallers without a signal.

Getting forward in the dark of the witching hour proved tricky. The ground was broken and unfamiliar; squat, square shapes of enemy pill-boxes rose like stumpy demons. Each had to be skirted with care. Ahead, quite far ahead it seemed, bursts of fire crackled, glimpses of flame and red hot tracer arcing. 'Fucking radios,' he grumbled to himself. The bad feeling lurking in his gut rose like bile, having been half dispelled by the thrill and fury of action, it now came back.

He'd slung the Beretta, drawn his .38 Smith and Wesson with Fairbairn-Sykes knife in the other. He literally collided with the Italian who'd stepped outside for a pee. Short-lived relief. Joe thrust up under the ribs, the wicked stiletto blade slicing through tissue to pierce the heart. The man gave up with a sigh and crumpled. There was nobody else.

Next, he nearly bumped Campbell's rearguard – ultimate irony to be shot or bayoneted by your own side. The Major, when he found him, had plenty of worries of his own. 'We got forward OK or so it seemed, up a handy wadi. Turned out the bloody place was mined.' This hadn't been anticipated; getting through proved to be something of a trial. The sappers had carefully cleared a path. This was both dangerous and hugely time consuming. Time was a commodity they did not possess.

'It was nearly bloody midnight by the time we got through. Seemed to go fine for a few moments, then we tripped a sentry post, I had to send Mike Roberts up with a section to flush 'em out, driving the Wops back onto our guns, just like woodcock really.'

'Did you see our flares?' In the stark, flickering light of tracer, Campbell looked ghastly, pain and exhaustion etched deep.

'We saw them, yes, put the wind up us even more. We're no-bloody-where near where we're supposed to be. This Brighton is about as far off as the south coast original.'

Joe was wondering where they went from here. The advance was stalled and this flank was effectively in the air. 'Look,' Campbell went on. 'I can't spare any blokes but take yourself and Tommy here and do a quick recce of the cove, bloody boats will be here soon and at least you've seen the place.'

With Tom Langton in tow Joe managed to find the beach. It was deserted, just the rush of waves filling the cove, no sign of enemy presence. This definitely was reassuring, but time was running out faster than the swiftest tide. Doggedly they retraced their steps, fearful as much of their own blokes as the enemy. Now, on Joe's advice, Campbell's commandos tried to filter in eastwards hugging the coast, one flank covered by the open sea. Each section proceeded almost independently, seeking out targets of opportunity. Mike Roberts was the first to brush an enemy pillbox and charged in, Tommy-gun blazing. Next, they came across a communications post and this was cleared in classic commando style. Joe was still bloody worried.

By now Mike Duffy's section had located the main gun emplacements but found them unoccupied, isolated pockets remained and were systematically being cleared. Their deadline loomed very close indeed.

They'd advanced perhaps a mile or so. Both Langton and Joe were fretting about the need to get back to the cove, and pronto.

Here was a gamble. 'Should we send up the flares?' Joe asked.

Campbell looked inexpressibly weary. 'Right, yes, go on do it, I'm pretty sure we've got this door bolted.'

It was now 01.15 hours and the raid was on. By the time Haselden could get the coded message *Digger* transmitted, and by the time this was received then decoded, it would be almost 02.00 hours. At least the landing cove was safe.

Joe and Tom Langton set off, yet again, to reach the cove in time to signal the MTBs. Campbell's commandos reformed and continued their eastward march in search of the alluringly-named Brighton Rest Camp. 'Have you got your lamp?'

This was basic, but Langton had stashed his Aldis back at the villa. 'Christ no, I thought the bloody thing would be safer in the villa.' The original time frame would have allowed for the detour back to retrieve it. Present realities did not. They had no lamp. The present whereabouts of Pilot Officer Scott and the status of his gear were unknown.

'We'll just have to use our fucking torches,' said Joe, 'good news is it worked for me last time.'

A torch isn't an Aldis lamp, far less powerful and throws a white rather than a red beam. Langton stayed on the east side of the cove, Joe jogged over the shingle to the other. Shingle. Once he'd been on a rare family holiday to the real Brighton, the one back home. Shingle beaches there, too, and he remembered the sound his plimsolls made as he ran delightedly over the unfamiliar, sinking surface. Then the bright summer sun, warmer than any he'd experienced in cooler Northumberland, reflected off bold, white-capped waves breaking in from the Channel while holidaymakers crowded the front, summer frocks and straw boaters.

Four years before the war, a whole different world.

Their signalling had been due to commence by 01.30 hours; three long flashes every two minutes on a northeast and easterly bearing. There was no sign of the MTBs. The beach was very lonely, just the sibilant hiss of waves and a fitful moon that reflected off a very empty sea. Joe realised he'd lost his watch in the earlier scrapping, bugger. He stared as their feeble flashes were swallowed up in the indifferent darkness but then, not long after 02.15 say, he saw two of the unmistakable MTBs slide into the cove. His spirits surged but what the hell should he do now? Keep signalling or get down to the beach?

As a compromise, he wedged his torch and left the beam on, but no sooner had he covered a couple of hundred yards than he saw a light out to sea, apparently signalling. So now he dashed frantically back to his own and re-commenced flashing. Nothing happened. He couldn't communicate with Langton, who was several hundred yards east. He could hear noises from the shoreline; those first two boats had obviously made it in. Joe headed back to the beach.

The pair of MTBs was busily unloading the Northumberland Fusiliers detachment with their Vickers machine guns. The infantry seemed very smart and clean. Still, the newcomers were only a single platoon, led by a burly NCO who introduced himself as Sergeant Miller. Joe's old regiment — but he didn't recognise any of the faces.

'Where the bloody hell's the rest?' He was aware of how plaintive he must have sounded, and nobody had an answer. As though in training for some Forces' Olympics, Joe pelted back to his torch and started signalling again. By now the hornets' nest was thoroughly stirred. Searchlights were quartering the skies and coastline. A battle was obviously raging westwards. Tantalisingly, the lights showed up the rest of Blackburn's flotilla, still searching for the cove, but the sleek MTBs got caught in the searchlights and he could see plainly their tell-tale wake and tracer bouncing off one of them. Joe reckoned, dismally, that there was now very little chance of the boats getting safely into the cove.

Dawn was fast approaching, grey light just beginning to filter out the darkness. It was hi-ho and down we go, back to the beach for Joe. The Fusiliers and their kit had gone, moved off inland as he'd ordered. One of the boats had gone too. The other remained stuck fast in the shingle, abandoned. Crewless and forlorn. He could identify with that. It was definitely getting lighter. He took stock, both flanks of the breach were holding, further over in the west he could hear the thump and flash of eighty-eights and what he assumed to be our naval guns answering. There seemed to be a lot more of theirs. Far nearer, he could definitely hear the crackle of small arms around the Italian villa intensifying.

He made it back, just in time it seemed. The Axis had woken up and discovered the raiders' nerve centre. 'I've got the wireless truck close up,' Haselden told him, unnecessarily given that he was crouched next to it. You had to keep low, as random shots were pinging in. He could sense the net tightening. 'I sent your Geordie lot to keep the door open, got to keep the corridor going.' Haselden no longer looked like a genial schoolteacher, he was a man whose every doubt and fear was breaking loose and dancing on his shoulders. Without comms, he was pretty much isolated, unable to direct any aspect of a fight that was already passing out of his control.

'Looks like they've got around our flanks,' he confessed, 'just got to hold on.'

Joe could have asked 'for what?' but didn't, no point really; with only one platoon of Fusiliers and a perimeter already under attack from just about all sides, they weren't going anywhere.

Surprise, audacity, dash and courage had won possession of their piece of enemy North Africa, but a bridgehead without a bridge is just a trap. And it was. Aside from the Geordies and their two Vickers guns, they'd no reinforcements. The enemy was awake and recovering from any initial shock. They had thought to fight low grade Italians but were battling high grade Germans. The two arms of the commando deployment were flung out east and west forming a fragile salient. Their HQ was under attack. There was no hope of the LRDG getting close enough from inland to open up an escape route.

'SNAFU, as we'd say.'

'FUBAR as our former colonial allies would put it.'

Both correct.

*

Joe took a quick look round. Archie, Angel and the SIGs were still forming a forward block, though God knows how long half a dozen of them could hold out. The commandos had bashed loopholes through the thin walls of the villa and fortified a kind of verandah running along two sides with looted sandbags and their few Brens. It wasn't quite the Alamo, though the similarities were increasing.

'How much ammo have we got?'

Haselden just winced and looked at him. The unspoken answer was clearly *not a lot*. The rotund Trolly and his Scaley Backs were manning the perimeter, given up on wireless. Gibbo's MO station had got very busy, crammed with more serious cases, the walking wounded were bandaged and back out again. In all, Joe estimated they'd perhaps two weak platoons in and around the villa. He'd no way of knowing how strong the enemy was, but at least a couple of companies and getting stronger, the unmistakable zipping staccato of MG42s was getting more insistent by the minute.

Poynton and his tiny team of gunners had abandoned their westerly vantage, desperately low on ammunition. 'Old' John had watched with an artilleryman's eye as the shore defences swung into action against Blackburn's MTBs.

'No chance of them getting in,' he confirmed flatly. 'Like rabbits in a car's headlights. Jerry's got every bloody shore gun he possesses in action and theirs aren't like the Eyetie relics we took; they work and those boys know what they're doing. It looks even worse further up, I could clearly see one of our destroyers, far too close in and taking hits, lots of hits ...'

Joe could see it all: searchlights probing like bright scalpels, paring back the thinning vestiges of dark, the small, vulnerable craft shown up as they dodged and swerved. Each fingering beam of light instantly followed by a hail of shells, bright fireflies of tracer swooping along the cones. Still the little ships wouldn't give up. There would be no famous victory for the Royal Navy that night but he knew that wouldn't be for lack of will, or effort, or endurance. The MTBs would keep coming back, sea wolves beyond the sheepfold till, each time, the sheer weight of fire drove them off. Only dawn would bring an end to this very one-sided game. Joe was all too aware their time was running out.

Campbell's men had gone off the radar again so David Sillito had gone off to find out, retracing the route Joe had taken. 'It was bloody difficult. God knows how many enemy posts are still manned. We must have missed the buggers in the dark first time round, mines everywhere. I ran clear onto the business end of a 20 mm Breda, a very nasty sensation, till Sergeant Swinburn shot the Eyetie gunner, bloody close call though.'

'No bloody rest at Brighton either.' Jerry was as alert as alert gets, defences fully manned. 'We were greeted by a bloody storm as we tried to infiltrate the bunkers and pillboxes. They've got interlocking fields of fire with support laid on by the bigger guns north of the port. Campbell got hit in the leg, not serious, and Mike Roberts pulled him clear. We knocked a few of 'em out, chucking grenades down the air vents but that's as close as we got.'

As if to prove him right, knots of Campbell's men were coming in, the wounded major supported by two others. He wasn't the only casualty. The east flank was gone. More men were filtering back from the west, dodging the tightening noose.

'Welcome to the bleedin' Alamo.'

As night retreated, dawn showed just how many enemy outposts had been missed, the hornets' nest was buzzing. Shells from those same big guns across the harbour were now falling into the narrow salient, a Wagnerian dawn with fountains of earth, rock and dust kicked up by the impact.

His two mates plus the SIG contingent also fell back. 'There's hundreds of the bastards,' Buck concluded grimly. 'I told my blokes to dump their Axis kit, for any of us to be captured is a passport to Buchenwald. This isn't quite what we'd hoped for, is it?' Buck went on. 'We were supposed to hare off looking for POWs, there was even talk of a high ranking Axis defector and loaded pay-chests.'

'Yo, ho, ho and a bottle of fucking rum,' Tiffen added sourly.

'How did you get British gear?' Joe asked, but looking at their uniform gave him the answer.

'We had to borrow stuff from our deceased comrades I'm afraid — and there's no shortage.'

It was obvious that, as the commandos had originally stormed the Italian house, a number of the garrison entrenched nearby or just bolting from the building had got clear and raised the alarm. They'd now been able to guide several Axis companies directly onto Haselden's HQ, around which the unequal battle was raging. Full dawn meant certain annihilation for defenders, virtually surrounded, hopelessly outgunned and running low on ammo.

Haselden's dream was evaporating but he hadn't lost hope, give the bugger his due, he was equal to the situation. 'Right ho,' he said. 'I really don't like this place anymore and you can tell the landlord I said so. In the meantime, I want to get our wounded blokes clear. We've got two trucks, so let's get the stretcher cases mounted up and away.'

The two surviving three-tonners, in the lee of the building, hadn't attracted too much hostile attention though that would change as surely as the rising sun. Gibbo, with four badly wounded in the first truck and Barlow with more in the second, got moving, stray rounds careening off the metal, ripping through canvas. 'I'll ride shotgun on the first, Joe you're on the second. We jump ship as soon as they're clear.'

All a bit bloody John Wayne, Joe thought as he crammed a fresh mag into the Beretta. He had another two left, less than a minute's shooting on full auto. Every flat surface was covered in spent brass, tinkling, rolling underfoot. More walking wounded were crammed into the wireless truck, despite frequent ventilation by Jerry, it still ran. Buck drove, Angel had a Thompson. 'Bit like *Stagecoach*,' Gibbo suggested as he helped the injured Taylor, still protesting that he was perfectly capable of fighting, into the three-tonner.

The trio roared off in the dusty dawn. There was nothing subtle, a fixed charge in soft-skinned trucks against everything that could be thrown at them. And there was a lot. The windscreen in front of Joe disintegrated. Barlow cursed, wiped the blood from his eyes and floored the accelerator. Joe emptied one magazine in the enemy's general direction, no chance of hitting anything as the three-tonner bounced and skidded. Fuck – Jerries had humped oil drums and heavy stones across the track. He saw Haselden jump down as the lead truck slowed and launch himself up the shallow slope towards the enemy, Sten spitting.

Joe dismounted, yelling at Barlow to keep going, try and burst through. He was aware of Angel behind him, Thompson thumping. He could hear the hysterical sounding of German orders. As suicide clubs go, this one was pretty select. He saw Haselden go down, he raced towards the Colonel but a stick grenade tossed him, lifeless, over the sand. Bullets were spurting dust all around. He and Angel dived into a slight fold which offered the barest of cover. Joe was down to his last mag; they both were.

From the corner of his eye he saw the desperate charge had worked. The lead truck had somehow slid round the barrier, rear wheels racing then finding grip and getting clear. Barlow's truck made it too but Buck's had its front tyres shot out and ploughed into an oil drum, grinding to a screeching halt. Axis swarmed around, he didn't see what happened to Buck but there were no more shots so presumably the SIG was in the bag. Thank God he wasn't still in Axis kit. In the brief lull, they rose, crouching, and made a mad run back to the refuge, however temporary, of the villa. An encore of shots followed them but mercifully, impossibly, they made it.

'You're a lucky bastard,' Sergeant Swinburn grunted as they scrabbled onto the sandbagged verandah. 'The Colonel?' Joe shook his head, Swinburn just grunted again. Geordies might get depressed over a poor pint but Armageddon and the end of the world was treated with casual equanimity. 'Looks like you're in charge then, any orders?'

'Make every shot count, don't anybody waste ammo. Any regular churchgoers have my full permission to pray as hard as they like.'

'Most of the sappers didn't make it.' John Poynton looked no happier but then no more worried either. 'One of my lads heard tracks rumbling, so the bastards are bringing up armour, just to make sure.'

The beleaguered villa was shuddering under the increasing tempo of fire, like an earthquake in the offing. As it got lighter the shooting became more accurate and ever more intense.

'Feckin' stuffed, ain't we? Archie concluded, still quite cheerful. And indeed there was no hope. They kept on fighting because that's what they did and despite the fearful odds no one was minded to surrender.

Then out spake brave Horatius/ The Captain of the gate/
To every man upon this earth/ Death cometh soon or late/
And how can man die better/ Than facing fearful odds/
For the ashes of his fathers/ And the temples of his gods.

He'd thrilled to Macaulay in school, but now he wasn't quite so sure. A stick of planes, Messerschmitts he assumed, whizzed overhead, buggered all ways. Graham Taylor was still among the walking wounded, he'd escaped the MO's tender clutches just as they drove off. A good few others were in similar clip.

'Look here,' he wheezed at Joe, ashen-faced but not out of the fight. 'I know we're pretty much stuffed whichever way it goes from here. I thought I'd round up the rest of the zombies like me who can just about walk and we'll make a break for the beach, who knows, we might just make it and we might even get picked up.'

Joe was about to say *don't be daft* but then thought, *why not?* 'OK,' he replied, 'go for it. We'll cover you as far as we can, oh and good luck.'

'Thanks, and to you too, we'll both be needing it.'

As Taylor's tattered group stumbled and clambered towards the temporary haven of the cove, Joe could hear the battle raging out to sea. Oddly, the Axis didn't seem to fire at the weary, blood-shod little group of pilgrims. He knew they'd never make it as far as the cove, but at least they'd be captured and survive. Joe now had no more than a single polyglot platoon left to defend their tiny island. There was no sign of the Fusiliers or of Duffy or any other survivors, but he could hear the furious rattle of the RNF machine guns keeping the enemy busy off on the landward flank. This might just be enough to let Barlow and Gibson get clear.

Pilot Officer Scott had abandoned his lonely vigil down by the cove vainly waiting for more of the MTBs and made a dash back to HQ. It was quite a sprint, every Axis gun in North Africa seemed to be firing at him. Happily unscathed he reported that a German E boat, nosing unexpectedly into the cove, also opened up with its formidable firepower but only succeeded in shooting up some of the Afrika Korps. Scott, dodging from rock to rock, somehow jogged clear and fell in with Mike Roberts and Lieutenant Murphy with more survivors from Campbell's commando. They all struggled in.

The Italian House would never be a pretty seaside villa again. Small arms and mortars were raining down on the makeshift defences. Daylight now, and there was hardly any cover, a regular Rorke's Drift. More enemy were massing, getting steadily closer, ammo stocks were nearly exhausted. Joe, John Poynton and Sergeant Swinburn were in charge. The Axis came in at a rush. Sustained fire drove them back. Joe steadied his SMG on one of the sandbags, accuracy was impossible. He fired short three to five round bursts, aiming as best he could. A few of the enemy went down.

They kept on fighting. Minute by minute the odds grew heavier, but the commandos had managed to create a kind of improvised blockhouse linking some straggling tin sheds on the blind side of the villa. This Heath Robinson redoubt had room for no more than a dozen men. The rest held the sand-bagged verandah of the main building, now in some need of repair. Rounds were zinging off or punching through the tin sheets, ripping into sandbags.

As the enemy pressed ever closer, the British chucked grenades but the bombs couldn't clear the nearest ridge. 'Right lad, just hang onto that sack like a good 'un.' Swinburn got another commando to hold open an empty sandbag while he pulled the pins from two grenades and placed them inside. Leaping to his feet the big Geordie, an admirable target, whirled the sack, sling style, and sent it on its way. As this appeared to have the desired effect, he repeated the performance several times and cleared the Axis from their immediate vicinity. Amazingly, and not for lack of trying, they failed to hit him.

'Sarge, if we ever get out of this I'm signing you up for Bedlington cricketers,' Joe bellowed. 'No disrespect sir, but I'd rather play for Rommel than bloody Bedlington. Ashington for me every time.'

Most of the commandos were armed with automatic weapons, Tommy guns. Whilst these were very effective at close quarters, they lacked the rifles' range and were far more prone to jamming. They also consumed ammunition at a prodigious rate. An enemy machine gun team found a particularly good vantage and opened up, the jagged, tearing sound of the fast-firing MG42 unmistakable. Rounds clawed at the flimsy sandbags, hammered the shuddering tin plate huts. Swinburn now went into action with a Bren, firing from the hip. Again he was exposed and tempting fate, but again he came through safe and the enemy were suitably discouraged. Joe was out of ammo, he found some nine mm and a jammed Sten, loading the spare rounds into his mag. It wasn't much.

Stirring as this defence might be, it was only a matter of time. Fire from the porch side of the building slackened and the place was overrun. Grenades were practically showering down around them. Joe waited for the bomb which had just landed by his left foot to explode and kill or maim him. It went off and amazingly, he was unscathed. There wasn't much to be said for going on, most had only a few rounds left. Joe decided he wasn't quite beaten, not yet. He yelled to Swinburn that he'd lead a group of volunteers, well they were all volunteers, up onto some higher ground to the rear. The rest would cover and then leapfrog back in their wake. As desperate plans go, this was pretty bloody desperate.

Tiffen and Shai were up for it, as were Archie and Angel. 'If this is it,' Shai commented, as calmly as though he was asking for a fag in the NAAFI, 'then I'd rather go down fighting than throw in the towel.'

Tiffen nodded. 'We, my people, we've too much history with these bastard Huns already and I'm too far in to spend the rest of the war curtsying to some fucking Aryan twat and taking endless shit in some khazi of a POW compound. So let's just do it.'

They sprinted inland, aiming for the dunes that lowered sullenly above the shot-up villa. Bullets rained around them. This clearly couldn't end well but suddenly Joe, panting, tripped over one of their Italian prisoners, one of a whole bunch who'd been cowering collectively and largely overlooked by both sides. The commandos' sudden arrival, accompanied by a crescendo of so much automatic fire, provoked a collective panic. The captives rose as one man and bolted, happily in the same direction as the Brits wished to travel.

Joe was a sheepdog driving a stampeding flock, a persistent sheepdog, and drove the bleating sheep to the top of the ridge, despite a final burst of enemy fire that nearly did for everyone. A few of the Eyeties tumbled but the rest kept on running. The ruse had succeeded, but to what point? Swinburn had signalled that he couldn't follow, a second group wouldn't be so lucky and the enemy now certainly had their range.

They slid into a handy depression atop the ridge of dunes. 'Right, get fucking going,' Joe ordered the rest. Amazingly, they'd got through unscathed. 'And that's a fucking order!' He had the half-mag in the Beretta, six rounds in his .38. After that long instant's hesitation, they slid away down the far side of the dune into one of the innumerable wadis. They might just make it.

Germans were storming up after them. He waited till they were just about on him then opened up. A couple went down, the rest to ground. Searching rounds sought him out. They'd be working around his flanks. Still in the cover of the sand and harsh grass, he slithered along the lip of the dune. *I used to do this at Newbiggin*, he thought, cowboys and Indians. Today he'd rather be with the Indians.

A couple of started Huns rose up before him. He shot them both. There were more. He dodged a bayonet, shot the owner in the face. Then another came at him, no time for them to shoot. He had to grab the rifle with both hands, losing his grip on the Smith and Wesson. He pivoted and twisted, heaving his opponent spinning down the slope. He groped for the dropped gun.

Below, back at the shattered building he saw, just before the butt end of a Mauser sent him sprawling, Sergeant Swinburn take off his tattered shirt and wave it above his head. The NCO's luck, which he'd pushed to the bloody limit, somehow held. The shooting stopped. Force B would fight no more. The battle was over, we lost.

Joe had grit in his mouth, over his face and in his hair. On his knees, he tried to gather his scrambled senses. This wasn't too easy, but what *was* easy enough was to recognise the business end of an MP40 hefted by a classic four-square son of the master race, just looking for an excuse to pull the trigger.

Joe barely registered any more detail because next to the stocky landser stood a pair of immaculately polished riding boots. Idly, he wondered how you kept up such a gleam in all that dust. He didn't need to look at who was wearing them. It had to be Oberst Erich Hahnemann — and Joe sensed the jaws of his very own pit of deepest hell opening before him.

Chapter Seventeen

SNAFU

No drums they wished, whose thought were tied
To girls and jobs and mother,
Who rose and drilled and killed and died
Because they saw no other,
Who died without the hero's throb,
And if they trembled, hid it,
Who did not fancy much their job
But thought it best and did it.

   Michael Thwaites: *Epitaph on a New Army*

*

Lt. Aldo Raine: *You probably heard we ain't in the prisoner-takin'*
business; we're in the killin' Nazis business. Business is a-boomin.'

   Inglourious Basterds (2009)

*

'Drink the water,' Hahnemann advised. 'Obviously you need it after
such great exertions and it isn't poisoned, not this time.'

Joe shrugged and drank from the glass tumbler. Water had never tasted so good, as he tried not to gulp feverishly, his mouth was like a long ago dried up riverbed, slicked with the muck of ages. The glass even had Afrika Korps insignia, now *there's* finesse.

'I've paid particular attention to your career Herr leutnant, our last meeting was a most memorable one as you put me to a great deal of inconvenience. I'm heartened to see you've fully recovered. You will be needing all of your strength.'

'That's the problem with cheap muscle,' Joe mumbled, his tongue just beginning to work, 'you just can't get the staff.'

Hahnemann laughed, a dry, unconvincing sound. Joe doubted he did it very often.

'I confess, I was rather hoping we might meet again. And for the record, I bear you no malice. You are after all, a soldier fighting for your country, as am I. The mere fact you are here proves you to be a very brave man if not necessarily a prudent one.

'I find in fact we are not at all dissimilar. This might surprise you but we both owe much to National Socialism. For my part had it not been for Adolf Hitler, I'd now be a boring schoolteacher somewhere in Bavaria. You, well what might you be; an artisan perhaps, an aspiring clerk in some dingy office? Now at least you are an officer, a gentleman almost, and I know how much importance your countrymen place upon such matters.'

'I wouldn't be going around shooting POWs in cold blood, gentleman or not.'

'Ah yes, the business on Crete, I think it was, that you alluded to at our earlier meeting. It distresses me to say I've no recollection of the incident. We were all very busy. And besides, your own hands are far from clean. You shot down a bunch of our airmen in the midst of their dumplings and then there's the unfortunate Sergeant Essner whom you executed summarily and without trial.'

Joe assumed he didn't need to reply. The German was clearly at ease, enjoying himself. And why not? His side was well ahead on points.

'You may wish to know about Bruckner,' Hahnemann went on. 'It seems we're giving him a medal and no, he wasn't an agent of mine or anybody else's, just a traitor and a coward who panicked at the last moment. The man you murdered was innocent of any role in his duplicity but that's the nature of war of course, the moral high ground quickly gets covered in mud and the more you go on the deeper the filth gets. Sometimes it sticks to your boots. Shakespeare says something of the sort I recall. *I am in blood stepped in so far, that should I wade no more, returning were as tedious as go o'er.* The Scottish play, I believe?'

'Tell that to the Jews. How many have you murdered? And what exactly is their crime, just being different?'

'Ah yes, our Hebrew friends, we may have touched on that last time. A stupid business all round and such a waste of resources. Trouble is, we have to defeat the communists and so many of them are Jews as well. Tidy in one way I suppose, and the Fuhrer has always equated the two. It's really a shame you British can't just see things our way. You should be fighting alongside us, not against us. What we do here in this godforsaken desert is just a sideshow, a diversion; the real war is being fought in Russia, though I'll freely confess I'm in no hurry to see the place.'

Joe knew Hahnemann's style. This was pretty standard interrogation fare. Put the prisoner at his ease, bond with him. It saved time later with the thumbscrews. At least it gave him the chance to think. Think about what, though? Chances of escape were less than zero. If he'd wondered what lay behind the basement door in Abwehr HQ, now he knew and it was pretty much as he'd expected. They sat on either side of a battered wooden desk, bare except for a single angle-poise that cast pools of light and shadow over the scarred surface, dank concrete walls and a pair of likely lads in civvies. Two slab-faced thugs with shirts, ties and braces, not the sort you'd expect to find at the church social; ex coppers, like as not, and not exactly the homely PC Plod type.

'Hans and Karl,' Hahnemann introduced. 'Yes, those are their names, just like in your comic books. They don't speak much English, not much call for it in Munich. Both ex-policemen, as you'll have guessed, and skilled enough in their way at extracting information. It's as much a hobby as a job, and they've had years of practice on kikes and commies. They're pretty bored here too, so frankly they can't wait.'

Hahnemann let that sink in, his meaning pretty clear, *talk to me or they'll beat it out of you.* The twins certainly looked as though they were really hoping that Joe would prove obstinate. Chance for a bit of torture was probably something of a bonus out here.

'You may not believe this,' Hahnemann went on, still in that lightly conversational tone, a civilised discourse between near-gentleman. 'But I don't much care for the rough stuff, never have, so before, and with reluctance, I'm obliged to hand you over to Hansel and Gretel here, I'm going to make you an offer.'

Joe would have said 'fuck off' if he could have mustered the energy, his imagination was already filling in the blanks and the jigsaw wasn't looking too pretty. His hands weren't bound, but both heavies had automatics in shoulder holsters and they'd be looking forward to any chance to demonstrate their fast draw.

'Here is what I am able to offer. As a POW it's our duty to hand you over to our Italian friends. They're much braver off the battlefield and when their enemies are unarmed. You seemed to have killed quite a number of them earlier, mainly while they slept. To be fair, they're rarely awake and this may serve to sharpen their instincts — but I doubt it. So your choice is an Italian camp or a German one. And you'd be a whole lot better off with us.

'Now, obviously I know why you attacked Tobruk — you intended to destroy the port but I don't fully know who or how. We've a real good haul of prisoners and some will certainly talk. The amphibious landings, well that's all pretty clear, very shoddy planning if you don't mind me saying and apparently your improvised landing craft were death traps.'

'Looks like you've got it all worked out, you don't really need me.'

'Ah well, there you're wrong. Like your phantom major, I've as many enemies in my HQ as he has in yours. If I can go to them with a full breakdown of your order of battle from the landward side; who was leading, what units were involved, vehicles, direction of march, escape routes, all that sort of thing, then that would be a big feather in my cap. You know all of these things of course. I'm assuming that with your LRDG friends you came in over the desert and from the south, an astonishing feat.'

'You seriously think I'm going to tell you?' Joe spat back with a good deal more bluster than he felt, bowels churning with fright. Hans and Karl perked up noticeably, their time was getting nearer.

'Why not?' Hahnemann continued. 'The beauty of what will be our little arrangement and ours alone, is that only we will ever know. I'll keep your name out of it, nobody on my side needs to be aware. In time we'll work it all out anyway; this way I'm just front of the queue. Nobody on your side will ever realise either. You go straight from here into the cage and sit out the rest of the war ogling the frauleins; both of us win.'

Was he tempted? Of course he bloody well was. It was an easy way out. The Axis had won hands down. They'd hundreds of prisoners on their books and, as Hahnemann said, they'd work it out soon enough anyway. He could imagine Alice urging him on, what did it bloody matter, the whole show was totally fucked up anyway, it didn't really matter.

Except that it did.

'Sorry,' he said, and meant it, 'no can do. They'd drum me out of the golf club.'

Hahnemann smiled thinly. 'I'm afraid your golfing days may already be over before they've begun. And you do realise when we use such uncivilized means, we prefer not to leave any witnesses?' He barely moved his head but Joe felt himself gripped by arms of iron and dragged from the chair, playtime for the boyos.

'You can thank the Spanish Inquisition for this little trick, one of their more refined techniques. It would be best for you if we don't have to graduate onto any of the others.'

Joe was bound, his feet in shackles, wrists in fine, very tight cord, pinioned on a sloping wooden board, spread-eagled, now stripped naked and exposed. 'I'm led to believe there are those who pay for this sort of thing; gives them sexual pleasure. Can't see it myself but at least for you it's free, courtesy of the Reich.'

A fine muslin cloth was draped over the upper part of his face, the sort his mum used for cheese, so he saw through the dim light, just vaguely, suggestions of shape and shadow. It didn't matter really; he knew what he was in for. Hahnemann's tone never changed, no ranting or screaming, just the merest hint of distaste that Joe's unreasonable behaviour had driven him to this. They had moved him into a back room, possibly in a former life intended for bathing.

This was to be an altogether different type of water sport. The twins had thumped him about a bit first, just a softener or more probably simply because they could. As far as he could tell nothing was broken, thank God. Due to the stale stifling heat, bashing him was just too much effort and both goons were sweating heavily, their cheap cologne not really up to the effort; 'guaranteed to keep the most ardent torturer smelling sweet and fragrant' – probably a ready market in Abwehr and SD circles.

'Last chance,' Hahnemann suggested flatly.

Save my breath, Joe told himself, *probably need it for screaming*.

He was right. Karl, he thought it was, had picked up a watering can; how oddly incongruous this innocent piece of gardener's kit. It was painted bright green as far as he could tell and had probably never been used for anything more draconian than refreshing someone's roses. The objective part of his brain, still sort of functioning despite the funk, realised that this was part of the treatment, the everyday transformed into instruments of terror. So far it was working quite well.

They were pouring water over the muslin. He could feel it weighing on the thin fabric, then pressing down on his eyes. A surge of panic clawed through his belly. He thought he'd very likely piss himself. The cloth was pulled down, so that now his whole face was covered, the soaking material blocking nose and mouth. Somebody had once told him that drowning was merciful and painless — they were misinformed, it was instantly agonising. His mouth gaped like a floundering haddock's. Time had no meaning. They were still pouring, a steady relentless stream that mocked every twisting agony of his tortured lungs.

He must die, his whole body wracked by spasms of imminent extinction. Nobody had spoken. Then the cloth was removed and his lungs clawed for the clear sweet air of the dingy bathroom, clogged with the half hidden stench of previous torture. He'd no idea how long he could hold out before he blabbed every detail they were after — and he'd be sure to make up a whole lot more just to make the story believable.

'If we have to continue with this, and even if you don't die, there's every possibility your lungs will be irreparably damaged, your brain too I'm told; must be to do with the lack of oxygen. Ask yourself, is it worth it?'

This question was clearly rhetorical. After only three or four heaving gasps of air, the cloth was re-applied. He would have screamed now, if his breathing had been up to the job. This time it seemed even longer, surely his lungs would burst. He hovered on the brink of consciousness but Hans and Karl knew their trade, understood just how close to the shadow of death they could tread. He vaguely recognised they were chatting to each other in German, jocular, inconsequential stuff, all in a day's work for two wholly dedicated sons of Hitler's Germany.

They brought him back, again the desperate, retching gobbling of air from his anguished lungs, every effort an agony. There seemed no point in it. Nobody asked him anything. A few seconds relief and his head was forced down again, the hateful, saturated cloth draped over once more and the watering can that never seemed to empty. Heaving breath in was part of the game. Once your gasping lungs were full and the water flowed, you couldn't breathe out so the air you'd craved became a torture in itself. You had to hand it to those fucking Dominicans; they were real pros.

It seemed, as his senses reeled and buckled, that he'd been in this room for half a lifetime, the objective shard he was clinging onto guessed it was probably less than half an hour. Hans and Karl were in no hurry, a frontier posting probably brought few distractions and these were lads who clearly loved their calling. Hahnemann was right, Joe had no idea of how much of this he could take but it wouldn't be that much. He tried to fight the mounting surges of despair, twinned with panic and terror. He thrashed frantically each time the cloth was draped over his face, bloodied fingers clawing at the rough pine board. He'd never have dreamed such an everyday scrap of fabric could induce such stark terror. He knew he was gibbering.

Hahnemann had left the room, probably had paperwork to do. The boys took a break, their casual banter a further refinement in itself. He was ignored as he heaved in air. They'd get back to work in just a mo.

The door opened but they barely looked. Karl was in the midst of some funny story. Hans had probably heard it before, but laughed anyway.

Then Archie Dunmore came in with a Colt .45 in each hand, best Cagney style, and shot them both, blasts filling the small space like the clap of doom. Karl fell like a wet sack, flung over Joe, his one remaining eye fixed on Joe's. He did seem very surprised.

Was he delirious, could he have lost his marbles already? 'Get the fuck up,' Archie ordered as he and Angel, who'd followed him, unfastened his shackles. 'Can you walk?'

'I'll bloody well walk out of here,' he heard himself croak. That might prove ambitious. As he stood, the room seemed to distort like some surrealist nightmare, shapes magnifying then shrinking, the walls pressing closer. 'I bloody well *will*,' he mumbled again.

'We have rooms like this in Spain,' Angel confided, 'no good,' he added, unnecessarily. 'Not many come out.'

Joe's reeling consciousness registered that they were in Axis kit, Afrika Korps again, (few battles have seen so many swift costume changes), and he was being stuffed into a spare set. 'Worst room service I've ever had,' he managed. Angel tied his boots on then, with Archie on the other side, they marched him out. His legs were sort of functioning, but clearly not really interested in working in tandem.

They came out through the front door, 'shitty little lock,' Archie commented, 'me mum could 'ave picked it.' Nobody seemed to have heard the shots, the sentries must have buggered off somewhere. Nobody would have been expecting this sudden resumption of hostilities from a beaten enemy. And there was no sign of Hahnemann, master of the disappearing act. 'The bastard must have sixth-bloody-sense or something,' Joe mumbled.

There was a lot of activity in the square, much coming and going, knots of sullen Allied POWs in various states of disrepair — hell of a lot of navy types, the raid had been an epic shambles all round.

Tiffen and Shai were waiting with a Sd.Kfz.251 Hanomag half-track, snarling with machine guns. 'Sorry, the taxi got stuck in traffic.' He didn't ask any questions as they bundled him in, plonked him on the hard rear bench and the vehicle, with much clanking and spewing of dust, roared off. Nobody paid them any heed. If he'd been in a more philosophical frame of mind, Joe might have reflected that doing a runner from downtown Tobruk was becoming a regular fixture. And they took the same route, clattering through the battered streets, alive with Axis troops towards the east. Columns and knots of sullen allied captives were being marched through the town, the shock of failure etched on every face.

'Where are we headed?' he croaked, 'the balloon's got to go up at any moment.'

'It'll take your nasty mate a bit o' time to organise a posse, we got a few minutes to get clear.Lucky for you the pair up front saw them draggin' you off and knew you'd be in for it, no great shakes guessin' where you'd be took neither, just a shame we missed that bastard.'

His lungs still protested shrilly at each grateful gulp of air and every bump and shudder of the hard suspension sent him retching. Cold sweat clung like a shroud. He decided he'd rather shoot himself before surrendering. He was a marked man anyway. They chugged clear of the town and back across the scarred and gutted plain, bunkers sooted in black, smoke still eddying over.

It was oddly empty; a theatre after the show has finished and only the patrons' rubbish left. Detritus of battle was still everywhere and the shop-worn Italian House was in need of a complete makeover. Discarded brass lay like confetti, the walls ravaged, no bodies but plenty darkening bloodstains. It was now mid-morning and time to dump the getaway.

'We'd best get dahn to the beach,' Archie advised. 'Jerry's got east of here sewn up tight. There's still a boat, we might just get the bugger going. If not it's a fakkin' long walk.'

The main battle might be over. Theirs wasn't. With Joe stumbling, supported by Archie and Angel and flanked by the two SIGs, they retraced their steps, exhausted, to the temporary sanctuary of the cove. It too was eerily deserted but for the shell of the abandoned MTB, still hopelessly aground. This was one of his more surreal moments. The wrack of war all around, yet not a German or Italian in sight. It couldn't last. They'd be back to salvage or strip the boat. The two SAS, veteran scroungers blessed by a natural gift, went aboard. Clearly she couldn't be got going, but they picked up whatever grub there was. This included the rum jar and Joe took his ration neat, temperance be buggered — and it helped. He took another hefty swig, just to be sure.

They were joined by a couple of other survivors, Lieutenants Sillito and Russell who'd been skulking in the lee of overhanging rocks. 'Like bloody *Treasure Island*,' Tiffen commented sourly. And what a motley crew they were, some in knocked off Axis gear, the newcomers in what was left of khaki, all with suitably distressed finish. A bit more colour and a parrot and they'd have looked like Stevenson's characters. Archie had gone below to see if he could fix the engines. 'No such luck,' he confirmed, 'and the bugger's stuck fast. Only way we're gettin' out of 'ere is on foot.'

It was hard to leave the boat behind, how easy if she could have been floated off and those blessedly powerful engines revived. They would have roared off back eastwards waving two fingers at Regia Aeronautica. An easy deliverance would have been nice, but the aftermath of the botched operation was living up to its evil repute. Try as he might Joe couldn't think of anything that had gone right.

Moving up off the sand they navigated a belt of mines and tabbed into a sheltering wadi. They'd see much of such sheltering wadis in the weeks to come. Their tiny handful was boosted by the irrepressible Sergeant Evans, another one who'd evaded the net, and they began the long, very long, trek east. Constantly, they had to duck and dive away from the eyes of prowling planes or searching ground patrols. The ridgeline, though very tempting, was too risky by far so, like creatures from under rocks, they clung to the shadows.

Hahnemann had probably organised the search parties, he'd have something to prove, the Axis version of the Gaberdine Swine would be chortling into their sauerkraut. He doubted Hans and Karl would have many mourners. The enemy had a general idea where they must be hiding and enemy guns from 'Brighton' sought them out, odd ranging shots from eighty-eights plunging into the barren ground, some throwing up those eviscerating showers of whizzing stone chips. Scrambling on into yet another happy depression, they came across a larger squad of fifteen to twenty survivors.

Most of these were Fusiliers who, after firing off their last rounds, had spiked the guns and made for the cove led by Lieutenant McDonald. Altogether, this was what remained of Operation Agreement, and their joint and only objective was escape and evasion. Few as they were, they were too many for a single group so they split up. Sillito and McDonald led their team east via the coast, hoping against hope that they might be picked up by the MTBs. 'I don't think they've the slightest chance of succeeding,' Russell drily observed.

Joe and Russell, as the surviving officers, now led their own squad, together with eight other assorted waifs and strays. They struck off southeast to find a landward route. Nobody would have given much for their chances either, hares constantly dodging the hounds. And this was a big pack with the scent fully in their nostrils. Lying up in yet another arid, scree-sided defile, their luck held throughout that first day. As darkness fell, they opted to split into still smaller groups. Joe, despite his sorry state would lead Archie, Angel, Tiffen and Shai. They divvied up their meagre shares of water and rations and said their brief goodbyes. They were all on the run.

Travelling only by night, lying up during the dwindling late summer days, *Famous Five Go Wild in Libya*. The enemy had not forgotten them, would not be likely to forget them. Still, after a few days, they'd got as far as Bardia. Between them they had only one and a half bottles of precious water and bugger-all rations. Then they struck scavengers' gold. By the old airfield at Gambut they chanced on a real treasure trove; a quarter-full tin of jam and some additional water.

Skeletal planes scattered the abandoned runways as the cooling wind blew in sand, traces of men's lives quickly obliterated and reclaimed. 'Ghosts of Libya,' someone commented, though Joe didn't know if he meant them or just the planes. It was vaguely surreal; here they were haunting one of the places they'd often targeted, like one small footnote in a history that had already moved on.

Joe didn't seem to have suffered any lasting damage from his ordeal. His lungs were still raw and his ribs hurt from the preliminary beating. Sometimes he found concentration difficult and his fitful sleep was haunted by the exquisite terrors of near-drowning. Bizarrely, at times he also felt a kind of exhilaration. They had escaped and there was more chance now — it would be the desert that did for them. At least he could ask for no finer company. These men had all risked their lives for him. The bonds which bound them could never now be severed. Somehow they would come through, with a bit of luck anyway.

Both Archie and Tiffen were born storytellers. This helped ease the crushing monotony of their nocturnal marches, eased the hunger, thirst, boredom and pain from their blistered feet in gaping boots which, like the flies, were their constant companions. Archie, despite being at the desperate end of history's greatest crime, hadn't lost his appetite for the more macabre historical versions.

'Spring-heeled Jack, 'e were called, like a phantom, 'cept 'e were real. Neither man nor ghost, he'd leap from roof to roof in a great black cold. Kept jumpin' on servant gels an' the like, breathin' fire an' eyes like 'ot coals, fair scared the life out of folk. An' it's true an' all, me granny told me she'd seen the blighter an' in broad daylight.'

'So your grandmother actually saw him?'

'She did, or at least she knew someone as 'ad.'

At night, when not moving, they huddled together against the cold, like old beggars under railway arches. Day's heat vanished as though someone had thrown a switch and temperatures plummeted, no fat Tropal coats on this trip, just the infested odours of their own stink, matted, bearded and filth-encrusted.

'Yer know,' Archie confided, 'I used to watch all them old Foreign Legion movies back in the day, Gary Cooper, George Raft an' all. I always thought being out 'ere in the desert was dead romantic like, clean uniforms, white 'ats an' stuff. Christ now bloody look at us, the real bleedin' thing I am. I'll never watch another film without loads o' water an fuck-all bloody sand.'

The hope that the Navy would send additional boats to Mersa Shegga, nine or so miles north of Bardia, had buoyed them up. They got very near; close enough to attract the hostile attentions of Italian coastal troops, 'just our bleedin' fakkin' luck, innit?' Having, as it seemed, been written off by the senior service, Joe decided it would be easiest just to highjack a truck from one of the Italian convoys motoring along the main highway between Bardia and Tobruk.

'Fucking bright idea this was then,' someone chirped, 'another fine mess you got us into.' The coast road turned out to be less fruitful than they'd hoped. 'Nuffink but bleedin' convoys and more bloody convoys, where's that plump little ration truck just puffin' along on 'is own?' There weren't any, and seeing all those fat, well fed Italians in their fat, well filled trucks just added to their prevailing misery.

Aside from the tortures of hunger, memories of meals past and eaten, of oceans of cool beer, he thought much about Alice. Not just pleasing nocturnal reminiscing of their many amorous moments but also in daytime, during the unending, draining, unchanging marching, of how their life together might be. After the war, some domestic idyll under an English heaven, of ripe cornfields and thatch, he might yet be that staid provincial solicitor, she the midwife perhaps, warm ale in ancient pubs by timeless, somnolent rivers. He could almost hear the sigh of the waters, if it wasn't for the fucking flies which dogged their every breath, clogging eyes and ears and nostrils.

They did bump into one friendly tribesman who gave them bread and took them to water. Their new guide, one of those hawk faced Senussi with no love for the Italians, if less scrupulous about their cash, did warn there was no more to be found this side of the El Alamein line. Still undeterred, Joe opted to march inland avoiding the more heavily patrolled coastal strip. Frequently, they could only move under cover of darkness, their tiny supplies dwindling and then gone. Shai was a tremendous asset; he was able to communicate with a party of Bedouin who took them in.

'Funny buggers, this lot,' Archie commented as they squatted beneath canvas and ate a thick glutinous stew that could have contained traces of most things. 'One day you shares their dinner an' the next they sell you off to Jerry or cut your bleedin' throat.'

'We're all just the same to them,' Shai commented, 'one invader looks much like another and they've had nothing but shit and bullets from the Eyeties. Why should we be any different? Besides, they've seen plenty stragglers from both sides over the last couple of years, we're a commodity to them, made use of, traded when opportune.'

As if to prove his point, they found supper wasn't charity. The Senussi accepted weapons, watches, fags and anything else that could serve as currency. Joe made sure each man kept a pistol or revolver, ammunition and his fighting knife. The rest they weren't likely to need, they'd no chance of winning any kind of firefight. 'I feel bleedin' naked,' Archie groused, 'I mean we've scarpered often enough before, did our share o' runnin' on Crete, but never felt like a bloody mouse with the cat on me tail.'

'That's the one good thing about being a Jew,' Tiffen replied, 'you get to know the feeling pretty early on.'

The tribesmen claimed they'd known all about the planned raid on Tobruk though the LRDG's epic journey all the way up from Kufra astounded even them. Having suitably impressed their temporary bene-factors, the escapers were now passed as human cargo across a chain of tiny desert settlements. These were straight from the Old Testament; low, dingy awnings, scruffy camels and scrawny goats, heavy on squalor. They'd probably covered say, seventy miles from Tobruk, lots more to go.

'I reckon Moses must have kipped in gaffs like this lot on 'is way to the Promised Land an' bugger all 'as changed.'

'You're right, and we're still not quite there ...'

Even keeping inland they still ran the risk of bumping enemy outposts. They had to skirt a *Beau Geste* Italian fort to reach the Wadi Kattara, yet another dry defile though likely, as they so often did, to burst into flood beneath an autumn monsoon. As yet there were none. They discovered their Senussi hosts operated a thriving sideline in selling eggs to local Axis units, a handy source of information. Enemy morale was low, it seemed. The Allies were gaining ground. Worsening weather didn't help, the season was changing. Now, even if it didn't pour, it rained; the dank, grey veil of autumn. Both Archie and Tiffen contracted dysentery, the soldier's curse from time immemorial. Both became so weak they had to be helped on the grinding, unending slog.

What did they have? They had a map, some cans of bully beef, goat's meat and ten bottles of water. Joe kept them heading east, zigzagging to avoid hostile eyes till they passed unnoticed through the old frontier wire, the surreal junkyard of industrial warfare rusting in a primeval landscape, the battles of winter 1940 seeming like just more ancient history. Their boots had long given out, so they bound their feet with scraps like poor men's puttees, torn from what remained of their kit.

All suffered from desert sores, ulcerous lesions abrading arms and legs, any exposed part really, horribly debilitating. Like medieval lepers on some desperate pilgrimage they stumbled on, half sun blind, dehydrated, ragged. Yet nobody talked of surrender. There was that something which kept them going, propelled each painful step on blistered feet. They had survived not just the enemy but the worst incompetence Allied planners could throw at them, making the desert seem almost benign in its timeless indifference.

It was Friday the thirteenth of November; they had been nearly two months on the run. Joe thought they might have reached Himeimat, some thirty miles south of Alamein, but he couldn't be sure. He had more and more difficulty in concentrating and he could feel all his painstakingly learnt skills slipping away in the mirage. He'd only heard of these in books or movies, something from *Arabian Nights*, but now they were real, just another refinement of their daily torture — vast green oases opened up, so close it seemed you'd be there in minutes, only to disappear. The pain of reality, when it kicked back in, was exquisite.

He was finding it harder and harder to keep a grip on reality. His mind had taken to rambling off on its own and dredging up memories. One was of an argument he'd had with his father, back in '38 at the time of the Czech crisis. He realised now that at the time he'd known far too little and his father far too much.

'We went to war for gallant little bloody Belgium and what good did that do? They told us that's who we were fighting for and it was bollocks, pure and simple. The war was just a put up job by filthy rich, bloody capitalists and Jews so they could sell more guns and get richer while the people just bled for 'em in the trenches. Well, not this time.'

The bosses' conspiracy was a frequent refrain from his father and his socialist friends.

'They were so bloody clever then, these aristos and profiteers, they sent their own sons to the front as officers and got most of them killed, what kind of useless conspiracy is that?'

In this fresh war, at least the offspring of proles got a chance to be almost on a par with the sons of gentlemen, even if the attrition rate was just as bad.

*

The armoured cars appeared over the lip of a rising dune, sun behind them, the roaring of engines suddenly surrounding them. Joe guessed they might be Allied, Eleventh Hussars possibly, hopefully. Heavy, chunky little vehicles loaded with Brens and Vickers. The Hussars were none too sure.

'Looks like a bunch of fakkin' Wop deserters dunnit, you blokes Eyeties then?' A blaring Kentish NCO demanded, pink and scrubbed in the turret. Numerous Stens were lined up on them. Joe needed to say something but found he couldn't seem to speak.

An officer appeared, the gangly, sporty type you couldn't really imagine fitting into the armoured coffin of a Marmon-Herrington, all bones and sculpted planes.

'I rather think these fellows are ours, Corporal, ragamuffin as they might be. So if we're not going to shoot them I suggest you get a brew on, pronto.'

Other Hussars crowded round, they got smokes, their first for weeks. They'd arrived at Heaven's gate.

'Tobruk?' the officer asked. 'We've picked up a few odd strays and runaways, pretty sure you're the last though. Damn rough show but no fault of your lot. Well done and welcome home.'

Joe might have cried, if he'd had the strength.

*

They got a brew, hot food and medics. Joe was numb, he guessed they all were. His mind, when not far away, could only dwell on his torture and the rigours of their escape. Three-tonners arrived to take them back to Alamein, the line they'd crossed so very long before. They'd missed the battle, the biggest of the campaign and a resounding defeat for Rommel.

Everyone had forgotten about Operation Agreement. Stirling and the rest of SAS had tried to have another go at Benghazi and that hadn't gone well. LRDG had really biffed the Axis at Barce, but none of that mattered anymore either. The Yanks had landed in Vichy held territory and the Afrika Korps was in full retreat everywhere. It seemed like a different war.

Joe was still an officer, newly showered, clipped and shaven, kitted out in borrowed gear but that was enough to get him a ride back in a jeep. They drove east through a landscape of battle, bowling along the coastal highway that had witnessed so many swings of the desert pendulum. Burnt out tanks and trucks littered the track, blown up eighty-eights and A/T guns, split barrels gaping. It was dank, a uniform blanket of dismal grey just added to the prevailing desolation. Dumped and tattered webbing lay everywhere, theirs and ours, mostly impossible to tell. And more crude wooden crosses bearing the names of men who had lived very far from here and would never be going back, leaving just their bones in the sand and their stories unheard.

His driver, a stocky nearly-Geordie from some incestuous mining enclave in East Durham, chucked Joe a week old copy of *Crusader*, the Eighth Army magazine. Normally, he'd never bother reading it but this time, as the Willys bounced and rocked, he thumbed through. The paper confirmed in ringing tones what he'd already heard, editorials blaring as though the bloody war was as good as over. The wags, thank God, were still busy.

Sir — in response to the heartfelt plea from a Home Guard unit assigned to lonely nights on the Kent coast and seeking donations of home comforts as they're a good five miles from home. Can we please have some too? We're on the coast of Libya and we're five hundred miles from anywhere, we've sand in our char and Rommel just down the road. Any contributions gratefully received.

Then he saw the short column feature on page six:

351

Italian bombing of Alexandria hospital — following the cowardly attack on the medical facility, all of those patients and staff killed or injured has now been identified…

Alice's name was fourth from the top, *her* name in black and white. This wasn't possible, not this final twist, surely? But Alice was dead; his mind could grasp that, even if his heart could not. He knew then that it wasn't for herself she'd wept that last time, but for him.

His war wasn't over, it was just beginning.

Author's Note

This is a work of fiction and sticklers for precise historical detail are warned accordingly. I have attempted generally to remain within the correct timescales, details of weapons and kit should be an anorak's delight. Where I have introduced real characters, I've attempted to portray them as accurately as possible and placed them where they ought properly to be. When it comes to locations, I can safely claim to have some form on, having walked most. I've written up the Cretan Campaign, the Desert War, LRDG and Operation Agreement in previous works of non-fiction.

In terms of the history of the SAS in the Western Desert I'd recommend Ben Macintyre's excellent and lively *SAS Rogue Heroes* together with Gavin Mortimer's *Stirling's Men*. Fitzroy Maclean provides a lively account of his time in the desert in his classic *Eastern Approaches*.

To list what went wrong with Operation Agreement could fairly easily be summarised as 'everything' and this would not be too blasé or cynical. Attempting to list the failures has to start with the overall concept and planning. Haselden's original idea was sound, risky, bold to the point (but not past) of rashness and essentially do-able. Once the whole plan grew so astonishingly, involving air and sea elements, it got totally out of hand and into the near fantastical of wishful thinking. It grew too big, too many interdependent elements, too many split second timings. At the time the failure to light the landing beaches was stressed and this is undoubtedly correct. But it was a failure of intelligence and communication that the SBS Folbot team and the officer commanding submarine *Taku* did not appreciate just how vital their assigned role was, or the dire consequences of failure.

Those damned lighters, badly, cheaply and wrongly put together, were another prime cause. Their limitations were not picked up because of the inadequacy of training and rehearsal. Properly undertaken, this would have revealed the inherent problems. Sending in the bombers before rather than after as the original *Waylay* plan had called for was another principal error. The enemy's defences were not compromised, very little real damage was inflicted and the Axis ability to deploy to meet the attack barely inconvenienced. Lack of adequate aerial reconnaissance prior to the raid and the bland assumption that only Italian troops of questionable quality would be present were avoidable mistakes. Lack of adequate comms was another.

Whilst we armchair strategists, writing with the inestimable benefits of hindsight and under no operational pressure whatsoever, find it easy to be critical, in war mistakes will be made. What the many successes of LRDG had demonstrated was the need for limited objectives, the fewer cogs the better and getting in and out fast. Barce, the sole success in that September, underlines the point. Later, in 1943, the LRDG were to become victims of similar muddled objectives and slack planning when they were pitch-forked into the mess of the Dodecanese campaign. Military success cannot rely entirely on wishful thinking and political expediency. This led to disaster in Norway, Greece and Crete, nearly losing us the Desert War in the process.

The fallout from Operation Agreement and its outcome was very quickly eclipsed by events. Montgomery had been careful to distance himself from the raid, though by no means slow in adding his powerful voice to the wailing chorus of mourners when it failed. Yet the next month, October 1942, he launched his great offensive which became the second battle of El Alamein. This was the deciding swing of the pendulum. Hard fought, a grinding struggle of attrition, Rommel's forces were ground down, and finally hurled back.

Admiral Harwood said *I much regret the heavy losses, but I feel it is better to have tried and failed than not to have tried at all.* He did, naturally, have to put on a brave face. In public at least, behind the scenes the blame game was in full swing and would continue for some time. Monty stood clear but wasn't shy with his *I told you so.* In terms of the unrealistic scale and complexity of *Agreement*, Montgomery might have reflected more fully on these whilst planning or conceptualising *Market Garden*, where not dissimilar planning failures resulted in an even worse disaster.

This failure had still been expensive. Some 280 naval personnel, 300 marines and 160 soldiers and commandos had become casualties, though many of these were captured. HMS *Coventry*, the venerable light cruiser, together with destroyers *Sikh* and *Zulu*, four MTBs and two Fairmiles, all went down, a diminution on strike capability the Mediterranean Squadron could well have done without.

Axis losses were minimal; perhaps a dozen Germans and an unaccounted number of Italians, probably, in the early stages of Force B's attack, quite high. The Official History pithily sums up the causes of failure: *the great hazards of the plan, the distance to the objective — beyond the reach of all but a few of the British fighters — lack of experience of landing operations and of suitable craft, and underestimates of the enemy.*

This is essentially correct, if nicely understated. The plain facts are that it was a bad plan, hastily extemporised, without a single guiding mind behind it. Haselden's original concept was hijacked and expanded beyond all recognition. As the Americans might say — FUBAR!

Anyone wanting to know more about Operation Agreement immediately owes a debt to Gordon Landsborough's *Tobruk Commando* (London, Cassell 1956), the first and probably best account of the raid. This is followed by Peter C. Smith with *Massacre at Tobruk* (London, W. Kimber 1987, re-printed by Stackpole Books in 2008) and David Jefferson's *Tobruk — a Raid Too Far* (London, Robert Hale 2013). I do, of course, rely upon many of the very good books written about the Desert War generally (including my own). In terms particularly of the Jewish soldiers of SIG, I rely heavily upon Martin Sugarman's *Fighting Back* (London, Valentine Mitchell 2010). Much of the primary source material has been included in a compendium volume published by the national Archives *Special Forces in the Desert War* (2001) which reproduces two earlier works by Brigadier H.W. Wynter, and I have relied upon the second of these *The History of Commandos and Special Service Troops in the Middle East and North Africa — January 1941 to April 1943* (CAB 44/152).

Joe Milburn is a fictional character yet the photo he might have taken of the commandos just prior to the operation does exist, (IWM HU 3708), and it encapsulates the spirit of these men far better than any words of mine.

As for the verse quotations: *Waiting* is reproduced by kind permission of Samantha Kelly, *Rare as Fairies* appears in quite a few histories of the Greek and Cretan campaigns and I'm not aware of who may hold any original copyright. *Belisha's Army* of course refers to Leslie Hore-Belisha MP, Minister for war 1937–1940 who was not infrequently the butt of Anti-Semitism. *Ode to a Desert Flower* — the latrine trench is to be found in *Crusader* volume 57, 31st May 1943. *Tobruk Heroes* and *Libyan Handicap* are included by kind permission of the trustees of the Fusiliers Museum of Northumberland. *Hitler has only got one ball* is ancient doggerel and *If* is again used by kind permission of the Fusiliers Museum of Northumberland. *Ode to Bully Beef* has been around since 1941 and *There was a Servant Girl* is included by kind permission of the trustees of the Northumberland Hussars. *Land of soap and water* is more antique doggerel and the extract from *D-Day Dodgers* appears by kind permission of Margaret Ward. The poem by Yates is included by courtesy of Durham County Records Office (Yates was an officer in the Durham Light Infantry, killed in action in 1943). *A Prisoner of War is* included, again by courtesy of the trustees of the Northumberland Hussars. *Epitaph of a New Army* comes from *More Poems of the Second World War* editor, V. Selwyn (London 1989), p. 39.

For fluency in the rougher side of the German language, I am, as ever, indebted to my close accomplice Silvie Fisch.

Joe, Archie and Angel haven't finished campaigning. And certainly last time I was there, Andreas Hatzidakis was still running his wonderfully jumbled and eclectic war museum in Askifou.

ENDEAVOUR QUILL

Endeavour Quill is an imprint of Endeavour Media

If you enjoyed *Blitzing Rommel* check out
Endeavour Media's eBooks here:
www.endeavourmedia.co.uk

For weekly updates on our free and discounted eBooks
sign up to our newsletter:
www.endeavourmedia.co.uk/sign-up

Follow us on Twitter:
@EndeavourQuill

And Instagram:
endeavour_media

ENDEAVOUR MEDIA